Rubies of
the Viper

To Susan and Gary —
    I hope you'll enjoy
reading my novel as much
as I enjoyed writing it!

           Martha Marks
           Santa Fe
           Nov. 18, 2010

Rubies of the Viper

A NOVEL BY
Martha Marks

Rubies of the Viper

Published by Martha's Art®
PO Box 31493
Santa Fe, NM 87594
marthamarks.com
505-690-9601

ISBN: 978-0-9795193-4-5 (paperback)
978-0-9795193-3-8 (Kindle)
978-0-9795193-5-2 (EPUB)

Cover art © 2010 by Bernard Marks
Cover design by Laura Feuerer

DEDICATION

To Bernie Marks, the talented,
patient, and supportive love of my life.

And to the memory of my parents,
Truman and Margaret Alford,
who took me at an early age to Rome, Pompeii and
Herculaneum and, among other things,
taught me to appreciate history and good books.

TABLE OF CONTENTS

SHOW ME A MAN WHO ISN'T A SLAVE.
ONE IS A SLAVE TO SEX.
ANOTHER TO MONEY.
ANOTHER TO AMBITION.
ALL ARE SLAVES TO HOPE AND FEAR.

—Seneca, 4 B.C. - A.D. 65

YOU HAVE AS MANY ENEMIES
AS YOU HAVE SLAVES.

—Roman proverb

PART 1

A.D. 53, MAY

CHAPTER ONE

ROME

Gaius Terentius Varro lurched out of the riverfront brothel, snapped his fingers at the four slaves snoring on the pavement, and crawled into his litter. The bearers hoisted their belching burden and set off through the dark toward the Caelian Hill. It was a trip they had made every third or fourth night for years.

The two men waiting behind a pile of discarded lumber were not there by habit. As the litter neared, they pulled hoods over their heads, drew curved Syrian daggers, and moved into the street. One blade sought the Roman's heart, spurting hot blood onto his white tunic. The other slashed wide and deep across the patrician throat, nearly severing the head. The groggy, unarmed slaves offered no resistance, and within moments the master of one of Rome's greatest fortunes lay dead on his plump silk cushions.

CHAPTER TWO

THE VILLA VARRO, ON THE COAST NORTH OF ROME

Her brother's murder lay heavily on her mind as Theodosia Varra pushed aside the sapphire-blue curtain and stepped into the blackness of the library that their father had added to his ancestral villa eighteen years earlier. It was late, and the bouncy journey up from Rome on the old Via Aurelia had exhausted her, but she had to spend a while here—the one place where she had always felt safe—before she slept.

Accustomed to the well-lit dining room, her eyes could make out little in the library. One small lamp flickered on a table straight ahead; another burned in the corner to her right. The air was thick with the familiar, fragrant mix of old leather and costly Egyptian oil.

Groping toward the nearest lamp, she bumped into a bulky object.

Father's couch.

Her fingers played along its carved wooden back as her eyes, gradually adjusting to the dark, explored the room. The oversize strongbox still stood against one wall, flanked by the Etruscan urns from the necropolis at Caere. And the scrolls that generations of her family had collected were still there, too, neatly stacked in their niches.

She walked over and chose a scroll at random. Its leather sheath felt warm and familiar in her hand as she held it down to the lamp.

Terence. Father's favorite playwright.

Aulus Terentius Varro and his daughter had read the comedies aloud here together many times, taking turns at the roles, pitching their voices high or low as the parts required.

Gods, we'd laugh till our cheeks hurt!

Returning to the couch, Theodosia was about to unroll the scroll when, from the corner behind her, came the sound of a man noisily clearing his throat.

She jumped.

There had been too much violence lately for calm nerves.

Then she saw him—beyond the circle of amber light cast by the other lamp—standing on the far side of her father's desk.

Moments passed. The two stared at each other across the great gulf of the room... he stiff as a pillar, she struggling against her fear, feeling alone and vulnerable.

"Who are you?" she said at last. "What are you doing here?"

"My name is Alexander, mistress. I am the steward."

In an instant, Otho's mocking words flooded her memory.

Alexander the arrogant. Alexander the conqueror. Alexander the slave.

Through her mind ran snippets of information gleaned from Tribune Marcus Salvius Otho, a senator's son and her brother's best friend who had become Theodosia's own friend and ally in the two weeks since Gaius' murder.

An insolent Greek who insists on calling himself Alexander...

Refused to accept the name Gaius gave him...

A strange one...

Insufferably arrogant...

Capable but dangerous...

Only slave allowed off the villa grounds without permission...

Wields as much power at the villa as Nizzo does on the farm...

And then Otho's final advice, just yesterday afternoon.

Take control fast.

Don't believe a thing he tells you.

Don't ever turn your back on him.

Theodosia remembered her surprise that her brother would bring in a stranger and turn the estate over to him to manage.

"I'll run the place myself, as Father did," she had promised Otho. "You won't catch me deferring to a slave!"

Still unmarried at the shamefully old age of nineteen—and with no living male relative to direct her affairs—Theodosia had unexpectedly become the sole owner of the family fortune. Her unique situation placed unique burdens on her. No one else had any claim to her property, but she had to prove she could manage it.

She gripped the scroll and looked at the man in the shadows.

My slave.

"I can't see you over there. Come here." There was nothing gentle in the command.

5

The steward obeyed, then bowed and stood silently. It was not his place to speak first. His comportment was perfect for a servant except for his dark, deep-set eyes, which remained fixed on her face.

She kept him standing awkwardly before her as she inspected him at leisure. Otho had said the steward was Greek, and he looked it. He was taller than Theodosia and lean, with intense eyes and high cheekbones that carved strong angles on his face. The lamplight picked out a deep, jagged scar on his right jaw.

Without saying a word, Theodosia stepped around him to replace the scroll on its shelf. Determined not to reveal her nervousness, she returned to the couch, rested her hands on its back, and faced him again.

Finally, having prolonged the silence as long as she cared to, she spoke. Her voice had lost none of its pique.

"Why didn't you make your presence known when I came in?"

"I stood up when you entered, mistress, and thought you would see me. It wasn't fitting for me to speak."

For some reason, Theodosia was annoyed by the correctness of this Greek's Latin. Though accented, it sounded as educated as her own.

"I was told my brother gave you a more appropriate name. 'Servus,' I believe."

"Your brother called me many things, mistress, but my name is Alexander."

"Your name is whatever your master chooses to call you."

Silence.

"Isn't that so?"

"I had a name," the tone was soft but insistent, "long before I had a master."

Astonished by his self-assurance, Theodosia let the matter drop.

What does a slave's name matter, anyway?

"What were you doing there?"

"Compiling a list of household slaves for your inspection. I would have finished it by now, but Tribune Otho sent a message late this morning that he wanted delivered to the farm today. Since I'm the only one from here who goes there—"

"Does Tribune Otho often send you on errands?"

"On occasion, yes. My lord Gaius told me that I was to treat an order from Tribune Otho as if it came from him, my own master." Alexander paused. "Tribune Otho also sent word that you would arrive tomorrow, mistress, instead of today... as we were originally informed. I intended to present myself to you then, along with a full inventory of your property."

6

Theodosia looked aside, puzzled.

Otho knew I was planning to travel today. This Greek must have misunderstood.

"Why were you doing your work here?"

"This is my office. My lord *Gaius* instructed me to work here."

"Are you telling me that my brother turned our father's library—the most beautiful room in the villa—over for the private use of a slave?"

For the first time, the man hesitated.

"My lord Gaius hardly ever came here, mistress. And I have done no harm to anything."

Theodosia breathed deeply.

If I must battle for control of my estate, then let Father's library be the first conquered territory.

"Well, Alexander," she said, exaggerating the syllables of his name, "this room is now reserved for my use. You're not to come here unless I've summoned you. There must be plenty of cubicles in the house that will do for you. Find one. And you will bring me that inventory first thing in the morning. We have much to discuss tomorrow. Now," she flicked her hand impatiently, "be gone, fellow!"

Alexander dropped the pile of papyrus sheets on top of the chest in the tiny room where he slept and collapsed onto the narrow mattress.

"Damn these Varros!"

Eight years spent trying to please the haughty, irascible Gaius were enough. Alexander had hoped Theodosia Varra would be different.

Damn the great Tribune Otho, too.

If he hadn't sent that message—or at least if he'd gotten it right—Alexander's updated inventory would have been finished before the new mistress arrived; the kitchen staff would have known to prepare an appropriate dinner for her, instead of having to rush something out at the last minute; and Alexander would have been here to welcome her properly, instead of coming in from his farm errand while she was eating.

Damn you, too, man. Only a fool would believe anything Otho says.

He lifted the top sheets off the stack and spread them across the bed, smoothing the worn blanket so the pages lay flat. "First thing in the morning," she had said. "Much to discuss tomorrow."

Tomorrow sounds delightful.

The lamp burned low. Alexander sat hunched over his inventory when he heard a tap on the door. In the next instant, Stefan ducked his head and shoulders under the frame.

"She's here!" A smile played across Stefan's shaggy face. "Got in about dinnertime."

"I know. We met."

"Well...?" The smile grew wider.

"Oh, she's a charmer!"

Stefan grinned.

"What'd I tell you?"

Alexander glanced sidelong at his friend and shook his head. Irony wasn't something Stefan ever understood.

"Have you had a friendly little chat with her yet?"

"Not yet. Too busy with her carriage and horses."

"Well, you better plan on sticking with the goatherd's daughter. Not even your legendary luck with the ladies is going to help you much with Theodosia Varra."

"I don't understand." Stefan's grin faded.

Of course not.

"That sweet girl you remember has grown up." Alexander rubbed his burning eyes. "Become a Roman."

Lucilla was busy unpacking. Theodosia could hear her singing in the second bedroom.

She never sounded so happy before.

Over the past two years, Theodosia and her only slave had worked out a mostly amicable relationship despite a hostile start and Lucilla's occasional surly moods.

Getting out of Rome will be good for her, too.

Theodosia strolled into the sitting room, still unable to believe it belonged to her. It was to this magnificent suite that Aulus Terentius Varro had brought the first Theodosia twenty years before. As a child, their daughter had come here often, sometimes inviting the slave children who were her playmates upstairs for a giggly game of hide-and-seek among the master's bulky furniture.

Theodosia had always loved this room, where tall bronze lamp-trees cast their golden glow into every corner and Odysseus reenacted his exploits in vibrant frescoes of crimson, green, and gold.

8

On this warm night, the shutters stood open to the balconies on two sides, offering panoramas of the sea and gardens and filling the suite with crisp, salty air. The mosaic floor had been polished to a high gleam, and an enormous bouquet of sweet-smelling red roses dominated a low chest. There might have been some confusion about the day of her arrival, but someone had prepared the room well.

"Juno," Theodosia said to herself, "it's really mine!"

Gaius had been the heir. Only through an advantageous marriage could a girl with a brother hope for splendors like this, and no such match had ever been arranged for Theodosia.

She walked onto the western balcony, propped her arms on the railing, and looked out at the Etruscan Sea. The upturned crescent of Juno the moon, goddess of women, floated above the water, and Theodosia fancied that she smiled.

It's over eight years since Father died, right here.

She peered down into the garden, remembering how she had huddled there with her friends that night, crying and wondering what would happen now that the despotic Gaius had taken his father's place as master of them all.

In her mind, she called up those slave playmates: Simi, so dainty and finicky about what she ate; Gerta, smarter than any of the rest of them, Theodosia included; the lovely little Arisata, whom Theodosia always envied for her fine, curly hair; and Stefan, so funny and gentle, with his bright-blue eyes... the son of a housemaid and Aulus Terentius Varro's life-long body servant. As a child, Theodosia had been unable to say his true name, Stefanus, so she dubbed him "Stefan" and it stuck.

She could hardly wait to see her childhood pals again.

Why haven't any of them come in for a visit tonight?

Lucilla joined her on the balcony and took a deep breath of the briny air. Born in Rome of German slave parents, she had never seen the sea before this evening.

"Well, what do you think?" Theodosia asked with a smile.

Lucilla turned her broad, blonde face to her mistress and shook her head in wonder, jingling her glass-bead earrings. Her long, looped yellow braids glistened in the lamplight. She stood a full hand's length taller than Theodosia.

"Oh, miss, I didn't know places like this even existed!"

"Well, they do, and this is not the finest. Just the best."

Theodosia stepped back into the room, dropped into a cushioned chair, and stuck her feet out for the slave to remove her sandals.

"Try to be happy here," she said to the kneeling Lucilla. "I don't intend to live in Rome ever again. This house is what matters most to me. So... start making friends, because we're going to be here forever."

"I talked with a few of the houseboys at dinner. They're all so good-looking!" Lucilla rose and took the silver pins from her mistress' hair, then smoothed it with a tortoise-shell comb. "And there's a stable hand who's an absolute giant."

"Well, I'll not stand in your way this time. That's a promise."

Theodosia closed her eyes, surrendered to Lucilla's big-boned fingers on her neck and shoulders, and let herself be lulled nearly to sleep.

Suddenly—as unwelcome as a nightmare—the face of the man in the library came into her mind, shattering her peace for the second time that night. She jerked her head as if for another confrontation.

"Did I hurt you, miss?"

Theodosia shook her head and pulled her maid into a crouch.

"Tell me something. During your dinner tonight, did you hear the man Alexander mentioned?"

Lucilla's brow furrowed.

"Alexander? Oh, yes. His name came up a lot. Someone said he had gone somewhere, to see somebody. A couple of men wanted his permission to do something. I'm sorry! I can't remember any details."

"How did they sound when they talked about him? Like they resented him?"

"It was more like they felt sorry for him."

"Why? What did they say?"

A wary look appeared in Lucilla's eyes.

"Do I have to report everything I hear in the kitchen?"

"Of course not. I don't need spies in my own house. But there may be some danger. After what happened to Gaius..."

After what happened to Gaius in Rome, only the gods know what might happen to me... all alone out here.

"Tell me what you heard, Lucilla."

"Just some men complaining about how you was planning to live here full time and take charge. Someone said it ain't natural to be owned just by a woman. It seemed to slip out before they realized I was there. Then they shut up. But first, a bunch of them was saying that maybe things wasn't so bad before, that at least the master left this Alexander in charge. And that he was one of them. You know... a slave and a man."

"So that's it. I'm not a man."

"Someone said this Alexander was going to get the worst of it."

10

Theodosia sat in silence, remembering her sharpness with the steward in the library. Roman women were notoriously harsh with their slaves. No doubt she'd already managed to confirm that reputation.

Well, so be it. Better a strong start than a weak one.

"There's something else." Lucilla stood and went back to massaging her mistress' shoulders. "Maybe I shouldn't say it, but I get the feeling this Alexander's way too powerful around here. Sounds like he thinks he's the master himself." She bent to Theodosia's ear and whispered, "Oh, miss, please do be careful with him! I get the feeling he could be real dangerous!"

A wave of affection for her maid swept over Theodosia.

"I'm not worried. If he can't adjust to me, I'll get rid of him."

"That'd be good. But still... I think it'd be better if you was married. Then all those fellows would be dealing with a man again. They don't think a woman can run a place like this, especially a young woman and... a pretty woman. There was plenty of comments about that, too."

Theodosia chuckled grimly. Gaius' reputation for abusing his slaves was so bad that even the most jaded Romans had snickered about it for years. And the gossip had increased since his murder. Theodosia had anticipated a better reception from those who had been the easy targets of his fury.

She left her chair and propped an arm against the wall next to the balcony.

"I'm not asking you to spy on anyone, Lucilla," she said, staring at the stars. "But lots of people think it was my brother's slaves who killed him. I wouldn't have come out to the villa by myself if I believed that, of course, but still..." She looked over her shoulder. "You're the only one I know for sure I can trust. If you hear anything that you think matters, you must tell me."

Lucilla made no response. Theodosia faced back toward the sea.

"Living here may not be easy for either one of us, you know. We just have to make sure it isn't life-threatening as well."

CHAPTER THREE

Alexander watched from the shadows of the atrium as Theodosia Varra lingered over her breakfast in the sunny, flower-filled peristyle. Her yellow tunic and ankle-length blue stola fluttered with each gust off the sea, echoing the blue and gold of the frescoed walls behind the colonnade that surrounded her. The breeze caught her hair, too, sending golden-brown wisps flying.

The late-May morning was perfect, so when the houseboys had finished scrubbing the atrium floor, Alexander had instructed them to set up a table beside the pool, next to the bronze figure of Adonis dressed as a hunter. The statue was Greek, of course, as was all the art in the house except the Etruscan antiques collected from the nearby necropolis.

Alexander had selected Dabini and Selicio, the tall Ethiopians who were the best waiters in the household, to attend the mistress this morning. He noted now, with satisfaction, that the two had made no mistakes.

Theodosia Varra even deigned to smile at them as she rose.

She sauntered along the pool, stopping every few paces to observe a goldfish, catch a scent, or admire a blossom.

Alexander's eyes never left her slim figure.

What a lovely thing this must be for you. Home again, after years in exile. What wouldn't I give for such a homecoming?

"Morning, Alexander," she said in Greek as she passed, trailing behind her a subtle clove-oil fragrance.

"Good morning, mistress."

How odd to speak his own language with her. Gaius Terentius Varro always flew into a rage if the Greeks in his household did so, even though he, like all educated Romans, spoke Greek fluently.

Alexander held the sapphire-colored curtain aside and stood behind Theodosia Varra in the doorway as she surveyed the library, awash now with light flooding through the eastern window of the five-sided room, whose views of the sea to the west were spectacular all day long. The morning sun gilded the walnut tables with their mother-of-pearl inlays, the finely wrought chairs, the bronze lamps, the blue-veined marble floor. In the late afternoon, the sun would turn it all to flame.

Alexander never failed to marvel at this room. Window glass was a luxury enjoyed by the wealthiest Romans only; he had never seen it before he arrived here. Having such a wonderful space all to himself had done much to ameliorate the bitterness of his slavery. Now—after eight years—he was losing it.

"You finished your work last night?" There was no hint of a smile in his new mistress' voice as she marched to the big, sun-washed desk.

There's no softness in this woman, for all her looks. Maybe I should have told... He sighed. *Too late for that.*

"Everything is ready." He pulled out the chair for her.

Theodosia Varra sat; then she twisted in her seat to peer through the window, giving Alexander the chance to inspect her as leisurely as she had inspected him last night. He was struck by the beauty of her skin and hands and hair. Her complexion was flawless. Her fingers lay like cream against the deep blue of her stola. Though her hair was wind-blown now, she obviously preferred loose waves to the tightly curled styles favored by most Roman women. The sun burnished highlights in it that, when she turned back toward him, framed her face in gold.

"Well, Alexander, what have you to show me?"

There were sheets for each of her properties... the residences—this ancestral villa, with its enormous swath of surrounding land and a long stretch of seacoast; Gaius' mansion on the Caelian Hill in Rome; and the little house in the Subura where Theodosia Varra had been living... and the revenue producers—the vineyards near Reate, the farm, the two marble quarries in Italy, and the three silver mines in Spain.

Alexander spread each set out in turn as he explained them. He had organized the data in columns detailing land, equipment, furnishings, artwork, and slaves; business expenses; gross and net profits and losses for each of the past eight years. It was no mean fortune. Any one of the mines produced enough in a few months to maintain an ordinary family in Rome for a lifetime. All told, the estate included four thousand slaves.

The delicate creature studying those pages might be the wealthiest unmarried woman in the whole Roman Empire.

His fellow slaves could stop their grumbling.

There'll be a new master around here soon enough.

"Why do these go back only eight years?" Theodosia Varra asked after an interval. "Didn't my father keep records?"

"I couldn't find any when I came, so I started keeping them."

It was a matter of pride to Alexander that he wouldn't have administered the estate any differently—or any better—had it belonged to him.

"Show me the list of slaves here at the villa."

Alexander pulled out the appropriate sheets. One hundred and fifteen labored in and around the villa. He had categorized them by occupation, noting the age, nationality, and specific tasks of each. On the last page, she would find his name: Alexander, 29, Greek, steward.

The list covered eleven pages, and as Theodosia Varra read through them, Alexander saw her expression change. The eager look he first took for greed vanished, replaced by a furrowed brow. Her eyes scanned top to bottom, quickening with each sheet until she reached the last one.

"Why is it that I don't recognize any but the oldest servants?"

"That was the master's doing, mistress." He paused for her response, but her face was blank, so he went on. "He sold almost the entire household—over a hundred—and bought new slaves to replace them."

Her mouth fell open. Red blotches popped out on her cheeks.

"But he was raised with them, same as I was!"

"Apparently, that didn't matter much to him."

"Uproot an entire household?" Her voice was faint. "On a whim? Gods, how unfair!"

"Where is it written that a Roman can't indulge his whims? That a Roman must be fair?"

Theodosia Varra turned toward the window, as if to hide her consternation. Alexander regarded her curiously. Up to now, their exchanges had reflected the usual balance of formality and intimacy between a slave and his owner... a self-conscious reserve on both sides.

Suddenly, there was a break in that reserve.

After a while, she leaned back and raised flushed cheeks to him, making no effort to hide her distress.

"The young women... the girls who were around here when I was growing up..." Her eyes were liquid. "All gone?"

"The only females he left were the laundresses and the wives and daughters of the shepherds, goatherds, and gardeners... who live by themselves a distance away."

14

Theodosia Varra swung toward the window once more and sat with her back to him, obviously wrestling her emotions into submission. When at last she faced him again, that break in the reserve had yielded to the mask of command that he associated with Roman faces. The red blotches and liquid eyes had disappeared.

"You've done a fine job on these records, Alexander."

The unexpected compliment surprised him.

"Thank you, mistress."

"And I understand you're also responsible for the good service I've been enjoying. The waiters told me you trained the entire staff, or at least the younger servants... which I now see is just about everyone. Your talents are remarkable, it seems." She paused and regarded him at length. "Tell me something about yourself. What part of Greece are you from? How on earth did you end up here?"

Alexander sucked in a breath and considered his response. He'd won on the issue of his name, she on the issue of the library. Here was another issue to negotiate.

"That is a long story, mistress, and a very personal one. I would prefer not to talk about it."

And then he waited. It was unheard of for a slave to refuse to answer a question, much less tell his owner that something was none of her business. In most Roman houses, a remark of that sort would quickly earn him a whipping for insolence.

Alexander looked his new mistress in the eye and awaited her anger.

Theodosia Varra stared at him in obvious disbelief, her eyes remote and appraising. After a long interval, she bobbed her head.

"As you choose."

◇ ◇ ◇

They were still in the library when Theodosia caught the sound of horses in the driveway. It was nearly noon.

"Go and see who it is."

Alexander bowed and left. Theodosia knew she should wait, but she followed right away... too curious to hold back.

She was standing at the top of the wide steps in the main entryway, shielding her eyes from the glare, when a stable hand strode around the corner, coming to take the visitors' horses. Theodosia exhaled sharply through her mouth.

Juno, what a man!

15

Tall and robust, with brawny arms and shoulders and a full beard, the slave looked as if he could haul Emperor Claudius' ceremonial chariot with just one of his massive hands. Though he wore the same coarse brown tunic as all the others in the household, on him it hung differently.

This must be the giant that Lucilla was talking about.

Two riders were accompanying an open carriage up the driveway. The burly fellow held the horses as the men dismounted. One was balding and heavy set, the other clearly his son by their identical jaw line.

Alexander offered his hand to a girl inside the carriage; then he lifted out a fat-faced boy of three or four, who immediately took off for the rocks along the shore. Alexander chased him and—to Theodosia's great surprise—swung the squealing child into the air and around his head for a few turns before returning him to his sister's arms.

"Theodosia?" said the heavy-set man. "I am Titus Flavius Sabinus Vespasianus the Elder. Of Reate and Caere."

"Hero of the conquest of Britain, then quaestor, then praetor... and one of my father's dearest friends." She smiled and gave him her hand. "See, General? I know all about you."

"Guess you do. That's dangerous in a woman."

Vespasian turned to his children.

"This is Titus Flavius Sabinus Vespasianus the Younger," he said, drawing the name out for effect, "my daughter, Flavia Domitilla, and troublesome little Domitian."

Already, Theodosia was charmed by Vespasian's Sabine accent. The laugh lines around his eyes testified to the earthy humor and tongue for which he was famous. She had heard much admiring talk about the general from Reate.

"So, you live in Caere now?" she asked.

"This side of town, near the tombs. Inland, so Flavia's nagging me to build a new villa by the sea." He cast his daughter a pseudo-malevolent frown. "But I'm an honest man, so how am I to get the money?"

"Guess she'll have to wait till she marries her rich lawyer," Titus said.

Titus was already taller than his father, though he looked no more than fifteen. Thick black hair rippled around his face; thick black lashes fringed his eyes.

"Sorry about Gaius' death, Theodosia," he said. "Must be scary for you, all alone here."

Theodosia stifled the urge to wince. The last thing she wanted was for her servants to think her new situation frightened her.

16

"I understand you've been seeing a lot of Lucius Gallio lately," Vespasian said.

Theodosia nodded.

"He was my father's lawyer and friend. My brother's lawyer, too."

"Flavia's to marry him sometime next year," Titus said. "Father's big catch for her. He's only thirty years older than she is!"

"But he's the emperor's advisor," Flavia said. "He'll present me at court when we're married."

"Gods, is Lucius in for a surprise. He thinks he's getting some meek little thing for a bride."

"No, he doesn't. He's known me all my life."

"Anyway," Vespasian went on, "it was Lucius who told us you were coming home this week. Since we live out here—so far from all the sons and daughters of bitches in Rome—Lucius keeps us supplied with the latest news and gossip." Vespasian shook his head, eyes twinkling. "By Juno's tits, it's hard to tell the difference these days. So, my dear, don't pay any attention to what you hear, especially from a young pup like this." He pointed his thumb at his son. "He likes to think he's got Gaius' murder all figured out."

"It was the litter bearers killed Gaius," Titus said. "But don't worry. Your slaves have been well warned by what happened to those four in the Carcer Tullianum."

Theodosia shuddered at thought of the notorious prison.

"Titus!" said Flavia. "You know they'd have put the whole household in Rome to death if they thought the slaves did it. Lucius says street thugs murdered Gaius."

A year or so younger than her brother and pretty in an immature way, Flavia exuded warmth and self-assurance.

"I've been dying to meet you, Theodosia! Actually, everyone's been curious, even Father."

"But we really didn't come just to gawk," Vespasian said, "despite what Flavia says. So... just ignore her."

"That's all he ever does," Flavia said. "Ignore me."

"We came to invite you to dinner—"

"See? Ignoring me!"

"To meet the neighboring landowners. Important folk, all of them. Interested?"

Theodosia laughed at this example of resolute ignoring.

"Yes, but... only if you'll stay and have lunch with me today. Eating alone is going to get old fast. I can see that already."

◇ ◇ ◇

"Did you know my mother?" Theodosia asked Vespasian as they strolled through the masses of spotted lilies and red and yellow roses that separated the house from the pergola.

"Actually, no. I knew Terentius' first wife, but your mother never joined us. I understood she was having a difficult pregnancy. And then, of course, she died."

"Giving birth to me, I think."

"You *think*?"

"Father never told me how she died. Never talked about her, just said he loved her so much he gave me her name."

"Shame he didn't give you a Roman name," Titus said from behind them. "You'd have made a wonderful Terentia."

"Oh, no!" said Flavia. "Greek names are lots more interesting."

The girl bounded toward the pergola, ran up the stairs under the lilac-covered entryway, and skipped across to the stone wall.

"Theodosia," she said as the others stepped through the fragrant purple arch, "this is absolutely the most gorgeous place I've ever seen!"

Theodosia laughed and nodded. Her earliest memories were of sunny afternoons in this airy, vine-covered arbor built on a flat rock projecting out over the sea. The breeze carried a fine spray from below as gulls swooped and called.

"Haven't you ever been here before?"

"Gods, no. Gaius never invited anyone to his villa."

"Except his buddy, Otho," Titus said. "Folks used to say Otho spent as much time at Gaius' villa as Gaius did. Of course, with Otho around, nobody else wanted to be here."

"Someday," Flavia said, "I'm going to have a villa by the sea, with a pergola exactly like this. Wait and see!"

Just then, Alexander came into the arbor bearing an ornate silver tray, pitcher, and cups, each of which—Theodosia noted as he drew closer —was adorned with a large ruby in an intricate raised setting.

"To your new life, Theodosia." Vespasian raised the cup of Falernian that Alexander offered him.

"Oooooh, what wonderful goblets!" Flavia turned hers around and inspected it closely. "This is biggest ruby I've ever seen, and... what an amazing design!"

"Looks like a serpent eating an apple," Titus said.

"Is that your family crest?" Flavia asked.

"I've never seen it before." Theodosia turned toward Alexander. "Are these family pieces?"

"No, mistress. My lord Gaius brought them from Rome last year."

"Oooooh, they're exquisite!" Flavia ran her finger around the edge of her goblet and down the raised silver face of the ruby-eating snake. "Look at this... even little rubies in the eyes. You're lucky to have such beautiful things, Theodosia." She made a show of pouting. "Father's just so tight. Won't spend money on anything. Everything we use is as dull and practical as what our slaves use."

"Soon, my girl," her father said, "you can squander Lucius Gallio's money. Let's hope he's rich enough to buy you all the things you want."

Titus strolled across to stand beside Theodosia, who was leaning against the waist-high stone wall.

"Bother you to talk about Gaius' death?" Titus wrapped his fingers around a vine as thick as his wrist.

"No. We weren't close at all. I don't think he ever forgave Father for marrying my mother. When Father died, Gaius banished me to Rome with Phoebe, my old Greek nurse. He wouldn't give her to me legally, so we were always afraid he might decide to take her back or—" she shot a glance at Alexander, who was standing apart from the Romans, "even sell her to someone else. My poor Phoebe died before it occurred to him."

Theodosia pulled a leaf off the vine, tore it into pieces, and dropped them one by one into the sea below.

"Gaius never gave me any money, either."

"What'd you live on?"

"Well, he bought me a tiny house with a couple of shops on the street and let me keep the rents."

"I didn't know you lived by yourself in Rome," Vespasian said. "Just assumed you were with Gaius."

"Out of the question! He wanted nothing to do with me. No, I was in the Subura."

Titus looked as if he might choke on his wine.

"The Subura? I wonder you didn't get killed yourself, what with all the drunken foreigners and freedmen in that miserable slum."

"Well, I never went out at night, and not all that much in the daytime either. Couldn't afford to buy much. The rents never amounted to anything. One of the shops mostly stays empty, and in the other there's an old sandal maker who's sick a lot. Lately he's paid me nothing, so nothing was just about all I had these last few months."

"You didn't even have a maid?" Flavia was shocked.

"It was four years after Phoebe died before I saved enough to buy a maid, but at least then I had something that Gaius couldn't take away from me. Lucilla's the only slave I ever owned till now."

Just then, a troop of houseboys arrived with a round wooden tabletop, a stone pedestal, five chairs, and cushions, and began arranging them under Alexander's direction.

"I never wanted to live in Rome," Theodosia went on, "but Gaius wouldn't let me stay here in our home. Not once did he invite me to that mansion he built on the Caelian Hill. And guess how often I saw him in those eight years." She paused for effect. "Three times... and it was coincidental each time. He would be out in his litter with his friends, and I would go say hello to him. My beloved brother always acted as if I were some trash blown up on the street."

Soon came the Ethiopian waiters with an assortment of fresh fruit, bread, olives, and an array of cheeses. The bowls and trays they carried all bore that same ruby-serpent design.

Titus sat down next to Theodosia and laid his hand on her arm.

"How is it that you're not married yet?"

"Never found anyone I wanted to marry who wanted to marry me. And at this point, I'm probably too old."

"Not a chance!" said Vespasian.

Flavia had pulled a roll apart and was stuffing it with cheese. Now she stared into Theodosia's face.

"That's unbelievable. Someone as beautiful as you had no suitors?"

"Nobody I'd consider. A couple of greasy freedmen. What Roman patrician wants an orphaned, half-Greek girl with no dowry?"

Flavia shook her head in mock sympathy, her eyes agleam.

"Oooooh, well... I guess that's one thing you needn't worry about any more!"

Theodosia felt a blush creep into her cheeks. Titus' hand on her arm suddenly felt very warm; she slipped out from under it on the pretense of reaching for a roll.

As they were eating, Domitian bolted from the table, raced down the steps, and headed around the side of the pergola, toward the cliff.

Alexander sprinted after him again and hauled him back.

"If you wish, sir," he said to Vespasian, "I can find a playmate for him."

"Yes, please." Vespasian smiled as he spoke.

Theodosia blinked in astonishment.

A famous general... cordial to a slave!

She'd never heard of such a thing before.

Alexander set off for the house and soon returned, hand in hand with a curly headed boy of six or seven. Before long, the two children were chasing each other along the graveled garden paths.

"It's hard to believe that Gaius is dead," Vespasian remarked, watching the boys. "I remember when he was just Domitian's age. What a brutal way to go." He sighed. "There are so many thugs around nowadays, and not all of them are poor foreign folk. I know for a fact that some of our finest young patrician blood runs wild and rough at night."

"But the Praetorians never seem to catch them," Titus said, "as long as their rich papas are in the Senate."

"So the gossips have it. Just remember, my son... I'm not rich, and I'm not in the Senate. There'll be no bailout if you ever get into trouble."

"Have things really gotten so bad in Rome?" Flavia asked. "I knew street gangs beat people up sometimes, but I didn't think they were murderers, too."

"It was robbers killed Gaius," Theodosia said.

"Maybe. Maybe not." Titus glared at the silent slaves standing off to one side. "I still think it was the bearers."

"My son, they questioned them thoroughly."

"Tortured them?"

"Of course, and their stories all matched. Two men. Hooded. Armed with daggers. Some of the slaves even had stab wounds."

"They could have done that to themselves."

"Titus, that's silly." Flavia looked disgusted. "If they murdered Gaius, why would they wait around to get caught? Even a litter slave has more sense than that!"

"Well," said Theodosia, weary of the topic, "the investigators must have been convinced they weren't guilty. Otherwise—as Flavia said— they'd have put to death all of Gaius' slaves in Rome, not just the ones who let him get killed. That's the law, isn't it?"

"Suppose the killers weren't strangers?" It was plain that Titus was enjoying this game. "Suppose someone had a grudge against Gaius?"

The others simultaneously burst out laughing.

"Zeus!" Theodosia said. "My brother was a wastrel and a brute... and everyone knew it. But who would deliberately set out to kill the son of Aulus Terentius Varro?"

She looked the young man squarely in the eyes.

"It was a random act. Nothing more."

21

CHAPTER FOUR

The houseboy on duty in the atrium responded to the clap of Theodosia's hands.

"Tell Alexander to come here at once."

"But Alexander is—" The boy fidgeted nervously. "He was just starting to eat, mistress."

Theodosia hesitated. Alexander had stayed in the pergola with the waiters to serve her and her guests. In fairness, he should be allowed to finish his own lunch. But there would be others with him in the kitchen.

Good chance to show them all who's in charge now.

"Do as you're told, boy."

Before she knew it, Alexander was standing in the curtained doorway, no expression on his angular face.

"As I told you last night," Theodosia said in Greek, "we have many things to discuss and do today. My family's personal items, to start. It's time you turned them over to me."

Without a word, Alexander stepped to the enormous strongbox and unfastened a leather loop from his leather belt. The iron keys jangled against each other as he selected one, inserted it into the lock, and turned it with both hands. Theodosia remembered when it was a punishable offense for a slave to loiter near her father's strongbox.

Now a slave keeps the key.

The ancient lock snapped as it gave way. Alexander lifted the lid, retreated a step, and motioned toward the chest.

The mustiness of long-stored goods half choked Theodosia as she looked in at scores of wooden boxes stacked to fill three quarters of the large space. She could reach the top ones, but it would be difficult—and undignified—for her to lean over and rummage through the chest.

She looked at Alexander.

"Shall I hand them to you, mistress?"

"Yes, please."

As soon as she spoke, she realized that she had mimicked Vespasian, answering a slave with all the politeness she would accord an equal. That "please" had come naturally, though. She decided not to sour the moment by retracting it.

She sat near the chest as box after box of treasures passed across her lap... more money and jewels than she had ever imagined existed in the world. Boxes of gold and silver coins. Boxes of long gold bars. Boxes of necklaces. Boxes of bracelets. Boxes of rings. Boxes of earrings. Boxes of pearls. Boxes of unset gemstones of all sizes, colors, and shapes. And boxes and boxes and boxes of rubies.

At first, Theodosia marveled at each piece, taking it out and holding it up to catch the warm afternoon light, delighted by what she saw.

But the delight didn't last long.

After an hour, she began to grow restless. Alexander continued handing boxes to her, placing each one's predecessor on the floor in an ever-widening circle around her chair. Another hour later, she was no longer picking up even the finest pieces. Her eyes could no longer focus on them. Her head hurt. Her mouth felt dry.

Alexander was still standing by the chest, holding another unopened box. Theodosia let him take the previous one from her hand; then she shook her head and glanced at him, catching a faint smile in his eyes.

"No more. Leave the rest where they are."

"You are tired, mistress?" Alexander spoke indulgently, as one humors a child, but there was irony in his voice.

Theodosia chewed on the inside of her upper lip, feeling ludicrous.

"I had no idea we were talking about anything like this. Where did it all come from?"

Alexander shrugged.

"Who knows? Some of the mounted pieces are family heirlooms, but my lord Gaius acquired many others, and all the unset gems. He couldn't resist a beautiful stone, especially a ruby. He'd buy whatever the dealers showed him, no matter what it cost. A few dozen pieces he had made into jewelry and the dinnerware we served you on today, but everything else ended up here, unset and unworn."

Theodosia stared at the large circle of boxes on the floor. Nothing in her past had prepared her for the way she felt right now. She had been raised with the standard Roman indifference to inferiors; never before had she stopped to think about the source of her family's wealth. Now, gaping at the absurd fortune at her feet—a sight far more evocative than lists of men and mines and machinery—she realized what it meant.

Immortal gods! Four thousand slaves!

In shock and guilt, she struck out at the bearer of the bad news.

"So... Alexander! The slaves in the mines and quarries and fields spend their lives sweating to produce vast sums of money, and Gaius squanders it on useless baubles and pretty boys. That's disgusting! Didn't you ever try to stop him?"

Alexander shook his head slowly and deliberately.

"He had a right to spend his money as he wished. He was the master, not I."

"But you could have said something! You were his steward!"

"A steward is still a slave, mistress, and a slave does not tell the man who owns him what he may or may not do with his property." The smile had faded from Alexander's face, but the bite was not gone from his voice. "That's not the way to live a long and happy life."

Half blind with a fury that even she didn't fully understand, Theodosia leaped to her feet.

"But why should you care so much about his money when he was determined to waste it? Why keep such meticulous records of his property? Why exert yourself so far beyond what was required?"

Her rising voice sounded odd to her, as if it came from someone else.

"I don't understand you, Alexander! You had the key to that chest! Why didn't you help yourself to a few of these boxes and head straight for the port at Martanum? Nobody would've stopped you. You could've gotten away without being challenged, and just a fraction of this would've bought a secure hiding place for the rest of your life. By all the gods, I wouldn't have hesitated an instant in your place!"

Suddenly aware of what she was saying, Theodosia jerked her head around and fled to the nearest window.

What a fool!

She was sweating now.

Forgetting every common-sense rule of how to deal with a slave... Suggesting that he steal and run away...

She turned to face him, propping her hands on the window frame behind her, as if braced for an attack.

How do I recover from this?

Alexander exhaled through pursed lips, his intense eyes piercing hers as he produced a crooked smile.

"Want to take that speech back, mistress? I can pretend I never heard it."

Theodosia stared at him.

Juno, help me! What do I say now?

"You have my word," Alexander went on. "I'll never mention it again. Not to you or to anyone else."

Theodosia leaned against the window frame and closed her eyes.

"No." She looked into his face. "It was a mistake for me to say what I just said, and we both know it, but it's no good pretending I didn't say it. My questions to you were improper and unwise—not to mention unfair to you—but I did ask them and, in truth, I'm curious to know. Don't feel compelled to answer though." She risked a smile of her own. "As you reminded me this morning... no one has the right to probe too far into the privacy of another, not even that of her slave."

Alexander stepped closer. Last night, he had frightened her, but now, for some reason, he no longer did. The fragile air of trust she felt would have seemed impossible, even that morning.

"Thank you." The irony was gone from his voice, replaced by a warmth that Theodosia hadn't heard there before. "I appreciate your frankness and your sensitivity, mistress. There are many things—many memories—that are painful for me."

As he spoke, Alexander rubbed a finger absentmindedly across the jagged scar on his jaw.

Theodosia made no reply. He might volunteer more information than she could ever force out of him.

"My lord Gaius once tried to make me talk about myself, and I refused, as I did with you this morning. Only he didn't let me out of the fire so quickly as you. But," his tone sharpened a bit, "if we may go back to your dangerously honest outburst... There's no reason why I shouldn't give you some answers. Why take such pains? Why not steal a box or two? Why not run away? Fact is, I've asked myself those same questions and others, many times. I don't have any answers."

"Maybe you were afraid."

"Afraid. That must be it." The irony was back. "If you say so, anyway."

"You're insolent, you know."

"Can a slave be both insolent and afraid?"

Theodosia paused, studying the angles of his face.

"Probably not."

Her eyes lingered on his, and after a while she shook her head.

"No, Alexander, I don't think you're afraid. It's something else. Am I right that you once were free?"

"How do you know?"

"It shows. The look on your face. Your voice. The way you carry yourself. You don't have the bearing of a man born to slavery. And didn't you tell me last night that you had a name before you had a master?"

"You were listening. I wasn't sure."

"I was listening. I just didn't like what I was hearing." She gave him another tentative smile. "Anyway, what I suspect is that you opted to serve Gaius better than he deserved to be served as a way of proving something to yourself, about yourself."

"You've read Seneca, it seems."

"So have you, it seems."

Theodosia was still propped against the window frame, facing into the room. Alexander came up beside her and peered out through the glass.

"As a way of proving... what?"

"Well, you're a proud man. Odd thing to say about a slave, but it's obviously true."

"A lot of good pride does me."

"So one might think, but— Look, I know what my brother was, and so do you. Everyone in Rome knew he was a monster and a fool. Gaius was nowhere near you, mentally and morally, and you knew it, but things like intelligence and morals don't matter much between Roman masters and Greek slaves. His power over you was absolute, and that galled you."

Theodosia stopped to give Alexander a chance to respond, but he said nothing. After a few breaths she went on, feeling her way through the tangle of her thoughts.

"I think you saw your mind as the only thing that Gaius couldn't command. By serving him better than he deserved to be served, you stripped a bit of power from him." She chuckled at the idea forming in her head. "I think your dedicated service was a form of rebellion that my brother was just too stupid to see."

Alexander stood gazing out the window as Theodosia watched his face. When he finally spoke, it was as if to the sea outside. His words were open and honest, and there was no hint of servility in his voice.

"Well, we're certainly being candid today." He nodded, eyes still on the sea. "You're right about one thing, at least. It did gall me to be forced to serve and obey a man who had absolute power over me simply because he was a Roman and I a Greek. And yes, you're right. I hated him."

"No doubt you feel the same way about me."

"I did, till just now."

"What changed your mind?"

Alexander turned his head and looked directly into Theodosia's eyes at close range. The sudden intimacy caught her off guard, yet she didn't seem able to move.

"Perhaps I see that you possess all the attributes your brother lacked. You're bright, intuitive, and clearly a moral woman. If it's true, as you say, that my face and voice and bearing betray my former freedom, then it's equally evident that you would do no harm to anyone."

Theodosia wanted to look away but couldn't.

"So, you see," Alexander said, "no matter how stern you'd like your slaves to think you are, it's a pose as translucent as the wings of a butterfly."

Now it was Theodosia's turn to be speechless. After a moment, she freed her eyes from the grasp of his and moved to the next window, propped her palms on each side of the frame and turned her head slightly toward him.

"All this makes me wonder what form your rebellion will take... now that I've discovered your secret and you mine."

"Perhaps I will feel no need to rebel against you. It should be a pleasant novelty to serve a Roman who is not only wealthy and powerful but intelligent and moral as well. From what I've seen, that's a rare combination indeed."

Theodosia threw her head back and laughed aloud at that sally, feeling at ease with him for the first time.

"Oh, Alexander! I'm sorry to disappoint you, but I'm afraid you're in for a terrible letdown."

"Why? Which of those attributes doesn't fit? Your morality? Your wealth?" Irony again.

"Actually, I wish that were it." She snickered. "Look, I'm just a woman, which means that the foulest free-born Roman male sleeping off his cheap-wine stupor in the street has more legal rights than I. And just wait till I marry. If I marry. Watch what happens then to my freedom, my property, and my so-called power. Besides," she said, over-enunciating for effect, "my mother was Greek, which makes me a half-breed, neither fish nor fowl. A huge social obstacle. So you see, Alexander, we are both pawns at the mercy of Rome."

Alexander frowned at that. Without a word, he went to the chest, which still lay open awaiting the return of its plundered contents. Reaching in, he removed another—much smaller—box. Then he stood

27

before her again, his deportment much more formal than before. With a stiff bow, he handed the tiny box to her unopened.

Puzzled, Theodosia dropped her eyes and lifted the lid. Inside, nestled into a white linen cloth, lay a gold signet ring.

Father's seal. The symbol of our family's prestige for generations.

"Lucius Gallio," said Alexander, "took it off your brother's hand the day after the murder and gave it to me for safekeeping."

Theodosia slipped the ring onto the index finger of her right hand. It was much too big.

"Why did you wait till this moment to give it to me?"

"You forbade me to bring anything else out of the chest, remember? But maybe it's not such bad timing, after all, since you appear to need consolation for your hopeless position in this cruel world that has treated you so savagely."

"I guess to someone in your position, my position doesn't seem too bad at all."

"No, miss, it doesn't."

It was the first time that Alexander dropped the stiff "mistress" in favor of the diminutive commonly used by close family servants. It was a natural shift that reflected the changing tenor of their relationship.

Their meeting had taken most of the day; soon it would be dinnertime. Theodosia remembered with regret that she had deprived Alexander of his lunch.

"Return the boxes to the chest and lock it up. Then, I suspect, you'll want to finish that meal I forced you to abandon."

She was almost to the door when he called to her.

"One more thing, miss, please. With your permission, I'd like to burn some old documents that I recently found in the chest. Nothing you'll ever need."

Theodosia glanced back.

Those old things are part of my heritage.

"No. Hold on to them for now. I may want to take a look at them someday."

CHAPTER FIVE

Alexander completed his task and returned to the cubicle that was a perquisite of his position. Most of the household slaves slept on straw piles in dank barracks below the kitchen. The stable hands enjoyed fresher air, but their loft above the horses was a firetrap. The shepherds and goatherds lived in mud huts a mile to the north, with their own families, kitchen, garden, chickens, and dogs... a self-contained community. The only ones who slept in the villa were the porter, Lucilla, and Alexander.

His tiny room at the service end of the peristyle had little in common with the rest of the house. No frescoes brightened its tufa walls. No mosaic enlivened its cement floor. Besides the low bed, there were only a small chest and a lamp. No chair. No window. The rear wing was far from the hypocaust that heated the family rooms; it was cold in winter.

But this was Alexander's sanctuary. Here alone he found privacy.

Tired and tense after the astonishing afternoon with Theodosia Varra, he closed the door, stretched out, and tried not to hear the voices of waiters carrying her dinner to the dining room. Yesterday at this time he hadn't even met the new mistress. Now they knew one another, but the master-slave formality that Alexander had expected—and used so well to keep his distance from Gaius—had evaporated in just a few hours.

Wide-eyed, he stared at the ceiling, thinking of that evening a week ago when he had followed Stefan up the creaky ladder to the stable loft. He remembered his amazement as Stefan pulled a gunny sack from under a pile of straw and handed Alexander his treasures: a painted wooden doll, a child's silver cup, and a lock of the same golden-brown hair that would later catch Alexander's eye in the library... keepsakes of a girl Stefan had loved all his life and never expected to see again.

But Alexander had just told him that she was, in fact, coming back.

Now, as he lay on his bed in the black cubicle, two faces appeared on the ceiling, as if by some magic of his mind. The gold-flecked eyes and creamy features of one were sharp and fresh. He knew Theodosia Varra's voice, her clove-oil fragrance, the way her hair gleamed in the sun. The other face was harder to recall... just an olive-toned oval surrounded by dark, curly hair. The vagueness of Antibe's features haunted him.

Sweet gods of Greece, I can't even remember the color of her eyes!

After a time, he lit the lamp, took a sheet of papyrus from the chest, and began to write in Greek. The poem came slowly... a love lyric to the young wife whose face and voice seemed harder to recall with each passing year. When it was done, he lay back and let himself fall asleep.

When he awoke, he knew by the din in the kitchen hall that the mistress had finished her meal. He bundled the poem with others in the chest, stepped into the bright night, and made his way—as he often did—to an ancient pine at the edge of the garden, beside the sea. Most times when Alexander had gone out like this, his master had been in Rome and the suite on the second floor dark and shuttered. But tonight the shutters were open, and between them he could see the crimson, green, and gold frescoes aglow in the light of the lamp-trees. Soft notes of a cithara drifted out. A clear, lovely voice was singing in Greek.

He stood for a while staring at the water, enjoying the music.

Then, abruptly, it stopped. He glanced up to see a white-clad figure step onto the balcony. It was Theodosia Varra.

She leaned against the railing and raised her face to the sky, apparently unaware of the man in the shadows below. Alexander watched her briefly, then slipped away to the kitchen.

The new mistress had respected his privacy. He would not spy on her.

Theodosia paced restlessly in her suite. Worries chased each other through her head like angry squirrels.

Fear from the unsolved mystery of Gaius' murder...

Anxiety about her too-frank conversation with Alexander...

Guilt for the absurd fortune in her strongbox...

And a strange new emotion that she couldn't yet define...

Lucilla had unpacked the cithara that Phoebe had taught Theodosia to play so long ago. Hoping to take her mind off her worries, Theodosia picked out a few ballads before laying it down. The muse was absent.

With the cithara came memories of early days in the Subura. After Phoebe's death, Theodosia had kept honing her skill at improvising. In recent years, Lucilla, the cithara, and a few books had provided companionship at times like this. But Lucilla had disappeared tonight.

The soft night beckoned, so she went to her balcony. A hum of voices from the kitchen formed a counterpoint to the waves breaking on the rocks below. Lucilla would be there with the others.

Love to know what they're talking about.

Theodosia propped her arms on the railing and gazed at Orion.

My only companion tonight, I guess.

Then she knew. Loneliness was that new emotion tormenting her.

It was one thing to be a poor girl living with her maid, and quite another thing to be the mistress of an estate like this. For years, she and Lucilla had ignored the social gap between them as they shopped and cooked and ate every meal together. But that gap had widened fast in the last few days and would continue to grow.

Can I ever confide in Lucilla again if I think she'll be out there every night, gossiping about me with my other slaves?

As the hubbub from the kitchen heightened the silence of the elegant apartment, Theodosia realized how thoroughly alone she was.

Everyone has someone to talk to but me.

She decided to take a walk.

Downstairs, she tiptoed past old Jason, the porter—one of the few servants left from her father's day—who was dozing as he always had on his couch by the main door, and hurried out to the gardens. Meticulously designed when the villa was new, they swept along three sides of the house, engulfed the pergola, and fanned out to embrace the shore.

Enjoying the silver light that fell through the vines and leaves onto the stone floor, Theodosia made her way to the far side of the pergola and stared into the cove below, where she had often played as a child.

Juno the moon winked conspiratorially, slipping from cloud to cloud, teasing her to the beach. The rocky steps were moss-covered and slick. Weeds whipped her ankles, but she reached the bottom without slipping.

Halfway across the beach, she kicked off her sandals and squished through the sand to a flat boulder lying just above the tide. There she climbed up, dangled her feet into the water, and reclined on the rock. Spellbound, she savored the mass of stars and the rustic silence—so unlike the cacophony of Rome at night—and lost track of time.

After a while, hearing voices, she glanced toward the pergola overhead. Staring down at her were Alexander and the gigantic stable hand. She turned her face away, hoping they would ignore her, but when she looked again they had reached the bottom of the steps and were headed in her direction.

"What are you doing here?" she said in Greek, sitting up but making no effort to pull her feet from the water.

The steward came as close as he could without wading into the surf, leaving his companion a few paces behind. He answered in Latin.

"Lucilla was worried about you, miss."

"I'm perfectly fine," she said in Latin. "I'll be along in a bit."

The giant came forward now, too, and addressed Theodosia. It was a terrible breach of protocol since she hadn't acknowledged him, much less given him permission to speak. Furthermore, as if to compound his impudence, he used the familiar form of address.

"It ain't safe for you to come here alone, miss," he said in uneducated Latin, and suddenly Theodosia understood why Alexander had switched languages. "There are brigands up and down the coast. Bet they wouldn't like nothing better than to get their hands on you."

"What would it be to you if they did?"

"I'd feel bad, as an old friend... if you'll let me use that term with you." The big man looked anxious. "You don't recognize me, do you? I'm Stefan, miss."

"Stefan?" She frowned in disbelief. "Little Stefanus... who used to bring sweets from the kitchen for all of us to feast on down here?"

He nodded as his shaggy face relaxed under a grin.

"And once took a beating when I snitched a honey cake intended for the master's dinner party. Have I changed so much, miss, that you didn't know me?"

Theodosia lifted her feet from the water and rose to her full height on the boulder. The stable hand was standing in the sand, but still he towered above her.

"Stefan? Oh, yes, you have changed. Quite a bit! I had no idea who you were."

She gave him her hands and let him help her off the rock.

"Why didn't you come in last night to say hello?"

Stefan stared at her, saying nothing. It was Alexander who answered.

"He hasn't been sure how to deal with you, miss. You spent many years in Rome, and he didn't know how you'd feel now about people who knew you as a child. Especially since your brother sold off almost everyone else he'd grown up with."

"Well, I'm not my brother! But, Stefan, why didn't he sell you, too?"

"Oh, he threatened to many times, up to a couple of days before he got killed. Alexander always managed to talk him out of it. Kept telling him how much more I'd be worth in the market once I stopped growing."

Theodosia turned grateful eyes to Alexander.

Then she went to find her sandals, slipped them on, and headed for the stairs. Back in the gardens, she looked once more toward the cove.

"I love it down there. Doesn't the army try to capture the brigands?"

"They go on raids every month," Alexander said, "and they do get some each time, but they can't get all of them."

"Escaped slaves, no doubt. Have any of ours ever joined them?"

Then she blushed, suddenly uncomfortable with the topic.

"Not to join the brigands," Alexander said. "But three fellows did run off together several years ago."

"What happened to them? Did they get away?"

"My lord Gaius hired men to hunt them. It took many months and lots of money, but they caught two in Sicily and returned them to him."

"What did Gaius do?"

"You know the usual punishment for running away."

"Flogging," she said softly. "Crucifixion, sometimes, if the escape is part of a slave uprising."

"My lord Gaius decided to do both, to teach us all a good lesson, so the next day he sent for a meatman."

"Meatman?"

"A professional flogger, miss." Alexander's tone was cool.

"With a set of mean-looking whips." Stefan was more passionate. "Sharp pieces of metal set into the thongs."

"You know that big double oak by the kitchen?" Alexander's voice remained chillingly placid. "Well, the meatman crucified those two on it early one morning. Drove his long iron spikes through their hands and wrists... one man on each side of the double trunk, so they faced each other through the gap. They hung there the whole day, screeching and begging for mercy. That evening, your brother made all the rest of us watch as the meatman whipped them to death, right there on that tree."

"What about the third man who ran away?" Theodosia asked when she trusted herself to speak.

"We never heard anything more from him."

Without another word, Theodosia set off at a clip for the house. Halfway along the path, she stopped and turned again.

"Something's just occurred to me. That runaway you mentioned, the one who never was caught— Couldn't he have been one of the thugs who ambushed my brother? Maybe he recognized Gaius during the robbery and decided to kill him."

"Not likely," Alexander said.

"No, listen. Wealthy patricians don't tend to get murdered on the street in Rome. Robbed, yes, but not killed. However, if one of the thugs was the third man who escaped from here... wouldn't he have had reason for wanting to avenge his friends? That's got to be it! He was involved in a random street crime when he saw his chance to get even."

Alexander's eyes darted from Theodosia's face to Stefan's.

"It wasn't a robbery, miss. The master's gold signet ring was still on his finger when the officials recovered his body later that night."

"Well... robbers wouldn't take anything so identifiable."

"There were no robbers involved. And it wasn't a random act."

Theodosia paused for a moment. Alexander spoke with conviction, yet this information, if true, would shatter everything her fragile sense of security was built on.

"How do you know that?" she demanded.

The steward merely shook his head.

"Alexander, statements like that don't come out of the blue. You must have some reason."

"Please don't ask me for reasons. I'm telling you the truth, but I can't tell you how I know about it."

Theodosia felt a surge of anger.

"Just because you refused to answer a few questions this morning—"

"That's not it, miss."

"Then... you're saying the bearers really were guilty and the investigators covered it up. A lot of people thought so, and when the litter slaves were put to death it seemed to corroborate that rumor. But I didn't believe it since the emperor didn't order the execution of every slave in Gaius' household in Rome." She paused again. "There's no getting around a certain question. Tribune Otho told me he saw you in Rome the day Gaius was murdered. Said he talked to you and—."

"That's not true."

"You're accusing Tribune Marcus Salvius Otho of lying?"

"No. Just that... the only patrician I spoke with was Lucius Gallio."

"What were you doing in the city?"

"I went there on the master's business."

"So, why weren't you there when the authorities sealed his mansion the next morning? After Gaius died, they wouldn't let anyone in or out until Emperor Claudius decided the fate of the slaves."

"I left Rome late that afternoon, several hours before the murder. Ask General Vespasian. I stopped by his villa that evening on my way through Caere, bearing a message for him from Gallio."

"You could have turned around, gone back, and used that as your alibi. Gaius was killed around midnight. You see how easy it would be for someone to suspect you in this business? And you've already told me how much you hated my brother."

"I had nothing to do with your brother's murder, and the authorities wouldn't have covered up a slave revolt if they thought that's what it was. They'd have executed every one of his slaves in Rome. No, miss, the fact that robbers didn't kill him doesn't automatically mean his slaves did it."

"You sound like Titus."

"Maybe he's on to something. Think about it. What was my lord Gaius doing in the brothel district in the middle of the night without bodyguards? Nobody expects litter bearers to provide any protection."

"Gaius went there all the time without guards. You know that. Gods, everyone in Rome knew that."

"Yes, miss, everyone in Rome knew that."

"Look, he was in a bad area and got jumped by robbers, who killed him. Either that or he was extraordinarily obnoxious that night, and his bearers rid themselves of him. No other alternatives were investigated."

"And why weren't they?"

Theodosia started to answer but stopped short. Robbers would have taken a gold ring. Slaves had nothing to gain from murdering their master. Their claims of innocence would not be believed, even when made under torture. Gaius' late-night trips were predictable. If anyone had wanted to murder him, that was the perfect time and place to do it.

Alexander shouldn't have known anything about his master's death, and he shouldn't have said anything about it to Theodosia. She'd be justified in turning him in to the Praetorian Guards. And now he was insinuating conspiracy with a calm and confidence that unnerved her. She had no reason to believe him, and yet...

Vespasian's words returned to her memory.

"There are so many thugs around nowadays, and not all of them are poor foreign folk."

Theodosia shivered in the warm spring night.

Was Gaius murdered by someone with enough power to influence the investigation?

She shivered again.

And if so, what does that mean for me?

35

CHAPTER SIX

Full of energy despite a sleepless night, Theodosia rose the next morning with plans to explore every corner of her villa. She felt confident today—her second full day at home—as if confronting her fears in the dark had strengthened her.

She began with the storage area behind the peristyle, sticking her head into every cubicle she passed. There were sacks of barley and other grains; amphorae of olives in their oil; tubs of fruit and nuts from last fall's harvest; honey and pungent spices. One room was locked; she supposed the wine was stored there. Nearby was a tiny sleeping chamber.

Everything appeared to be in order, so she headed to the kitchen, hoping it would be as she remembered... a noisy finch singing in its cage by the door, something fragrant simmering in a kettle over the fire pit, and rough-hewn tables, chairs, and benches scattered around the room.

Since time began, it seemed, their slaves had gathered here for after-work camaraderie. Theodosia's father had followed the philosophy of his famous grandfather from Reate, Marcus Terentius Varro, among whose prolific writings were treatises on humane slave management. Even Gaius—who abused his servants in many ways—had not chosen to deny them the evenings of unfettered leisure that were a family tradition.

As she neared the kitchen this morning, Theodosia heard a harsh voice railing at someone. Stepping to the door, she saw Milo, the bald-pated head cook, sitting with his back to her, jabbing his finger into the chest of the same curly haired boy whom Alexander had brought to play with Domitian. The kitchen staff sprawled around the table, laughing.

The scullion stood before Milo, his head down. Abruptly, Milo leaned forward, grabbed his shoulder with one hand, and slapped him in the face with the other. The boy tried to pull away, but he couldn't break

36

Milo's grip. Only when he looked up did anyone notice Theodosia in the doorway.

The child's eyes seemed to grow larger and freeze as he spotted her.

The others followed his gaze, their laughter stopping as they jumped to their feet, scraping benches across the floor and rocking the table. Milo, his face reddening, released the scullion. As Theodosia stood wondering whether to interfere, the boy ran over and dropped to the floor beside her.

"What has he done?" she asked after a moment.

"He is uncooperative and disobedient, mistress. Shirks his duties every chance he gets." Despite being called to account before his staff, Milo's voice sounded steady. "This morning, I sent him to bring buckets of water to wash the dishes. Instead, Denos here," he gestured to one of his assistants, "caught him in the garden, drawing in the dirt with a stick."

Theodosia thought of the piped-in, heated water that supplied the lavish bath in the house. Apparently, such conveniences didn't extend to the working parts of the villa.

Before she could reply, she heard footsteps behind her and turned. The scullion dashed out the door to Alexander, who had stopped a few paces away. To Theodosia's surprise, the boy buried his face in the steward's tunic and clutched him about the legs.

Without acknowledging her, Alexander took the child in his arms and whispered something that Theodosia couldn't hear.

She stepped outside.

"Bring him and come with me."

She led the way into the garden, to a circle of pink oleanders surrounding an elaborate Etruscan urn that had been made into a fountain. Reaching out to the boy in Alexander's arms, she pushed up the long curls that fell over his forehead. There were three old scars on his face, and one cheek was red from Milo's slap. Still, he was beautiful.

"What's your name?"

The boy clung to Alexander's shoulder.

"Don't you have a name?"

"Philip of Macedonia." The voice was expressionless.

"Tell the mistress your real name," Alexander said in Greek, "and speak to her in our language."

The child stared at Theodosia. Finally, he answered... in Greek.

"My mother and father called me Lycos."

"Well," Theodosia replied in Greek, "I think we should call you Lycos, too. Don't you agree, Alexander?"

Alexander gave her a look she had not seen on his face before.

37

"I certainly do, miss. It was the master who mocked him with the name of our great Greek king. It amused him to give us ludicrous names. He became angry if Lycos used his real name or mine."

"And I'll be angry if anyone calls you anything but Lycos." She patted his arm. "Now, you go play in the garden."

Alexander set the child down and whispered again in his ear. Lycos grinned and scampered away.

"You're fond of that boy," Theodosia said.

"He's a sweet child. Reminds me of another boy I used to know."

"Your own son, perhaps?" The hunch came to her in the instant she articulated it. "You said yesterday that many of your memories are painful. I know I've no right to pry, but am I wrong to guess that you once had a wife and family?"

Theodosia thought he would reproach her, but he just shook his head.

"No, miss, you are not wrong."

"Where are they now?"

"I don't know. I wrote three letters to my wife in Corinth after I came here, but never got an answer."

"How did you send those letters?"

"Bribed sailors leaving Martanum and Ostia for Corinth. Only the gods know if they were ever delivered. A slave's letters, you know. They all probably ended up in the sea."

"Probably so, if they went without a Roman seal."

Alexander stared into the fountain.

"Have you ever loved someone you were powerless to protect?"

"Only Phoebe, my nurse."

"Then you know how terrible it is."

"Maybe I can help you." She snapped a blossom off an oleander and twirled it. "Any letter that Theodosia Varra writes will be delivered."

That unfamiliar expression returned to Alexander's eyes as he looked at her. Theodosia felt as if she had cracked the shell of a very hard nut.

"You would help me find my wife and son?"

"If I can."

"Oh, miss!" Alexander gave an odd half-laugh. "You've no idea how often I have begged the gods to let me know they are alive somewhere. Just to know they are still alive." His voice was husky but controlled. "You asked me yesterday why I hadn't run away. Well, it did occur to me to do so, many times. I kept thinking of Antibe and my little Niko, and also of the fear we would all live in, even if I could get away and find them. So maybe you were right yesterday, when you said I was afraid."

He turned back to the fountain.

Don't interrupt. Let him talk.

"When I was a boy in Corinth, my parents drilled into me the most important lesson a Greek can ever learn. The Romans are all powerful, and there's nowhere one can go to escape the reach of Rome. And they were right! All the jewels in that chest couldn't buy safety with so much money and influence chasing me. Your brother was vindictive and cruel. He'd have hunted me down like he did those two in Sicily, just for the fun of it. I couldn't stand being torn from Antibe and Niko again and brought back to face the punishment given to runaways. I'd seen what he would do, and it was dreadful, as I told you last night."

He paused, but Theodosia—sitting now on the fountain edge, letting the water cascade over her fingers—still made no comment.

"I know how the Romans operate," Alexander went on. "They surely sold my wife and son into slavery when they sold me, so I'd be risking that same punishment for them if I tried to free them, which I can't do, because I don't have any idea where they are. They might be in Lusitania, or in Africa, or in Britain. I wouldn't know where to start searching for them, even if I were free and could do it openly."

After another silence, Theodosia looked up.

"I'll write a letter and see if I can locate your wife and son. If so, maybe I can find a way to bring them here. The stewards of estates like this often have their own families; no reason why you should be any different. But... there's a catch."

She rose and confronted him, eye to eye.

"In return for my help, I'm going to demand more of you than Gaius ever did. I want your frankest advice. Your total honesty. I want your friendship, too. I don't want to spend my life worrying that you might be my enemy... somehow conspiring or working against me."

"There's no way I could be your enemy, under the circumstances."

"Oh, I think you could be a real enemy if you chose to be, regardless of the circumstances. But I want more from you than just not to be my enemy. I want us to be friends." She waited for his response, but none came. "Friendship is not something I can order you to give me. Friendship must come freely, as a gift. Can you accept a Varro as your friend?"

"It's a bit hard to think of the person who owns you as a friend."

"Willing to give it a try?"

Alexander turned and stepped away.

"You say you want my honesty? Well—in all honesty—I don't think we can be friends. That's not possible, under these circumstances."

"If not friends, then, at least not enemies. I'll help you, voluntarily, if you'll do the same for me. Well, no… maybe it won't always be voluntary on your part, because—as we both know—I do hold the power in this relationship, and I'll use it if I have to. I'd prefer your voluntary help, though." She went to stand in front of him. "Look. Between what you told me last night and what Lucilla says all my other slaves think of me… I'm sure I have enemies I don't even begin to know about. It doesn't seem too farfetched that you might be one of them."

"Miss, I—"

"So, just in case, I'm willing to take some steps to ensure that you have a stake in my survival. Since my father was once governor of Corinth, I should be able to get some answers. We'll write a letter today, and you may take it to Ostia tomorrow. With my seal on it, you can be sure that it will be both delivered and answered."

Alexander regarded her warily.

"What do I have to do to earn that favor?"

"Well, since you're not willing to tackle something as difficult as friendship with me… we'll make it easier. First, you will tell me everything you know about my brother's murder."

"Miss—"

"Everything." She paused to let the word sink in. "And second, you will escort me to the farm the day after tomorrow."

"Aren't you going to wait for Nizzo to call on you?"

"No. I want to see the place for myself, and I intend to arrive unannounced. Just look at all I've learned this morning by showing up unexpectedly in the kitchen."

"Nizzo won't be pleased. He isn't used to being supervised."

"You go there on occasion."

"As an errand boy, nothing more. Nizzo is free and a Roman citizen, thanks to your father. He's not about to take orders from a slave."

"Well, he will take orders from me. Alexander, that farm belongs to me. I have every right to visit it."

"You said you wanted frankness from me. So, miss, I'll be frank. You own some of the best farmland in the Roman Empire, plus a horde of brute laborers. Your crops are sold in markets from Ortobello to Pompeii. Your vineyards produce a wine that's among the most esteemed in Rome, and wool from your sheep may well be in the toga the emperor's wearing today. It's a huge, complicated agricultural operation, and for decades Nizzo has run it all. There's a reason why your father lifted that one man above a thousand others who started exactly where he did and placed him in charge of them, even while he was still a slave. Nizzo isn't polished, but he's smart and tough and honest and ambitious."

"But it's *my* property. I want to see it."

"You won't like what you see."

"That's no reason for me not to go."

"No? Here's another reason. You say you're worried about enemies? Well, threaten Nizzo's authority and you'll make a formidable enemy."

"He's just a freedman."

"Don't underestimate him. He has many influential friends in Rome. Antagonize Nizzo and you'll have more enemies than you can imagine."

Theodosia turned and studied the roses.

"I know I asked for your advice, but that doesn't mean I have to take it." She laughed, amused at the curious situation she had gotten into. "Look, Alexander. I didn't ask to inherit all this. All I ever wanted was to live here at home. I never envied Gaius his property."

"Well, envy it or not, you've got it now."

"True. I've got it now, and I'm going to see every bit of it that I can."

Alexander reacted with the sigh of one who is not being heeded.

"How do you intend to get there? The place is deliberately isolated. There's no road at all from this side, so you'd have to take your carriage into Rome, then out on the Via Clodia. It would take four days round trip, and you'd probably have to spend a night in that wretched place."

"How do *you* get there and back in one day?"

"Through the woods. On a horse."

"Then I'll go that way, too."

She turned around in time to see a remarkable series of expressions cross his face... as comprehension gave way to disbelief and then to astonishment. He opened his mouth, but no words came out.

"What's the matter? Never seen a woman on horseback?"

"Not a Roman woman, no. Do you ride?"

"I haven't in years, but I used to ride very well. Father taught me, and we'd go galloping off somewhere every day, right up to the afternoon he died. After lunch today, I'll take a horse out and get some practice."

"You'll be sore. General Vespasian's party is just three days off."

"Let me worry about that."

Alexander's astonished look slowly evolved into a grin.

"Well, it's obvious I have no choice."

Theodosia matched his grin.

"No, you don't." Motioning him closer, she changed her tone. "Now... tell me more about that boy, Lycos."

"My lord Gaius bought him in Rome last summer. He speaks Greek, as you saw. Says he was stolen from his parents by pirates. All he knows is that they lived on the coast, but there's a lot of coast in Greece."

"Why did Gaius buy such a little fellow? I'm sure it wasn't out of compassion."

"He bought him for a plaything, to put it as delicately as I can. The boy was to be trained to serve him flawlessly, in every way your brother might think up."

"So, why is he working for Milo in the kitchen? I'm guessing you didn't assign him to that."

"You are even more intuitive than I suspected. But in fact, I did cause it by befriending him. Shouldn't have, but... It was easy to imagine he was my son, speaking Greek and all. Same curly hair as my Niko."

"Gaius didn't like that much, I'm sure."

"I guess not! He ordered him to stay away from me, but Lycos kept coming to the library. Every day, except when the master took him to Rome to serve as entertainment at his parties." Alexander made a face and waved his hands. "You don't want to know. Anyway, there were times when he left Lycos here, so I began teaching him to read and write. Then one day, my lord Gaius caught us reading. I'd never seen him so angry." He patted his cheeks. "Lycos and I were both well slapped that afternoon. Slapping in the face was your brother's favorite form of correction."

Theodosia closed her eyes briefly as Alexander went on.

"My lord Gaius was so angry that he banished Lycos from the house. Gave Milo complete authority over him and ordered him to report it if Lycos and I even spoke to each other again."

"I wonder... would you care to add tutoring to your other duties? Train Lycos to be your assistant some day?"

Alexander's face brightened. He smiled and visibly relaxed, as if their conversation were over. But it wasn't.

"There's still one thing left for you to do," Theodosia said, "to earn my letter to Corinth. Tell me what you know about my brother's murder. No information, no letter."

Alexander's smile had faded as she spoke. Now he winced.

"You're forcing me to do things that shouldn't be done."

She made an impatient little gesture with one hand.

"All right," he said, "but I'm really not the one you want to talk to."

Theodosia dropped her head back in exasperation.

"The one you want to talk to is over there," Alexander nodded sideways, "drawing his letters in the flower bed."

CHAPTER SEVEN

"Get the boy."

No answer was required, so she headed for the pergola and settled into a chair. Lycos bounced in soon after, carrying a spray of lilacs. Alexander strode in behind him.

"Thank you, Lycos," Theodosia said in Greek as she accepted the fragrant bouquet, a momentary distraction from the unpleasantries ahead. "Sit down, both of you."

Alexander quizzed her with his eyes. A favored slave child might sit beside his mistress on occasion, but that familiarity was forbidden an adult slave by centuries of custom.

"I said... sit down. Let's have a conversation, not an interrogation."

Alexander sat, took Lycos on his lap, and was silent.

"Let me guess," Theodosia said to start the conversation. "You were both in Rome the day my brother died?"

Lycos leaned into Alexander's chest, his eyes apprehensive. Alexander wrapped his arms around him and nodded. Theodosia recalled his words: *"Have you ever loved someone you were powerless to protect?"*

"Lycos had been in Rome with the master all week," Alexander said, "and I rode in that morning. A message had arrived the evening before, ordering me to the city the next day."

"Why?"

"The message didn't say, and I never found out. When I got there early in the afternoon, the master was at the baths. By the time he was murdered, Lycos and I were safely back here."

"You didn't wait to find out why he'd sent for you? And you took Lycos away without his permission? Why?"

43

Alexander leaned his head over the boy's shoulder.

"Tell the mistress what you told me that afternoon."

"It was two men," Lycos began in a frightened tone, "at the dinner the night before. I heard them talking."

"Lycos heard them, but he couldn't see them. He'd decided to hide before they sent for him," Alexander's voice grew hard, "to have their usual sport with him. He was behind a curtain when he heard the conversation."

"Did you recognize the voices?"

Lycos shook his head.

"What did they say?"

"Kept talking about the viper. One of them asked if everything was set for the viper, and the other one said, 'I told him about all the new whores down by the river. He'll be so drunk when he comes out, he won't know what hit him.' And they laughed and laughed and laughed."

"Viper," Theodosia said, drumming the tabletop. "That's the design on those silver serving pieces. A serpent with a ruby in its mouth."

She looked at Alexander.

"Where did you say Gaius got that set?"

"He brought it from Rome about a year ago. Rubies were his favorite gemstone, but that serpent design meant nothing to me. I really never thought anything about it."

"Until Lycos told you what he'd overheard."

"Correct. After we talked, I began to put things together. That message I'd received was odd, for one thing. No indication at all of why my lord Gaius wanted me, or what I was to do once I got to Rome. It wasn't his writing, either."

"He could have had a secretary write it."

"True, but it looked almost like his writing, as if somebody wanted me to think it was his. A hired messenger brought it, too, not one of his slaves. He'd often ordered me to ride to Rome before, but it was always one of his own men who brought the message."

"So, after you talked with Lycos…"

"I knew why I was there. Our master was going to be killed, and somebody wanted me in Rome when it happened."

"To take the blame? But why would anyone suspect you?"

"The authorities don't find criminals in cases like that, miss. Just scapegoats. Litter slaves, street thugs… a Greek steward perhaps. It wouldn't have been hard for them to find a motive for me, because so many people knew how much I hated him. He used to taunt me about my slavery in front of his friends, or slap me in front of them. I got into lots of trouble trying to protect Lycos, and when your brother started talking with some of his friends about selling Stefan as a gladiator—"

"Gladiator?"

"Well, he's the kind that circus masters search the world for, and here he is, tending horses just up the road from Rome."

Stefan in the arena? Damn Gaius!

"You still haven't explained why you brought Lycos back with you that night. If Gaius hadn't been murdered..."

"Don't you see, miss? They were arranging it to look like some of his slaves did it. So, according to your gentle laws, all his slaves in Rome could be executed, even the children."

"So... you made sure Lycos wasn't there when they sealed Gaius' house the next morning."

"I wasn't eager for my own execution either."

"I guess not." Theodosia tapped Lycos' knee. "Go play."

Alexander stood up as the boy skipped away.

"An old habit."

"Suit yourself. I see why you didn't want to tell me any of this."

"Information of this sort does a slave no good. Leads right to the torture chambers of the Carcer Tullianum."

"Why did you hint at it last night?"

"Mistake. But I hated to see you inventing scenarios that had nothing to do with the truth. It's time to put your brother's murder behind you."

"That's not so easy." She rose to her feet. "All right, you've satisfied my demands. Think you're up to riding to Ostia tomorrow, to send a letter to Corinth?"

"Whenever you wish it."

He followed her to the library, and together they composed a letter to Marcus Viticus, the Roman governor of Corinth. Theodosia dictated and Alexander wrote, supplying data about his wife and son.

"Now," Theodosia said as she pressed her ring into a drop of red sealing wax, "go to the barn and tell Stefan to pick out a horse for me to ride this afternoon."

Alexander took the scroll and bowed. As he turned away, Theodosia caught the sleeve of his tunic.

"One more thing. On your way through Rome tomorrow, go to the shop of Sordus, the fine-fabric merchant on the Argiletum, and buy a good length of the most brilliant green silk you can find. I want to be stunning at Vespasian's party."

<> <> <>

"Well, Stefan... are you going to put me on your gentlest horse or your most spirited?"

Stefan had been lounging against the open barn door; he straightened as Theodosia approached.

"Somewhere in the middle." He smiled shyly, but his manner was formal. "And they're your horses, miss, not mine."

"Well... you work with them so much, they... must seem... like your own." She floundered to a stop and took a deep breath. "Do you have a favorite?"

Stefan nodded and ushered her to a sleek, well-groomed black filly ready with a blanket, bit, and reins.

"I call her Lamia, miss, but you can call her whatever you like."

"Lamia. The mythic sorceress. I like that!"

Theodosia patted the filly as she led her into the sunlight. Stefan made a step with his hands and gave Theodosia a boost; then he walked beside her up and down the driveway.

"Get a horse for yourself," she said, "and let's go somewhere."

He disappeared into the barn and soon emerged on a roan gelding. Theodosia trotted between the sycamores that lined the long driveway linking her villa to the Via Aurelia, with Stefan following a few lengths behind. At the road, she urged the filly into a gallop. Stefan hung back, though Theodosia was sure he had to rein in the gelding to do so.

Rolling pinewoods stretched for miles on both sides of the Via Aurelia, broken only by occasional patches of once-cultivated land. A century earlier—before the rise of rich landowners like her family—those had been small farms. Now they fed no one. Few farm families could compete with the big, slave-worked plantations.

Theodosia felt a quick flash of guilt. Still, there was no denying that those overgrown fields were beautiful. Gray-green leaves of gnarled olive trees rustled in the breeze. Strips of wildflowers carpeted the spaces between them and spread out along the roadway, mixed with fennel and rosemary. The scent was incomparable.

She led the way across a stone bridge toward a hill that promised a fine view of the sea. Guiding the filly off the paving stones, she threaded her way up the slope through pines and plane trees. At the top, she reined in to savor the panorama of her property. To the north and east lay forests and hills. Somewhere inland was the farm. To the southwest, beside the sea, sat her villa... its red-tile roof seemingly afire in the afternoon sun.

"How's it feel to know all this belongs to you?" Stefan's voice was close behind her.

"Feels great! But this was Etruscan land, you know, long before it was Roman, and it's only mine temporarily. Just an instant or so, as the world goes. Then it will all 'belong' to somebody else."

They rode again the next morning—despite aching muscles that threatened to paralyze Theodosia—and headed south along the shoreline toward Caere. As before, Stefan lagged behind. When they were out of sight of the villa, she slowed the filly and motioned for him to join her.

"Ride up with me when we're alone like this. I invited you to come for companionship, not as a bodyguard."

Stefan made no answer. He didn't even look at her.

"Look, I get lonely sometimes. I need someone to talk to."

Still he kept silent.

Frustrated, Theodosia raised her voice.

"Stefan, you're such an old friend. Relax!"

"It ain't easy for me after all these years."

"You think it's easy for me? Just talking to you is an ordeal."

"At least it ain't dangerous for *you*."

"Is talking to *me* dangerous for *you*?"

"It was always dangerous to talk to my lord Gaius."

"Gaius is gone. This is *me*." She tapped her chest. "The same person you used to call 'Theodosia.' It's no more dangerous to talk to me now than it was before."

"I can't just forget who you are."

"Really? Well, maybe you do belong back there, after all!"

Angry now—and hurt—she kicked the filly and raced off under the trees that lined the shore, aware of the gelding's heavy hooves behind her. She rode until she thought Lamia might not be able to stand much more. Stopping at a grove by the water, she waited for Stefan to draw near.

"Help me down."

He dismounted, looped his reins around a low branch, and reached out to help Theodosia off her horse. Holding on to the filly's neck and Stefan's hand, she swung her right leg over the blanket and slid to the ground. Her muscles stabbed as she landed, and she cried out in pain.

"You all right?" Stefan bent over her, then a hasty, pent-up apology tumbled out. "I'm sorry, miss. I didn't mean to upset you."

His contrition swept away the remains of her anger.

"It wasn't your fault. You don't make the rules."

She tottered to a flat rock beside a gnarled cypress and sat down facing the sea. After an interval, she turned. Stefan was still standing by the horses, one hand clasped around a thick branch above his head, watching her.

"Please... come sit and talk with me."

He released the branch and moved closer, eyeing her as if to confirm the invitation. Amused, Theodosia pursed her lips and nodded. Stefan lowered himself to the rock, bending his enormous legs and wrapping his hands around his knees, plainly uncomfortable with the situation.

For a time, neither of them spoke. Theodosia reached down, scooped up a handful of pebbles, and began tossing them, one by one, into the water below, increasingly aware of the tantalizing difference between the size of Stefan's arms and her own.

"You never had any qualms... about sitting next to me..." she said between tosses, looking him full in the face, "when we were children."

Stefan bent and picked up his own handful of pebbles. Then he imitated her tossing with an odd mixture of humility and humor.

"You weren't... my owner... in those days."

"How much do you know about Alexander?"

"Not much. He don't talk about himself."

"But you must know something about his background."

"Just that he was twenty and had a family when the Romans made him a slave. He's faithful to his wife, even though he ain't seen her for over eight years. Swears he'll go looking for her one of these—" Stefan glanced at Theodosia. "Guess I shouldn't tell you that, should I?"

"It doesn't matter. He already told me much the same thing."

"Slaves can love, you know, miss, no matter what you Romans think, and Alexander still loves Antibe very much. I don't know nobody else like him. He can read and figure, and he writes poetry, too."

"Poetry?"

"You didn't know that? Something else I shouldn't have said. He'll be furious at me if he finds out. Please don't let on that I told you."

Theodosia nodded her promise.

"One more question. Can I trust him?"

"The master trusted him with all his money. So can you."

"Can I trust him with my life?"

"I don't understand." Stefan's eyes were wary.

"Alexander was in Rome the day Gaius was murdered. He says he left there before it happened, but..."

"Don't you believe him?"

"To be honest... I guess I really don't. He admitted he hated Gaius. That would be stupid if he were guilty, and Alexander's not stupid. On the other hand... admitting up front that he hated Gaius would be a clever tactic if he actually were guilty. And Alexander is very clever."

She stared out to sea and tossed a few more pebbles into the water.

"Did you or anyone else see him come in with Lycos that night?"

Stefan was slow to respond. Finally, he shook his head.

"So nobody," Theodosia said, "can vouch for him."

"Don't worry about the murder, miss. Forget it!"

Why is everyone so anxious to get my mind off the murder? I've every right to know why Gaius died.

Then a new thought occurred to her.

That whole scene with Lycos could have been a set-up, an elaborate ruse to keep me in the dark.

"You'd tell me the truth if you knew it, wouldn't you? I've got to believe that. You and Lucilla are the only ones here I know for sure I can trust."

"What're you afraid of, miss? Alexander ain't no killer, but even if he did what you're thinking, you don't have to worry. It was your brother he hated, not you."

"This is an odd thing to say, but... I might actually be glad to learn that Alexander was the murderer. I understand what might have motivated him. It's more frightening to think that maybe he didn't do it."

"I didn't know you cared so much about your brother."

"I didn't. But if Alexander's telling me the truth... if his theory is correct... if it wasn't a random thing... if someone other than robbers or the litter slaves killed Gaius... then the men who killed him may have some reason to kill me, too."

She looked into Stefan's azure eyes.

"I've got to find out who killed Gaius, if only to protect myself."

CHAPTER EIGHT

Lucilla was in the driveway, flirting with a slender houseboy who had first caught Theodosia's eye earlier that morning. He was, without a doubt, the handsomest of all the youths Gaius had brought to the villa. His skin was smooth, his nose and chin so perfectly shaped that a sculptor might have chiseled them, his eyes round and a sensuous brown.

"Remember," Theodosia said to Stefan as he helped her dismount, "not a word to anyone about our conversation."

She turned to the houseboy as Stefan led the horses away.

"What's your name?"

"I am Marcipor, mistress."

The young man stood before her without obvious discomfort, his voice respectful, his eyes politely lowered. Though dressed in the drab brown of a country slave, Marcipor had the look, sound, and deportment of a servant from a sophisticated city household.

"How long have you been here?"

"Almost a year, mistress. Before that I belonged to Tribune Marcus Salvius Otho."

Marcipor. Marcus' boy. I should have known he once belonged to Otho.

"You were born in his father's household?"

"Yes. The Senator gave me to him when we were children."

"How did my brother happen to buy you?"

Marcipor threw a sidelong glance at Lucilla. Her face turned red, which was odd, because she didn't usually suffer from the quick blushes that plagued Theodosia.

"He didn't buy me, mistress," Marcipor said in a hushed tone. "My former master made a gift of me."

"A gift? Why?"

"I don't know. My lord Otho simply said I was now his friend's property. He gave my lord Gaius other gifts, too. Not just me."

Theodosia turned to Lucilla.

"Go draw my bath. Hot water, and lots of it."

Lucilla reacted with a curious look, but she left obediently. Marcipor watched her until she disappeared into the house.

"You strike me as a bright fellow, Marcipor," Theodosia said when her maid was out of earshot. "I have a few more questions for you, but you're to tell no one about them. Understand?"

Marcipor's eyes met Theodosia's for the first time, and he nodded.

"What did you think about all this gift-giving?"

"Not much, mistress, since I didn't have a say. The only thing..."

"Was what?"

"Just the way my new master gloated about getting me from my old master. It didn't seem the right way to act after someone gave you a gift."

"That's odd. Did you ever—any time you were in Rome—hear anyone refer to my brother as 'the viper'?"

Marcipor shook his head.

"Those silver serving pieces—the ones set with rubies... Were they here when you first came to the villa?"

"I don't recall."

"Did you ever see them in Rome?"

"No."

"Does the design have any meaning for you?"

"No, mistress."

Another dead end... unless someone's lying to me.

The vaulted, gaily frescoed bath sat on the ground floor, but it was accessible only by an interior stairway leading down from the second floor. Once the door was shut, it was private.

Aulus Terentius Varro had had this room built twelve years ago. Theodosia remembered her awe when her father first showed her the two marble pools... one for cold water, the other for hot water piped in from an underground chamber, where the houseboys kept a fire stoked year round. From the start, this room had been reserved for the Varros and their guests, hence the limited access. Their servants still used the original bathhouse at the edge of the woods.

51

Aching from two days of unaccustomed exercise, Theodosia tossed aside her sweaty clothing, sprawled naked on the massage table, and allowed Lucilla to work on the sore spots with her fists and a vial of perfumed oil. Half an hour later, tired of the pounding and rubbing, she slipped into the hot water that now filled the pool, grateful for its sting.

"Have you talked much with Marcipor?"

"Some." Lucilla waded in to scrape the oil off Theodosia's skin. Later, she would rinse and comb her hair. "He really hated to leave Tribune Otho. Says the tribune's a fine man and a good master. Marcipor told me about your brother, too, miss. Said his moods was awful. He'd change like—" She snapped her fingers. "Marcipor said that whenever he was angry he'd hit them. He'd hold his hand right in front of their faces when he asked a question, and if he didn't like the answer—or if it didn't come fast enough—he'd smack them on the cheeks, over and over."

"Slapping in the face was the master's favorite form of correction." Alexander's words. And what was it Stefan said? "It was always dangerous to talk to my lord Gaius."

She remembered the old scars and newer, healing cuts she'd seen on almost every face around the villa... except Marcipor's.

Wonder if there's something to be read into that?

"He did that to everyone? Even Alexander?"

"Alexander most of all, according to Marcipor. Said he loved to humiliate Alexander in front of his rich friends."

"Alexander must have hated him a lot."

"Sure did. He was glad your brother spent so much time in Rome. Bet that's why he was upset when he heard you was coming here to live full time. He figured you'd be just like your brother."

Alexander returned from the big seaport at Ostia in midafternoon. Theodosia was sitting in a sunny corner of the pergola—sipping wine and letting her hair dry in the wind—when he appeared.

"Successful trip?"

"I have the word of the captain of the fleet that the letter will go on the next ship that sails for Greece. Thank you, miss, for that." He made a little bow to her. "I ran my other errand, too. Ended up dragging half of Rome back with me."

"You did *what*?"

Just as she asked the question, she heard wagons in the driveway.

"The fabric merchant. Once he knew it was you I was shopping for, he wouldn't just sell me a roll of silk. He insisted on showing you his other wares. And I paid a visit to the goldsmith who did work for your brother. He's here, too, so you can have that ring sized to fit your finger."

"The man came all this way to adjust a single ring? Hmmm. Couldn't wait to start getting his hands on my money. Well... I'll indulge Sordus. My old clothes are a disgrace. Unfortunately for the goldsmith, I have enough jewels to last a lifetime."

The merchants followed Alexander into the pergola, accompanied by a dozen sturdy slaves bearing wooden chests on their shoulders. Lucilla arrived with a silver-backed hand mirror, followed by Lycos, who stood wide-eyed... as if watching a troop of mimes in the Forum.

Theodosia felt like Cleopatra on her throne, surrounded by a flock of obsequious minions.

Reuben ben Judah, the goldsmith, was a somber, middle-aged Jew with the squinty-eyed look of a man who had spent too much time at his craft. Pride in himself, his heritage, and his workmanship showed in every line on his face as his slaves knelt at Theodosia's feet with an extensive sample of their master's wares.

Ben Judah was disappointed in failing to tempt her and reluctantly confessed that all he needed was a forge and a correctly sized ring to do the job he had been asked to do. Lucilla fetched the signet ring and a plain silver band that Theodosia had worn for years; then she took ben Judah to the barn with instructions for Stefan to prepare the forge.

Theodosia was delighted by the rainbow of silk, cotton, linen, and woolen goods that Sordus—the legendary cloth merchant to the elite of Rome—had brought for her inspection. At one point, she felt a flutter of conscience, but she managed to brush it off.

No way this compares with what Gaius spent. I could dress well for a year for the price of just one pretty boy in Rome.

When she had selected all the fabrics she wanted, Alexander took Sordus into the library to negotiate the price. Lucilla and Lycos left, too. Reuben ben Judah returned to the pergola just as Sordus' slaves were hauling away the last of their burdens.

Theodosia slipped the heavy ring onto her finger. It was a perfect fit.

"It's beautifully done." She smiled at the goldsmith. "When I'm ready to have some jewels made up, I'll send for you."

"Thank you, lady." Ben Judah's eyes looked straight at hers. "I hope you also like that last commissioned piece I made for your brother."

"Which piece was that?"

"A very different kind of gold ring, with a special design I created just for him. A serpent with an enormous ruby in its mouth. Your brother picked it up late in the day... only a few hours before he was killed. He was wearing it when he left my shop."

The goldsmith shook his head to show his sympathy.

"I'll be glad to size that one for you, too, whenever you can bring yourself to wear it."

"Thank you," Theodosia said, revealing none of the questions in her head. "I'll call on you when I'm ready."

Theodosia lingered in the pergola, admiring the family ring that now actually *felt* like it belonged to her. She had just finished a cup of red wine when she heard footsteps. Alexander was back.

"Is there more wine in the pitcher?"

Alexander refilled her cup and wiped its edge with a white linen cloth. It was the same attention to detail that she had seen in all the servants at her villa.

"Thank you," she said as he returned the cup to her. "Watching you at work makes me glad you're the one who trained the rest of my staff."

She took a sip.

"I'm glad you appreciate what I do," Alexander said. "May I ask, then, why it is you still don't trust me?"

Theodosia choked; the wine spattered the front of her stola. Alexander lifted the goblet from her hand and offered his service cloth. Tears blinded her as the blood rushed to her cheeks. She accepted the cloth and buried her face in it. It was a while before she could speak.

"Stefan had no business—" she sputtered, "telling you about— our conversation."

"Nevertheless, he did."

"Leave me. Go to the house."

"You can't banish your fears so simply, miss," Alexander said, making no move to obey. "Might as well confront them right now."

"Very well." Theodosia wiped her eyes, certain that her face was still as red as the wine stain on her stola. "Did you have anything to do with my brother's murder?"

"No, miss, I did not."

"Of course, you wouldn't admit it if you did."

"Probably not, so does it do you any good to ask me?"

"Probably not. That story about the viper... Rather farfetched, don't you think?"

"Too farfetched to invent, don't you think?"

"I don't know. What Lycos told me..."

"I put no words in his mouth. What he told you was the same thing he told me that afternoon in Rome."

"Can you produce the note you claim you got from Gaius?"

"I destroyed it. On purpose."

Theodosia cocked her head and cast him a lingering glance.

"Reuben ben Judah made an unusual ruby ring and delivered it to Gaius the very day he died. What do you know about that?"

The genuine surprise on Alexander's face answered her question. Carefully, she sipped the wine again.

I may be foolish, but I've got to trust him.

"You will take me to the farm tomorrow. If I survive the trip, I'll know I can trust you."

"Oh, you'll survive the trip, miss. Just don't hold me responsible for your encounter with Nizzo."

The trip took longer than Theodosia had expected.

They left the Via Aurelia a few miles north of the villa and headed east toward the western spur of the Apennines. Unlike Stefan, Alexander rode alongside Theodosia for most of the first hour... and even took the lead once they entered the forest. Determined to prove she trusted him, Theodosia followed him into a thicket she would have called impenetrable. Alexander stopped at intervals to lift branches so she could pass through unscratched.

It had rained the night before, and an intoxicating scent rose from the lichens and last year's fallen leaves. Shafts of sunlight swept the ground. New leaves whispered overhead as birds trilled provocatively to their mates. Smelly, raucous Rome seemed very far away.

Neither Theodosia nor Alexander spoke much until they moved out of the forest and passage became easier. Soon the sun was directly above them. Accustomed to the shelter of the woodlands, Theodosia began to feel its heat in a short time.

"The farm's just ahead," Alexander said a while later. "This would be a good opportunity for you to eat."

He led her to a grove of sycamores atop a hill, where he dismounted, helped her down, and pointed toward a gray line in the distance.

"There it is... the outer limits of Nizzo's empire. No farm slave is allowed near that stone wall."

"I can see groups of men farther on, I think."

"Women, too. Chained together at the neck. Those iron rings bear the name Varro. They wear them all their lives."

Alexander pulled a blanket from his pack, spread it in the shade, and returned for the provisions Milo had packed. Theodosia settled onto the blanket as he placed bread, cheese, olives, and a small cup before her.

"You need to eat, too," she said, deciding to give friendship another try. "Care to join me for lunch?"

A flicker of amusement crossed Alexander's eyes.

"This is not a social outing, miss, nor am I your invited guest. We must both remember that."

So, he stood as she ate, keeping her cup filled from a wineskin. When she was done, she dusted the breadcrumbs from her lap.

"Eat something before we go on. I'll stroll around a bit."

She wandered under the sycamores, peeking over occasionally as Alexander finished the leftovers before leading the horses to her.

"Sure you want to go through with this?" he asked.

Theodosia nodded but said nothing.

"Well," he went on, "I can't stop you. I do have a request, though, if I'm not being too bold."

"A bold man would have joined me for lunch."

Alexander chuckled, but his eyes remained serious.

"Please don't order any major changes today."

"Don't do anything foolish, you mean."

One corner of Alexander's mouth angled up.

"Just realize that what you do could impact your income. And as someone who wishes you well—whether you trust me or not—I must repeat my warning. Nizzo won't be bullied, and he can be dangerous."

"You always make me think you know more than you're saying."

"Maybe I do."

"Don't be so cryptic! And don't give me any more argument either."

She turned to the filly and waited for Alexander to help her mount. The pleasant part of the day was over, and she knew it.

CHAPTER NINE

The noon sun boiled the air, sending waves of visible heat rolling across the fields. Mounted, whip-armed overseers rode back and forth, forcing a steady work pace. Angry shouts and agonized cries rose simultaneously and died in the stifling air. Spring planting was underway.

As far as Theodosia could see, ragged, dirt-encrusted figures bent low, dropping seeds into long, muddy furrows. Men with bulging ribs and raw sores and women with leathery faces gazed at her as she passed, showing more curiosity than resentment.

Do they have any idea who I am?

Those iron rings were everywhere. After years of wearing such a collar, a slave's neck would have the texture of a tree trunk.

Four thousand slaves!

She began to sweat.

The farther they rode, the more her discomfort grew. The soft wool horse blanket she was sitting on seemed of goat hair, so badly did it chafe her legs. Her nostrils clogged with dust. Hair stuck to her neck, plastered with sweat. Rivulets ran between her breasts. Her heart pounded. Her vision blurred. Her lunch rose to her mouth. A thousand bees came out of nowhere to swarm inside her head.

Alexander was leading the way across the fields. Theodosia tried to get his attention but found she had no voice. She was swaying to the left, desperately trying to hold on, when he turned to say something. In an instant, he whirled about and grabbed the filly's reins.

"Dismount before you fall off," he ordered, leaping to the ground as he spoke and holding up his hands to her.

Theodosia obeyed and pressed her forehead to his chest as the world dissolved around her in a roaring hum of bees.

Gradually, the vertigo passed. Theodosia came to consciousness on the ground between two crop rows, propped against Alexander, aware of his arms supporting her.

"Drink some wine?" His voice sounded far away.

Theodosia nodded.

Keeping one arm around her shoulders, Alexander yanked the wineskin from its pouch on his horse and pressed it to her lips.

They stayed there—waving away the overseers who offered assistance—until finally Theodosia looked up at Alexander. He helped her stand, boosted her onto the filly, and from then on rode at her side, watching her closely. But she felt no further nausea.

"You were right," she said at last. "I wasn't prepared for this. How can you remain impassive at the sight of so much wretchedness?"

"I've been here many times, remember? I will admit though... whenever I catch myself cursing the gods for my lot in life, I have only to think of this place. It does wonders for one's perspective."

Whatever image Theodosia had of her father's freedman, Aulus Terentius Nizzo lived up to it. Nearing fifty, he was a humorless man, as gaunt and baked and dirty as the slaves he ruled. Around his neck—still visible after two decades of freedom—was a ring of toughened skin.

Nizzo's response to Theodosia's visit was not warm, but he greeted her respectfully and led her into the compound at the heart of the vast farm complex. Alexander followed a few paces behind with the horses.

The first gangs in from the fields were gathering for their only meal of the workday. They would, Nizzo assured her, be fed again in the evening. There was no conversation, no acknowledgement of friends. The air reeked of unwashed bodies, including Nizzo's. Despite her sweat-soaked tunic and gritty hair, Theodosia felt so out of place, so clean.

She glanced at a bowl that a slave had just received. Inside was a mound of brown pottage and some brown beans. The man immediately began devouring the stuff, using a chunk of brown bread as a scoop.

"What will they eat tomorrow?" she asked Nizzo.

"The same."

"What do they drink?"

Nizzo pointed to children hauling jugs to gangs sprawled on the ground. The chained laborers passed the jugs from one to another, gulping water directly from each spout.

"Show me the kitchen and the barracks."

Still unsmiling, Nizzo escorted her to a building with a single door and two smoke vents in the roof. Theodosia glanced briefly at several old women who were kneading bread.

Old women? She looked again. *They can't be more than thirty.*

Outside once more, she passed mules turning wheat into flour with their endless haul around six grinding stones. Decades of plodding had worn circular tracks into the dirt. Nearly naked, sun-blackened men emptied and filled the millstones and kept the mules moving.

The expressionless Nizzo led the way to the far end of the compound. There he lit a torch and accompanied Theodosia down a steep flight of stairs, through a pair of heavy doors, and into an underground hall. The torch illuminated a series of cave-like rooms behind iron bars.

Theodosia took the torch and entered one chamber alone. Something scurried in a corner. The fetid combination of moldy straw and human excrement assaulted her nostrils as nausea swept over her for the second time that day. She retreated, thrust the torch into Nizzo's hands, fled past Alexander to the stairs, and—once in the open air—inhaled deeply to clear her lungs and settle her stomach.

"Is there some place where we can talk privately?"

Nizzo guided her to a stairway that provided the only access to an odd structure built high above the ground, affixed to the outside wall.

Before going up, Theodosia turned to Alexander.

"Come along, but don't interfere."

Nizzo's room was small and crudely furnished... two old wooden chairs beside a table, a chest, a narrow bed. Straw and a thin blanket were piled in one corner. As they entered, a plump woman with red hair rose from one of the chairs. Her roundness and pale skin offered a startling contrast to the slaves in the fields and the compound below.

"That's Persa, my woman."

Nizzo offered Theodosia one chair and sat in the other.

She was tempted to ask if Persa was actually his woman or her own property, but decided against it.

"Wine," Nizzo said to Persa.

The woman deposited two black pottery cups and a chipped jug on the table, then turned and left... making no effort to serve them. Alexander poured the wine before stepping behind Theodosia's chair.

"You do a fine job of managing the place," she began, hoping to flatter Nizzo into cooperation.

"Why'd you come here? Alexander's idea?"

59

Theodosia shook her head, picked up one of the cups, and sipped. It was typical slaves' wine... thin and vinegary.

"He tried to dissuade me, but I insisted. I wanted to see it."

"Now you've seen it."

"Yes." Theodosia leaned forward. "And now that I've seen it, I'd like to suggest a few changes."

Nizzo drained his cup and motioned to Alexander to refill it.

"What changes?"

"Feed them three times a day, and give them some variety."

"Can't do it. Costs too much."

"I'll pay for it. Also, clean out the barracks and replace the straw a couple of times a year, at least."

"You done that in the slave cells at your villa?"

Theodosia hesitated, realizing that she'd been distracted from her explorations and never got to the sleeping chambers under the kitchen.

"Yes," she lied, silently commanding Alexander to hold his tongue.

I will make sure they're cleaned out, if they're anything like these.

"Well, you can do as you like at your villa."

"This farm is my property, too."

The freedman named after Theodosia's father took another drink.

"I'll have no frivolities here while I'm bailiff."

Theodosia bit back an urge to snap at him.

An ultimatum won't work.

"Where do the slaves bathe?" she asked instead.

"No facilities for that. Water's too scarce."

Theodosia thought of the streams they had crossed that morning and the irrigated fields. Water was anything but scarce around here.

"They must bathe at least once a month. I insist on it!"

"Then you can find yourself another bailiff."

Theodosia stopped cold at that. Following Nizzo's example, she drained her cup. Alexander refilled it.

"Do you bathe?" She fixed her eyes on Nizzo's.

"When I'm in Rome. But I'm no slave."

"Not now, thanks to my father, but you have been. Don't you feel compassion for those who haven't had your good fortune?"

"Fortune ain't got nothing to do with it. Aulus Terentius Varro didn't set me free because I was fortunate, but because I knew how to run this place. Then he and your brother were shrewd enough to stay out of my way. No, lady, fortune ain't had nothing to do with it. I bent and sweated in those damn fields long before you was born. Never needed no bath."

"But now—"

"My neck still remembers the caress of that iron collar, and for years I slept in those cells you'd have me go prettying up. No, lady, get yourself another bailiff if you ain't satisfied with me. Just make sure he knows what he's doing and don't steal all your profits."

Theodosia had forbidden Alexander to interfere, and he had obeyed, but in her head she could hear his arguments. A thousand brutes couldn't be left without the one man they most feared. The government would step in and take over. Rome had fought too many slave wars already to take any chances on another. Theodosia could lose a lucrative property.

"I got a better idea, lady. Sell the place to me. The whole thing. Land, equipment, slaves. I'll pay a fair price."

With what?"

"Gold. You think you're the only one who profits here? Well, I've taken my legal share for twenty years, and you can see I ain't spent much. It's all been honestly earned, saved, and invested. Ask your steward. I bet he seen the contract your father wrote when he freed me."

Theodosia lifted her eyes to Alexander, who nodded.

"But you couldn't have saved enough to buy the whole thing."

"What I ain't got now I can get. I got friends—"

"I'll not sell my land and slaves."

"They'll loan me whatever I ask 'em to."

"I will not sell any part of my inheritance to you."

Nizzo smiled then, a chilling sight.

"Funny. That's exactly what your brother said a month ago, last time I proposed the deal to him."

"Get the horses," Theodosia said to Alexander.

I'll be damned if I'll play games with Nizzo.

As she approached the gate, her eyes fell on a scene that threatened to bring on her nausea a third time. Near the high wall—in plain view of all the slaves inside the compound—a man and a woman hung by their wrists from a raised wooden scaffold. Both had buckled at the knees and would have fallen but for the ropes. They had been whipped.

Gods! How did I miss seeing that when we entered?

Theodosia wanted to turn away, but her feet set a course of their own. Without consciously willing it, she walked until she stood directly in front of the scaffold.

61

At that close range, she could see the crudely stamped VARRO on the iron rings the couple wore. Their bloodless hands were distorted into crab-like shapes by the weight of their bodies against the ropes. Both were caked with dirt and blood, their lips crusted white, their protruding tongues swollen with thirst. Naked and unable to shoo away the flies that swarmed over them, they twitched reflexively. Only that faint response let Theodosia know the woman was still alive.

The man, however, looked straight at Theodosia. There was no anger in his face, just pain and the same dull curiosity she'd seen on so many other faces that day. She stared into his bloodshot eyes, then swallowed, turned her back, and strode away.

She found Alexander and Nizzo standing beside the horses. The freedman's expression betrayed no emotion. Her steward's mixed annoyance and pity.

"Those two," she said to Nizzo, "what have they done?"

"The woman lost control of herself. Went wild."

"And the man?"

"One of the overseers was going to discipline the woman, and that fool interfered. Attacked the overseer."

"Why did she 'go wild'?"

"Something about a baby."

"Whose baby?"

Nizzo shrugged with disinterest.

"I got a farm to run, lady. No time for personal chit-chats with every slave on the place."

"I'm not asking you about every one of them. Is he her husband?"

"We don't use words like that around here. Lots of stuff happens in a place like this, but marriage ain't one of 'em."

Theodosia looked at the pair on the scaffold.

A field slave cared enough for a slave woman to risk torture and death to protect her.

The idea was revolutionary.

"What happened to the baby?"

"Died. It wasn't well, even when she was nursing it. After we took it away so she could get back to work, she thought we let it die on purpose. Total nonsense, of course. Nobody lets good property die on purpose."

Slaves can love. Stefan said so.

She looked again at the man and the woman on the scaffold.

"Has she any other children?"

"One."

"How long since they've had food and water?"

"Two days. They'll be dead by tomorrow night."

"I want them taken down. Right now."

Nizzo cleared his throat and spat on the ground.

"Every slave here knows I've sentenced 'em to death. Can't go back on that."

"There's only one person with the authority to sentence my slaves to death, and you are not that person!"

Furious, Theodosia flicked her eyes toward Alexander. Disapproval hung heavily on his face.

Damn them both!

"Tell you what," she said to Nizzo, "I'll let you run the place as you see fit, but you *will* take those two down. Do it after the others are locked in for the night. Give the word out tomorrow that they died."

"What in hell do I do with 'em then?"

"Put them in a wagon after dark and have them taken to my villa. The surviving child, too. I'll find a place for all three."

"That man is brutal!"

They had crossed the fields in silence and now were reaching the gray stone wall. Alexander dismounted to open the gate.

What do you know about brutality? Ever been in a Roman prison? On the receiving end of Gaius' rages?

"No, miss," he said as he remounted his horse. "Nizzo's tough, but he takes no pleasure in his punishments. Wish I could say that about everyone with power over slaves."

"Tell that to those two back there."

"I'm more concerned about what they'll say at the villa about our soft-hearted mistress who can't stand to see anyone in pain. A fine chance I'll have of keeping order if your slaves get the idea you'll interfere whenever one of them is punished. That is necessary at times, you know, even at your beloved villa. And you shouldn't bring new slaves into the household without knowing something about them. No telling what vermin and superstition will come along."

"I'll take the responsibility." She looked at him. "Damn it, Alexander. It's *my* farm and *my* villa. Those are *my* slaves hanging up there half dead. And—I swear by every god on Mount Olympus—I'll have my way on something today!"

"Well," Alexander knew his tone was testy, but he couldn't stop himself, "I'd say Nizzo got off quite nicely, all in all. Traded a couple of near-dead troublemakers for a promise of no more interference from you. Not a bad deal."

"You'd like to figure out some similar deal, wouldn't you? I guess that's one big disadvantage of being a slave."

She gave the filly a sharp slap with the reins and trotted away.

I guess so. Just one of many.

They reached the villa two hours before dusk and found a set of horses that Alexander knew too well standing beside the barn. A cluster of green-liveried slaves mingled with those wearing brown.

It's Otho, damn him, come for another state visit.

He glanced toward the pergola. There sat the young patrician, as much at home as if surveying his own domain. Marcipor was there, too, as always, standing silently in the shadows behind his former master.

Alexander dismounted to help Theodosia Varra down, but she ignored him and nudged the filly through the yews toward the pergola. He followed on foot.

"Your porter said you were gone for the day." Otho rose from his chair. "Off on a horse, and to the farm of all places. If you weren't old Gaius' sister, I'd never have believed it."

Alexander stopped beside his mistress' horse and glanced up into her delighted face.

"Otho! I'm so glad you've come! I trust my servants have made you comfortable."

"I feel quite at home with Marcipor looking after me."

Alexander's eyes shot to the other slave's face. Marcipor looked subdued, all expression carefully veiled.

"Hope you'll forgive me," Theodosia Varra said, "but I've got to bathe and change. Alexander," her voice became imperious, "you will stay and see that the tribune has everything he needs."

Alexander suppressed a sigh.

I'm every bit as tired and gritty as you are.

In the next moment their eyes met, and he saw that she knew that. Theodosia had had the last word at the farm gate. She intended to have it again now. And Alexander would have to spend an hour with the only person he had ever hated more than Gaius Terentius Varro.

CHAPTER TEN

Tribune Marcus Salvius Otho slouched against a post in the pergola, a smirk on his thin lips. As usual, he was perfectly turned out, with a fresh shave, immaculate clothing, and manicured, squared-off fingernails. Despite the obvious effort that went into Otho's grooming, Alexander always found the smell of him repulsive, as if too much wine, sex, and power had left their mark on him... the very stench of Rome.

The long nose inherited from Otho's royal Etruscan ancestors flared as Alexander approached and bowed.

"Well, Greek... what do you think of your new mistress?"

There was a dangerous edge to the question. Otho enjoyed getting slaves into trouble, and he was good at it.

"She is kind, sir."

"Oh, really?" Otho's voice rippled with amusement. "I hear she's stripped control of the place from you." His lips curled in derision. "Makes me wonder what else she's stripped from you. You know, Greek, I bet you'd enjoy being stripped down by such a lovely woman."

Alexander could think of no appropriate response to that.

"Fetch more wine," Otho barked at Marcipor, who hurried from the pergola. "Isn't she a lovely thing, Greek?" His plucked eyebrows rose, inviting Alexander's response. "So young and innocent."

"It's obvious that my mistress is young, sir."

"And lovely? Don't tell me you haven't noticed that, too."

"Her appearance is of no concern to me, sir."

Otho regarded Alexander with studied arrogance.

"I never would have guessed, Greek, what a diplomat you would turn out to be. Don't recall seeing 'diplomat' written on that tablet hanging from your neck in the slave market."

Alexander clinched his teeth. Otho never failed to mention the day eight years ago when he and Lucius Gallio had accompanied Gaius to buy a steward. It was not a day that Alexander cared to remember.

"Aren't you afraid your mistress will decide she doesn't need you and send you back to market?" A malicious smile. "Don't imagine you'd look forward to being sold again."

"I would prefer not, sir."

"But it's quite likely, from what I hear. Of course, there are ways for you to stay right here, as much in charge as you were before." Otho's eyes wandered toward the house. "A new master would certainly take your mistress with him to Rome."

Alexander kept silent, wary of the guile on the Roman's face.

"Would that not please you, Greek?"

"Whatever my mistress chooses to do will please me, sir."

"But you might be in a position to influence her, and the man she marries might reward you... if you'd been helpful."

"The man she marries will become my master, sir."

And if I'm going to help anyone become my master, it sure as hell won't be a sonofabitch like you.

"All the more reason to win his favor before the marriage."

Theodosia returned to the pergola wearing still-damp hair, a fresh dab of clove-oil perfume, and a diaphanous silk stola in aquamarine, her most becoming color. Alexander pulled out a chair for her, but before she could sit, Otho rose, took her hand, turned it over, and pressed his lips into her palm. Theodosia felt a fiery blush race up from her throat.

"You're too bold," she said, embarrassed at being embarrassed in front of her servants.

"I'm known for courage in battle." Otho's eyes sparkled as he raised them to hers. "I've killed many enemy chieftains, taken many captives, brought many slaves to Rome. Should I be less bold in seeking the affection of a beautiful woman?"

Eight years in the Subura had taught Theodosia how to rebuff the advances of all sorts of low-born men, but she had no idea how to react to such an overt expression of interest from a patrician.

"Don't gawk!" Otho snapped at Marcipor. "Pour her some wine."

Theodosia started at the sudden harshness in his voice. Marcipor's hand trembled, she noticed, as he obeyed.

66

"First, a toast." Soft-toned again, Otho raised his cup and looked her up and down. "To as lovely a woman as I've ever seen, in or out of Caesar's court."

Theodosia felt another surge of fire. Otho's eyes lingered on her breasts, as if the searing blushes had burned away her stola and tunic. Speechless, she shook her head.

"You don't believe me?" Otho said with overly dramatized shock. "Tell you what... we'll ask that Greek." He shifted his eyes to Alexander. "What have you to say on the subject, Greek?"

It wasn't a question, but a command.

Theodosia caught a momentary flash of dismay on Alexander's face. It would be impudent for a slave to praise his mistress' physical charms to her face, and equally impudent for him to denigrate them. Yet he was required to obey the order.

"Come now, Greek, speak up!"

Alexander mumbled something inaudible.

"Never knew the fellow to be so shy. Hmmm. Maybe he's taken a fancy to you himself." Otho chortled loudly. "Shame on you, Greek! Such a hot-blooded fellow!" He looked at Theodosia. "Well, trust my judgment. I'm famous for my taste in women."

"I thought you were famous for your courage in battle." She was relieved to turn the conversation away from herself.

"I'm famous for both."

"Does your refined taste extend to anything other than women?"

"Horses. Sculpture. Slaves." Otho wagged a finger in Marcipor's direction. "Take this boy, for example. Father gave him to me when we were ten... because I asked for him. An excellent choice, as I'm sure you'll agree. What was it they were calling you back then, boy?"

"Phaon, my lord."

"Silly Greek name. So, when he became my boy, I changed it to Marcipor. A more appropriate Roman name." Otho scrutinized the slave. "I've often been sorry I gave my boy to Gaius. Wouldn't mind owning him again some day. Is he working hard enough to suit you?"

Ostensibly, Otho was addressing Theodosia, but his eyes never left Marcipor's face, and his voice carried a teasing familiarity that could only be directed at the slave he was raised with.

Marcipor studied the floor as Otho regarded him with the cool superiority of an aristocrat comfortable with his power.

This doesn't look like the relationship between a slave and the master that—how did Lucilla put it?—Marcipor hated to leave.

"Is my boy working hard enough to suit you?" Otho repeated, shifting his eyes to Theodosia.

"I find his work satisfactory."

"Well, that's good to know!" Otho's voice bubbled with sudden mirth. "And you, boy, what have you to say about your new mistress? Has she had occasion to beat you yet?"

"She is a kind mistress, my lord." Marcipor looked directly at Otho. "And no, sir, she has not yet had me beaten."

At dinner that night, Theodosia found Otho charming once again. The uncharacteristic meanness that he had displayed in the pergola had vanished. It was fun to have company, and Otho's presence drove unpleasant memories of the day's activities from her mind.

"Why in blazes did you go to the farm?" Otho asked as Selicio served him seconds of the roast lamb.

"To see it. It does belong to me, after all."

"Our dear Gaius never put himself to so much trouble. Had you warned Nizzo you were coming?"

"No. I surprised him the same way you surprised me this afternoon. Have you ever met Nizzo?"

"He came to report to Gaius occasionally when I was here, but I doubt he even knows who I am."

After dinner, Theodosia and Otho strolled to the pergola. The wind had picked up since afternoon. Now it whipped across the rocks, lifting her hair, swaying the trees, and spraying everything with a salty mist. Juno the moon had chosen to go elsewhere tonight.

Theodosia stepped to the wall, looked down at the hard-pounding surf, and inhaled the pungent smell of fish.

Otho wrapped an arm around her waist and bent to her ear.

"Don't you know it's dangerous to be out with a lustful lad like me?"

"Lustful lads don't frighten me. Life in the Subura isn't for the timid, you know."

"So, if lustful lads like me don't frighten you... what about this lustful menagerie that Gaius collected out here?"

"If my slaves are lustful, they do a superb job of hiding it from me."

"For now. This is—what—your fourth day here? I wonder how you can sleep at night with all these oversexed fellows hanging around. And not kept under lock and key either, as they should be."

"I sleep quite well. But what makes you think all the men here are oversexed?"

"That's what Gaius bought them for."

"Not Alexander!"

"Well, no. Gaius bought him to manage his business. But he's probably the only one Gaius wasn't buggering. If his boys weren't inclined to it naturally, he trained them himself."

"He trained them?"

"With a stick. Or a whip. Or both."

"To make them—" Her voice cracked as she pulled away from him. "Gods, Otho, I knew Gaius was abusive, but I... Gods, that's awful!"

"No, that's life... for a slave. Anyway, the practice came from Greece. Our Greek boys were the ones who taught it to us, so they can't complain much now, can they?"

"Well, it's perfectly fine if they want to do that, but to force them..."

Gaius was even more repulsive than I thought. No wonder somebody wanted him dead.

"What about Marcipor?" she asked.

"That's what Gaius wanted him for."

"Was he 'inclined to it naturally,' as you put it?"

"Marcipor? Hell, no! He couldn't keep his eyes—or his hands—off a girl in my father's household."

"You knew that, and still you gave him to Gaius?"

"Of course. I'm generous to my friends."

Theodosia curled her fingers around a vine and gave it a shake.

Did he force Stefan? Little Lycos?

Alexander's words came back to her in the wind.

"Have you ever loved someone you were powerless to protect?"

Another shake on the vine.

And what was it Stefan said? "Alexander's no killer, but even if he were, he wouldn't kill you." Blessed gods, I think Alexander did kill Gaius, to protect Lycos. And I don't give a damn if he did.

Otho wrapped his arms around her and nuzzled her hair.

"Sweet, innocent Theodosia. Weren't you curious why Gaius sold all those women your father kept around the place? And speaking of Aulus Terentius Varro... now there was a notoriously lustful lad. Especially when it came to buying—and forcing—voluptuous slave girls!"

"Don't talk about my father like that!"

Father forced the slave girls?

She extricated herself again and dropped into a chair.

"Alexander told me that Gaius sold off all the women because he didn't want servants who'd known him his whole life."

"Don't you remember what I told you a few days ago? You can't believe a thing that Greek says. He'll lie to you every time."

"I don't think he meant it as a lie. He was trying to shield me from something even more unpleasant."

"Don't be a fool! He doesn't give a damn about you. He hates Romans. He'd like nothing more than to see you as dead as Gaius." Otho sat down beside her. "I'm worried about you, Theodosia. You're much too trusting… jaunting off to the farm with him. Ever think what he might do to you out there in the woods?"

"I came back safely, didn't I?"

"Today, yes, but tomorrow? Gaius was foolish, too, and look what happened to him."

"I don't care what happened to Gaius."

What a relief to say that!

"Gaius was vile," she said. "He deserved to die."

"I told you, I saw that Greek in Rome the day Gaius was murdered. I talked to him."

"Alexander admits he was there but denies seeing you."

"That's another lie."

"He says he was back here by midnight. I believe him, Otho."

"Then you are just as much a fool as Gaius was, and you'll soon be just as dead." Otho's eyes narrowed. "Turn that Greek over to me. I have friends among the guards at the Carcer Tullianum. The professionals there will put him to the question. They'll get the truth."

"You think I'd let them torture the most valuable slave I own?"

"He should've gone on the rack after Gaius died. I'd like to know why that didn't happen."

"Enough of this!" Theodosia felt lighter, released from her fear.

Gaius died because he was twisted and cruel, like a viper. I'll live because I deal humanely with my slaves.

"I've got a question for you," she said to change the subject. "If you're such a lustful lad, why aren't you married yet?"

"Oh, I will be soon if my old man gets his way. Says he'll disinherit me if I don't wed General Silvanus' daughter. Silvia's thirteen and flat as a floor, but her old man is Father's best friend, so I'm to marry her."

Theodosia stood and returned to the wall overlooking the sea. Otho followed, slipped an arm around her shoulder, and took her hand.

"I've told Father I won't have her. Told him that a year ago, after Gaius and I ran into you on the street. Remember that? 'Theodosia Varra,' I said to Father that very day, 'is the only wife for me.'"

Theodosia shook her head in disbelief.

"When I was just Gaius' paupered half-sister?"

"Pauper or not, it was a beautiful woman I saw that day."

And he planted his lips on hers.

The kitchen was a bi-colored patchwork of chaos as a score of green-clad slaves belonging to Tribune Marcus Salvius Otho thronged around the tables, eating dinner with the brown-clad Varro servants. Their voices were subdued. No one wanted to disturb the tribune, who considered silence one of the cardinal virtues in a slave.

Alexander came in later than the others, having taken a bath to get rid of the farm grit and spent an hour alone in his room.

Otho's got marriage on his damn mind.

It was all he could think of tonight.

He filled a bowl with stew from the kettle, took a chunk of black bread, and poured a cup of the sour wine that was the slaves' standard beverage. Dodging a few stout fellows in green, he picked his way through the crowd, inhaling the fragrant steam rising from his bowl. Rabbit stew would never replace the herbed roast lamb on Theodosia Varra's table, but it was a far cry from the verminous pottage that Nizzo's laborers were forced to eat.

He spotted Stefan, Lucilla, and Marcipor sitting with Calchas, the tribune's body servant. Marcipor and Calchas were old friends from Senator Salvius Otho's household. Calchas was another Greek... a quiet, nervous fellow, as were all those who served the same master. Right now, he was whispering across the table, as if afraid his voice would carry to the pergola.

Stefan slid closer to Lucilla to make room for Alexander. Lucilla slipped her hand through his elbow and snuggled up to him.

"He's been preparing for this visit for two weeks," Calchas was saying under his breath. "I've never seen him so picky about his clothes."

"You can see he's determined to have her," Marcipor said. "What'll his father say?"

"Threaten to disinherit him, like he always does."

Stefan laughed loudly, then ducked his head as the others shushed him. Despite the reprimand, a grin spread across his face.

"That won't matter if he marries Theodosia Varra!"

"You won't be laughing if he does." Alexander tore his bread in half. "We'll all be right back where we were before."

"Well," Lucilla said, rubbing her fingers up and down Stefan's arm, "I think it'd be great if she married the tribune."

"Then you're mad!" Alexander dug a spoon into his stew.

"No, I ain't mad. I'm thinking about her, which is more than you can say. All you're worrying about is who's going to be your next master."

"Maybe that's something you should worry about, too."

"Hey, I'm the one who attends our mistress every night, sees how lonely she is. It ain't right for a young lady to be living out here with nobody but us. She needs friends, and we can't never be that to her."

"I can think of a couple dozen other patrician men I'd rather see be her friends… or her husband. For her sake, as well as ours."

"Well, I can't see much difference in any of the rich Romans I know." Lucilla squeezed Stefan's arm and smiled into his eyes. "They all think they're gods, don't they?"

Calchas gave a soft, resigned chuckle.

"Far as we're concerned, I guess they are."

"Far as you're concerned, you mean," Alexander said.

"Far as my master's concerned, I mean," Calchas said, "and I'm sure as hell not going to be the one to tell him otherwise."

Theodosia leaped out of bed as a massive thunderstorm slammed full force into her villa. The room flashed with yellow-white light as a torrent of water blasted across the open western balcony. The walls that for two centuries had defied Neptune's fury shuddered in trepidation.

"Get back in bed, miss," Lucilla said as she ran out of her bedroom. "You'll be sick for the general's party!"

Lucilla got drenched struggling with the shutters.

Theodosia sent her out to dry off, then pulled up her blanket and snuggled in to muse about the disturbing green-eyed tribune in the bedroom down the hall. After a while, she drifted off to sleep, dreaming of making love in this bed, in this storm, to Marcus Salvius Otho.

They ate breakfast in a recess off the peristyle as a cold rain battered the roof and splashed through the terra cotta downspouts into the cisterns. Despite the heavier stola that Theodosia had put on this morning, she shivered several times. Finally, Otho wrapped his arm around her.

"Better?"

Theodosia nodded and leaned into him, welcoming the warmth of his body. She sat up straight later as a houseboy, his hair and tunic soaked, came scurrying through the colonnade, plainly perplexed as to why Alexander considered the arrival of a wagonload of slaves from the farm important enough to interrupt the mistress and her guest.

"You really are a fool," Otho said after Theodosia had told him the story. "Poor Nizzo, having to work for a woman."

"'Poor Nizzo' tried to buy the farm from me."

"Thinking of selling it to him?"

"Not even the tiniest parcel."

"Why not?" He kissed the top of her head and gently pulled her toward him. "I'd sell, if I were in your shoes. Keep this old villa as your hideaway, then come to Rome with me and live like a lady."

"But how would the slaves out there fare if someone didn't hold that brute accountable?"

"They survived when Gaius was alive, and he never laid eyes on them. Only a woman would think the way you do."

"You sound like Alexander, except he puts it more tactfully."

"First time that Greek ever told the truth about anything."

Otho ordered out his entourage at midday, when the rain subsided. A fine mist hung below the still-threatening sky as Theodosia accompanied him to his horse. Suddenly—right in the middle of a cluster of slaves—he seized her shoulders and pulled her close. His hands slid to her waist and hips as he bent and gave her a long, passionate kiss.

The heat of a hundred fires shot up from Theodosia's neck. She tried to push him away, but Otho was too strong.

When he finally released her, she stepped back and looked around. Old Jason, Stefan, Alexander, Lucilla, Marcipor, a trio of other houseboys, and all of Otho's green-clad men stood watching. He could have bid her farewell inside the house, or in a less embarrassing way.

Theodosia started to remonstrate, but Otho's sly grin stopped her.

Damn the man! An audience was exactly what he wanted.

CHAPTER ELEVEN

Neptune tossed his trident about the heavens all afternoon, bellowing in rage—as Lucilla put it—at not being invited to Vespasian's party. Theodosia laughed, but she also kept an eye on the brooding storm.

When Theodosia emerged from her bath, Lucilla dried her and smoothed a rich cream over her skin. Then she combed her hair and pinned it into the loose curls that her mistress liked. With Lucilla's help, Theodosia slipped into a gold-colored linen tunic, then into the stola that Lucilla had fashioned of Sordus' deep-green silk, and finally into an elegant matching palla and sash, both edged with gold braid.

"You'll be prettier than anyone at court, miss, like the tribune said."

"How'd you know he said that?"

"Word travels. Are you going to marry him? He sure is handsome!"

"Well, don't get any ideas. Stick to your own kind."

"You still say I can have anybody I want at the villa?"

"Of course," Theodosia said absentmindedly as a deafening crack announced the arrival of yet another thunderhead. "Now... fetch my new sandals, perfume, and the jewelry."

Theodosia had asked Alexander to dig into her strongbox and find jewels appropriate for the green silk. He had selected an heirloom necklace of emeralds and gold and a matching pair of looped earrings that dangled provocatively over her shoulders.

Delicate gold silk sandals, a gift from the fabric merchant, completed her dressing.

She pivoted before the polished bronze mirror, feeling as sunny as if Apollo, not Neptune, ruled the day. Then she headed to the atrium.

Water had been pouring through the roof opening all afternoon; now it splashed in a widening circle around the flooded pool.

Stefan, in a heavy woolen cloak, and Alexander, holding Lycos by the hand, stood talking in a dry space near the foot of the lamp-lit stairs. They fell silent as Theodosia came down to them, and she could see her sparkle reflected in their eyes.

"Well, Alexander," she said, pausing a few steps from the bottom and tilting her head coquettishly to show off the emeralds against her skin, "what do you think?"

Her steward responded in an equally indecorous manner.

"Of the jewels or... the lady?"

"Is there anything wrong with either?"

Such talk was shamefully close to flirtation, but Theodosia felt lovely and, after her talk with Otho, safe for the first time in weeks.

Alexander answered with a look of frank admiration and a shake of his head. A simple "no"—low, soft, and unexpected—was all he said.

Theodosia felt that embarrassing warmth rising to her cheeks. Quickly, she turned her attention to Lycos.

"Think they'll let me into the party, Lycos?"

The boy nodded, but it was Stefan who spoke.

"You look so beautiful, miss."

The unmistakable wistfulness in his voice sobered her.

Better put a stop to this.

"Thanks, Stefan," she murmured. "Is the carriage ready?"

Long before she reached Caere, rain blasting across the Via Aurelia had soaked the curtains of Theodosia's carriage, permeating the interior with the pungent smell of wet wool. She could hear Stefan shouting at the horses from his perch overhead, and she worried about him... with nothing but a cloak to protect him from the angry god.

After an eternity of bouncing, the carriage pulled up under Vespasian's portico. A bolt of lightning exploded just as Stefan jumped down to open the door. Grooms scurried to hold the jittery horses.

Vespasian greeted Theodosia in the atrium and introduced her to his other guests. Primus Sullus, the patriarch of one of Rome's first families, was her nearest neighbor to the south. Sullus held her hand for a moment and murmured a few compliments before introducing his wife. Decades younger than her husband and a great beauty, Annia was notorious for cutting the locks of her German slave women to make blonde wigs for herself.

Annia smiled coolly and gave Theodosia an equally cool kiss on the cheek. Stepping back, she eyed her emeralds and brilliant green silk.

"I've never seen a patrician wear a color like that," she said by way of greeting, "but it does look right on you."

"Sordus brought this silk out the other day." Bright colors had been Theodosia's main indulgence throughout her years of poverty. Although she knew society women disdained them as the mark of a courtesan, she still enjoyed wearing them. "I really do love the color!"

"Brought it out?" The sharp tone contradicted Annia's fixed smile. "Sordus traveled all the way to your villa?"

"He made the trip with Reuben ben Judah. I didn't even know they were coming till they got there."

The smile on Annia's face soured quickly, but before she could say more, Vespasian presented his other guests. Sabinius Lucan, a centurion grown wealthy in the conquest of Britain, stood beside his wife, the matronly Julia. Flavia and Titus stepped forward to greet Theodosia, along with Lucius Gallio. Gallio, the emperor's chief legal advisor and Flavia's future husband, completed the perfect set of nine for dinner.

Theodosia was surprised, then, when Otho came up behind her and noisily kissed the top of her head.

"What're you doing here?" she asked.

"The storm caught me just outside Caere, and you know… a dinner party makes an appealing refuge."

Theodosia looked at Vespasian, who shrugged.

"We've squeezed one couch in a bit. I can always find room for an old friend's son."

The dining room was plain by Roman standards and the pottery positively Spartan, but at least there was a slave at each couch. Vespasian escorted his guest of honor to the center, then took his place to her right. Titus sat to her left as the other guests assembled on the remaining two couches. A slave moved around the table, replacing each guest's sandals with soft slippers before they reclined on their sides for dinner.

The conversation focused quickly on Theodosia and her new situation. The wife of Sullus, seemed especially curious.

"Don't you feel vulnerable? You wouldn't catch me stuck out like that by myself, especially after what happened to poor, dear Gaius."

"I don't feel vulnerable in the least. My servants keep an eye on me."

"I bet! All those gorgeous men Gaius bought." Annia snickered. "But who keeps an eye on them?"

"So far, I've had no trouble. Not expecting any either."

"You're used to managing slaves, then? How many did you have in Rome?"

"Two."

Just not at the same time.

This confession of Theodosia's previous poverty appeared to satisfy Annia, who busied herself with a platter of leeks with mussels, snails, and oysters being passed around on the outspread palms of a well-trained boy.

"You spent a lot of time with your maid, didn't you?" said Flavia.

Theodosia swallowed her first oyster and nodded.

"Lucilla and I got to be quite close."

"That's nice," said the matronly Julia, "when you're young."

"Close to your maid?" Annia made a face.

"Oh, the maid's a sweet thing," Otho said. "Really devoted to Theodosia, and she's got good sense, too."

"How do you know?" Theodosia was astonished.

"I talked with her for a while yesterday, before you returned from gallivanting to the farm on a horse with your steward."

After a period of embarrassed silence, Lucius Gallio turned toward Theodosia.

"How're you getting along with Alexander?"

"Just fine. He's going to be a big help to me, I think."

"I've been warning her not to turn her back on him," Otho said.

Theodosia frowned. That refrain was becoming tiresome.

"Why?" Vespasian asked. "Alexander's one of the finest stewards anybody ever had. Wish I could afford to own one like him."

"Oh, the fellow's clever, for sure... and sly," Otho said. "Too sly for my taste. Been in charge so long he resents the situation now."

"And how do you know that?" Theodosia asked.

"I talked with him, too. You should hear what he says about you."

"It seems you had chats yesterday with all my servants."

"Not all. That would take months. Remember not to turn your back on that Greek, Theodosia. He's dangerous."

"Nonsense!" Lucius Gallio said. "I'd trust him with—"

"I hear her slaves just *hate* having a woman own them," said Annia.

"How would you know that?" her husband asked.

"One of my maids said so."

Theodosia couldn't resist the temptation.

"I thought you weren't close to your maids."

"Listening to their gossip isn't the same thing as being close to them! Besides... they do know everything that's going on."

"Well, Annia's right as far as that Greek is concerned," Otho said.

"I'm sorry, but... I really don't agree," Theodosia said. "Alexander has accepted the situation well enough. He may not like it, but he knows where he stands. In these first few days, he and I have established the foundation for a good working relationship."

Otho grunted.

"A slave is like a horse, Theodosia. Gaius let that one run loose for years. So, here you come along and think you can break him, but... are you sure you'll have the strength to control him when he begins to buck?"

"Nonsense!" said Lucius Gallio again. "I've known Alexander since Gaius bought him. I'd trust him with anything I own. I respect him. The man may be a slave, but he's honest, hardworking, and competent."

"Oh, he's competent all right," Otho said with an impatient gesture, "and arrogant and impudent."

"Of course." Gallio chuckled. "Alexander is convinced he's superior to us poor, piddling Romans."

"What that horse needs," Otho droned on, "is a strong master. If he belonged to me, I'd slam a bit into his mouth and yank the reins hard."

"The fact is," Theodosia said, "Alexander belongs to me, and with me he is anything but impudent."

Annia snickered louder at that and whispered something to Titus.

"You must have found some magic method of dealing with him." Otho seemed determined to pursue the subject. "I can still see Gaius in a frenzy one morning, slapping that impudent bastard in the face, back and forth, over and over and over again."

"I thought you said Gaius kept this Alexander fellow on a loose rein," drawled Sabinius Lucan in a slow, ironic tone.

"Oh, when it came to handling Gaius' business affairs, the slave was on his own. But Gaius still liked to make him jump." Otho turned to Theodosia. "You know that scar on the Greek's jaw?"

Theodosia nodded.

Otho refuses to dignify Alexander with a name.

"You're wearing the instrument that made it, right there on your finger."

Theodosia studied her heavy signet ring, noticing the sharpness of the triangular projections surrounding the "V" in the center... any one of which could gouge out a chunk of skin if it landed with enough force.

"My ring?"

"It was Gaius' ring, too. So, don't forget what a wicked weapon it can be on an impudent slave's face."

Theodosia stared at the ring, remembering how graciously Alexander had presented it to her... and also how many of her other household slaves bore facial scars similar to his. Even little Lycos.

"Have you ever loved someone you were powerless to protect?"

No wonder Alexander hated Gaius! Gods, I'd have killed Gaius myself if I ever saw him hit that child with this.

As the main course arrived, Vespasian began telling her of his son's genius for rhetoric and his prowess with horses and swords. Titus would enter the Centuriate next spring; that would be—Vespasian assured her—the start of a glorious military career. Theodosia nodded, amused. Vespasian's elder son was tall for his age and bright, but it was hard to picture such an immature youth bringing the enemies of Rome to heel.

After dinner, Vespasian offered a series of toasts. Boys with pitchers kept the wine flowing. For entertainment, the general had hired a freedman and his company. The freedman chanted classic tales of heroism, plus newer tunes popular at court, which his wife interpreted in dance as his kneeling slaves accompanied them on cithara and pipes.

After listening to the music for half an hour, Theodosia turned to Vespasian and confided that she, too, played the cithara.

He reacted with surprise, for music was a servile art, not practiced by patricians. Emperor Claudius' nephew and son-in-law, the prince Nero, was a notable—and much-criticized—exception.

"My friends," Vespasian remarked above the noise of clinking cups, singing musicians, and passing servants, "Theodosia has just told me that she also plays the cithara. Perhaps we could persuade her to perform."

There was a sudden silence as everyone stared at Theodosia. Annia's eyebrows rose, and she glanced toward Julia, who shot back a look of equal amazement. Annia's husband applauded with inebriated enthusiasm as his wife whispered behind her hand into Otho's ear. Otho laughed.

Theodosia moved around the table and took the cithara from the slave who had been playing it. At a gesture from Vespasian, one of the waiters ran to fetch a chair. Theodosia sat and let her fingers play across the strings a few times, then she closed her eyes and began to sing one of the old Greek poems that she had set to music long ago in Rome.

When she finished and raised her eyes, they met a variety of expressions. Sabinius Lucan was asleep. Titus and Vespasian wore astonished, trying-to-look-polite looks. Lucius Gallio, Primus Sullus, and Lucan's wife seemed embarrassed. Annia's eyes gleamed with undisguised malice, while Otho's bore an expression that Theodosia couldn't interpret. Only Flavia was smiling.

"That's beautiful!" the girl said. "Who taught you to play?"

Theodosia wanted to hug her.

"My Greek nurse. I like to compose music spontaneously to go with poems I enjoy."

"How wonderful!" Flavia's appreciation sounded genuine. "Hey, I've got an idea. Bring a book of Virgil," she said, snapping her fingers at a slave. "Theodosia, if you don't mind, I'd love to hear you compose something spontaneously for us."

When the man returned, Flavia took the scroll and chose an eclogue.

"This one."

It wasn't the most pleasing marriage that Theodosia had ever made of poem and melody, but her audience wasn't the most discerning she could imagine, either. She was still singing when the wife of Sullus sat up and gestured to a slave for her sandals.

"Please excuse us, Vespasian, but my husband and I must go. Never have we seen such coarse behavior in one who purports to be a patrician."

Theodosia stopped in mid verse and stared around the room. Then she rose with as much dignity as her reddening face would allow.

"General, Annia has been baiting me all evening. I suggest that it is she, not I, who exhibits coarse and unbecoming behavior."

"The family of Primus Sullus does not socialize with riffraff," said Annia.

"Since when are the descendants of the illustrious Marcus Terentius Varro considered riffraff?" Theodosia demanded.

"Since they began marrying Greek sluts."

There was another stunned silence.

"I expect an apology," Theodosia said at last, "for that insult to my mother and my family honor."

"You'll get none from me. I'm only saying what everyone in Rome is thinking. And I don't apologize to riffraff."

Annia stood, nodded with exaggerated respect to all but Theodosia, and marched from the dining room.

Every other pair of eyes in the room had been swinging back and forth between Annia and Theodosia. Caught in the middle of a spat, but not sober enough to mediate it, Vespasian reached for the comfort of his cup, downed its contents, and emitted a deep burp. Titus rolled onto both elbows and gaped at Annia as she disappeared into the atrium. Otho appeared to be barely stifling a laugh. Primus Sullus and Lucius Gallio exchanged discomfited glances. Sabinius Lucan snored on as his wife swung her legs to the floor.

"We should leave as well," Julia said, nudging her husband awake. "Sounds like the storm is getting worse."

"I must go, too," Theodosia said, trying to sound unaffected by Annia's affronts.

Regretting that her unorthodox behavior had hastened the party's demise, she called for her sandals and offered her hand to the general.

"Thank you for hosting this wonderful dinner on my behalf. I hope I haven't disgraced myself."

"Of course not, my dear."

Titus sent a waiter with instructions to have her carriage brought around. Shortly afterwards, he escorted Theodosia through the atrium to the front entrance. Stefan was waiting a few feet outside... his wet, billowing cloak giving him the look of a dolphin fished up from the sea.

"May I come for a visit in a day or so?" Titus asked Theodosia.

"If you still want to, after what happened tonight."

Before Titus could answer, Otho stepped between them.

"Just because you're our host's son, that doesn't give you the right to monopolize Theodosia's attention. I'm sure she'd prefer the company of a man with experience in the world." He took her arm. "I'll see you home. You shouldn't be out alone."

"Thanks," Theodosia said, twisting away, "but I'm not alone. My coachman will take good care of me."

She stepped around Otho and rose on tiptoe to give Titus a sociable peck on each cheek.

"I look forward to your visit."

Without warning, Otho seized her arm, drew her to him, and kissed her hard on the mouth until Titus pulled him back. Otho reacted with his characteristic grin, but Theodosia saw fire in the younger man's eyes.

"Horrible night!" Theodosia muttered as she pulled up her lap robe for the rough ride home.

If that's society, they can keep it.

But at least it was over. Nothing else could go wrong tonight.

A short time later, Alexander met her at the door with news of her first big crisis.

CHAPTER TWELVE

"We've got trouble." It wasn't Alexander's way to mince words. "Lightning hit the old double oak. The kitchen's demolished."

Demolished?

Theodosia whirled about, sped through the peristyle to the rear entry of the villa, and leaned out into the horizontal rain as wind whipped her clothes and hair. In the next flash of lightning, she saw the broad, leafy top of the broken tree lying across the crumpled building where most of her servants ate and slept. Alexander came and tugged her back into the sheltered passageway.

"Anyone hurt?"

"Not seriously. Two men were pinned against a wall. It took us a while to free them. Half a dozen others have cuts and broken bones."

Theodosia let out a relieved breath as he continued.

"General Vespasian lends us his Egyptian physician whenever we need him. I'll send for him at first light."

"How bad's the damage?"

"Bad. The barracks are flooded."

"Where's everyone now?"

"The injured men are in a storage room. We made them as comfortable as possible."

"And the others?"

"I sent them to the barn, though I'm afraid the roof may not hold. It's leaking in several spots."

"Why didn't you bring them into the house?"

"That's always been forbidden, miss."

"Well, it isn't now, and you should know that. Go get them!"

◇ ◇ ◇

Soon Alexander returned, leading a dripping group into the atrium. About half of the slaves had followed him.

"I can't get the others to come. That woman," his voice was taut, "the one from the farm. 'Etrusca' she calls herself. She's been haranguing them about demons from the sea. Now they're afraid to leave the barn."

"Tell them I insist."

"Sorry, miss, but I tried that." Alexander sounded weary. "They don't even hear me. She's got them in some sort of trance."

"Then I'll go. No!" she said as he began to protest. "You just find places for the ones who came. Anywhere but upstairs or in the library."

She took his hooded cloak, lifted it over her head and shoulders, and set out for the barn some ninety steps from the peristyle. Lightning provided perfect illumination. So buffeted that she feared she might unwittingly imitate Icarus and take flight, she gripped the flapping cloak at her neck and above her knees and bent into the gale.

"This isn't the Roman way of doing things," she muttered to herself, with a curse for the irate god hurling fire bolts over her head.

But even as she sloshed through the muck on her way to do battle with the sea-demons of a slave's imagination, she couldn't help smiling.

Wouldn't Annia love to see me now?

The barn doors were open. Wading through ankle-deep water, she found several dozen terrified slaves in the rear. Streams of water poured through sagging timbers. She saw lightning through the roof.

The woman from the farm was crouched near the outside wall, her thin, battered arms raised toward the sky, her puffy eyes shut as she held forth in a high-pitched wail that Theodosia didn't try to understand. The others seemed oblivious to anything but Etrusca's howls.

"Get up!" Theodosia shouted over the din of creaking timbers, splashing water, thunder, whinnies, wails, and moans. "Get up this instant!"

Realizing that the only solution was to force Etrusca outside and on to the villa, she pushed through the crowd, took her hands, and tried to tug her to her feet.

Toughened by a lifetime of labor, Etrusca resisted without effort.

Theodosia grabbed her emaciated shoulders and shook her. At last, the woman opened her eyes and fixed them, wide and wild, on Theodosia's face. Senseless words continued to tumble from her mouth.

"Be quiet!" Theodosia commanded, desperate to get out before the roof gave way over their heads. She shook Etrusca again. "On your feet! You're going to the house!"

She discovered that night how quickly frustration and fear can outwit self-control. Cold, wet, and afraid, she seized Etrusca's lacerated wrists and yanked them repeatedly, without success. Furious at her own failure, she drew back her hand and slapped the hysterical slave in the face. Then—horrified at having done what she loathed in others—she made a quick decision to abandon Etrusca and all the others and return to the house alone.

The slap, however, had its effect. Etrusca stopped wailing and stared at Theodosia... almost as if she recognized her. Her eyes blinked several times. Her mouth closed.

Changing tactics, Theodosia wrapped an arm around the woman's shoulders, reached out with the other hand to help her stand, and began talking softly of the comfort and safety to be found a few steps away.

They were halfway to the barn door when Alexander came in.

"Make sure the others follow," Theodosia said to him.

All was going well until they stepped outside. Etrusca slowed, eyed the sky with the same wild look as before, and began to wail again. Theodosia tightened her grip, determined to press on. A few steps later, a massive flash split the darkness. Etrusca screamed, jerked free, and raced back to the door, where Alexander caught her.

"Knock her out if you have to," Theodosia called to him over the thunder, "but get her to the house. I'll see to the others."

Working her way in and out, barking orders like a centurion in battle, she herded the crowd of terrified slaves through the storm to her villa.

Marcipor was waiting for her with a blanket. Tossing the sopping-wet cloak she was wearing onto the floor, he bundled her into the dry wrap. Lucilla brought a towel for her hair.

The marble floor was slick with water as the atrium and the dining room—and even the alcove dedicated to the household gods—filled up with dripping bodies. In the wind that howled through the atrium, Theodosia heard her ancestors protest the desecration of their sacred space.

She was about to go upstairs to change when an agonized cry rose from the other side of the center pool. Etrusca raced toward the peristyle as the man from the farm sprinted to stop her.

A few moments later, Theodosia reached the struggling pair.

"What's the matter now?"

"My baaaaaaaabyyyyyyyy!" the woman wailed.

The eyes that had won Theodosia's compassion as they stared at her from Nizzo's scaffold pleaded with her now for still more.

84

"What's wrong?" Theodosia said again, her voice much less harsh.

"Our girl ain't nowhere here," the man said as he clung to Etrusca. "She got left in the barn!"

Etrusca was still screeching, trying to break free.

"I'll go see if I can find her," Alexander said.

"No!" Etrusca cried. "I go!"

"No!" Theodosia again traded her blanket for Alexander's cloak. "I'll go look for her."

Alexander started to object, but Theodosia cut him off.

"Don't argue! I caused this mess, it seems, so I'll fix it." She flung the cloak over her head. "You're not the only one who's had a tough time tonight."

Turning away, she confronted the man from the farm.

"What's your name?"

"Nicanor, mistress." The slave made an awkward attempt to bow while keeping his grip on Etrusca.

"Nicanor, listen to me. I'll find your baby, but you must quiet this woman and keep her quiet. There'll be no place in my household for her if she can't control herself."

Theodosia retraced her steps to the barn as what was left of her delicate sandals disintegrated in the mire of the driveway. Stefan had shut one of the doors and was struggling against the gale to close the second. He stared in astonishment as he recognized the face under the coarse woolen cloak. Then they both darted into the barn.

Dropping the hood to her shoulders, Theodosia plucked at the strands of hair plastered to her face. Water ran down her cheeks and dripped from her nose. Stefan had been soaked hours ago; now Theodosia was every bit as wet as he.

He shook his head.

"Gold. Silk. Emeralds. Mud. Bare feet. Slave's cloak. Quite a sight."

Theodosia smiled into his eyes.

"I dressed up just for you."

Stefan held her gaze for so long that Theodosia began to wonder what might happen next. It was an oddly intimate moment.

A woman and her coachman...

Alone in the barn at night...

In a thunderstorm...

What would it be like to spend the night out here with him?

Shocked at herself, she dropped her eyes.

"I came to look for the child from the farm."

Together they poked through the hay and into nooks filled with tools. The horses whinnied and shied away as they moved among them.

After a while, Stefan found the child cowering in an overturned barrel in an empty stall.

Theodosia cuddled the girl to her chest and folded Alexander's cloak over her. Unable to cover her head with the toddler in her arms, she submitted to the full blast of wind and rain as she emerged into the storm.

Stefan won his duel with the door and ran up beside her... two drenched refugees eager for sanctuary.

"There's a blanket and a jug of good wine waiting for you inside," Theodosia said. "You've earned them tonight."

Etrusca sobbed when Theodosia put her daughter into her arms.

Acknowledging Nicanor's thanks, Theodosia dropped the cloak to the floor once more, reclaimed her blanket, and shooed Lucilla upstairs to get some dry clothes out for her.

Having settled most of the other slaves in the dining room, Alexander was standing in the atrium with Stefan.

Theodosia stepped over beside them.

"You found places for everyone?" she asked her steward in a tone that forgave his previous petulance.

Clearly amused at the sight of a Roman heiress soaked to her skin, Alexander nodded. He was soaked now, too; the scar on his jaw glistened with the dampness. Theodosia smiled to herself, realizing that tonight she no longer felt even remotely afraid of him.

What do I care if he did kill Gaius? Under those circumstances, I would have killed him, too.

She pulled off her earrings, unfastened her necklace, and deposited them in Alexander's hands.

"Put those away. Then... go pour a pitcher of Falernian, bring three goblets with you, and wait for me in the library. Tonight," she said, deliberately paraphrasing his words of yesterday, "you *are*—both of you—my invited guests."

Alexander and Stefan stared at her in disbelief. Slaves not did sit or take refreshment in their owner's presence.

"In my own house," she said, "I can break any rule I please."

Alexander stood up when Theodosia Varra entered the library.
Hard to believe that's the woman who bedazzled us on the stairway.

The heiress had put on a tunic that a housemaid might wear to mop the floor. Her still-wet hair was tied back with a ribbon.

"Ready for that wine?" She motioned to the ruby-serpent pitcher and cups that Alexander had placed on a table.

"Sounds like you're ready, miss," Stefan said.

"Yes, I am. I'm ready for some friendship, too."

Stefan made no response. Neither did Alexander.

"Why can't we be friends," she demanded, "the three of us?"

"No reason at all," Alexander said, "as long as you're sure you know what you're doing. You've already behaved in a most un-Roman way tonight. Sure you want to continue the experiment?"

In reply, Theodosia filled all three goblets, handed one to each man, took the last for herself, and lifted it in toast.

"Here's to a part of the experiment that I think I will enjoy very much. It can't be any more disconcerting than dinner with my peers."

She drank, but neither Stefan nor Alexander made a move.

"Look," she said after a few moments, "I'll not force you to stay here if you'd rather be with the others. I would appreciate it, though, if you'd stay and give this little experiment in friendship a chance to work."

Alexander turned to Stefan and delivered a set of mock-patrician lines, aiming for the aplomb of the best actor in Rome.

"What about it, my friend? Shall we cancel our plan to hit the hot spots of Caere tonight? We can always go another time. Weather's rather foul for traveling anyway, don't you think?"

Theodosia and Stefan both laughed at that, and Alexander was glad he had found the right note to put them all at ease. Raising his cup to his lips, he took a sip. The sweet bouquet of rare white Falernian flooded his senses. He shut his eyes to savor the precious liquid that had always been reserved for the Varros and their guests.

Since Alexander had the key to the wine-storage room, he could easily have taken some. But it was a matter of honor for him not to cheat. When he was free—he had been promising himself for eight years—he would buy a jug of top-quality wine to share with Antibe.

He opened his eyes and watched as Stefan tasted something other than vinegar wine for the first time in his life.

"What's this?"

"Falernian," said Alexander. "You've got a cup of the finest in your hand, my friend. Don't spill it."

Stefan nodded impudently in their mistress' direction.

"Is this what she drinks every day?"

"No," said Alexander. "It's saved for special occasions... like this. But her everyday stuff isn't bad either." He glanced at Theodosia Varra to make sure she wasn't offended by their blatant insolence. The grin on her face reassured him. "Not a bad life, eh?"

"I guess not." Stefan sipped again. "If you can't do no better."

Still grinning, their mistress sat on the couch, kicked off both sandals, and tucked her feet under her tunic.

"There are two chairs," she said, stating the obvious.

After a brief hesitation, Alexander sat. It was difficult to break the habits of slavery.

Stefan lowered himself into the other chair and remained quiet.

"You shouldn't treat us this way, miss," Alexander said after an interval. "It's bound to make things harder for us tomorrow, back in the real world. Harder for you as well."

"I can handle it."

They sat quietly as rain pounded the windows and thunder rocked the house. Once again, it was Alexander who broke the silence.

"Didn't you enjoy the party?"

"Not really. I felt out of place all evening." She gave him a lopsided smile. "Probably the same way you two feel right now. It wasn't the Flavians' fault, though. They did their best to welcome me into their social circle. Do you know the wife of Primus Sullus?"

"By sight. She's a lovely woman."

"Her slave girls grow lovely hair."

Alexander laughed, knowing he was expected to, and glanced at Stefan, who looked puzzled.

He doesn't get it.

"Care to tell us what happened?"

"It's hard to explain. Annia was hostile from the instant we met, as if she came prepared to dislike me. I can't imagine why."

Alexander set his cup on the table.

"Want to hear my theory?"

"Sure."

"Well... just think about her. She's beautiful, and she knows it. Comes from a comfortable family that married her off to rich old Sullus before she was sixteen."

"Just like Flavia, about to be married off to rich old Lucius Gallio."

"Exactly. So, there she is—with her nice house and her children and slaves—feeling satisfied with her life. Then she hears about you... younger, equally lovely, fantastically wealthy, and with the remarkable bonus of having complete control over your fortune and your fate. No one is going to force *you* to marry anybody, and you don't need to snag a rich old man to be wealthy for the rest of your life."

Theodosia Varra reached for the pitcher and poured more wine into all their cups, but she said nothing.

Alexander took another sip, then continued exploring his theory.

"And, of course, the lady Annia knows that you'll soon have the cream of Roman nobility lined up at your door with marriage proposals. If you haven't already," he added pointedly.

"No. Not yet."

"You will. Very soon." He paused. "So you see, miss... old Sullus was the best deal she could get. But you..."

He gave her a chance to reply, but she just gazed at him, so he pushed into territory that he knew might be dangerous.

"There probably isn't a well-born unmarried male in Rome who hasn't spent the last two weeks weighing his chances with you. It's only a matter of time before they all show up. Let's hope it's not all at once!" He laughed at the chaotic potential scenario. "The process has started already, you know, and you've only been here five days. You could marry a prince and wind up as empress someday, if you set your sights that high. Is it so hard to imagine why someone like the wife of Sullus might be jealous?"

"Is that what you think, Alexander? That I'm out to parlay my name and my inheritance into an 'important' marriage? Well, I'm not. But even if that were the case, would it make any difference to you?"

"None, except... well, certainly you realize that... I mean, surely you know this matter of your marriage is... it's never..." Alexander floundered to a stop, waving his hands a bit and shaking his head.

How much should I say? She keeps asking for friendship. Don't friends tell each other the truth?

He took a deep breath and plunged ahead.

"Truth is, we have as much at stake in your choice of a husband as you do. More, really. You'll always have some degree of legal protection. We won't. And while some men would make fair, reasonable masters, others definitely would not. So you see, miss, no matter how well you treat Stefan and me right now, we know we'll soon have a new master. Can you blame us for wondering how he'll react when he learns you've shared your wine and your friendship with two of your male slaves?"

"Do you want me to submit a list of candidates for your approval?"

"Of course not. And I really don't think you're looking for a title. My guess is, you'll choose a man whose company you enjoy. He needn't even have much money, since you've got plenty of that." Alexander sipped his wine. "I'm only telling you this so you'll know what we're thinking when a Tribune Marcus Salvius Otho comes calling."

"Or a Titus Flavius Sabinus Vespasianus the Younger," Stefan said.

"Oh... not Titus, surely!" Theodosia Varra laughed. "He's so young and immature."

"Mature enough for you to have to stand on tiptoe to kiss him goodbye tonight."

The mistress ducked her head. Even by lamplight, Alexander could see that familiar flush creeping across her cheeks.

"He's just a boy!" she protested again.

Stefan seemed to be enjoying this turn in the conversation.

"The Titus I saw tonight—sparring with a military tribune for your attention—didn't act much like a boy."

"He's just a friend."

"I thought you were in such dire need of friends," Alexander said, "that you came to us in desperation."

"Hey, I'm not *that* desperate." Her eyes twinkled, and she took a few more sips. "You needn't worry about my marrying Titus. Unlike my brother, I do prefer grown men to pretty boys."

"What about Marcus Salvius Otho?" Alexander asked, repeating the name that set his teeth on edge. "Should we be worrying about him?"

Theodosia Varra's expression slowly changed to an enigmatic smile.

It was Stefan who broke the long silence that followed.

"How come folks at the party spent so much time talking about Alexander?"

Theodosia Varra looked incredulous.

"How do you know about that? You weren't in the dining room."

"Hang around a kitchen sometime, miss. You'll see how fast the comments of the master's guests wind up as gossip for his slaves."

"The waiters tell...?" Her voice trailed off in dismay.

"Want proof?" asked Stefan with an impish gleam as his eyes moved back and forth between the other two. "The wife of Sullus thinks you're in danger, all alone out here with no one to protect you from us. She thinks it's a scandal that you consider Lucilla a friend. And General Vespasian wishes he had a steward just like Alexander."

Stefan downed the rest of his wine as Alexander leaned forward.

"Why was I the topic of conversation?"

Theodosia Varra let out a noisy breath and glared at Stefan, whose impish gleam was fading fast.

"I wasn't going to mention that," she said.

"But since *he* did... I'm curious. Why would a group of patricians spend 'so much time' talking about me over dinner?"

"Lucius Gallio asked how things were going here."

"It doesn't sound like you'd need very much time to answer that."

"I didn't, but Otho picked up the subject."

Otho would.

"What did he say?"

The mistress pointed her finger at Stefan.

"You got us into this. You can tell him what you heard."

Looking chagrined, Stefan rapped a thumb against his cup and made no response.

"Go on," she insisted.

"Well," Stefan said with obvious reluctance, "it seems the tribune gave our lady some advice on how to deal with you."

"And that advice was...?"

"Something about putting a bit in your mouth and yanking the reins."

Damn Otho!

"Anything else of interest?"

"He told her how you got that scar on your jaw."

"Which, of course," Theodosia Varra rubbed a thumb over the circle of prongs that surrounded the seal on her finger, "immediately explained the scars on almost every other face around here."

Grateful for her reminder that he hadn't been singled out for special punishment, Alexander bowed his head.

"I told you... your brother's favorite form of correction was a series of sharp slaps in the face."

"He didn't bother to remove his ring first?"

"It wouldn't have occurred to him."

There was another heavy silence. Alexander stood and walked to a window, where he watched the rain hit the panes.

Anger does a slave no good. It beats away at you till it wears you out. I won't give Otho the satisfaction of destroying me with anger that I have no chance of turning back on him.

After a long interval, he returned to his chair and sat down again. Theodosia Varra handed him his cup, filled once more with Falernian. He took a drink.

91

A moment later, Stefan laid his hand on Alexander's shoulder.

"Want to know something else I learned tonight?"

"Probably not."

Stefan leaned close to Alexander's ear, but he made no effort to lower his voice.

"Remember that music we heard a few nights ago? Well, it wasn't just the wind in the trees. And it seems our mistress don't mind shocking the patricians."

"You played for them?" Alexander asked, unsure if that was what Stefan meant.

"And sang," the mistress replied. "It would have been so much better if I hadn't. Certainly didn't do my reputation any good."

"'Riffraff' was the word I heard," said Stefan.

"Riffraff?" Alexander was astonished. "Theodosia Varra?"

"According to the wife of Primus Sullus."

Alexander whistled.

"You really *didn't* get along, did you?" He was glad to talk about something other than his own humiliation. "Well, just wait till you're married to some prince or other. Then you—not the lady Annia—will be the one deciding who's riffraff and who's not."

"You think some prince or other will want me after word gets out?"

"Positive. I can think of at least one who might consider that your talent makes you a perfect match for him."

Thanks to every blessed god that Nero's already married!

Alexander glanced at the window. The most flamboyant part of the storm seemed to be subsiding. He turned to Theodosia Varra.

"May I be so bold as to ask a favor, miss?"

"If we're friends... of course."

"Will you grant your friends a special performance?"

"If you'd like one." She sounded almost timid.

Alexander brought her cithara from the other side of the room.

Self-consciously at first, Theodosia Varra began to play. For an hour, she sang her favorites and impromptu interpretations while Stefan held the lamp close and Alexander selected poems from the scrolls in the rack.

It was then, as the dying storm beat itself out against the villa walls and the lamplight flickered seductively around the curves of Theodosia Varra's face and figure... It was then that Alexander first caught himself thinking the unthinkable, imagining the impossible. Not for a long time had anything or anyone stirred him so deeply. Not since he last held Antibe in his arms had he felt the way he felt right now.

Theodosia Varra had walked into his life this last week of May and opened up to him in a way that he never would have anticipated. Unexpectedly, he now wanted to give something of himself to her. He knew what it had to be. He had nothing else to give.

Without a word, he slipped out... leaving her singing to Stefan.

It surprised him to find Lucilla on the other side of the blue curtain. He grabbed her wrists and marched her across the atrium.

"What were you doing over there?" he whispered.

"You ain't my master," Lucilla whispered back, trying to shake his grip. "I don't answer to you."

"You'll answer to our mistress when she finds out you were eavesdropping."

"Go ahead and tell her. I'd expect you to."

"You were looking for Stefan, weren't you?"

"None of your business."

"He's occupied at the moment."

Lucilla broke free of his grasp and ran toward the stairs leading to Theodosia's bedroom suite. Alexander started to follow, then stopped.

Why let her ruin this special night?

He headed instead for his own room at the far end of the peristyle.

For a while, he sat on his bed, head in his hands, trying hard to see Antibe in his mind, but the only face that came belonged to Theodosia Varra. At last, he lifted the lamp off the chest and pulled the stack of papyrus sheets from their hiding place.

Giving his poems to Theodosia would shred what little remained of his privacy. But right now—more than anything else in the world—he wanted to hear them sung in her voice.

PART II

A.D. 53, JUNE TO DECEMBER

CHAPTER THIRTEEN

Alexander stepped out at first light and surveyed the storm damage with dismay. The kitchen lay smashed beneath the old oak, and the underground barracks were flooded. Large chunks of the barn roof had collapsed. Fortunately, the wind had caused no harm to the villa itself.

Grateful for clear skies, he lined up every hand along three ropes and joined in the palm-blistering pull that hoisted the tree out of the rubble. Then he divided the slaves into teams to begin the cleanup and repairs.

He was at the bottom of the pit that had been their sleeping quarters, fishing benches, branches, and beams out of the muck, when he spotted Theodosia Varra above him, picking her way around the puddles at ground level.

He knew that she had slept as little as the rest of them, but no one else would guess it. Her hair and skin glowed this morning, and he noted —as if for the first time—the slimness of her body, the swelling curves of her breasts, and the lovely lines of her arms and hips.

She passed by without seeing him, peered into the other end of the destroyed building, and nodded to the slaves at work there.

Waist deep in water, Etrusca grabbed Nicanor's arm. Then they climbed out of the pit and bowed to their mistress. For a while, the two stood before her, engaged in a conversation that Alexander couldn't hear.

The contrast between the radiant young Roman and the slaves she had rescued from the farm was poignant, and—to his surprise— Alexander was glad she had done it. Despite their lash wounds, the rope burns on their wrists, and their overall bad condition, Nicanor and Etrusca had been among the first into the pit this morning, lugging out the smashed timbers without being told, as if eager to justify their salvation and atone for the trouble they had caused last night.

Though no taller than Theodosia, Nicanor was broad-shouldered and accustomed to hard work. Alexander could find plenty for him to do. Etrusca was scrawny but surprisingly pretty when seen up close. Once their welts and bruises healed and they gained some weight, they would be indistinguishable from others at the villa... except for those bands of toughened skin around their necks, which would mark them forever.

When their conversation ended, Alexander crawled out of the rubble, uncomfortably aware of the mud on his hands, arms, legs, feet, and tunic.

Theodosia smiled as he approached.

"Good morning, Alexander. Get any sleep after I left?"

Alexander shook his head.

"Stefan did, though. He curled up in his blanket and fell asleep on the library floor, like a baby."

Theodosia's smile widened.

"It was nice, you know."

"Yes, miss. It was very nice."

They stood beside the pit, watching men pass buckets of water to the top. After a while, Theodosia looked at Alexander.

"I'd like to do all this differently when we rebuild. An above-ground dormitory with light, air, and a mattress for everyone. Will you see to it?"

What an improvement. She's asking, not ordering.

"It'll cost you a bit."

Theodosia threw him a teasing, sidelong glance.

"I can't afford it?"

"If you can't, we've got bigger trouble than just some storm damage. By the way, I'm hoping everybody can sleep in the barn tonight, so your life can get back to normal."

"Whatever 'normal' is these days."

"Well, 'normal' doesn't usually include singing to your slaves for several hours."

Theodosia reddened, and Alexander chuckled to himself. Her quick blushes had annoyed him before, but now he enjoyed seeing her flush.

Together they strolled to the barn. Half a dozen men were on the roof. After an hour in the humid heat, all had stripped to their loincloths.

Theodosia stopped, squinted, and raised one hand against the sun. Some of the men acknowledged her presence with waves and smiles.

That wouldn't have happened before last night.

Alexander was about to comment on the change when he caught a rapt expression on Theodosia's face. Her lips were parted, her eyes wide and tracking some movement on the roof. He followed her gaze.

Straddling the peak of the roof—with his back to them—stood Stefan, obviously unaware of the scrutiny from below. The sweaty muscles of his arms and shoulders and thighs bulged as he hoisted a log to the ridgepole. Alexander looked again at Theodosia, who appeared oblivious to anything but the big man on the roof.

It seemed forever before she lowered her eyes.

"What are you staring at?" she demanded.

"At you, staring at Stefan."

Once more, the blood rushed to her face.

"You shouldn't embarrass me, Alexander."

"Nothing to be embarrassed about. You have every right to inspect your slaves at work."

"Well, it's not as if he's totally naked!"

"Naked or not, that's up to you."

She turned her back to him.

"You really *are* trying to embarrass me, aren't you?"

"That flush becomes you, miss. Don't hide it."

"I don't have to take this from you, you know."

"I know," he said, amused. "But there's no reason to be embarrassed. There aren't many men around, anywhere, like Stefan."

Theodosia turned on him then with the glee of a triumphant fox. Her eyes drifted suggestively down his mud-soaked tunic.

"No, there certainly aren't."

Now it was Alexander's turn to blush.

When his eyes met hers, she grinned. He returned her grin, glad that last night's freedom and friendship had not vanished with the daylight.

The joint visit by Otho and Titus was unexpected. Theodosia and her steward had just stepped into the barn when two horses splashed up the driveway. The slave that Alexander had sent at dawn to Caere had already returned with Vespasian's physician. Apparently, word of the calamity at Theodosia's villa had spread to the general's family and overnight guest.

"I wasn't about to let Otho come alone," Titus said as he jumped to the ground. "A man has to look out for his interests, you know."

"A man does." Otho tossed his reins to Alexander. "And a boy usually stays out of his way."

"No boys around here that I know of," Titus retorted.

Theodosia let the two share her smile.

"Nor I." She looked at Alexander. "See that the horses get water. I'll show these gentlemen what fun we had around here last night."

Sunny with pleasure, Theodosia took Titus' arm... and also Otho's. Alexander watched as they turned to inspect the work on the roof, wondering how the visitors would have reacted had they arrived in time to catch the enraptured expression in those beautiful, gold-flecked eyes.

There were few days that summer when Theodosia had no guests. As Alexander had predicted, an array of blue-blooded suitors soon began streaming out from Rome in hopes of winning her fancy and her fortune. Some were invited back a second time, but no one—no matter how rich or noble or handsome—secured an invitation for the coveted third visit.

Once a week for the first month, Vespasian rode over alone from Caere. There was no flirtation to it, just the easy friendship of a man and a woman young enough to be his daughter. Theodosia knew that a proposal of marriage would follow if she encouraged him, but she did not. By early July, Vespasian was coming only with his children.

Flavia dropped by every day for lunch in the pergola, which she repeatedly proclaimed her favorite place in the world. If Theodosia hadn't sensed so much affection in her, she might have wondered if Flavia came to visit her or that lovely perch by the sea. Indeed, if anyone appreciated her villa as much as Theodosia, it was Flavia.

Titus was another frequent guest. He liked to escort Theodosia on her rides, and only when he was along did she go out without Stefan or Alexander. Titus was a fun companion. The four-year difference in their ages mattered less as the summer wore on. Vespasian was right, she decided after a few weeks. There were great things in store for Titus.

Otho's overnight stays increased in number and duration through June and July, as if he expected to win Theodosia by sheer persistence. If he arrived when she was riding with Titus, he would demand a fresh horse and gallop into the hills in pursuit of his rival. Theodosia continued to find herself drawn to his sardonic-affectionate charm.

Otho and Titus were different types of men, and the times she spent with them reflected their differences. There was no trace of tension around the villa when Titus was there. Her servants seemed at ease in his presence. Honest and open with Theodosia from the start, he confided his dreams and fears as if laying the groundwork for a long-term relationship. Theodosia felt happy and relaxed in his company.

But if Titus was a comfortable friend, Otho was her most exciting suitor, though his visits never failed to stir up her household. In mid June, he began campaigning for the Senate. Now their time together was filled with talk of the powerful men who were his allies, and of the emperor's nephew, Nero, who—since Gaius died—was Otho's new best friend.

Otho was unashamedly ruthless in getting what he wanted. He bragged about it. His name and wealth and connections all but guaranteed him a spot in the Senate later that year. From there, he planned to rise to the highest office the empire could bestow.

"I'll be emperor some day," he said one morning, his wicked green eyes flashing an invitation for Theodosia to join him on the throne.

And she believed him.

By late June, Theodosia knew how sweet kisses could be... and how different, depending on the man who shared them.

But Otho and Titus were not the only men in her life that summer. Alexander and Stefan weren't suitors as the Romans were, but they became her friends just as surely.

Several days a week, she went riding with Alexander; occasionally, Stefan came along. They might travel for an hour, then dismount and sit together under the trees or on a rock by the sea, talking of everything from Alexander's approach to poetics to the serious business of Theodosia's estate. The change in her steward amazed her. He had grown ebullient since the night of the storm, laughing and joking with a spontaneity that Theodosia would not have thought possible before.

One morning in June, the three made a trip to the Etruscan necropolis outside Caere. They approached from the west, walking their horses through narrow streets still rutted from the processions that had carried long-dead chieftains to their rest. Mint and wild garlic mingled with yellow calendula on the roadsides, their fragrances shouting down the dusty smell of old tufa. Swallows swooped and shrieked overhead, as if angered at this intrusion into their nesting grounds.

Pausing at the first beehive-shaped structure, Theodosia touched the ridged stones and wondered about the people who had sculpted them.

Stefan was leading the way along the street, with Theodosia in the middle and Alexander in the rear. Suddenly, he stopped between a pair of large tombs.

"Race you to the top!" he said, taking off without warning.

"You cheat!" Alexander shouted.

Theodosia whirled in time to see him drop his reins and head for the mound nearest him. She eyed a third tomb on the opposite side of the street and decided to accept the challenge. It was a tough climb up the weed-covered dome, but when she reached the summit—panting and sweaty—her companions applauded from atop their perches.

"What do I win?" Stefan called.

"He does cheat, doesn't he?" Theodosia shouted in Alexander's direction. "You decide what he wins."

"We all win... a spectacular view." Alexander pointed toward the southeast, behind Theodosia. "Just look."

Theodosia turned and gasped. Scores of grass-covered burial mounds filled the valley all the way to the distant hills, each one containing the remains of a family dead for half a millennium.

"Hey," she said after a while, "somebody needs to help me down."

Stefan hurried over and reached up to give her confidence. Near the bottom, her foot slipped. She would have fallen, but he caught her. Shaken, she clung to him for a bit, looking into his blue eyes. Then she jumped to safety.

Further along the street, Theodosia stopped at another tomb. Narrow steps led to the below-grade entrance.

This is it.

"Let's see if I can still do this." She slipped her right hand into a crevice at the edge of the slab that sealed the tomb. "They all have catches somewhere. Father showed me how to release this one. The trick is finding the right pressure point."

After a few more tries, the latch loosed its hold, and the door clicked open. Theodosia grabbed its smooth edge with her left hand.

"Find something to prop this with," she said. "We don't want to get trapped. There's no way to release the catch from inside."

Stefan left, returned with a rock that only he could have lifted, and dropped it in front of the open door.

"Think that'll do?"

"Probably be here as long as the tomb is."

"I'm certainly not going to try to move it," said Alexander as he led the way into the underground chamber.

Theodosia followed, guided by a shaft of light from the stairwell. The air was clammy and cold. As her eyes adjusted to the darkness, she saw stone cornices and benches around the perimeter and frescoes of leaping dolphins, sea horses, and nobles at table.

"The Etruscans were extraordinary people," she said. "Treated their women as equals... which is something the Greeks and the Romans have never seen fit to do." She dropped onto one of the carved benches. "Father once brought me to this tomb. It was his favorite, and he wanted me to see it." Her voice echoed in the vaulted room. "Hardly anyone ever comes here anymore."

Stefan threw the bolt on one of the interior doors and opened it. A swell of dankness billowed into the outer chamber.

"Somebody could live here," he said, "and nobody else would ever know it."

"Father said they built their tombs just like their houses. When people died, they laid them on stone beds and surrounded them with everything they had used and enjoyed."

"But there's nothing here."

"It's all been stolen. Sad, isn't it?"

"Well," said Alexander, "you own lots of Etruscan urns and statues. You could bring 'em all back."

"I don't feel that sad."

They left the necropolis through the woods, planning to picnic by the river a mile or so away. The riverbed took a sharp bend where they came upon it.

"How odd," Theodosia said. "The bend seems to point straight to the necropolis. It's almost like a sign from the gods!"

"Maybe the gods want us to have our lunch here," Alexander said. "Looks like a divine spot to me."

Theodosia wasn't sure when Titus first learned of the extraordinary privileges she was now granting her two favorite servants, but from the very beginning, Otho knew everything she did.

If she had spent an afternoon in the barn with Stefan, Otho berated her. If she had ridden alone with Alexander, he called her a fool. And once—when the three had planned a picnic trip to Lake Bracciano—he showed up on the road and accompanied them, changing the nature of the outing considerably.

Theodosia often wondered which of her slaves was Otho's spy.

Still, she was happier now than ever before and—no longer fretting over Gaius' brutal life and death—content to enjoy the summer as Titus and Otho battled for her favor. Though she expected to marry one of them some day, she never failed to experience a thrill when Stefan wrapped his hands around her waist and lifted her off the filly. And, with increasing frequency, she wondered what it would be like to kiss *him*.

Alexander was updating the record books in his room one steamy morning early in July when a houseboy brought a summons to the library. He straightened his tunic and smoothed his hair as he walked through the peristyle and into the atrium. When he pushed aside the sapphire-blue curtain, he found Theodosia sitting at her desk, twisting the ring on her right index finger.

"Lucilla's sleeping with someone," she said without a greeting. "She slips out of her bedroom at night when she thinks I'm asleep." Her eyes hardened. "Got any idea who it is?"

Alexander threw up his hands in mock self-defense.

"Hey, it's not me!"

She's more upset than she's letting on.

"Oh, I know that. Ever devoted to your Antibe."

Alexander let his hands fall and looked away.

Antibe.

"It's not just that she's gone at night," Theodosia went on. "It's her whole attitude lately. She seems to resent everything I ask her to do."

"Want me to speak to her?"

Theodosia shook her head and absentmindedly picked up a reed-pen.

"She's my maid. I can certainly tell her if her behavior displeases me." She rapped the pen a couple of times against the edge of the desk. "It's just that... I gave her my word I wouldn't interfere again in her romances."

"Again?"

"It's not much of a story." The pen began rapping harder on the desk. "Do you know who she's sleeping with?"

"No, miss," he lied.

The rapping increased in intensity, then it stopped.

"I'm pretty sure it's Marcipor." A few more thumps of the pen. "I can't blame her for falling for him. He's such a handsome fellow."

104

"She knows about you." Alexander kept his voice low.

Lucilla looked up from the corner table where she was sitting with Stefan. Her eyes widened suddenly, and she wrinkled her nose. Lucilla always reminded Alexander of a rabbit—jumpy, with big ears and feet— but never more so than now.

"What're you talking about?"

Alexander glanced cautiously around the rebuilt kitchen.

Theodosia had been true to her word. Her slaves' airy, new, above- ground barracks—with straw compacted into mattresses instead of spread on the floor, plus equally modern shuttered windows—was a model of benevolence, their improved bath far more conducive to cleanliness. There was greater space between the kitchen tables now, but still it was easy to hear what one's fellows were saying.

He pulled a chair from a nearby table.

"She knows you're sleeping with someone," he whispered to Lucilla. "She knows you leave her suite at night."

"If she don't like it," Lucilla said with a shrug, "she'll let me know."

Alexander turned to Stefan.

"She suspects it's you, although she's trying to convince herself it's Marcipor."

"It might have been Marcipor." Stefan smiled at Lucilla as she laid her hand on his knee. "'Cept she found somebody better."

He put his hand atop Lucilla's and gave it a gentle squeeze.

"But why should the mistress care? Slaves was sleeping with slaves a thousand years ago. What's a healthy man supposed to do around here? Rape Theodosia Varra?"

"She'd probably like that." Lucilla giggled. "You know how she teases you."

"She don't know she teases."

"Look, Stefan." Alexander tried to be patient. "You're not just a stable hand any more. You're the mistress' oldest friend. Her dearest friend."

"He's my dearest friend, too," Lucilla said.

Alexander ignored her.

"Don't you realize how much she cares about you?"

"Too bad." Lucilla's hand slipped out from under Stefan's and slid along his thigh. "Because the one *he* cares about is *me*."

"That attitude will get both of you into trouble. We're not talking about Rila, the goatherd's daughter."

Stefan was unimpressed.

105

"Hell, I was sleeping with Rila before Theodosia Varra came back. What's the difference if I sleep with her goatherd's daughter or with her maid?"

"Well, for one thing, Theodosia Varra doesn't wake up in the night and call for her goatherd's daughter to attend her."

Alexander turned his attention to Lucilla.

"If I were you, I'd be worried about what happens when she decides to find a maid who's more interested in serving her than in screwing her coachman."

"Mind your own business. I've been with her for two years. I know her better than you."

"You can go ahead and take a short cut to the slave market, for all I care. But I'll be damned if I'll let you drag Stefan along with you."

"I ain't dragging him nowhere! He's man enough to decide who he sleeps with. Besides... she promised I could have anyone here I wanted."

Lucilla's arms encircled Stefan's waist. Then she stuck her tongue out at Alexander.

"Don't think I'll give him up just because she's itching to get her hands on his prick!"

CHAPTER FOURTEEN

Nizzo showed up the morning of the last day of July. Alexander led him to the library and went to find Theodosia. It was too hot to ride these days, so she had taken to spending a few hours each day in the barn, talking with Stefan as he worked among her horses.

Alexander knew exactly what would happen today. Nizzo would argue for her to sell him the farm, and she would argue for him to make changes, and neither would budge. At least, that was what had happened at the end of June when the freedman last came to the villa.

From the peristyle an hour later, Alexander saw them pass by, headed for the service yard.

She's giving him a tour.

Curious, he stepped out and strode along behind them.

Theodosia's new kitchen-bath-and-barracks building was everything Nizzo opposed. He made sure that she knew it.

Neither was he impressed by the sight of Nicanor in his clean brown tunic, his wounds healed and his belly fuller than it had ever been before.

That afternoon, Alexander was in a storage room, supervising one of Milo's assistants as he measured grain, when he heard someone call his name. He stepped outside and flagged down the houseboy.

"The mistress commands your presence. She's real angry."

Alexander left the kitchen worker to finish his task and strode through the peristyle to the atrium. He found Theodosia Varra standing in front of the sapphire-blue curtain.

"Get in here."

Astonished at the fury in her voice, Alexander followed her into the library. Euripides' *Andromache*, which they had taken turns reading aloud last evening, lay on the floor. He remembered leaving it open on a table when they parted. Now he bent, picked up the scroll, and handed it to her.

"I don't want it," she said. "I threw it down there."

"Then what—"

"Open it." Her voice was icy, her eyes equally cold.

Alexander unrolled the scroll. Inside was a sheet of papyrus identical to those in her desk. On the sheet, scrawled but legible, was a laughable attempt at a rhymed couplet.

THE SAD FATE OF THE BROTHER

WILL SOON COME TO THE SISTER.

Alexander looked up. Theodosia's face was pale and pinched; her hands trembled despite an obvious effort to steady them.

She's more frightened than angry.

"This is nonsense," he said, laying the sheet on the table.

"I wonder."

"You wonder... what, miss?"

"Why you wrote that and left it for me to find."

"I thought we'd gotten past suspicions like that. I didn't write this, you know."

"No, I don't know that."

"Well, it's true. Threatening you is the last thing I'd ever do."

"If you didn't write it, who did?"

"Someone who wanted to make you mistrust me."

"Who else knows you write poetry?"

"Just Stefan. But he can't write, so even if he—"

"I'd never suspect Stefan of something like this!" The confidence in her voice was devastating.

You'd suspect me, but not him.

Never before had Alexander been jealous of Stefan's special, life-long relationship with their mistress, but jealousy swept over him now.

"You have access to my library," Theodosia continued.

"I never come alone. Not allowed to, remember?"

"You were here last night."

"You invited me in."

"You knew what I was reading."

"So would anyone who saw that scroll on the table."

"You *are* the one who wrote that."

"No!"

"I say yes!"

Jealousy quickly gave way to panic as Alexander realized there was no way he could prove his innocence. He hadn't seen that frozen look in Theodosia Varra's eyes since their first encounter back in May.

"Miss, I— If you've learned nothing else about me by now, you should know—" He faltered again, groping for a credible defense. "If I'd written this, it would be better poetry!"

He felt the blood congealing in his veins under her fixed, icy stare.

Gods, I will run this time. I can't stand being sold again.

After a terrible, lengthy interval, Theodosia blinked. Crossing the space between them, she put a hand on his shoulder and shook it.

"That's what I thought. I'm sorry, Alexander. I had to make sure... test you... see how you'd react."

Her face was close to his, her eyes intense, her clove-oil fragrance almost too delicious for him to bear. He turned his own eyes away as relief coursed through his body.

Theodosia released his shoulder then, and though for a time he could not face her, he knew she was still very close.

"You frightened me, miss. Please don't do that again. If you have a doubt about me or a question about something you think I've done... give me the chance to answer you in a normal way."

"Actually, I wasn't sure I could frighten you."

"Oh, you can. Don't worry!" Alexander met her eyes again. "A slave's greatest fear—at least for one like me, who lives or dies on his owner's confidence—is losing that confidence."

"Then you, at least, can relax now." Theodosia rubbed her temples with her fingertips. "I, on the other hand, still have to figure out who wants to see me dead."

She hasn't looked this frightened in months.

Alexander wanted to wrap his arms around her, to comfort her, but he resisted the temptation. Such gestures weren't for slaves.

"It's Nizzo," Theodosia said, fingering the sheet. "Didn't you leave him here alone this morning when you went to find me?"

"Don't jump to conclusions."

"Hey, I've been threatened in my own home! I'll jump to any conclusions I like. I don't want that man here ever again. Don't ever want to see him again. You'll deal with him at the farm. Understand?"

Alexander nodded.

"Damn Nizzo!" She wadded the sheet and threw it to the floor. "I thought I was over Gaius' death. Felt really safe again. I was so afraid when I first got here, especially of you. Now, just when I'd relaxed—"

She broke off in mid sentence, knelt beside the wad, and stared at it.

Can't you see that somebody wants you afraid again?

An instant later, she raised her eyes... bright with discovery.

"Nizzo murdered Gaius!"

Alexander gave half a laugh.

"Impossible. He had no motive, nothing to gain."

Theodosia stood and nodded.

"But he did! Think about it. What does he want to own so badly that it's eating him up inside?"

"The farm he worked as a slave."

"Yes. So, he gets his rich friends—all those wealthy freedmen in the palace—to agree to lend him the money to buy it. Then what happens? Gaius refuses to sell to him. Remember Nizzo's comment that day at the farm? 'That's exactly what your brother said the last time I proposed the deal to him.' But Nizzo's no fool, so he thinks, 'I can fix it so there's another owner. The little sister will be easier to persuade.' And so, by Juno, here I am a few months later, listening to his arguments."

"You could be right about the murder. Nizzo might have figured a young, inexperienced woman would be easier to deal with."

Bet he's rethinking that now.

"And if so, you're perfectly safe now. A plot like that wouldn't work again, because, as you say, you were there to inherit the family estate."

"How does that make me safe?"

"Well, you're not married. You've no family. Who would inherit your property if you died right now?"

"Emperor Claudius."

"Exactly. And do you think that old bird would sell a big chunk of the most valuable farmland in Italy to a freedman? Not a chance. He'd keep it himself, for the income... and Nizzo knows it."

"You're probably right." She chuckled once, then after a few moments chuckled again. "Of course you're right! Gods, I feel better than I have in months!"

Alexander's face must have betrayed his confusion, for Theodosia's hands came up in a sidewise flutter of fingers.

"Never mind why. It's just something stupid I'd been believing about you since May." Her face puckered, and she laughed outright. "Oh, it's all so clear now! Nizzo took a slave from the farm to Rome and forced him to help murder my brother; then he killed him, too—right there—and dumped his body into the Tiber where nobody could identify it." She laughed once more. "Have you ever heard of a more perfect crime?"

She sat at the desk, smiling broadly.

If thinking that her bailiff murdered her brother makes Theodosia Varra so happy, who's her steward to argue?

"May I ask," Alexander said, "why you were so afraid of me last spring?"

"It was just something I'd heard. Doesn't matter now."

"It matters to me. Was it something Tribune Otho said? He hates me, you know."

"And you hate him."

Alexander hesitated. The truth might be dangerous, but this was no time for lies.

"I won't deny it."

"What happens if I marry him?"

"Then I'm in trouble."

"If that's what I decide to do... how could I help you?"

Alexander glanced down and sighed.

"Sell me before your marriage." The words came hard. "Didn't Vespasian say he'd like to own a steward like me? So... give him that opportunity." He looked at her. "You're not old enough to free me, you know, even if you wanted to. The law says you must be twenty-five to manumit a slave."

Theodosia filled the silence by drumming on the desk. After a while, she rose, laid both her hands on Alexander's shoulders, and looked directly into his eyes at close range.

"Why does Otho hate you so?"

"No idea, miss." He shook his head as if to answer her question, but in reality to steady himself against the unsettling effect of her intimacy. "I'm in no position to do the tribune any harm."

"He made you sound like a real monster last spring, before I left Rome."

"He'd like to see you dislike me as much as he does."

"Well, it hasn't worked."

The smile returned to Theodosia's face as she lowered her arms and took a step back from him. But still... her eyes never left his.

"I'm not afraid of you any more, Alexander. Nor do I dislike you in the least. In fact, I've become surprisingly fond of you."

111

Alexander made no response.

"I haven't told you that before, have I?"

Am I the one she's going to start teasing now?

"Well, I am fond of you. But right now, I need to be alone." She flicked her fingers toward the door. "Leave me. Please."

That night, after dinner—and two hours of reading in her suite— Theodosia drifted outside, drawn by the hum of cicadas.

Wispy clouds ambled by overhead as Juno's crescent glided among them. The hottest July in memory would pass into history on a still, starry night.

She strolled past the pergola into the woods and kept going to the far edge, to a rocky clearing where the coastline jutted out into the sea. She had often ridden this way by day, but never before had she ventured such a great distance at night. And never had she come alone.

It was dark under the big pines. She could see her villa shining in the moonlight across the curve of the shore.

Feeling the same exhilarating mix of freedom and danger as on that earlier venture into the cove, she dropped to the ground, leaned against a tree, and closed her eyes.

For another hour, she listened to the lapping of waves against the rocks and held a series of fantasy conversations with the four men who were growing in importance in her life.

She told Titus that she planned to marry Otho.

She told Otho that she planned to marry Titus.

She told both Titus and Otho that she would marry neither of them.

She told them that she was taking Stefan as her lover.

She told Stefan to come to her suite tonight.

She told Alexander that he now belonged to Vespasian.

She told him that his wife and son had been found in the household of a kindly Athenian, who was selling them to Theodosia.

She told him that Antibe and Niko had never been enslaved and were looking forward to his return to Corinth in six years... as her freedman.

When her fantasies were exhausted, Theodosia stood and made her way home. It was the first of many solitary nocturnal walks that she would make before the summer ended.

The next afternoon, Theodosia returned from riding with Titus to find Alexander pacing in the driveway.

"A legionary brought a letter from the governor of Corinth."

"You opened it?"

"It's addressed to you, miss."

Dearest Juno, for his sake... let it be good news!

Alexander stood just inside the blue curtain as Theodosia slit the wax seal and read silently, aware that the wait was torment for him. Then she handed the scroll to him.

Alexander's eyes were the only things moving as he absorbed the words on the page.

"No record at all? But it was the governor's own men who arrested me. I spent three months in his damn prison." His voice was growing louder. "There must be some record of that!"

"I'm sorry."

"If he said he knew about my case but not what had happened to my family... But to know nothing at all! He's got to be lying!"

"It's been almost nine years."

"You don't think they just lose records, do you?"

Theodosia toyed with the objects on her desk, not sure how to deal with his disappointment and anger.

"You know they don't!" He was almost shouting. "Those bastards have the records all right, they just don't want to bother looking for them. What are a few miserable Greeks to the masters of the world? They've been sending us off in their stinking slave ships for two hundred years!"

Abruptly, Alexander checked his tirade, drew a breath, and exhaled it. Then he stepped over to Theodosia and returned the letter to her.

"Forgive me, miss. I've no business talking to you like that."

"We'll have to try again, I guess."

He stared at her.

"You'll write another letter?"

"What else is there to do? Just don't expect too much."

So, Theodosia wrote a second letter to Governor Viticus, reminding him of her father's service in the same capacity, declaring the matter urgent, and promising to keep on until she got the information she needed.

The response came—with remarkable swiftness—the last week of August. Theodosia and Alexander read the letter together.

Clerks had indeed found records of one Alexander, son of Demosthenes, a well-to-do Corinthian shipper. Both had been convicted of defrauding a dozen Romans doing business in Corinth. Their assets were seized, and the son, Alexander, was enslaved as punishment.

"Is that true?"

"That is what happened, but as for the accusation... No, it's not true. We were set up, miss. You may not believe me—I know that's the oldest excuse in the world—but it's true."

"How did it happen?"

"The Romans who accused us were investors in our main competitor's business. Treachery isn't limited to politics and war, you know. I'm sure the Roman investors and their Greek puppets got very rich with us out of the way."

"But the trial...?"

"The trial! The magistrate, the clerks, the lawyers, the witnesses, the plaintiffs... all Romans. Nobody gave a damn about a couple of Greeks hauled up filthy and ragged after three months in prison."

"What happened to your father?"

"He was almost fifty. Not worth much as a slave, I guess."

Alexander stopped cold. Theodosia waited for him to go on.

"I was right there," he said after a while, "chained to the wall, when they slit his throat."

Theodosia winced and briefly touched his arm.

After a few moments, she continued reading. Yes, the governor wrote, since it was a criminal case, the records on the man Alexander were intact. Data on his wife and child were unavailable, but the governor supplied the name of the official in charge of the census a decade earlier.

That evening, for the third time, they composed a letter for Alexander to carry to Ostia in the morning. Theodosia dropped her head into her hands as he left the library, wondering which of them would tire of this process first.

It was at the far edge of the woods, in that clearing around the curve of the shore, that Otho proposed marriage two nights later. None of Theodosia's rehearsed speeches had prepared her. She stood looking at her hands, at the trees, at the sea... everywhere but at Otho.

"It's too soon. I don't yet know what I want."

"You haven't promised yourself to Titus?"

114

"No. I'd give him the same answer right now. I can't decide between the two of you, or if I even want to marry at all."

Otho's laughter roared across the water.

"It's hard enough to believe you can't decide between me and that baby-faced boy, but to think of remaining a spinster… What else is there for you but marriage?"

"That." She waved her hand toward the cluster of lights across the water. "My home. My land. My servants."

"Sentimental rubbish."

"Guess I shouldn't expect you to understand. You've known all your life that you'd inherit your father's name and money and villas and slaves and power. Not me. I never thought I'd have anything, and now I do. I have everything! But on the day I marry, I lose it all."

Otho's face seemed stuck between a laugh and a sneer.

"I can't believe you're such a fool. You'll ruin this place. You know nothing about managing money and property."

"Gaius relied on Alexander. So will I."

"That impudent Greek still has to be dealt with. He and that big fellow who puts his hands all over you."

"Stefan helps me on and off my horse."

"Well, you'd better watch yourself with him or nobody of any worth will touch you. Your wealth might land you an ambitious plebeian for a husband, no matter what your reputation—"

"There's nothing wrong with my reputation."

"And maybe you can keep Titus hanging around like a lapdog… ruffling his fur… tweaking his ears… But no woman makes sport of me."

Without warning, Otho seized her wrists, pinned them behind her back, and came down roughly on her lips. Wedged between his arms and chest, she could only submit to his tongue as it probed ever harder and deeper into her mouth. He had kissed her that way once before, but he was gentle the first time. This time, he was not gentle.

Fearing her neck might snap, she tried to escape his grasp, but it was impossible. She struggled to breathe and push him away.

Juno, help me!

She felt so weak, so powerless.

This must be what the slave girls go through!

Then, as unexpectedly as he had begun, Otho released her and stepped aside. A sardonic grin spread across his face.

"Baby-faced Titus never kissed you like that, did he? And that big barbarian slave better pray I never find out he did so, either."

115

CHAPTER FIFTEEN

Theodosia had the same circular conversation with Alexander several times that summer.

"You ought to visit the house that my lord Gaius built in Rome," he would say. "Aren't you curious to see it?"

"I'm not going back to Rome," she would say.

"Then you should sell the house."

"But I haven't even seen it."

"So... go see it!"

Finally, once the heat of August had passed, she gave in. Lucilla, Alexander, Stefan, and Marcipor accompanied her to Rome.

After exploring her brother's mansion on the Caelian Hill, Theodosia knew for sure that Gaius had been mad. There was much too much of everything... golden lanterns by the dozens, golden roses on every ceiling, golden shells around every doorway, African ivory on every table, rare serpentine marble on every floor, ornate frescoes on every wall, Athenian sculpture throughout the house and garden...

By comparison, their ancestral villa looked like a peasant's abode.

But that wasn't the worst of it. Three hundred slaves lolled about under a single overseer whose job it was to keep them all busy and in line.

That day, Theodosia instructed Lucius Gallio to sell the mansion, furnishings, and slaves. She would stay a week, then go home for good.

Just as Gallio was leaving, Otho showed up with his friend Lucius Ahenobarbus... the prince called Nero. After their last encounter, Theodosia wasn't thrilled to see Otho. And she was puzzled.

How did he find out so fast that I was here?

She was curious, however, to meet the emperor's nephew. A devotee of music and the theater, Nero had performed in public on several occasions. It was a scandalous act for a nobleman that had created even more sensation than Theodosia at Vespasian's dinner party.

"So... this is the young woman I've been hearing about. A fellow artist. A lady who sings. Plays the cithara. What a delectable novelty!"

"His Highness craves novelty in his entertainment," Otho said with the pride of one who possesses privileged information.

"And, my dear," said Nero, "surely you appreciate how very hard novelty is to come by. Everything they offer me is so trite and boring. You must promise to perform for me at the palace."

"Whenever Your Lordship wishes."

Juno, keep me from ever having to fulfill that promise!

Nero chatted on, but his appearance distracted Theodosia from the conversation. Rings on every finger and half a dozen bracelets on each arm clanked with his smallest gesture. Sculpted tiers of reddish curls around his face created a disconcerting air of femininity. Though he wore imperial purple, Nero was hardly a figure to inspire girlish admiration.

A series of chins launched a single flabby ripple that extended from his fleshy lips through his blotchy, bloated neck and on to his protruding belly. Below his fine toga, a pair of spindly legs seemed barely enough to support his ponderous body. Despite the heavy musk he wore, the stench of rotting teeth forced Theodosia to outperform the most skillful of actors, keeping her face sociably close to his.

All Rome had rumbled last year at news of the marriage of Claudia Octavia, the daughter of Emperor Claudius, to this adopted member of the Julio-Claudian family. In a city accustomed to political marriages, theirs was exceptionally significant, because Britannicus—the emperor's only surviving son—was still a child. So now, even the poorest urchin in the street could tell you who would assume the throne when the ailing Claudius went to join Caligula, his demented predecessor, in hell.

"I share your sorrow at the loss of our beloved Gaius," Nero was saying. "He was my good friend, so I feel I've known you, too, my dear, for many years. And of course, Tribune Otho speaks constantly of you."

"I don't know what Otho has told Your Lordship, but—"

"I trust the marriage will not be long delayed." Nero's malodorous mouth came closer and whispered in her ear. "My friend is most eager. We will hold a great banquet at the palace to celebrate the consummation of your marriage."

Remembering the insistent force of Otho's tongue, Theodosia felt herself reddening, as usual. But she couldn't just turn her back on the next emperor as she did when her steward made her blush.

117

◇ ◇ ◇

The next morning, Theodosia offered Stefan a guided tour of Rome on foot. Lucilla begged to come, too, and soon their little entourage had expanded to include Alexander and Marcipor.

It was fun for Theodosia to see the city through Stefan's eyes. To a man whose idea of grand architecture was an old stone villa on the Etruscan coast, the marble temples, theaters, palaces, and baths gleaming in the sun around the Golden Milestone rivaled Mount Olympus.

As they meandered along the Argiletum, the Forum's busiest street, under the two-storied portico of the huge Basilica Aemilia, Stefan gawked at the shoppers, moneylenders, and street walkers jamming the entrances to the elegant shops.

Theodosia noted with pride that more than a few in the throng gawked back at him.

The Forum was, as always, a jumble of patricians and their clients and slaves, acrobats, legionaries, soothsayers, beggars, pimps, horses, dogs, and trained monkeys... all shouting and gesticulating and bumping into each other.

Theodosia and her retinue stopped at the Rostra to listen to a seedy-looking man in a threadbare toga harangue about the price of fish. She sat on a bench, smiling to herself as her slaves—standing behind her—made rude jokes about the shabby citizen at the podium.

"What's that?" Stefan pointed to an oddly shaped building on the north side of the Forum.

"The Carcer Tullianum," said Alexander.

"The famous prison? So small?"

"It's mostly underground."

"They say you go in alive through a hole in the floor," Lucilla said, "and come out dead in the sewer below."

"What happens in the meantime is anybody's guess," added Marcipor. "But if they want to keep you alive for a while, they stick you in some underground cave where the Cloaca Maxima enters the Tiber."

Alexander chuckled without mirth.

"And then they allow you the luxury of dying of fever and starvation, instead of torturing you to death."

"A place to stay away from," Lucilla whispered. "They say it's easy enough to wind up there without trying."

Around midday, they made their way down the winding Via Sacra, through the chaos of the commercial district, past stores whose stocks of pots, pottery, sandals, tin ware, and cheap fabrics overflowed into the streets. Eager shopkeepers pounced on anyone who slowed; their voices accounted for much of the din. Bakeries spewed delectable smells into the air, as did the cook shops and taverns.

Pungent, too, were the terra cotta urns placed on corners around the city to serve the multiple purposes of giving passersby a place to relieve themselves without fouling the streets, allowing tavern customers to continue their revels without interruption, and collecting urine for the fullers to use in cleaning the togas of the rich and powerful.

The hubbub stretched all the way to the immense market near the river, where slaves from the great houses fearlessly elbowed aside the free poor to buy nuts, dormice, pheasants, spices, and other necessities for their masters' tables. The assorted squawks, bleats, squeaks, and quacks of the live merchandise blended with the clamor of negotiation and the protests of those kept waiting, just as their odors merged with the more savory aromas of the produce stands.

Amid this tumult, Theodosia showed off bargaining skills honed in more frugal times. Then, in the quiet of a nearby temple garden, she shared with her servants a feast of fruit, bread, olives, and wine. Finally, they set out for the little house in the Subura that had been her home for eight years.

"Just to show you I know what the world is really like," she told the men as they headed into the maze of cramped and smelly alleyways that made up Rome's most notorious slum.

Overhead loomed the wooden firetraps where thousands of Rome's poorest, mostly foreigners and former slaves, found crude shelter but little else. So tall and tightly packed were the buildings that the sun made its way to the streets for only a few hours a day. An open window on the top storey of one building belched the sounds of a ferocious argument. Balcony-hung laundry—flapping and snapping in the breeze—formed a counterpoint to the slaps and curses and breaking pottery.

Nor was life any more pleasant on the ground. A pack of feral dogs —nosing through the offal and creating more—snarled if anyone came too close. Four naked toddlers played unattended in the dirt. A trio of drunks quarreled in a corner bar. The streets stank of urine, sewage, and rotting garbage.

Theodosia's house stood in a slightly better neighborhood in the heart of the Subura, where people owned their single-storey homes and attached street-side shops. Buildings were lower; there was more sunlight. At one time, the entire area had been like this, but the surrounding blocks had been razed over the years to pack in more cheap housing.

She stopped in front of the shop where Dinos—the elderly sandal maker who was her tenant—and his slave eked out a living and slept on the floor. Dinos' meager payments had been Theodosia's sole income for years, but she had charged him no rent since Gaius died.

Dinos was sitting on a shaded stool just inside the doorway, a bright-eyed spider alert for prey in the web of sandals spread out along the edge of the street. Now he hopped down... eyes agog at the sight of Theodosia.

"It is you, lady! I never expected to see you again."

"You're well, Dinos?"

"As well as possible, and still very grateful to you."

Dinos' slave, Rubol, stepped through the doorway and bowed. Sometimes in the past, when Dinos was out, Theodosia would slip food to Rubol, for she knew how little he got from his master. And she had talked with him enough to know his story. Long before Theodosia came here to live, Dinos had bought the boy, brought him to this shop, and taught him his trade.

Rubol was tall but stooped from years of hunched-over toil. Though he was no more than thirty, poor nourishment had depleted his body. A lifetime in the windowless back room had left his thin face gray. He winced now in the glare of the street.

"It's good to see you, Rubol," Theodosia said.

He bowed again and squinted to focus on her face.

"And you, lady."

"Give Dinos a hundred sesterces," Theodosia said quietly to Alexander, who was carrying her money. "Buy yourself and Rubol a good meal, Dinos, and hide the rest. You may need it someday."

"The gods bless you, lady!" the old man said as Theodosia turned to her own doorstep.

The lock resisted the key in Lucilla's hand, but at last it gave way. The slaves stood aside so Theodosia could enter first.

A legion of real-life spiders had invaded the tiny atrium. The flowers that Lucilla had planted in the narrow peristyle last spring had died of thirst. Theodosia headed for the kitchen where she and Lucilla had prepared and eaten all their meals together.

"You lived here by yourselves?" Stefan asked. "Just you two?"

Lucilla smiled pertly at him.

"I was here a couple of years. Miss was alone before that."

Stefan turned dismayed eyes to Theodosia.

"In this neighborhood? All alone?"

"Yes, for four years after my nurse died. I never went out past midafternoon."

"Someone could have come in over the roof."

"Well, I was prepared."

Theodosia stepped to the wall behind the kitchen table and pulled out a loose brick. In a cavity behind it lay a long-bladed knife with a bone handle. She pulled the weapon out and handed it to Stefan.

"It's sharp!" He fingered the blade, which showed no sign of rust.

"Very." She returned the knife to its niche and replaced the brick. "There's another in the bedroom wall. Phoebe pried the bricks loose soon after we moved in, and together we hid the knives there. She wanted to make sure I knew where they were and that I could get to them. Hard to believe I was only eleven at the time."

"Why didn't you ever show them to me?" Lucilla asked.

"I thought for a while I might need them to defend myself against you. We had some problems at first, remember?"

Alexander's eyes shot to Lucilla's face.

"Problems?"

"Nothing that concerns you," Lucilla said.

"Oh," Theodosia said with a slight laugh, "Lucilla was upset after her master died and they broke up his household. She seemed to blame me, for some reason."

"I loved a man there, and she wouldn't buy him."

"Couldn't buy him. I was barely able to buy you." Theodosia turned to the others. "Sometimes, I'm still not sure she's forgiven me."

Otho's promise of good behavior overcame Theodosia's reluctance to be with him again, and she accompanied him to banquets three nights in a row. He hadn't yet been elected to the Senate, but his father had put the requisite million sesterces in his name. Everywhere they went, his election was toasted as if it were a fact. Favors were sought and granted at those parties; new political alliances took shape. Every patrician in town wanted to be seen with the future emperor's closest friend.

On the fourth day after her arrival in Rome, Theodosia received an invitation to dinner from Livia, the wife of a consul whose support Otho had just won. "No men allowed!" the message read.

Intrigued, she decided to go.

Gaius' litter bearers had been executed in May and no more had been bought, so Otho lent Theodosia his litter and a team of bearers, plus a set of liveried guards to clear a path.

Stefan went along, too, walking close by to protect her from the rabble in the streets.

Theodosia had ridden with Otho in his immense two-person litter; she found it an unsettling experience. The eight men were closely matched in height and trained to carry their load steadily, but Theodosia disliked the jostling as they made their way through the crowds.

She felt uncomfortably conspicuous, too. Few litters were more opulent than Otho's, so everyone recognized it. Not only that but... how could anybody fail to notice the green swarm of identically clad slaves who accompanied Otho on all his outings?

Theodosia also knew that her return to Rome had renewed gossip about Gaius' murder. People in the streets pointed at the heiress passing by in Marcus Salvius Otho's litter. Otho liked to be seen as he traveled about, but she did not. A few blocks into this solo trip, she pulled the curtains closed.

The dinner was exactly what Theodosia had expected... too much food, wine, and witless chatter. Though not pleased to see Annia, the wife of Sullus—again with a slave's blonde hair atop her head—Theodosia resolved to treat her civilly.

She had met her hostess and several other patrician women earlier in the week at the Baths of Agrippa, where both the common people and the flower of Roman aristocracy went to be steamed, oiled, scraped, soaked, and invigorated. When they lived in the Subura, Theodosia and Lucilla had taken advantage of these free public baths, but never had they availed themselves of the other services favored by those who could afford to pay for greater indulgences than simply being clean.

At the baths this week, her new acquaintances had giggled at Theodosia's refusal to be massaged by one of the dozens of slave men available for that purpose. Sophisticated ladies, they assured her, paid no more attention to male slaves than to male horses or male dogs. Being unsophisticated, however, and unaccustomed to naked massages by any man, slave or otherwise, Theodosia declined the opportunity, though she sat by as the other women enjoyed vigorous rubdowns under the carefully controlled hands of the bath slaves.

Now, as Livia's dinner party neared its end, discussion turned to Theodosia's odd behavior in the baths.

"Do you have only females at your villa, Theodosia?" asked a dainty young patrician in yellow.

The other guests howled in laughter.

"Poppaea Sabina is the only one who'd think that!" said Annia. "Everybody else knows that Gaius would have only men around him. The handsomest men money could buy."

"Interesting household, Theodosia," said Marcia, the wife of Camillus, a popular and powerful senator who had not yet agreed to support Otho's bid for the Senate. Otho had told Theodosia several times how critical it was for him to get Camillus' endorsement.

Others chimed in.

"If it were mine, I'd love it! All those gorgeous men around, and no husband to spoil the fun!"

"And she pretends to be so modest."

"You're turning red, my dear. Are you ill?"

"Speaking of gorgeous men... anyone notice that big fellow who tagged along with her today?"

"I saw him, too!"

"Those were Otho's men, don't you know?"

"Not the one Claudia's talking about. He wasn't wearing Otho's livery."

"Did you all see the way he looked at her?"

"Now, that would be a great one to attend your bath, Theodosia. With those hands... what a massage he could give!"

"Which is it, Theodosia?" said Annia. "Is he yours or Otho's?"

"He's mine. My bodyguard."

"They grow big in the country, don't they? Got any more like him stashed away out there?"

"Hey, this isn't fair!" said Poppaea Sabina, who had unwittingly introduced the topic. "I didn't see him."

"Bring him in then," Livia said, "for Poppaea's education."

"Oh, Stefan may not be here right now," Theodosia said, hoping it was true. "I told him he might go see a bit more of the city."

Titters erupted around the table.

"He must be something special then," Poppaea said. "What good is a bodyguard if he's not around to guard your body when you need him?"

Livia snapped her fingers at the slave behind her couch.

"Go and see if the lady Theodosia's bodyguard has returned from sightseeing in the city." Her tone was droll. "If he has, tell him to come here at once."

Soon Stefan appeared in the doorway.

"Here he is," Livia said. "What did you say his name is?"

"Stefan."

Theodosia wanted nothing to do with this game but didn't know how to stop it.

"Come here, Stefan," said Livia, pointing to the space between her couch and the one occupied by Poppaea Sabina. "We all want a good look at you."

Stefan stepped warily across the room. Theodosia felt a swell of pride in him... until his eyes reached hers. They were seething.

Juno, I wish we were both anywhere but here.

Poppaea Sabina reached out and ran a single fingertip down Stefan's arm; then she let it wander on down his leg.

"He's magnificent! I've never seen a man this big so close up. Is he a gladiator?"

"He's fit for one, I'm sure," said Claudia. "Ever thought of having him trained?"

Numb with guilt at treating her old friend this way, Theodosia shook her head.

He'll think this was my idea.

"What a shame," Marcia said. "Pull out those pins at your shoulders, fellow. Give us a better look at you."

Stefan's jaw tightened, but he did as he was told.

There was a ripple of appreciation around the table as the brown tunic fell to his belt.

"Now... that *is* a man," someone said.

Theodosia saw Annia's eyes dally around Stefan's chest, waist, and legs. It was clear she would gladly force him to strip completely.

"Why not make a gladiator of him?" chirped Poppaea Sabina in her little-girl voice. Her yellow sleeve rippled as she poked a finger into Stefan's abdomen. "Turn around, slave. Oh, just look at the muscles on his back! He'd be the best of the lot!"

"Stefan and I grew up together," Theodosia said. "We were playmates as children. I'd never send him to the arena."

"Hogwash!" said Marcia. "You know, Camillus needs new fighters for the games he's sponsoring right before the election. He was negotiating with Gaius last spring to buy one of the Varro slaves. It must have been this fellow."

"Your husband was negotiating—?" Theodosia said, dumbfounded.

So it's true. Gaius really was about to sell Stefan.

"They'd almost reached an agreement when Gaius died. Camillus had raised his offer to fifteen thousand denarii. He's still interested, Theodosia. Has he approached you about it yet?"

Theodosia shook her head again.

"Well, the offer still stands."

Fifteen thousand denarii.

It was an immense amount of money.

Theodosia couldn't bear to look at Stefan, just shook her head.

"Nonsense, child." Marcia sounded like one unaccustomed to being thwarted. "What's one slave more or less to you?"

"She's right, you know." It was Annia. "Come on, Theodosia. Don't be so selfish. Share this magnificent fellow with all of Rome."

"Tell you what," Marcia said, "we'll list Tribune Otho as a co-sponsor of the games and give him credit for the new gladiator. Your Otho will win for sure once the mob sees this fellow in action."

"He's not *my* Otho!"

"Don't be so coy. Think about it. Your fortune combined with Otho's senatorial rank... You'll be one of the most powerful couples in the empire. That's not a bad swap for a single slave."

"Maybe she wants him for something else," Poppaea Sabina said, setting off another round of titters.

Theodosia felt herself flush again, even hotter than before. She was beckoning for her sandals when the hostess reacted with indignation.

"Friends, I am offended by your rude treatment of my special guest, and especially your insinuation, Poppaea. Theodosia is a lady from one of our most distinguished families. She'd never squander herself on a slave."

Marcia turned to Theodosia and smiled.

"Here's a deal. I'll go out on a limb and double my husband's offer. Thirty thousand denarii for that fellow. An incredible sum by anyone's standards, Theodosia. Even yours. But if you don't sell him to us, Camillus will deny Otho his support, and Otho will lose the election."

Marcia paused for effect.

"Otho *will* lose the election," she repeated. "I guarantee it."

Theodosia stood and offered her hand to her hostess.

"Thirty thousand denarii for you," Marcia said again, "and a seat in the Senate for Otho."

Theodosia caught Stefan's eye and motioned to the door.

"Stefan," she said, "is not for sale."

Stefan said nothing as he helped Theodosia into the litter. He said nothing as he helped her out. Then he disappeared.

Theodosia told Lucilla to find him and send him to the garden.

She strolled to an ancient stone wall at the end of a torch-lit path. Hundreds of other torchlights twinkled in the city that nestled into the valley below and spread onto the surrounding hills.

She didn't hear Stefan approach, but when she turned, there he was —stiff and angry—some distance away.

She studied his face, hoping for forgiveness, but found none.

"I'm sorry for what happened tonight. I know you were humiliated."

"A slave can't never be humiliated. No more than a cow or a dog or a chicken."

"Damn it, don't talk like that! We've been friends for so long. Don't spoil it now."

"I ain't the one who spoiled it."

"Well, it wasn't my idea to call you in there."

"You allowed it."

I guess I did.

"Look, I've said I'm sorry, and I apologize, but I can't undo what was done tonight." She held out her hand to him. "Come on, be a friend again. Take a walk with me."

He did not take her hand, and he said nothing as he marched behind her... a soldier obeying an order from his superior officer.

"We'll go home in a few days," Theodosia said over her shoulder, after an awkward interval, "and things will be as they were."

Before he could respond, Theodosia heard shouts inside the house. She turned to see Otho stalking along the path, followed by Alexander.

The steward stopped a few paces away and let the Roman approach alone.

Otho strode up to Theodosia, jabbing his thumb in Stefan's direction.

"I knew I'd find you with *him*. You'd risk my election for a slave?"

"My slaves have nothing to do with your election."

"That one does! Thirty thousand denarii, by Jupiter!"

For a moment, Theodosia feared she would laugh. Otho's purpling face nearly matched the stripe on his toga. But the urge faded quickly before the violence in his voice.

"What will people say when they find out that the woman I intend to marry values her stable hand—or bodyguard, or whatever the hell he is— more than she values my political career?"

Otho swung around to Stefan.

126

"Get the fuck out of my sight! Go to the house and stay there!"

"Stay here, Stefan."

"How dare you countermand my order?"

"How dare you give him one?" Theodosia was almost as angry now as Otho. "Stefan obeys my orders, not yours."

"He'll obey mine when you and I are married, and if he wants to save his skin then, he'd better obey me right now."

"Don't you think you're taking a lot for granted?"

"Ho! You're too smart to turn me down."

"Maybe I'm too smart to accept you."

"Don't play games with me, Theodosia. Nobody's going to stop me from marrying you. Not baby-faced Titus, and certainly not this stable mutt you've taken as your pet."

"You forget. There's someone else who'll have a say in that."

"Who?"

"Me."

Otho's lips curled into a sardonic smile.

"Oh, you'll marry me. You want what I can give you."

Without waiting for an answer, he grabbed Theodosia's shoulders and kissed her hard. His teeth dug into her lips as she resisted his tongue and struggled to push him away.

Almost instantly, another pair of hands hooked under the tribune's arms and jerked him backwards.

Theodosia's hands flew to her bruised mouth.

Bless Stefan!

But it wasn't Stefan who had saved her. It was Alexander.

"By all the gods, Greek," Otho shouted, "you'll die for that!"

CHAPTER SIXTEEN

The next morning, Theodosia and her little retinue left the city.

"If I never set foot in Rome again," she said to Lucilla as their carriage headed out on the Via Aurelia, "it'll be just fine with me."

"But when you marry Tribune Otho—"

"I'm not marrying Tribune Otho."

Lucilla looked stricken.

"But, miss, he loves you so!"

"What he loves is my money. I'll hear no more talk of him from you."

That night, she went for her usual walk to the seaside clearing in the forest.

Home!

The word reverberated within her.

I'll never leave here again.

There had been no rain since mid July; the woods were noticeably drier than a week ago. After a time, as she made her way under the pines, she grew conscious of a steady crunching some distance behind. She walked faster. Then slower. Then she speeded up once more, ears keen for the footsteps that seemed to adapt to her pace.

Gracious gods, who's there?

When she reached the clearing, she stopped. The crunching stopped. Cursing her own stupidity, Theodosia listened, but the woods were as silent as death.

Are even the cicadas asleep?

"Who's there?"

Everyone warned me of the dangers of coming out all alone. Blessed Juno, why don't I ever listen?

"Show yourself!"

There was more silence, then the renewed crunch of footsteps. Theodosia froze in terror. She wanted to bolt from the clearing and race past the demon in the forest, but her feet would not move.

Just when she feared her heart might explode, a gigantic figure stepped out of the trees.

"Stefan!"

He said nothing. There was no hint of a smile on his face, and for the first time in her life, Theodosia feared him.

It was only last night... He was so angry...

But this was Stefan, her oldest friend.

He'll do me no harm.

"Gods, you scared me so!" She ran to him and wrapped her arms around his waist. "Oh, Stefan, why do I do dumb things like this?"

"Don't know, miss. You just do."

"You followed me. Why?"

"Because of all the dumb things you do."

Despite her lingering fear, Theodosia laughed.

"Is this the first time?"

"No, you just didn't hear me before. Wasn't so dry before."

"Why didn't you ever let me know?"

"You wanted to be alone, didn't you? Most of the time, anyway."

Theodosia pulled back and peered into his eyes.

"You followed me... even when Otho was with me?"

He nodded.

"Don't you trust a Roman to protect me from brigands?"

"Even a Roman can be overpowered."

Theodosia thought of Gaius and agreed.

"So... you saw what happened out here that night?"

That terrible night when I thought Otho was going to rape me.

"Are you angry, miss?"

"Of course! You had no right!" Quickly, she relented. "No, I'm not angry. Does anyone else know what happened that night?"

"Alexander."

"You told Alexander? Why?"

"Well, actually, I didn't tell him. Actually... we both followed you and Tribune Otho that night."

129

Her nocturnal walks continued throughout a fine, balmy September. At first, Stefan and Alexander would show up together, as if by coincidence. After a week, Alexander stopped coming, but Stefan never failed to join her at some point, and she knew he was there, even when she couldn't see him. He appeared to read her mind and moods. If she needed quiet, he hung back. If she wanted to talk, he drew closer. That angry night in Rome was well behind them now.

With the election approaching, Theodosia saw no more of Otho, for which she offered daily thanks to Juno.

Titus came out from Caere every morning, and they rode in the hills until noon, when Flavia joined them for lunch. Then the three would linger in the pergola, laughing and gossiping and sipping Falernian until late afternoon. Theodosia didn't love Titus, but he was fun and easy to be with. She felt comfortable with the idea of marrying him someday.

When he grows up.

It seemed a long time off.

One bright night towards the end of September, Theodosia saw her escort waiting for her behind the pergola, near the woods.

"Good evening, Stefan."

He bowed his head, as always, and followed her along the path. As they reached the clearing, Theodosia moved to the seaside rocks. Stefan stepped up behind her.

"I heard such laughter a while ago," she said without turning around. "Thought maybe you all were tearing the new building down."

"Did we disturb you?"

"No. It sounded like fun."

"If I didn't know better, I'd think you was jealous."

"Maybe a little." She bobbed her head. "There are times, you know, when I really wish I could join you out there."

"Ain't none of us gonna say you can't."

"I know, but... You know I can't." She snapped a few needles off the nearest pine tree and twisted them into a knot. "You must miss a lot of fun. Evenings are supposed to be your free time, but here you are watching out for me. This isn't a duty you have to perform, you know."

"I don't do it out of duty."

Theodosia started to step away but stopped when she felt a faint touch on her hair. Stefan was lifting the ends, rubbing them between his fingers. She stood still before turning around.

"Forgive me, miss," he said.

Theodosia waited another moment; then she took his right hand and brought it to the side of her head. Stefan seemed puzzled. Then his hand began to move, slowly sculpting her temple and tracing around her ear. His left hand rose and mirrored the actions of the right. Soon both were on her forehead, her eyebrows, her cheeks, her lips, her chin.

She could feel the thick calluses on Stefan's fingers. This was no Otho with manicured hands. These hands belonged to a coachman, a stable hand. Coarse, gigantic hands, but they were gentle... and clean.

They stood like that at the water's edge—his hands swallowing her face, their eyes locked—for a long time. The moon highlighted Stefan's hair and cast his eyes into shadows.

Do I want to let this happen? Whatever comes next depends on me. He'll never force himself on me. Just pull away, and that's the end of it.

But she didn't pull away.

Instead, she reached up and laid her own fingers on his face, caressing it. The lovely static moment couldn't last forever. One of them had to do something, yet she was unable to move.

Then Stefan bent and kissed her softly on the mouth. She stood passively, stunned by his kiss, even though she had wanted it for so long.

As if sensing her conflicting emotions, Stefan retreated a step.

"I got no right to do that," he said, apparently struck by the enormity of the crime he had just committed. By law, Theodosia could do anything she pleased to him or with him, but Stefan could be put to death if he so much as touched her the wrong way.

Theodosia dropped her eyes and bowed her head.

This is my last chance to stop it. He'll follow my lead.

She took a deep breath and looked up again.

"Don't be silly. You have every right."

She raised her hand once more and drew his head down for another kiss. Then she lifted one of his hands and pressed it to her breast.

Stefan pulled back a breath away from her face.

"You're sure?"

Her answer was to wrap both arms around his neck and lift her lips to his. After a kiss that promised never to end, she tugged him onto the fragrant carpet of lichens and decaying pine needles and pulled the bronze pins from the shoulders of his tunic.

<> <> <>

Four nights passed before Theodosia left the house again.

Titus came the next morning and was told that she had hurt her back and couldn't ride. Flavia tried to lure her to the pergola; they ended up eating lunch in the sitting room. Of the household staff, only Lucilla and the waiters were allowed to see her.

It wasn't that she didn't want to make love to Stefan again. She wanted him more than she had ever wanted anything before, but suddenly she was afraid for a host of new reasons.

Afraid of her own emotions...

Afraid of what her peers would say...

Afraid of losing her chance for a good marriage...

Afraid of what a sexual relationship between herself and Stefan would do to her household...

Masters routinely took their slaves—both male and female—to their beds. Legally, Theodosia had the same right to make a lover of her slave, but socially such things were frowned on. The Romans had lost many virtues over the years, but chastity was still the rule for an unmarried woman. A liaison between Theodosia and Stefan would fuel many a crude joke in her kitchen and the gods only knew where else. She couldn't bear the thought of becoming an imperial laughing stock.

Uncertain what to do, she did nothing.

Lucilla noticed her odd behavior and commented on it a bit too often. Theodosia shouted at her for the first time ever and ordered her out of the suite. Lucilla was sullen from then on and stayed downstairs late each night, which did not distress her mistress.

After dinner on the third evening, Theodosia unwittingly caught sight of Stefan. The night was warm for late September, so she poured a cup of wine and carried it to the chair on her balcony. Over the splash of the waves, she could hear her servants laughing in the kitchen.

After a while, feeling sorry for herself, she rose and stepped to the railing, cup in hand. As her eyes drifted over the garden, she spotted the unmistakable silhouette of Stefan propped against the pine tree near the cliff, his face turned toward her. She was about to go inside when she noticed another figure coming around the house. It was Alexander. He could not have seen Stefan from that angle, yet he turned down the right path. Clearly, he knew just where to look for him.

Alexander approached and gestured toward the kitchen. Stefan pointed to Theodosia's balcony. Alexander looked straight up at her.

For a few moments more, she stood at the railing, staring at the two men. Then she closed the shutters—walling herself off from them in the crimson, green, and gold suite—slumped into the cushioned chair, and downed what remained in the cup.

Finally, the woman who owned four thousand slaves blew out the lamps herself, drew back the covers on her bed, and tried to sleep.

"May I speak with you, miss, when you have finished?"

Alexander knew he was taking a chance intruding on Theodosia's dinner, four days after he had last been allowed a word with her. Earlier, he had sent a houseboy to request an audience, which was denied. That in itself would fuel gossip, and the household was already rife with rumors.

Theodosia motioned him away with a flick of her fingers.

"I'm tired. Wait till tomorrow."

"It's important. Please... in the library?"

"I said no." Her voice was remote. "You may go."

Alexander bowed and left. In the atrium he stopped and waited, expecting her to walk right past when she emerged from the dining room. When she did come out, she halted instead and eyed him with irritation.

"I'm sorry, miss, but... I've got to try once more."

"Is it really that important to you?"

"It really is. It concerns my closest friend... and yours."

Theodosia pivoted abruptly and beckoned him into the library.

"Did he send you to talk to me?"

"No. He'd be mortified if he knew I was here."

"So... why *are* you here?"

"Because he's suffering. Beating himself up with worry that he overstepped his bounds with you. He hasn't eaten or slept for days. He spends every night—all night—either out there where you saw him from your balcony or walking in the woods." Alexander came a few steps closer to her. "May I tell you a quick little story?"

After Theodosia nodded her consent, he walked over to the window. Staring out at the sea, he told her about that day the previous May when Stefan had showed him his keepsakes of the girl who had gone away to Rome and was now coming home.

"He adored you when you were children, miss. You were all he talked about when I first arrived here. He was sure he'd never see you again, and it almost killed him. When you returned, he didn't know how

133

to act with you. Since then, the little taste of equality and friendship that you've given us has only complicated the situation for him."

Alexander glanced around. Theodosia had dropped into a chair.

"Shall I go on?"

She nodded.

"He acted strangely that night, after he returned to the kitchen from being with you. He didn't say anything, but everybody noted his odd behavior. Then, very late—when the household was asleep—he came to my room, which he hardly ever does. Said he had to talk to someone."

"So... he told you what happened?"

Alexander hesitated, unsure how truthful he should be.

Theodosia, of course, read an answer in his delay.

"I should have known he couldn't keep quiet about that."

"Actually, no... he didn't say anything. But it wasn't hard to guess." He met her eyes then, amazed at the intimacy creeping into his voice. "Slaves can fall in love, you know. And when we do, the emotions and desires... they're all the same, whether a person is slave or free. You've seen how much Nicanor loves Etrusca. He's a slave—born, bred, and probably forever—but he would gladly give his life to save hers. These past few months, miss, I've watched Stefan's face whenever he looked at you or spoke to you. He's a different person when you're around. Perhaps, because of his size, we tend to think of Stefan as invulnerable, but he's a man like any other. Slave or free, we all fall in love."

"Slaves don't usually fall in love with Romans."

Alexander allowed himself a quick smile.

"I suspect that depends on the Roman."

He left the window to stand beside her.

"Please understand, miss... it's absolutely none of my business what happened out there that night. But rumors about you and Stefan started long ago. Now your servants see you acting oddly, and they see him acting oddly. They're jumping to some very dangerous conclusions, and that's a problem. We slaves do like to gossip about our betters. Stories about you two—true or not—are already out and about. There's no telling how far they have spread. Add to that the way you've been acting these last few days..."

"You're saying that I'm making the situation worse."

"It's not my place to tell you how to conduct yourself, but you should know what your behavior is doing to Stefan and what others are saying about it." He paused and knowingly stepped into perilous territory. "I hadn't thought you were the kind to play such games."

"You think I'm playing games with Stefan?"

"It's hard not to think that. We've all seen how you've kept Tribune Otho and young Titus dancing on your string for months. If you'd toy around like that with your peers, is it likely you'd take your slave's feelings any more seriously?"

Theodosia's head fell forward into her hands.

"What should I do?"

Alexander looked at the soft curls shining in the lamplight.

"Go out and talk to him," he said. "Don't ostracize him like this. Give him some peace of mind."

She raised her eyes with a look of longing that jolted his heart.

"Are you sure he's out there?"

"Quite sure, miss."

Theodosia found Stefan under the pine tree. She approached and stopped a dozen steps away. Her heart told her to go to him, but her head kept repeating the alarm it had been sending for days.

That one passionate hour in the forest could be excused as an indiscretion, but there will be no retreat if we cross the next boundary.

As she considered her options, Stefan rose to his feet. Theodosia waited for him to come forward, but he made no other move, and she understood his meaning... the next step was hers to take. The mistress must go to the slave, and she did.

"Can you forgive me? I have treated you so badly."

"Ain't nothing to forgive, miss. You got every right to treat me as you choose."

"Forget my rights. If I wanted to pull rank on you, I'd summon you to my desk." She nodded jerkily. "I really did come out to apologize."

"Nothing to apologize for. I promise that I— That what happened the other night won't happen again."

Theodosia pointed toward the sandy cove below.

"Stefan, when we were children, we used to go down there every day to play. Do you remember?"

"Of course."

"Then you remember what you called me in those days." She reached out and took his hands in hers. "Say it. Say my name."

He opened his mouth and closed it.

"Say it."

"Theodosia."

She rewarded him with a big smile.

"That's it. Not so hard to say. Will you call me that from now on… when we're alone?"

"Don't know if I can. I got that sort of familiarity knocked out of me long ago."

"My name used to come naturally to you. I bet you can get used to saying it again."

Stefan was staring into her eyes.

Theodosia raised her hands and laid them on both sides of his face, as she had that other night in the woods.

"My dear old friend. I love you very much. I love you in every way it's possible to love another person. I *want* you. Yes… *you!* I want to give myself to you, again and again, every day and night for the rest of our lives. I want so badly to take you to my bedroom and shout from the balcony that we are one, now and forevermore. Nothing would make me happier. But I can't take that step just yet. I'm not that brave. I'm sure we'll get there soon, but at this moment I'm too afraid and confused by our new situation."

She put a finger on his lips.

"Don't say anything to anybody about this, please. But know that I love you more than I've ever loved anyone else in the world… and wait a bit. Give me time to figure it all out."

"Ain't easy for a man like me to wait."

"But you can wait. You *must* wait. I'm asking you to wait."

Stefan's nod came slowly and reluctantly, as Theodosia pulled her hands from his face.

"Thank you, my love, for helping me get through this. We will find a way to resolve our situation, and once we've done that, I don't think either one of us will ever be sorry that we waited." She smiled once more. "Now… let's see if the porter can find you something to eat."

Alexander was finishing his dinner when old Jason, the porter, wheezed into the kitchen.

"Where's Milo?" he asked in a too-loud voice.

"What you need?" the cook answered from across the room.

"The mistress wants food and wine. Now."

"She already ate."

"Well, she ordered it," Jason said, his hands trembling. "Just now, when she came in. Said to send lots of food."

"She can't be hungry." Milo scratched his earlobe.

"Don't argue," Alexander said.

It's not the mistress who's hungry, you fool.

He scooped up his last mouthful of boiled lentils with a piece of bread but found them hard to swallow.

"I'll go see what's wrong," said Lucilla, rising to her feet.

"Sit down," Alexander said. "She didn't send for you."

Lucilla scowled at him, but she sat again.

Dabini and Selicio departed with a few leftovers from Theodosia's dinner and the best of their own. They returned half an hour later, as shaken as Jason.

"Is she ill?" asked Milo.

Dabini shook his head; then he dropped to the bench beside Lucilla and stared into her face. Selicio broke into a wide grin.

"We just served dinner to Stefan," he announced, "in the dining room! The mistress sat right beside him on the couch, watching him eat."

The kitchen hall erupted... an explosion of voices.

Lucilla swung her legs over the bench, her face blank. Marcipor put his hand on her arm, but she shook it off and ran out. He sprinted after her. A few moments later, Alexander did the same.

Marcipor had caught Lucilla near the rear door of the villa and was struggling to hold her as Alexander drew near.

"He's mine! She promised! She can't take him!"

"She can take anyone she pleases," Marcipor said. "And she'll hear you if you don't shut up."

"I don't care! She promised! She don't love him!"

"Love has nothing— to do with it," Marcipor said, chopping up his sentence as he tried to keep her still. "It never does— when there's a slave involved— with a Roman master."

Lucilla bent, trying to shake his grasp.

"What do you know about it?"

"More than I care to." Marcipor winced as she stomped on his foot, and he released her. "Consider yourself lucky if you don't."

Lucilla whirled around. Alexander blocked her path and seized her.

"You did this, didn't you?" she cried, her face livid. "Couldn't stand to see Stefan with me, so you made sure she'd take him."

"Oh, right! I couldn't stand to see my fellow slave make love to a slave girl, so I arranged for the mistress to fall in love with him."

137

"She don't love him! And she won't want him when she hears how often he's slept with me!" Lucilla sounded increasingly desperate. "This is the second time she's taken away a man I love."

"She's not taking him away from you. He was hers long before you laid eyes on either one of them."

"But he loves me!"

"He may lust for you at times, Lucilla, but it's Theodosia Varra that he loves."

Lucilla's face twisted with hatred.

"What do you know about love? Same thing Marcipor knows? How many times were you summoned to your master's bed?"

Alexander drew a deep breath, feeling an inexplicable sympathy for this unhappy woman.

"I know a lot about love. Not lust. Love. I know about losing love, too, and what it is to love someone I cannot have." He loosened his hold and slipped an arm around her shoulders—more gently than he would have thought possible—as he guided her toward the kitchen. "You cannot have Stefan, Lucilla. At least... not right now."

"When, then? Next month, when she's bored with him?"

"Maybe."

"I don't want to wait till then!"

Lucilla began to sob and buried her face in Alexander's shoulder.

"You'll wait," he said, "along with all the rest of us, to see what comes of this."

Theodosia sat in her cushioned chair until almost midnight, reading and waiting for Lucilla to come and attend her. When the maid finally arrived, red-eyed and rumpled, Theodosia wondered why she had bothered. Lucilla was surly and careless. After she had tangled and pulled Theodosia's hair repeatedly, her mistress seized the comb from her hand.

"What's the matter with you? Take it easy."

Lucilla sulked, her eyes on the floor. Theodosia stood and tilted her chin up with the comb. The eyes didn't follow.

"What *is* the matter with you?"

Theodosia waited a long time; then she smacked Lucilla's cheek with the broad side of the comb.

"Answer me, damn you!"

Lucilla's eyes slowly made their way to Theodosia's.

138

"You broke your promise, miss."

"What promise?"

"That I could have any man here I wanted."

"I never said you couldn't."

"You've taken Stefan from me."

"I've taken nobody from you." Theodosia laughed. "Oh, now I see. You get a little sweet on Stefan and think that gives you a claim to him."

"It's not just that! We—" Lucilla's voice faltered. "Stefan loves me. I know he does, but..." Her eyes filled with tears. "How can I compete with you, miss? I got nothing to give him."

"Neither do I, Lucilla. I have nothing to give him." Theodosia tossed the comb onto her chair. "Now... you must stop being ridiculous."

Alexander was dreading his next encounter with Theodosia Varra. He sat alone, ignoring his breakfast and the kitchen commotion around him, seeing only that glossy head bowed before him in the library last night, remembering the longing in those gold-flecked eyes.

She loves Stefan as much as he loves her.

He could not imagine why that thought hurt so much.

Later, Alexander saw Lucilla head for the barn, where Stefan was working. After half an hour, she came out, bound for the house. Soon she was in the kitchen once more, refusing to speak to anyone.

Noon arrived without sight of Theodosia. Titus came and went, but Flavia came and stayed. Alexander went out to greet her.

"My mistress has not come down yet."

"Her back's still bothering her?"

Alexander hated to keep lying to Flavia Domitilla, who struck him as remarkably decent for a Roman.

"She may be feeling better by now. If you'd like to relax in the pergola, my lady, I'll let her know you're here."

He settled Flavia into a chair, sent a houseboy to tell Theodosia, and returned to the pergola with wine. Flavia fingered the ruby-eating serpent on her cup—as she always did—and looked up.

"Theodosia's acting odd lately, don't you think? Titus wonders if she's angry at him for something."

"My mistress has been preoccupied." Alexander retreated a bit from the table, wishing he could avoid this conversation. "She doesn't confide in me, of course, but I'm sure it has nothing to do with my lord Titus."

Flavia's eyes refused to budge from his face.

"I suspect she confides in you a great deal more than you admit."

"I'm just her steward, my lady."

"Of course." Flavia took a few sips of wine. "We've been hearing rumors, Alexander. Nasty things our slaves pick up at market and giggle about when they think we're not listening. You probably know the rumors I'm talking about."

"Probably."

"I don't pay much attention to them, but they do upset Titus. He's hoping to marry Theodosia, you know."

"There are many here who also hope he marries her."

"His main rival is Tribune Otho, I believe." Flavia gazed at Alexander, her arched eyebrows inviting a response, but he did not cooperate. "I'm right, aren't I?"

"The tribune has spent a great deal of time here."

"Is he closer to Theodosia than my brother is?"

"I don't like to gossip, my lady, and in truth I know little about things like that."

Flavia smiled wickedly.

"You know lots more than you let on. So, tell me what Theodosia likes in a man."

"That would be unforgivably presumptuous of me."

"Most people think she'll marry Otho." The devilish eyes never left Alexander's face. "My guess is… you wouldn't like that at all. So, would you care to form a political alliance with me, to make sure such a terrible thing doesn't happen?"

"Political alliances can be dangerous, my lady."

"Oh, Alexander, you disappoint me. I had you pegged for a braver man. Well, if you're not interested, maybe I can enlist the help of that big fellow who works in the stables."

Theodosia joined them a short while later, her hair still damp from her bath and smelling tantalizingly of cloves.

She took the chair that Alexander pulled out for her but avoided his eyes. Even in the shade of the vines, she glowed. There was something about her that jeopardized Alexander's composure this morning, yet he couldn't take his eyes off her.

Beloved gods, she's beautiful!

"Oooooh, Theodosia, you look wonderful! Titus came this morning, but the houseboy said you weren't awake yet. He'll be back soon though. He's planning," Flavia confided, with a mischievous glance at Alexander, "to ask you to marry him." She leaned forward and put her hand on Theodosia's arm. "You will accept him, won't you?"

"I... I wasn't expecting that so soon."

Flavia squeezed the arm under her fingers.

"Oooooh, you must accept! We'll be sisters! I'll come for a visit every day, let Alexander serve me this wonderful wine in these gorgeous goblets, and—" she flashed a sparkling grin over her shoulder, "make him tell me all the household gossip."

Alexander started as Flavia winked at him.

"He won't dare refuse to answer then, will he?"

Titus returned early in the afternoon.

From the pergola, Alexander saw Stefan come around the house... saw Theodosia's eyes follow as Stefan led Titus' horse away. Her mouth had fallen open a bit; her expression was soft. It was the same enraptured gaze as when she had watched him on the barn roof that first morning in June. Alexander stared at her captivated face as long as he dared, then forced his eyes away.

A few moments later, Titus arrived, taking the stairs in three strides.

"Hello, lovely ladies!" He dropped into the chair beside Theodosia and took her hand. "I came to see if you were up for a ride today."

"Oh, not yet. My back still isn't fully recovered."

"Well, if you'd rather not go out..." Titus turned a sly smile on his sister. "Mind giving me some time alone with our friend?"

"Rats! I always miss out on the fun." But Flavia hopped up and kissed Theodosia on the cheek.

"You, too." Titus snapped his fingers at Alexander. "Leave us."

Alexander looked at Theodosia for confirmation of the order. She glanced at him and nodded, her eyes veiled and distant.

Titus was watching him, too, with the look of a future master all over his boyish face.

Alexander's presence made Theodosia uncomfortable this morning. Something in his eyes disturbed her. She felt them on her... a physical presence that she couldn't escape. It was a relief when Titus sent him to the house.

Titus reached out now and took Theodosia's other hand, his face full of energy and excitement.

"My orders have come in! I enter the Centuriate the last day of January. After six months of training, I'm off to Britain."

"That's what you've always wanted, isn't it?"

"Absolutely. There's only one thing left for my life to be perfect, and it must be obvious what that is. I know I'm young, and I'm about to leave for the army, but... I love you, and I want to marry you before I go. During Saturnalia, maybe? We'll give our households something really important to celebrate!"

Titus' fingers were slim and smooth... so different from Stefan's. His eyes were disturbing this morning, too, but in a different way from Alexander's.

"What do you say? Will you marry me?"

Theodosia stared into those earnest eyes.

"I'm not ready yet. I'm just beginning to feel at ease here. I don't want to leave so soon."

"But you won't have to leave. Since I'll be gone so much these next few years, you can stay at your villa as much as you want."

"Well... if you know you'll be away that long... why don't we wait till you're able to be home a lot more often?"

"I'll have lost you by then. Otho's not going to stand back to give me an even chance."

"Oh, Titus..." She gave a little sigh. "I'm just not ready to promise anything to anybody. I already told Otho the same thing."

"How long do you need?"

She thought for a moment.

"Until the end of the year. Give me till Saturnalia."

"And if you agree, we'll be married soon after?"

"If I agree."

Titus released one of her hands; then he stroked her cheek and playfully tapped the tip of her nose with a finger.

"You'll agree." And he pulled her to him for a kiss.

CHAPTER SEVENTEEN

Lucilla had changed. Sullen and snappish, she wore the same increasingly dirty tunic every day, let unkempt hair fall around her shoulders, and seldom took a bath. Alexander couldn't understand why Theodosia put up with her.

Stefan, on the other hand, had never looked better. He shaved off his beard, changed into a clean tunic every day, and managed to find a lot of time to be with Theodosia. They spent six or seven hours together each day, with Stefan riding one of her best horses all over the estate and giving orders to the other slaves... even when Theodosia was present. Quite a few eyebrows were raised when he assigned another man to do his chores in the barn, so it was no surprise that the household staff began making sour jokes about their "new master."

Alexander was almost certain the mistress and her coachman weren't sleeping together, because Stefan spent every night in the barn, but their curious new relationship left him feeling like an outsider. Lonesome and inexplicably annoyed, he turned his attention to Lycos, throwing himself into the boy's education. Since Theodosia was seldom in the library these days, Alexander and Lycos reclaimed it... without asking permission.

They were there one morning early in November, reading on the couch, when Theodosia and Stefan came in. Alexander rose and took the scroll from Lycos, who jumped up and scurried out. Theodosia stopped a few steps into the room, with Stefan looming behind her. It was the first time all three had been together in weeks.

"I apologize for the unauthorized intrusion, mistress," Alexander said. "Lycos and I weren't expecting you to come here today. We'll go somewhere else."

"What's he reading now?" Her interest sounded forced.

"The *Odyssey.*"

"You must be doing well as a tutor." She managed a thin smile. "I'm going to teach Stefan to read, too. Any idea how we should start?"

"I've never taught an adult, mistress. It would be presumptuous for me to give you advice."

Theodosia turned to Stefan.

"I'd like to speak with Alexander alone."

When Stefan had gone, she moved forward and laid her hand on Alexander's shoulder.

"It's been a month since you called me anything but 'mistress.' Have I done something you disapprove of?"

"Who am I to disapprove of anything you do?"

"You are, I thought, our friend. We don't have so many friends, Stefan and I, that we can afford to lose any."

Alexander retreated from her lovely eyes... far enough to free his shoulder from her fingers.

"I told you once—mistress... I don't believe in friendship between a Roman and a slave. The power equation is too lopsided. The social barriers are too great."

"But we *were* friends for a while. Where were those barriers then?"

"Just because we managed to forget about them for a time, it doesn't mean they weren't there."

She peered into his face, then shrugged her shoulders.

"Fine. Perform your duties as my steward, and I'll not burden you with further attempts at friendship."

Stefan appeared at Alexander's door that same day, while Flavia was lunching with Theodosia.

"I got to talk to you."

Alexander made a half-hearted gesture of welcome. Stefan dropped to the floor and leaned against the wall.

"Why are you so angry?" Stefan asked after a moment.

"Who says I'm angry?"

"You don't talk to nobody. You avoid me, and Theodosia, too."

"You call her 'Theodosia' now?"

"To her face, yes. That's what she wants."

"So, then... why assume I'm angry? Maybe I'm perplexed. Maybe I'm jealous. Maybe I'm worried about what's going to happen when your great friendship dries up. Maybe I just don't know how to handle the situation. Maybe... lots of things."

"Because you act angry."

"Well, angry is one thing I'm not. But I am worried. Have you and the—your Theodosia—have you talked at all about the future? About Titus? About Otho? About Stefan? With so much gossip swirling around you two, what do you think is going to happen to you when she marries?"

Stefan had sat silently, tracing circles with a finger in the dust on the cement floor as Alexander spoke. At last, he raised his eyes.

"She ain't gonna marry."

Alexander snorted.

"That sounds like wishful thinking on your part and, if it's true, it's not smart on her part."

"Why? She's happy now. She don't need a husband to feed her or give her a home. She don't need nothing she ain't already got."

"Oh, of course not. She's got me to manage her estate and you to have sex with... just as soon as she works up the courage. What a cozy trio we'll make for the rest of our lives!" Alexander leaned forward. "Stefan, what happens when she decides she wants an heir? When the Romans begin to ostracize her? When she gets bored with you or finds out how many times you've slept with her maid? I don't know how much longer you're going to be able to keep that from her."

"Lucilla won't say nothing."

"Don't count on it. The mistress already knows Lucilla's wild about you. You better pray Jupiter she never finds out there's been more than amorous eyes between you two... or you'll be saying 'Yes, master' to Tribune Otho before you can saddle your fine new horse."

"We must be married right away. Otherwise, I can have nothing more to do with you."

Senator Marcus Salvius Otho stood with his legs apart, hands on his hips in the heart of Theodosia's garden, where the old Etruscan-urn fountain splashed noisy camouflage for a private conversation.

Stefan was busy in the barn this afternoon. Alexander had started a crew shoring up the sea wall below the pergola, in preparation for winter, and was down there with them right now.

Otho had been at the villa since yesterday morning, but Theodosia's discussions with him had focused on his recent successful election. So far, she had managed to avoid talk of marriage. He was leaving within the hour; further evasion seemed impossible.

"That's no way to propose marriage."

"I've already proposed properly, and brought you gifts, and treated you like an empress. Now I want your decision." He rocked back and forth on the balls of his feet. "I'm an important man, Theodosia, offering you an important marriage. Ride to Rome with me today. We'll have the ceremony at Nero's banquet this evening—with all the court as our witnesses—and put a stop to those vile rumors about you."

"You pay attention to rumors?"

"Rumors about you have a peculiar way of turning out to be true. Are you sleeping with that stable hand?"

"I don't have to answer that!"

"Are you sleeping with him?" Otho's voice rose as he grabbed her upper arms and pulled her toward him.

"No."

His fingernails dug into her skin.

"You expect me to believe that?"

"Yes, because it's true. It *is* the truth! But even if I were sleeping with Stefan, why should I be ashamed of it? Are you ashamed of the hours you've spent in bed with Marcipor or any of your other slave pets?"

"What has that scum told you?"

"Enough to know what you and Gaius used to do with him and Lycos and others." She wrenched her arms away from the livid, bug-eyed senator. "You truly are disgusting, Otho. The lowest, most menial slave in my kitchen has more natural nobility than you."

Rage washed across Otho's face. Theodosia turned to run to the house, but his hand was quicker. He seized her wrist, jerked her toward him, shook her violently, and slapped her with all his strength.

"Stefan!" she cried as Otho's hand descended again and again, but the cry died in a surge of pain.

"Whore!" He fired a hot stream of spittle into her face and shoved her backwards over the rim of the fountain, into the cold water. "Slave-fucking whore! Now I know why you wouldn't sell the bastard to Camillus."

Theodosia wiped her face with her sleeve. It came away red.

Otho bent, grabbed her once more by both wrists, and yanked her out of the water.

"Gods, what pups the great Aulus Terentius Varro spawned! A lying blackmailer and a slave-fucking whore. Gaius told me—" He interrupted himself with a rude laugh. "By all the gods on Mount Olympus! Gaius was telling the truth, for once. Nizzo said he was. You're no Roman lady, just a filthy Greek whore like your mother. Damn Gaius, he was right about you all along. Gods! To think how close I came to marrying you!"

Theodosia was struggling to escape his grasp, but Otho looped the fingers of his left hand into her hair, wrenching her neck as he pressed her against him, and delivered another of those horrid, invasive kisses.

With his right hand, he mashed her breasts for what seemed eternity; then he lifted her palla and under-tunic and rammed his long fingers— with their square, cutting nails—into the most private part of her body.

When he was done, he released her hair, made a fist, and punched her backwards. Theodosia crashed against the cement-filled urn in the fountain and crumpled up as the water spilled over her.

Through her pain and humiliation, she heard him stride away, shout for his horses and his slaves, and ride off.

Alexander heard shouts and climbed the embankment under the pergola in time to see Otho and his retinue gallop away.

In the next moment, his ears detected a different, softer sound. He followed it to the garden and found Theodosia Varra doubled over in the fountain, vomiting. Her hair and clothing were soaked, and he knew from personal experience what had caused the bloody cuts on her face.

I will kill Otho.

"Stefan!"

Alexander lifted Theodosia out of the water.

"I'm so cold."

He eased her to the pavement, threw his cloak around her, and held her close, trying to warm her. They were still there when Stefan ran up. Theodosia was too shaky to walk, so Stefan carried her to her bedroom.

Alexander sent Lucilla to tend their mistress.

The only thing he knew for a week was that Theodosia was not well. She saw none of the servants but Lucilla and refused to come downstairs or receive any visitors except Flavia. She took all her meals alone in her room, served only by Lucilla.

Stefan's beard was beginning to grow back. Lucilla bathed again and fixed her hair and gave every other sign of being content once more.

The fifth morning after Otho's departure, Etrusca was summoned for an unprecedented private visit with Theodosia. When she returned to the kitchen, the others—especially Lucilla—tried to get her to talk. Etrusca steadfastly refused. The substance of her conversation with the mistress remained a mystery.

Likewise, no one knew what had happened in the garden between Theodosia Varra and Senator Marcus Salvius Otho, but the kitchen theories grew more elaborate with each day of her second self-imposed isolation.

◇ ◇ ◇

It was late on the eighth night after Otho's departure; the household had been quiet for hours. Alexander was lying on his bed, reading the *Milesian Tales* of Aristides—borrowed from Theodosia's library—when he heard a pair of timid taps on the door of the storage cubicle adjoining his. In the next moment, the taps came on his door. He rose and opened it.

Theodosia Varra stood alone in the dark, her face wan in the light from Alexander's lamp, her hair disheveled, her soft sleeping tunic wrinkled.

"I'm sorry to bother you. I know it's late, but I couldn't sleep. May I please come in?"

Alexander smiled, genuinely amused. At times, she was imperious; other times, she acted as if the villa belonged to someone else.

"There's nowhere to sit, miss."

Her eyes explored the little room, and she shivered.

"You don't get heat back here?"

"That's why I wear this wonderful wool." It was a feeble joke, and he knew it. Slaves' clothing was notoriously coarse and scratchy. "Look, you didn't come here at this hour to check on my comfort."

"No."

Theodosia dropped to the thin mattress and let the words tumble out.

"I'm going to have a baby. I never realized that could happen after just one time. We only did it once! I've been thinking there was something wrong with me, but it wasn't until I talked to Etrusca that I knew for sure what was happening. I must've come close to losing it that day in the fountain." She let out a long sigh and looked at him. "Please, Alexander, this isn't easy for me. Don't lecture me about social barriers or lopsided equations. I've come to you as a friend. I trust you, and I need your help."

Alexander closed the door.

Theodosia Varra… pregnant with a slave's baby?

The ramifications of it stunned him. He stared at her, wondering what her fellow patricians would do to her when they found out. Then, shedding his usual reserve, he sat beside her and took her hand.

"Have you told Stefan?"

"No. And you mustn't tell him either. I'll decide what to do without pressure from him."

Of course, it wouldn't occur to you that a slave might have a right to knowledge of his own child.

It was easy, sometimes, to forget how very Roman she was.

"So... nobody knows except Etrusca and me?"

"And Flavia. I told her today."

Alexander let out a low whistle.

"Why?"

"I couldn't deceive her. She's such a true friend. Can you believe it? They heard rumors that I was sleeping with Stefan and decided to ignore them. She says Titus still wants to marry me, and their father approves."

They're just as greedy for your money as everyone else.

"Is that what you plan to do?"

"I might have, but... How can I marry Titus with someone else's baby—a slave's baby!—growing inside me?"

"What did the lady Flavia say about that?"

"Said she's heard of women who can get rid of it."

"That's a good way to die."

"Find someone to do it. Ride to Rome tomorrow and ask around."

"I won't do that, miss."

Theodosia pulled her hand away.

"I say you will!"

"You said you came to me as a friend. If so, you've no right to order me to do something that will risk your life. That's not something friends do to one another."

"It's my life. I'll risk it if I choose."

"It's not just your life. Think about Stefan and Lycos and Lucilla and Marcipor and Nicanor and Etrusca and the hundred-odd rest of us out here. What happens to us if you die in some grimy cellar in the Subura?"

"What do *you* suggest I do?"

Alexander took a few moments to think.

"Go away before your condition begins to show. Go to Greece. Tell everyone you're looking for your mother's people, to help them out now that you've got money. After the baby's born, bring it home and let Etrusca raise it."

"As a slave?"

"You can always set him free—or her—in a few years. And once you're back, you can marry my lord Titus if you want to without giving him a slave's baby for an heir."

"You make it sound easy, but— I'll think about it."

She stood and stepped to the door; then she turned around, sat again, and raised her hands to her face. Alexander had followed her up; now he followed her down.

"Alexander... Oh, this is so hard!" She took a deep breath. "Do you know anything about my mother?"

The question startled him even more than the news of her pregnancy.

"Why do you ask?"

"You do know something, don't you?"

"I don't know what you mean."

"It's true then!"

"You're not making any sense, miss."

Her control broke at that. Face contorted, she struggled to speak through long, shuddering sobs.

"Otho called m-my m-mother a whore. 'Filthy Greek whore.' He said Gaius... and Nizzo... both said it was true."

Impulsively, Alexander wrapped his arm around her shoulders, trying not to enjoy her warmth too much.

"My father wouldn't have m-married a... m-married a whore!"

"Of course not."

"He told me once how he m-met her." Theodosia smiled through her tears. "He was governor of Corinth, and his wife had died, and one day when he was riding with his m-men he saw her in the—" She hiccoughed and paused to get control of herself. "My mother was working in a field. He had his men call—" another hiccough, "her over to meet him, and he fell in— love with her right there. She was very poor, but— never in his life had he seen such— a beautiful woman."

"That's a lovely story, miss."

Her sobs were subsiding, but the hiccoughs continued.

"He was leaving Greece soon, and he— talked with her family and persuaded them to let her— go to Rome with him. He'd never have brought a whore home to— be the mother of his son, would he? Or— given his daughter the same name?"

"Of course not, and you shouldn't pay attention to malicious gossip. You know Senator Otho will say anything to hurt you for refusing to marry him."

Theodosia sniffed and nodded. After a few moments, she bent and wiped her eyes on her tunic.

"I'm sorry to be— such a nuisance. You must be tired."

"My time is yours." He laughed a bit at the unintentional irony. "Literally! Now... you should go back to bed, miss." He stood and lifted the sputtering lamp. "I'll see you to the stairs."

"No. I made it— here by myself. I can make it back— by myself."

Theodosia rose and opened the door; then she turned and kissed him on the cheek.

"See you in the— morning."

Theodosia lay awake for several hours, wrestling with her dilemma.

Alexander's right. I'll go to Greece, have the baby, and marry Titus when I come home.

Too restless to lie still any longer, she got up in the dark, fished blindly in a bedroom chest, and pulled out a cotton tunic too light for November. But that didn't matter; the library would be just as warm as her suite. She slipped the tunic on.

Not wanting to awaken Lucilla from her sleep in the small second bedroom, Theodosia held her sandals in one hand and tiptoed into the hall and down the stairs. Padding barefoot across the atrium, she reached the library curtain and stepped inside. Then she stopped and gasped in shock.

Alexander was standing beside the great chest, holding two boxes in his hands, with virtually the entire contents stacked around his feet.

"What on earth are you doing?" She pulled her sandals on.

"I'm not stealing anything."

"That sure is what it looks like!"

Alexander drew in his breath and held it a suspiciously long time.

"Last spring, I told you there were some old documents stored here. I've been looking for one of them."

"Why?"

Alexander made no reply.

"I asked you why. Please answer me."

"To destroy it." His words were almost inaudible.

"Destroy it?"

"Do you trust me enough to let me destroy something that could harm you?"

"Without seeing it myself?"

"A few hours ago you said you trusted me."

"Those documents are mine. You've no right to destroy any of them. Find the one you were looking for and give it to me."

"I'd rather not."

She sighed.

"It's an order, Alexander."

He sighed, too.

"May take a while."

Theodosia stepped around the boxes and sat down beside the chest.

Alexander sighed again. Then he reached to the bottom of the chest and searched through a collection of wax-stamped parchment rolls, looking at each of them. Finally, he turned to her, holding one in his hand.

"I should have destroyed this before you came home last spring," he said as—with obvious reluctance—he handed it to her. "That would have been the right time, and I did give it some thought. I'm truly sorry that I didn't burn it then, before you or anyone else had a chance to see it."

Theodosia unrolled the scroll. It was written in Greek and dated March of the year of the consuls Helvius and Palladius. She made a quick calculation.

Almost twenty-one years ago.

There were two wax seals at the top of the page.

The first imprint bore the design of a ship... the seal of a merchant.

The second had been made by the ring now lying on Theodosia's bedside table. She ran a finger around that familiar design pressed into the hard wax before forcing her eyes to the faded writing below it.

It was the bill of sale of a Greek slave girl named Theodosia, age eighteen, to Aulus Terentius Varro.

CHAPTER EIGHTEEN

Alexander's eyes never left Theodosia's face.

She dropped the parchment into her lap and stared at it for so long that her steward wondered if she was having trouble reading the Greek.

After a terrible silence, she turned those gold-flecked pupils to him.

"My mother was a slave. Otho knows it, and Nizzo, too."

"No, miss. No one knows it except you and me."

"But Otho said—"

"He said your mother was..." The word wouldn't come.

"A whore. He said my mother was a filthy Greek whore."

"He didn't say she was a slave."

"Isn't that the same thing?"

"No! There are plenty of slaves who aren't whores, and not all whores are slaves, as you well know."

"Seems a pretty petty distinction. So... my father bought my mother and brought her here against her will. And that sweet story he told me— Oh, Alexander, my whole life has been built on that lovely lie. It's all a sham!"

"Stop it, miss. You are still your father's daughter, and maybe your mother didn't come here against her will. Maybe she was happy to be with him. Aren't you the one who's always telling me that friendship— and even love—are possible between a Roman and a slave?"

"But if she was a slave... A child follows its mother's condition."

She's right, of course. And old Varro left no certificate of manumission for his daughter in his strongbox.

"I always knew I was half Greek," Theodosia went on, "but I preferred to think of myself as a Roman. To be a Roman is to have some prestige, some rights, some control over your life. To be a Greek is..."

153

"To be a Greek is to be a slave."

"Nowadays, yes. In Rome, at least."

"Well, your father didn't raise you as a slave. Ask anyone who was around here when he was alive. Aulus Terentius Varro loved you, educated you, relished the time he spent with you, presented you to the world as his daughter. Slaves aren't given family names. Even your brother wasn't aware of your mother's status. Much as he resented you, he'd have exposed you years ago if he had known."

Theodosia's head sagged forward, and she laughed.

"Blessed gods, this explains so much! Why I'm not named Terentia. Why Vespasian never met my mother. Why Father never arranged a marriage for me, never even gave me a dowry. Why he never made me behave like a proper Roman girl. He let me read anything I wanted, run a little wild, play with the slaves, eat with them... Do you really think he'd have taught a free-born daughter to ride a horse?"

"Maybe. Maybe he just liked a spirited daughter."

"You're certain Gaius never saw this document?"

"Certain."

"When did you first see it?"

"Soon after I came here, when I began cataloguing your brother's inheritance. I found that parchment buried on the very bottom of the chest. Deliberately buried, it seemed to me, so that's where I left it."

"And you said nothing about it to anyone?"

"Nothing."

"I find that hard to believe." Theodosia picked a loose thread off her saffron-colored tunic and balled it with her fingers. "A conscientious steward would have shown this document to his master. Or to the Praetorians after the master was murdered. Or to the lawyers when it became clear that a bastard slave was about to inherit the family fortune."

"Not after hearing Stefan talk for eight years about that beautiful little bastard."

"You protected me all those years?" Disbelief rippled through her voice. "A girl you'd never even seen?"

"You're here, aren't you?"

"I guess I have to believe you... and thank you." She stood and moved to the window, re-rolling the parchment. Dawn was beginning to creep up on the horizon. "But... how do we handle a secret that you can use to destroy me whenever it suits you?"

Alexander took the scroll from her hands, walked to the lamp, and held the parchment above the flame until it flared. Then he held it upright and let it burn toward his fingers before throwing the fiery remnant into the bronze brazier. Soon nothing remained of the bill of sale but a puddle of waxy ashes and the acrid smell of burning animal skin.

"Now it'll be your word against mine, and you know who always wins in a dispute between a Roman and a Greek."

"Oh, I didn't mean to offend you! If you wanted to use that against me, you'd have done so last spring when I was treating you so badly. Please forgive me... for everything!"

"You're entirely forgiven... for everything. I only wish I'd managed to find that thing and burn it before you came down."

"So do I. But destroying the document now doesn't change the fact. I'll always know about it, and so will you."

Alexander let his face contort in mock bewilderment.

"Know about what?"

Theodosia threw him a grateful smile and headed for the door.

"I've got to get out of here and just be alone."

Before Alexander could reply, she dashed through the atrium and the peristyle, out the back door, and into the early-morning fog. He pursued her, caught up with her near the barn, and took her arm.

"What're you doing?" he whispered, not wanting to create a stir. His breath froze in the air as he spoke.

"Taking my horse out."

"It's too cold."

"I won't be long."

"You're not dressed for it."

"I'll be fine."

"It's too dark."

"Let me go!"

Alexander was about to protest again when the barn door creaked and opened. Everything else faded as he saw Lucilla slip out wearing a sleeping tunic. Her loose hair billowed as she pushed the door to and swung around toward the house.

The instant she saw Theodosia, Lucilla stiffened like a cornered rabbit. Her eyes widened. Her mouth opened, but no sound came out.

Theodosia stared at Lucilla without speaking.

Alexander's pounding heart threatened to pulverize his ribs.

Damn you, Stefan. Nothing worse could have happened right now.

Theodosia pounced on her maid.

"Slut!" In the quiet air, the word echoed off the walls of the barn and the nearby barracks. "You're supposed to be upstairs in my suite!"

Gods... there's no need for everyone to know about this.

"How long have you been sleeping with Stefan?"

Lucilla's eyes bulged. She gaped wordlessly at her mistress.

Theodosia grabbed her wrist and shook it hard.

"By Juno, Lucilla, you will answer me!"

"Well, you made love to him!" Lucilla cried after a long moment. "Why is it all right for you and not for me?"

"Because Stefan belongs to me. I can do whatever I damn well please with him. With you, too, in case you've forgotten."

"But you said I could have him!"

"Alexander, open the barn door."

Alexander obeyed, glad to hear authority return to her voice, even though it meant trouble for his friend.

Oh, Stefan, I warned you so many times!

"Call Stefan out here."

Again Alexander did as she commanded. Soon a sleepy, disheveled Stefan climbed down from the loft and crossed to the door, where he, too, froze. Theodosia's eyes hardened as they made their slow way around the three slaves standing before her. Alexander thought they lingered even longer on him than on Stefan and Lucilla.

She thinks I tried to stop her from finding out about them.

"I'll deal with you all later."

Theodosia shouldered past Lucilla and marched into the barn.

Lucilla bolted toward the house.

The commotion had brought a score of men out of the barracks. Alexander saw their shapes approaching in the mist. He exchanged glances with Stefan as they followed Theodosia to Lamia's stall.

"What're you doing?" Stefan's voice sounded groggy.

Ignoring him, Theodosia lifted the filly's reins off a hook and opened the stall door.

"Let me help you, Theodosia."

Stefan grasped the reins she held. She yanked them out of his hand.

"Don't you ever call me that again!"

He stopped short and exhaled sharply. Theodosia began slipping the harness over Lamia's head, but it snagged on the ears. When Stefan tried again to help, she struck his arm with the leather straps.

"This is my horse. I'll handle her."

With a tug, she slipped the harness into place and pulled the filly forward. A bucket, a length of rope, and a pair of riding whips hung on a nearby post. Theodosia reached for the bucket, turned it over, and boosted herself up. Never had Alexander seen her mount without assistance.

"I'll ride with you, miss," Stefan said.

"You will *not!*"

Alexander stood apart from them, unable to believe what he was seeing. Stefan took the reins from Theodosia's hands again, held the filly securely, and shook his head. "Too dangerous" was all Alexander caught of his words.

Theodosia leaned to the post, snatched one of the whips from its hook, and brought it down hard, almost a dozen times, on Stefan's neck and shoulders.

Stefan grimaced in pain and surprise, dropped the reins, and stepped back, a stunned look on his face.

Theodosia gathered the reins once more and prodded the filly to the door, where a cluster of men stood awestruck.

"I'm telling you— No, I'm ordering you—" She slashed the whip against the door frame. "Don't follow me, any of you!"

Kicking the filly, she sped off toward the north.

Alexander and Stefan stood in the doorway with the other men, watching as Lamia and her rider vanished into the foggy coastal woods.

Alexander had not slept at all the night before, so after he replaced the contents of the strongbox and locked it again, he returned to his room and stretched out on the bed. But now he couldn't sleep.

A couple of hours later, he got up and went to the kitchen. Stefan and Lucilla sat in a corner, whispering. Alexander left them alone.

It was a long morning.

Flavia and Titus arrived around noon, as usual. Alexander met them in the driveway.

"My mistress has gone for a ride. I don't know when she'll be back."

"Is Senator Otho with her?" Titus sounded annoyed.

"No, sir."

"Then she's with that stable hand?" Equal annoyance.

"No, sir." Alexander hesitated. "She went alone."

Titus helped his sister out of the carriage, then confronted Alexander.

"Alone? You let her go riding all by herself?"

"I couldn't stop her, sir. She was very angry. She beat Stefan when he tried to restrain her."

"Why was she so angry?"

I can't tell him the truth.

"I don't know, sir."

Flavia came around and took Titus' arm.

"When did this happen, Alexander?"

"Just before dawn."

"Then she's been gone for hours."

"Damn you, man!" Titus shouted. "Why didn't you follow her?"

"She specifically ordered us not to, sir."

"Of course, you wouldn't follow her if she ordered you not to." Flavia's voice was gentler than her brother's. "But when she didn't come home... Do you have any idea where she was headed?"

"No, my lady. She rode north along the coast, but she could have turned inland at any point."

"Terrain's pretty rough up there, isn't it?" Flavia tugged on Titus' sleeve. "I think you should go look for her."

"If this fool hadn't let her ride out alone..."

"Perhaps she'll be back soon, sir."

I pray to every blessed god of Greece!

"She has to know you'll visit her today." Alexander gestured toward the house. "Come, sir. Will you let us serve you lunch and see if she's here by the time you're done?"

Titus looked at his sister, and she nodded.

"Fine, but if she's not back in an hour, we're going after her."

Theodosia was not back in an hour, so Alexander assembled a crew of men. Stefan appeared as they were about to leave for the search. The welts on his neck and shoulders were red and blistered now.

"I'd like to go, too, sir."

Titus gave him a lingering look, obviously noting the whip marks.

"Another pair of eyes can't hurt."

Titus led the way on horseback; the slaves were all on foot. The group moved into the woods and split up randomly at the first stream.

The afternoon passed too quickly. Shadows lengthened. Nighthawks appeared in the pink-orange dusk. The wind was picking up as Alexander met Titus and the others at the spot where they had separated.

Nobody had found Theodosia.

"Maybe she's home by now," Titus said to Alexander. "We can't do any more tonight, anyway. Get her men to the villa. Send word if she shows up. If I don't hear from you, I'll bring help tomorrow morning."

Theodosia's slaves kept a vigil in the kitchen throughout the night. The disastrous ramifications of her disappearance were lost on no one.

Lucilla had been crying in the corner since morning. Stefan had tried to get her to go to her room in Theodosia's suite, but she refused. Finally, after dinner, Etrusca took her to the women's side of the barracks, found her a mattress, and returned to sit silently beside Nicanor, her hand in his.

Around midnight, Alexander went to his cubicle and managed to get a few hours of sleep. Shortly before dawn, he rose and walked to the edge of the forest, where Theodosia and Lamia had disappeared about this hour yesterday morning. Leaning against a tree, he stared at the stars... ears primed for the cries of the forest hunters and the pitiful squawks of their prey. There were bears and wolves and wildcats out there, and runaway slaves, and temperatures far too low for a cotton tunic.

What a turn of events.

Yesterday's pre-dawn encounter with Theodosia in the library seemed a decade ago; the strange conference in his cubicle the night before that was like a memory from another lifetime. She had kissed his cheek then; now she might be dead.

I'd give my life to back up and do these last two days over.

Yesterday morning's fog had not returned. The moon, Theodosia's favorite point of divine reference, still hung low in the sky.

Maybe Juno's keeping watch over her.

But Alexander had little faith in such things. His own life had proved that the gods were indifferent—if not openly hostile—to human suffering.

Stefan joined him a while later.

"I know what you're thinking. This is all my fault. And you're right, of course." It was the first time they had spoken since Theodosia's departure. Even in the early light, Alexander could see the blistered stripes on his neck. "What happens if we don't find her alive?"

Alexander chuckled without humor.

"I'm sure I'll enjoy slaving for the emperor. You'll be a big hit in the arena. I'll make it a point to go and watch." He paused. "Why did you go back to Lucilla? Couldn't you have honored Theodosia's need for time?"

"Our situation wasn't gonna change. She was playing with me. Nothing more could come of our relationship, and... I needed a woman."

"Lots of men need a woman. I haven't had one in nine years, but I don't use that as an excuse to mess around with the mistress' maid."

"Well, that's your choice. Who says you gotta be loyal to a wife you ain't never gonna see again?"

Alexander resisted the urge to punch him.

"I guess that's not something you'll ever understand."

Vespasian, Titus, and their Egyptian physician, Timon, arrived on horseback an hour later, with a cartload of slaves rumbling up the driveway behind them. There would now be over a hundred searchers.

Alexander marveled at the efficiency with which the veteran general organized the search. Vespasian, Titus, and Alexander—each with a military horn to summon help—would lead the way on horseback in different directions, with three teams of men accompanying them on foot.

Before they set out, Vespasian turned on his horse and faced the crowd of slaves.

"Twenty gold pieces to the man who finds her!" It was a generous offer... more than enough for the average slave to buy his freedom.

For half an hour, Alexander led his men into the forest to the east before coming to a stop in a sunny clearing beside a quick-flowing stream. They had picnicked here once—he and Stefan and Theodosia Varra—in the easy, growing camaraderie of last summer.

In his mind, he saw Theodosia smiling in this same patch of sunlight, the shine of her hair matching the flashes of water as it bubbled over the pastel rocks. He recalled the warmth of that day, the pink and yellow wildflowers, the lilt of her laughter. Now the trees were bare, their leaves brown and crisp on the ground... already smelling of rot.

Alexander pursed his lips. Theodosia knew her land well enough to find her way home. Whatever her problems, she'd never flee the place she loved most. That certainty only deepened his anxiety.

She's hurt, or she'd have come home by now.

He directed the men in his team to fan out into the woods. Nudging his horse around a log that jutted out of the water, he followed the stream to where the Tolfa Mountains began their rolling rise. The crisscross of animal tracks on the muddy banks made him shiver. He could only hope that Theodosia had survived the cold night and the wolves.

<> <> <>

Some time later, Alexander heard a faint shout behind him, deep in the forest to the northeast.

He wheeled his horse around and plunged into the thicket, following the cries that grew louder as he approached a high bluff overlooking the Mignone River. Rocks crumbled as the horse moved along the precipice. Alexander backed the animal away, then dismounted and peered into the riverbed. At the bottom—amid a pile of loose boulders and smaller rocks—Nicanor stood waving his arms. Beside him lay the crumpled filly. A bit of saffron-colored cotton fluttered in the breeze.

Nicanor had found her.

Alexander tied his horse to a tree. Gripping roots that jutted into the slope, he climbed down the bluff. Rocks gave way at every step, tumbling to the ground below. He could see where others had given way before, plunging the filly and her rider into the riverbed. It had been a long fall. From the position of Lamia's body, it was plain her neck was broken.

"Good job, man." Alexander gave Nicanor a clap on the shoulder. "You've earned that reward."

He dropped to his knees, with the stench of dead horse in his nostrils.

Theodosia lay face down in the mud and rocks, pinned from the middle of her back to her ankles by the weight of the filly. Her neck had twisted sharply to the right. Her right hand was draped over a jagged rock near her head; a track in the mud showed she had pulled it away from her cheek. The other arm disappeared beneath her chest. Her mouth was slightly open, her eyes shut. Alexander placed his hand to her face for a moment and sighed his relief. She was still breathing.

"We lift the horse?" Nicanor asked.

Alexander shook his head. There was no way the two of them could move the animal without dragging it across Theodosia's body, which would worsen whatever injuries she had already suffered.

Better let one of the Romans give that order.

"Climb up to my horse and blow on that horn with all your might. Don't stop till Vespasian or his son gets here."

Soon the horn was blaring through the woods.

Alexander eased his fingers under Theodosia's head and cleared away the smaller rocks from her bruised face and neck. Then he tore a strip from his tunic and wiped the caked mud from her eyes, mouth, and nose, watching for some sign of movement. There was none, but still... she was faintly breathing.

He moved the rock she held and wrapped his hand around hers.

"Come back, Theodosia," he said, stroking her matted hair. Never before had he called her by her name. Now he repeated it over and over.

It seemed forever before Nicanor let up on the horn.

Alexander raised his eyes when the sound stopped. Vespasian, Titus, and Timon were just reaching the spot where Nicanor waited; they made their way down the embankment together. Stefan and a dozen other slaves were already in the riverbed, heading Alexander's way.

He released Theodosia's hand and rose to his feet.

"We were afraid to move the horse, sir," he said as Vespasian ran up. "Our mistress is still alive."

"Praise the gods! Timon, see what you think."

The physician knelt beside Theodosia, raised her right eyelid, checked her breath, and felt the bones of her neck. Then he ran his arm as far as he could reach underneath the horse's belly. His hand, when he brought it out, was streaked with blood.

"One leg broken below knee, master." Timon's Latin was poor and so heavily accented that even Alexander—who knew his own accent branded him a foreigner—found it annoying. "I not know all hurts. Lady lying in blood and too cold. Horse keep her warm some, but not enough."

"Get six of the strongest men over here," Vespasian said to Alexander. "Your big friend and five others."

Alexander shouted the names of those he wanted; soon they were grouped around the dead horse. He pointed to the stubby fellow bending over Lamia's neck.

"Nicanor is the one who found her, sir."

"He'll get his reward, soon as we're back in Caere."

At Vespasian's command, the slaves lifted the heavy corpse and dropped it a few paces away.

Alexander caught his breath at the sight of Theodosia's body covered with mud and blood. There appeared to be a clean break on the right leg, but the other one was badly twisted. He heard gasps from several of the brawny men who had raised the horse. Stefan looked sick, as did Titus.

Timon felt above and below the break on Theodosia's lower right leg. Then he ran his hands down her left leg, stopping and shaking his head each time he detected a break. He stopped five times.

"Maybe she not walk again, master."

"Can't you do something?" Titus said. "What do we keep you for?"

"I do if I can, sir," said Timon. "Right leg not bad hurt, but left leg and knee... Treatment not certain work."

"We'll discuss it later," Vespasian said. "Right now, we've got to move her out of here."

He turned to Stefan.

"Can you get her up the cliff?"

Stefan nodded and stepped toward Theodosia. In the next instant, Titus came forward and blocked his path.

"No! I'll carry her."

Titus eased Theodosia onto her back and with one finger gingerly touched her swollen, blackened left cheek. He was slipping his arms under her when Vespasian stopped him with a few quiet words.

"My son, the slave is stronger. He'll carry her more steadily."

Titus kept his head bowed over Theodosia for a long moment. When at last he stood, he glowered at Stefan.

"See that you handle her gently!"

Stefan looked into the young Roman's face and nodded again. Then he dropped to the ground, cradled Theodosia in his arms, and carried her up the embankment.

The pain in her cheek was as keen as the pain in her legs. Slowly, Theodosia willed her hand out of the muck, dragged it across the rocks, and clutched at the sharp edge that most tormented her. Little by little, she worked the stone out of the mud and away from her face.

Gradually, the pain in her legs eased; she felt only throbbing cold.

Finally, she felt nothing at all.

She didn't know when she first heard the voice. Voices and faces and disconnected memories had been bobbing through her darkness for an eternity of pain. But this voice was different.

Came close.

Knelt beside her.

A presence attached to the voice touched her shoulder, then shouted and shouted until she thought her head would burst.

Abruptly, the shouting stopped.

A different presence bent over her.

Cleared the rocks from her cheek.

Brushed the mud from her nostrils.

163

Took her hand.

Caressed her hair.

Spoke her name.

Theodosia faded to blackness again, vaguely aware that she was safe.

She awoke to movement, to pain. She heard herself cry as she clutched at the scratchy fabric pressed against her cheek.

More voices above her head...

More presences...

More pain...

A hand touched her forehead, slipped to her throat, her wrist.

Clearer voices...

"Much pain when lady wakes, master."

"Better get her to Caere fast."

"I'll take her on my horse, Father."

"No, we'll get the carriage at her villa."

Theodosia strained to move the fingers of her right hand. One of the presences took them. She tried to open her eyes. The left refused, but the right did open and, desperate to focus, made out several heads hovering above her. The light stabbed her open eye, but—when the voices and the heads connected—she knew it was Titus holding her hand.

Not Caere.

She tried to make her lips work.

Not...

"She's trying to say something, sir."

"Get her to Caere before she comes to. Bring her along, fellow."

Theodosia felt herself being lifted once again to the broad chest she now knew was Stefan's. She heard horses, then Titus' voice.

"It's taking too long like this. Why don't I carry her on from here?"

The hooves came very close.

"Hand her up to me, fellow. I'll get her to Caere."

"Not Caere!"

Forcing her right eye to open fully and focus, she saw a set of welts on Stefan's neck. She had a faint memory of striking him with a whip.

Juno, how long ago was that?

"What is it, miss?"

"Not Caere!" Although she felt she was shouting, she knew her words were barely audible, if at all. "Home!"

"Tell them yourself," Stefan said under his breath. "Ain't nothing I can do to stop it."

"She's saying something, sir." The voice came from behind her head.

"Not Caere!" A spasm of pain raced through her chest. "Vespasian!"

"She's calling you, sir." It was Alexander's voice behind her head.

A gnarled hand that felt like the general's touched her arm.

"What is it, child?"

"Not Caere! Home!"

"Nonsense," Titus said from atop his horse. "Father, someone responsible must supervise her care."

"Home!"

"Child, that's unthinkable." Vespasian's voice was kind, his words frustrating. "You can't lie helpless and alone... at the mercy of slaves."

If Theodosia could have laughed, she would have laughed.

I'll be no more alone than before and not much more helpless.

She gathered her energy for one more desperate, gasping effort.

"I must go... home please let... your physician stay... my people will... care for me!"

Totally spent, she collapsed against Stefan's chest.

"Theodosia, that's impossible," Titus said. "Hand her to me, fellow!"

"May I say something, sir?" It was Alexander again.

"What?"

"Just that... you are concerned for our mistress' well-being, sir, but you must know that we are also concerned. Our own well-being depends on her survival."

Through her exhaustion, Theodosia marveled at Alexander's daring.

That's his future master he's confronting, and everyone knows it.

"My lord," Alexander went on, "there's not a slave in this lady's household who would do the slightest harm to her. And it does seem that she might recover faster and better in her own bed, tended by the servants she's used to."

"You make the decision, my son." It was Vespasian. "Just let me suggest... there is a certain logic to what he says."

Titus sighed loudly, sounding very annoyed.

"Very well," he said after an interval. "But we will hold you personally responsible, Alexander, if anything happens to her."

CHAPTER NINETEEN

Each step brought searing waves of pain as Stefan carried Theodosia through the forest to her villa. And when her body touched the bed, her own screams echoed through the dense gray stupor of her consciousness.

Clutching at Stefan's tunic, she struggled to pull herself off the mattress. Someone restrained her as someone else held a bitter liquid to her lips and forced her to drink. Gradually, the pain faded as she escaped into blessed darkness once more.

Disembodied voices returned in the fiery air that threatened to consume her. Presences at her side and over her head and around her legs... singly and in pairs and in groups...

Forcing more foul liquid down her throat...

Doing things to her body that she couldn't see, couldn't resist, couldn't even imagine...

Talking, sitting, standing, coming, going...

Leaving only the faintest impressions in her mind...

Gradually, however, the impressions became more coherent. Little by little, she grew in awareness of the activities around her. Still too weak to signal her increasing lucidity, Theodosia began to notice a single presence in a disproportionate number of the memories she retained.

Is it just a coincidence that I'm conscious when Alexander's on duty?

Each time, she smiled as she glided into an ever-gentler sleep.

How like Alexander to take his responsibility so seriously.

Alexander yawned, shifted his weight in the chair, set Book XVI of Livy's *History of Rome* on the table, picked up the lighter scroll that a courier had delivered three days earlier, and read—for at least the hundredth time—"Sold to a slave dealer from Antioch-near-Daphne."

He re-rolled the document and glanced by habit toward that other small circle of light beside the bed. And then he started.

In the dim amber glow, Theodosia Varra was staring back at him.

Alexander rose and stepped to her side, peering with wonder into her eyes. Timon had removed the bandages from her hands and arms a week ago. The black bruises that once covered her body had paled to a light purple or a lemony green. Those on her face had already vanished, so—except for her tangled hair and gauntness—she looked almost normal.

A smile crept across Theodosia's face as Alexander laid his hand on her shoulder.

"How long have you been awake?"

"A while." It was the chirp of an injured bird.

"Why didn't you call me?"

"Enjoyed watching you read."

He took her hand and rubbed her fingers.

"There must be a lot of gods watching over *you*. It seemed the fever would never break. Timon wasn't sure you'd survive it."

"Timon?"

"Vespasian's physician."

"With a funny way of talking?"

"He's Egyptian. Vespasian bought him in Alexandria. They couldn't pronounce his name, so they changed it."

"A very Roman thing to do." Theodosia half-laughed, and her mouth twisted in agony. She squeezed Alexander's hand as she clenched her teeth. "How long's it been?" she asked when the spasm had passed.

"Three weeks. It's December now."

"Pull your chair over."

Alexander obeyed and sat down beside her.

"What were you reading?"

"Livy."

"Something else?"

"A letter from Corinth. I took the liberty of opening it."

"Of course. Where are they?"

"Syria, most likely."

"We'll find them. You'll see." She shut her eyes for a few moments, then looked at him. "You've been here every night."

"What makes you think that?"

"Your face. You're exhausted."

"My lord Titus spent many hours here, too. The lady Flavia. Their father. Your servants… including," he said with emphasis, "Stefan."

"But not like you. I may have looked like a dead fish, but I wasn't completely unaware. Thanks for standing up to them. I really didn't want to go to Caere. How're my legs?"

The gold-flecked pupils challenged him for the truth.

"Not pretty, but the right one will heal, according to Timon. He's not so optimistic about your left leg."

"Why can't I move them?"

"They're in splints. It was quite a process. You were in great pain, so Timon gave you opium. We had to keep you still while he pulled your legs into position and pounded on the braces. The general, his son, and Senator Otho, plus…" Alexander gave a self-deprecating chuckle, "this poor Greek. Each of us holding down a part of you. What a scene. Good thing you were unconscious, or you'd never forgive us."

"How embarrassing!" Theodosia rolled her head to the other side, then back toward him. "Otho was here?"

"He showed up the day after we found you."

"He already knew what had happened?"

"Everything. The slave grapevine works fast, remember? Later on— But that's a story for another day."

There was a long silence. She stretched out her hand once more.

"Will I walk again? The truth, please."

"It's too soon to say."

"Stupid, wasn't it? Stupid fit of temper. How's Stefan?"

"Angry about that beating you gave him. But he still loves you, and he'll be glad to know you're awake."

"I'm going to tell him about the baby."

"You've lost your baby, miss." It was an abrupt way to break the news. "There was so much blood out there that nobody suspected it, but since I knew…"

He turned his eyes away for a few moments.

"My wife miscarried our second child, right before the Romans took me away. We were in trouble, and the stress was too much for her. Anyway, I knew what to look for. Timon confirmed it later… just to me."

Theodosia's face contorted. Tears glistened in her eyes. From her throat came a barely audible moan.

"There's no reason now for you not to marry my lord Titus." Alexander enclosed her hand with both of his, hoping to divert her attention. "He spent many hours here. It's obvious that he loves you."

"Will he love a woman who can't walk?"

"He knows all about your injury. Hasn't given any sign that it's changed his mind."

Theodosia stared at the ceiling. Alexander waited a bit, then went on.

"He's a fine young man."

"I don't love Titus."

"Do you love Stefan?"

"I thought I did, a month ago. Now... I really don't know. What's clear is that I have to marry someone soon, if only to protect you and everyone else here from imperial confiscation. Just in case I do something else as dumb as this and don't survive it next time around."

Alexander gave her a crooked smile.

"If you were to take my advice—which of course you'd never do!— you'd marry Titus Flavius Sabinus Vespasianus the Younger, just as soon as you're able. For your sake and ours, miss. Considering the alternatives, we could all do a lot worse."

Theodosia managed a crooked smile of her own.

"Well, I might take your advice... for once." She looked into his eyes. "There's something I want to tell you, Alexander. No matter who I marry, I think you're probably the finest man I'll ever know."

Suddenly aware of how long he had been sitting there, holding her hand as if he had a right to, Alexander felt his face blaze.

"Well, you— I— That's some consolation, I suppose."

Theodosia slept for two more days, but it was a healing sleep, not the fevered blackness of the past. Feeling stronger the third morning, she ate a full breakfast for the first time since her accident.

Today I resume control of my life.

"I want to thank everyone in the household who sat with me," she said to Dabini and Selicio as they collected her trays. "Tell Alexander to bring them all here together."

Alexander came alone.

"You should rest." His voice was oddly insistent.

"I'm tired of resting."

Resuming control of my life starts with Alexander.

"Bring the others up!"

Soon an odd assortment of servants clustered around her bed... Marcipor, Stefan, Milo, Lycos, Etrusca, and Nicanor. The presence of the latter two would have been a surprise had Alexander not told her how they begged for the chance to keep watch over her. Theodosia spent a few moments talking to each of the six in turn. It took her a while to realize that something was wrong... a reluctance by everybody to catch her eye, a visible discomfort in her presence. She had never felt anything like it.

Something has happened.

Then she realized...

"Where's Lucilla? Didn't she sit with me, too?"

Nobody said anything.

"What's the matter with Lucilla?"

Lycos developed an interest in a gull soaring outside. Marcipor turned to Alexander, whose gaze had followed the boy's. Milo, Etrusca, and Nicanor began to inspect the frescoes above the bed. The only one looking at Theodosia was Stefan, and his expression was inscrutable.

"I asked a question," she said, "and I do expect an answer."

"I'll explain it to you, miss," Alexander said. "Will you please let everybody else get back to work?"

Theodosia nodded.

Something is very wrong.

"I didn't want to tell you so soon," Alexander began after the others had left. "I've had Lucilla locked in one of the storage rooms for a week."

"Locked up?"

"She tried to poison my lord Titus."

"What?"

Theodosia pushed herself onto one elbow, wincing as pain stabbed her legs and back.

"Please lie down." Alexander eased her onto her pillow. "May I sit?"

Theodosia made a little gesture of assent.

"One afternoon, when my lord Titus was here with you, I let Selicio into the wine-storage room to pour some Falernian for him. Selicio left, but I stayed behind to reorganize the supply and lock the room again. Lucilla ran up to Selicio in the atrium and said I had something else for him to take to your bedroom. He left the pitcher beside the pool and went to find me." Alexander shook his head. "I hadn't even spoken with Lucilla that day, so Selicio and I were suspicious. She was gone when we got to the atrium, but the pitcher was still there. On a hunch, we poured another, and Selicio took it to serve my lord Titus. I carried the first pitcher to the shepherds' compound and trickled some of the wine down the throat of their oldest dog."

"And...?"

"The dog went into convulsions and died."

"Immortal gods!" Theodosia tugged her blanket over her shoulders. "Are you sure Lucilla poisoned the wine? Couldn't Selicio have done it?"

"Then he wouldn't have told me about it."

"Unless he wanted to get her in trouble."

Alexander shook his head again.

"After the dog died, Selicio and I hauled Lucilla into the grain-storage room. I searched her and found this." He pulled a nearly empty blue glass vial from the pouch on his belt. "Lucilla hasn't been out since."

Theodosia took the bottle, swished its remaining contents, slipped out the plug, and whiffed. No odor. Mixed with wine, the stuff—whatever it was—would probably be undetectable. She replaced the plug, laid the vial on the table, and turned her eyes to Alexander.

"There's more," he said, digging deeper into the pouch. "That night, while I was sitting with you, I searched Lucilla's bedroom. I found this tucked under her mattress, beside the wall."

He handed her a round silver amulet... a tightly coiled serpent with a tiny ruby in its mouth.

Dear gods... Lucilla!

"You never saw this before?"

"Never, miss."

"Does she know you found it?"

"No."

Theodosia studied the little silver viper for a moment, then buried it under the blanket.

"Bring Lucilla to me. Right now."

Lucilla halted a few steps from Theodosia's bed.

"I trusted you."

"I never betrayed your trust, miss."

Theodosia lifted the blue glass vial.

"What's this, then?"

"Poison, I guess, but it's not mine."

"Liar. You tried to murder Titus."

"No, miss. Alexander's the one who wants my lord Titus dead. He slipped the poison into that wine jug, not me."

Theodosia glanced at Alexander, who looked remarkably unperturbed for one accused of a capital crime.

"That's ridiculous. He's been trying to convince me to marry Titus."

"It's a trick, miss, can't you see? To cover up the fact that he don't want you marrying nobody."

"That makes no sense."

"Oh, yes, it does. Everyone knows Alexander's in charge around here. You don't do nothing without his approval, and a new master would change that. He's scared to death you'll marry Senator Otho. Knows he'll get beat for his impudence."

"You sound like Otho."

"I'm telling you the truth, miss, just like the senator did."

"Why would Alexander want to make me suspect you?"

"He hates me 'cause I won't sleep with him." Lucilla gave a long, loud sigh... as if reluctant to tell the truth, but to Theodosia the emotion sounded contrived. "He comes around when I'm alone. Puts his inky hands on me and threatens all kinds of things if I don't give in."

"Why didn't you tell me this before?"

"You never believed nothing I said about him. Now that he knows I'm not going to have sex with him, he's making this all up to get even."

"Selicio was in the storeroom, too, miss. He saw me take that vial from her."

"Selicio's just as bad! They're all jealous of me and Ste—" The name froze in Lucilla's mouth as her self-confidence crumbled. "Oh, miss, you've got to believe me!"

Theodosia inspected Lucilla's broad face, studying the familiar pale pairing of eyebrows and eyes, wide open now in sudden desperation. Then she looked at Alexander, trying in vain to picture him threatening Lucilla... or even fondling her.

"I can only accept one version of this story, Lucilla, and Alexander's version makes more sense than yours."

"But it's not true!" Lucilla fell to the floor and clutched at the edge of Theodosia's blanket. "It's just like Alexander to turn you against me. He's dangerous! You don't know!"

I was able to frighten Alexander once. I should be able to frighten Lucilla now.

"I don't believe a word you're saying." Her tone was as cold as she could make it. "Get away from my bed."

Lucilla leaped up. Blood surged to her face as she stepped backward.

"What're you going to do with me, miss?"

"There's only one thing to do with a slave you no longer trust." Theodosia's eyes never left Lucilla's face. "Alexander."

"Yes, miss?"

"Tomorrow morning, you will take Lucilla to the slave market in Rome. She's not to speak to anyone before she leaves. Is that clear?"

"Quite clear, miss."

He understands what I'm doing.

"You can't sell me away from Stefan! I love him!"

"I absolutely can. I intend to."

"But you promised!"

Suddenly the emotion was real. Lucilla's face convulsed as tears overflowed her eyes. She dropped to her knees again, then leaned onto her forearms and began to wail.

"Stop it. Right now. Alexander, get her out of here."

Alexander bent over Lucilla and seized her wrists.

She snapped at his hand.

He wrapped an arm around her waist and began tugging her toward the door. Lucilla was a large woman. Wrestling with her was obviously no easy task for a man who had spent much of his adult life at a desk.

As Alexander was struggling with Lucilla, Theodosia managed to push herself into a sitting position, ignoring the pain.

"Wait," she said after he was in full control. "Bring her back here."

Alexander marched Lucilla to the bed. Theodosia did not speak until the reddened eyes focused on her own.

Now.

"Lucilla, would you like another chance?"

The girl's bobbing head answered the question. Theodosia reached under her blanket and brought out the ruby-serpent amulet.

"Tell me how you came by this."

Lucilla's eyes bulged; her chin began to tremble. She cast a glance at Alexander, who tightened his grip on her waist. She gasped and squirmed and moaned, but ultimately said nothing.

"Very well," Theodosia said as the silence grew. "Take her away."

"No, miss, I'll—" Lucilla sobbed. "It was a gift!"

"From whom? Remember, the first lie seals your fate."

"From Senator Otho... back when he was just a tribune."

"Why did he give it to you?"

"To get me to spy for him."

"Spy on me?"

"Yes."

"And have you done that?"

Lucilla hung her head and nodded.

173

Otho always knew everything I did, but... Dearest Juno, I never suspected the spy was Lucilla!

"Since when?"

"Since before we left Rome."

"Since May?"

Lucilla shook her head.

"He first met with me last December, before Saturnalia."

"A whole year ago? Months before my brother was murdered?"

Lucilla nodded again.

Theodosia's elbow gave out. She collapsed and began to choke.

Alexander released Lucilla.

"Pour some water," he said as he slipped an arm under Theodosia and lifted her upright.

Lucilla splashed water from a bedside pitcher into a cup and handed it to Alexander. When Theodosia's coughs subsided, he held it to her lips.

"The rest of this can wait," he said as she drank.

"No. I have to finish it. Lucilla, what did Otho promise you?"

"Freedom." The word was barely audible.

"By all the immortal gods. He couldn't promise you freedom!"

"But he did. He said he'd free me when he married you."

"Is that why you were always pushing his cause?"

"Yes, miss."

Lucilla had steadied a bit, but her eyes were still wide with fear.

"What else were you to do for him?"

"Let him know if you was thinking about marrying somebody else. Tell him anything interesting about your private life."

"You told him about Stefan and me, didn't you?"

A tiny nod.

"I suppose he bribed you, too. Gave you money."

"At first. Then—before we came here—he gave me that little snake."

"Did Otho say where he'd gotten it?"

"He said he'd had it made just for me. He said I'd see other things like it here. Big silver pieces with serpents and rubies. He said he'd had them made for your brother... just like he'd had this piece made for me."

Theodosia and Alexander exchanged looks.

"You're sure Otho told you that?"

"Oh, yes, miss. He promised me that the day he married you, I'd go free and he'd give me all those snake things for my own. He said he was giving me this little one as a token of his pledge. So later, when I saw the others here, I believed him." Lucilla's face crumpled into another sob.

"He was nice to me, miss. Real gentle. Always said how much he loved you, so I couldn't see nothing wrong with helping him. And every time he came here he added to what he promised, so it seemed like whatever I wanted I was going to get... just as soon as you married him."

Alexander pounced on that.

"What else did he promise you?"

"I don't answer to you!"

"You'll answer every question you're asked," Theodosia said. "What else did he promise you?"

Lucilla's answer was garbled.

"What?"

"Stefan. As my own slave."

"And you believed him? Oh, you fool. Don't you know that—for much of this year—Otho was trying to have Stefan fight in the arena?"

"The arena? Stefan?"

"Of course! To win popularity for Otho and votes in the election. You stupid, gullible fool! You really believed he'd not only give you your freedom but also piles of silver and gigantic rubies and a slave worth thirty thousand denarii?"

"I wanted to believe it." Lucilla blinked back her tears.

"When did Otho give you that vial of poison?" It was just a guess, but Theodosia was sure it was true.

"Two weeks ago. The last time he was here. I didn't want to take it, but he scared me. He wasn't talking gentle anymore."

Theodosia's eyes sought Alexander's again.

"He must have been getting worried," Alexander said, "realizing he'd blown his chance with you, after that episode in the garden."

"Well, miss," Lucilla said, "he swore if I didn't poison my lord Titus, he'd tell you everything I'd been doing for him, just as soon as you came to. He said you'd have me whipped for sure."

Theodosia slammed both her hands into the blanket.

"Are you so dumb, Lucilla? Don't you know what the punishment is for a slave who kills a Roman? It's crucifixion. The slowest, most painful way to die that anyone ever invented. It's much, much worse than a whipping! By Jupiter, girl, I would have every right to sentence you to both those things... for spying on me and attempting to murder a Roman. And there's not a soul on earth who'd raise a hand to stop it."

Lucilla gasped and shot Alexander a plea for help.

"May I say something in Lucilla's defense, miss?"

"I didn't know you two got along well enough for that."

175

"We don't, but... To be fair... The senator uses similar tactics on me. Sometimes he blusters. Sometimes he cajoles. Sometimes he tries to bribe. But there's always an implied threat. Either I cooperate with him now or I'll pay with my hide when I become his property."

Theodosia set the tiny serpent on the table beside the blue glass vial.

"Keep Lucilla locked up until I decide what to do with her. Come back when you've finished."

Then she closed her eyes, unwilling to watch as he hustled away her once-trusted maid.

"I am going to sell her," Theodosia said when Alexander returned.

"You all but promised you wouldn't if she told you the truth."

"I know, but if I can't trust her..."

"You still need a maid."

"Etrusca will attend me until I find another skilled girl. Can we assume Lucilla is the only one Otho got to?"

"No telling. He certainly worked hard enough on me."

Otho worked hard... at marrying me.

The realization hit her with the force of Otho's fist by the fountain.

There's something more to this.

"When did Otho give Marcipor to Gaius?"

"A little over a year ago, I guess. But please don't worry about all this just now. I should have waited to tell you."

"You couldn't have waited. I insisted, remember?"

Theodosia closed her eyes again and lay quietly for a while.

Otho first approached Lucilla a year ago.

He gave Marcipor to Gaius not long before that.

I didn't get to know Otho until after Gaius died, but he said he knew he wanted to marry me after I bumped into them on the street. "Pauper or not, it was a beautiful woman I saw that day."

Gods, when was that? Two years ago?

She opened her eyes and turned to Alexander.

"Bring Marcipor to me."

"Later, miss. First, you must rest."

"I'll rest later. First, I must talk with Marcipor. And you," she added with a slow, affectionate smile, "must do as you are told."

Alexander glanced at the other Greek as they stepped into the mistress' bedroom. Anxiety clouded Marcipor's handsome features. Theodosia looked anxious, too. She had twisted to one side, clutching the blanket as if somehow it could protect her from all the Othos of the world.

"Marcipor, when did Senator Otho give you to my brother?"

"Almost eighteen months ago."

"I'm not going to waste words. I believe he gave you to Gaius to spy on him, and I believe you've spied on me, too."

The fine brown eyes widened in alarm.

"I'd never spy on you, miss!"

"I think you did. To help your former master marry me."

"He didn't say anything about spying on my lord Gaius. After the master died, he did demand that I spy on *you*, but I— I don't ever want to belong to him again. I hope you never marry him. I'd help anybody but him. Alexander will tell you…"

Theodosia flicked her eyes to her steward.

"Tell me what?"

Alexander wasn't sure what Marcipor wanted him to say, but he knew what he could truthfully say.

"I don't know except that Marcipor dislikes my lord Otho as much as I do. The senator abuses him—both verbally and physically—every time he comes around. You've seen a bit of that, I think."

"I have."

"Then imagine how much worse it is when you're not around. If Marcipor is a spy then he must also be a very good actor, and I've never seen anything to indicate that he is either."

Marcipor blinked his gratitude, which Alexander acknowledged with a slight tilt of his head.

Theodosia lay motionless. Alexander wondered what was going on behind her impassive expression.

"Last spring, Marcipor," she went on after a long interval, "I asked you some questions that embarrassed you. Now I have to embarrass you again, because I need to know what was going on before my brother's death. Answer truthfully if you want me to believe you. First, tell me why Otho gave you to Gaius, if it wasn't to spy on him."

"Blackmail."

"I don't understand."

"The tribune had often lent me to him for a few days at a time." Marcipor's cheeks showed a few pink spots. "I think my lord Gaius finally decided he wanted me for good."

177

"As his lover?"

"There was no love in it, miss. He was very brutal."

"Did Otho take you, too?"

"Ever since we were boys."

"Were you the only one?"

"No, miss."

"Females, too?"

Marcipor nodded.

"Occasionally. There was a slave girl in his father's household whom I loved, but he took her for himself. He forced her to sleep with him for months. Mostly to spite me, I think. He knew I loved her, and he had lots of others to pick from. And then—when he was bored with her—he talked his father into selling her to another man. Pure meanness, if you ask me. It wouldn't have hurt him to leave her in the household where she had grown up."

Theodosia's eyes never left Marcipor's face.

"Were Otho and my brother...?"

"Yes, miss."

Alexander was listening carefully. Much of this was new to him.

Where in Zeus' name is she going with this?

Theodosia's fingers laced and locked across her chest.

"How could Gaius have blackmailed Otho?"

"Do you know the tribune's—the senator's—father?"

"Only by name."

"Well, the senator—the old senator, my lord Otho's father—believes in the 'traditional Roman values.' We Greeks are ruining Rome, he says. He hates what he calls 'Greek love.' He knows it's not only girls his son takes to his bed, but as long as they're just slaves..." He shrugged. "But if he found out that his son was having sex with another patrician man..."

Marcipor finished with a roll of his eyes.

"Was my brother threatening to tell the old senator?"

"I think so."

"Why would he blackmail his best friend?"

"I can't say."

"Wouldn't Gaius have suffered as much from that revelation?"

"No, miss. Your brother had already come into his inheritance. Besides... everyone in Rome knew he was hot for boys. Slave or free, it didn't matter one bit to him."

"What would Senator Salvius Otho have done?"

"Disinherit his son, most likely. He was always threatening it."

"Otho mentioned to me last summer that if he didn't marry General Silvanus' daughter, his father would disinherit him."

"He was lying to you, miss. That betrothal was broken off two years ago, at the insistence of General Silvanus. Calchas—that's my lord Otho's body servant—says his master is smitten now with Poppaea Sabina."

Poppaea Sabina?

Alexander remembered hearing Stefan talk about her behavior at the ladies-only dinner party in Rome.

Theodosia began rubbing her temples. She looked tired.

Alexander stepped up beside her bed.

"Please rest now, miss. You can talk to Marcipor another day."

Theodosia ignored him... as he knew she would.

"Got any idea why—if Otho's 'smitten' with Poppaea, as you say—he's so anxious to marry me?"

"Money, miss. Poppaea Sabina's family isn't rich enough. Neither is my lord Otho's. He wants to become really, really rich."

"By marrying me?"

"That would be the quickest way."

"I guess. Did you ever hear Otho discuss me with Gaius?"

"I once heard him tell your brother that he wanted to marry you."

"When was that?"

"Before my lord Otho gave me to him. You happened to be walking by and stopped to say hello to your brother. After you left, the tribune asked him who you were. And then, just a few moments later—we couldn't have gone more than fifty paces—he told him that he'd fallen in love with you and wanted to marry you."

"Just like that? Out of the blue?"

"Out of the blue." Marcipor raised his eyes from the floor. "I saw you that day too, miss, but you wouldn't have noticed me. I was in the crowd of attendants surrounding their litters."

"What did Gaius say to Otho's 'declaration of love'?"

"He said no. Flat out no. Said it was impossible."

"Did he say why?"

Marcipor licked his lips nervously.

"Just said you couldn't marry into a senatorial family."

"Because...?"

Marcipor flushed. His eyes went back to the floor.

"I can't repeat what he said."

Alexander held his breath as he watched Theodosia's face. Her resolution never seemed to waver.

179

"Because my mother was a filthy Greek whore?"

Marcipor's head jerked up.

"How'd you know that?"

"Because Otho made the same comment to me not long ago. Said Gaius once told him that." She paused. "Was that all Gaius said?"

"Just that."

Alexander exhaled with relief.

Secret's still safe.

But Theodosia wasn't finished yet. To Alexander's surprise, she offered Marcipor her hand.

"Thank you for the information, Marcipor. Before you go, is there anything else you want to tell me?" She gave him a slight smile. "To prove once and for all that you're not Otho's spy?"

Marcipor stared in obvious disbelief at the slender hand stretched out to him. After a few moments, he took it. The silence that followed seemed to last forever.

Blessed gods, don't let him say anything that will shatter her!

He watched as Marcipor battled his misgivings.

"I have a hunch, miss, but—please—my lord Otho is very angry with me, because I haven't done what he demanded after you came here to live. Please... is it certain you will never marry him?"

"Quite certain. I promise you will never fall into his hands again."

"And you'll never tell him what I said about the blackmail? Or that he tried to make me spy on you?"

Theodosia sighed.

"I promise. And it doesn't matter anyway, because you belong to me, not to Senator Otho. I will protect you. So, what's your hunch?"

"Well, I have no way of proving it, but..." Marcipor's voice dropped to a whisper. "I think he's one of the men who murdered your brother."

CHAPTER TWENTY

Later that morning, Stefan carried Theodosia to the cushioned chair beside the window in her sitting room. It was her first time out of bed in almost a month. Being lifted and set down still tortured her legs and back, and she clung to his arms until the spasms passed.

"Thanks." It was humiliating to be so helpless. "There's no one else I'd trust to do that right now."

Stefan regarded her indifferently. His beard was full again, his demeanor stiff.

Wonder what he thinks of Lucilla's confinement. Has he heard that I'm planning to sell her?

"Anything else you need?" His chilly tone said more than his words.

Alexander's wrong. There's no love left between Stefan and me.

Love was part of the past.

Before the sight of a slave girl sneaking out of the barn...

Before the smack of a whip...

Before the loss of an unborn baby...

It had been Theodosia's decision to put a stop to their relationship, but still it grieved her.

Does it grieve him, too, or is he just angry? Does love always end this way?

"No," she said after a moment. "You may go."

Theodosia sat stoically in the cushioned chair, her splinted legs propped on a stool, as her new farm-bred lady's maid struggled with the unfamiliar art of hairdressing. While her fingers worked to coax three weeks of bed-tangles from her mistress' hair, Etrusca murmured that she had never dreamed of such a high position, that Nicanor was so proud, that they were both so grateful, that Master Nizzo would be so amazed.

Etrusca had filled out a lot in half a year; now her latest pregnancy was beginning to show. There had been no more displays of superstition, and her personality—once she outgrew her original awe of her mistress—proved bright and warm.

No wonder Nicanor's devoted to her. What wouldn't I give to have a man love me so much just for myself?

Timon came in to check Theodosia's progress. She had found she liked this odd little slave with the strange way of speaking Latin. Timon might know a great deal about the human body, but the verbs and pronouns of his master's tongue seemed likely to befuddle him forever.

No sooner had the physician begun unwrapping her right leg than Vespasian strolled in—wearing what Theodosia guessed was his finest toga—followed by Flavia, Titus, and Alexander. As if flustered by the arrival of so many Romans at once, Etrusca dropped the tortoise-shell comb. Timon bowed to his master and continued his work.

"Now... this is a pretty sight," Vespasian said.

"Oooooh, you do look better! Not like that pitiful person they fished up from the river." Flavia fingered Theodosia's russet tunic. "You've got such superb taste. I wanted you to help plan my wedding, but—" She accepted the chair that Alexander offered her. "It's to be the day after tomorrow! We're off to Rome today, just as soon as we leave you."

"I thought you were planning a spring wedding."

"We were, but there've been changes."

"Father and I are the troublemakers, I'm afraid," Titus said. He took Theodosia's hands and kissed them. "We've been ordered into service."

"Both of you at the same time? Is that a coincidence?"

"The emperor's doing," Vespasian said. "I'm to command the legion in Africa. Leaving in three days. My son enters the Centuriate the very afternoon of Flavia's wedding. Way ahead of schedule."

"Why such short notice? Did Emperor Claudius order that, too?"

"I doubt it," Vespasian said. "The old goat doesn't bother with such details. Someone else in the palace rescheduled Titus' deployment."

Someone else in the palace?

Theodosia looked at Alexander, hoping to catch his reaction, but—as always when Romans were present—his face was blank.

"Training camp lasts six months," Titus said, "so if I start now, I'll finish in June. I'll be home in March, and off and on after that."

Trying to shake her uneasiness, Theodosia turned her attention to the man bending over her right leg. She laid her hand on his arm and raised her eyes to Vespasian.

"Your physician is wonderful, General."

Before Vespasian could answer, Timon lifted his head and rewarded Theodosia with a disarming smile. One of his front teeth was missing.

"I happy I serve she, lady, help she walk again someday."

"You do think I will, then?"

"I hope it, lady. I check leg now. Turn face please."

"No! Why should I be the only one to miss the show?"

Timon shrugged and removed the final bandage around her right shin; then he lifted the top splint and handed it to Alexander. Theodosia pushed herself forward to get a look at the swollen mass below her knee.

"Not move, lady." Timon ran his fingers down the shin that shaded from purple to yellow. "Splints maybe off this leg by Saturnalia."

"And the other leg? I'll have to work hard that night, Timon. Folks around here are stern masters at Saturnalia."

"Slaves not have lady's service this year." He shook his head.

"What a shame!" Theodosia smiled ruefully at Alexander. "My first Saturnalia at home in years, and I'm worthless as a servant."

"We'll move your chair out by the bonfire, miss," Alexander said in the same vein, "and do our best to get some singing out of you. Perhaps the lady Flavia will join you. We can exact your share of work from her."

"Count on it, Alexander." Flavia laughed. "Lucius leaves for Naples next week. Neither Father nor Titus will be home for Saturnalia, so I'll be available. And hey... I'm a lively serving wench at Saturnalia!"

"In the meantime, there are serious matters to discuss," said Vespasian in a tone calculated to put an end to the banter. "Wrap that leg up, Timon. Then, you three, leave us."

"We'll take lunch here in an hour," Theodosia said to Alexander as Timon hastened to obey his master's command.

Alexander and Etrusca brought two chairs, then headed for the door.

Theodosia glanced up to see Alexander looking back. Their eyes met, and she saw him nod, ever so slightly, before stepping into the hall.

"Well, Theodosia," Vespasian began when the slaves were gone, "I'm a simple man, a soldier. Not known for fancy talk. So, we've come to you as a family... to make a family offer."

Titus sat and took Theodosia's hand again. The moment of commitment had come. She would postpone it no longer.

"My son is younger than you and inexperienced, but he has a fine career before him." Vespasian paused, his brow furrowed. "Our line is not as old as yours. Our purse is not as deep. Nor is our name as celebrated as the Terentius Varro name, but it is honest, and we hope that you may accept our offer despite these considerable differences in circumstance."

"Oh, but you know my mother was not—"

"Your mother was good enough to marry Aulus Terentius Varro, and that's good enough for us. My daughter already considers you her sister, and it's plain to everyone that my son is hopelessly smitten. We all want you to be a true member of our family, Theodosia, so—on behalf of the entire Flavian clan—I ask you to marry Titus next summer, after he gets his commission."

Theodosia felt that familiar warmth creep across her cheeks.

Even knowing about Stefan and the lost baby, they still accept me.

She looked from face to face until she trusted her voice.

"You honor me, General. Yes, I will marry Titus next summer. I hope to *stand* that day at the shrine of my ancestral gods and give thanks to them for showing me the way to walk again."

"We'll all give thanks for that." Titus rose and kissed her forehead. "And at Flavia's wedding, I'll pour an extra libation to Venus in gratitude for her special gift to me."

A while later, there was a tap on the door. Flavia opened it.

Alexander and the two Ethiopian waiters were just outside, silver trays in hand.

"We've got good news," Flavia said as the slaves entered.

Titus was standing beside Theodosia's chair now, one hand on her shoulder, the other holding her hand. Theodosia knew that the rosiness in her face had not faded completely.

"Alexander, I will marry General Vespasian's son next summer."

Without a word, Alexander poured the Falernian and offered goblets to Vespasian and Flavia.

His eyes met Theodosia's again as he bent to serve her. Then he straightened and raised them to Titus.

"Congratulations, sir."

Theodosia felt a twinge of regret as Alexander offered the last cup to the young man who would soon be his master.

Five days later, Alexander herded a dozen men into the garden to begin preparing the flower beds for the reseeding that would start in a few months. It was a boring chore that the slaves disliked, but now, after last night's hard rain, the ground would be malleable.

He had talked with Theodosia about the flowers. Come summer, she could decorate her villa and her marriage bed with blossoms of her own choosing. The date was set. Theodosia Varra would wed Titus Flavius Sabinus Vespasianus the Younger on the last day of July.

Impulsively, Alexander took a shovel and joined the digging. It was almost unheard of for a steward to engage in physical labor alongside subordinate slaves, and the mud would soil his tunic, but right now he would do anything to keep his mind from wandering. Theodosia's wedding day would come soon enough without his dwelling on it.

Timon remained at the villa to care for Theodosia, but no guests were expected until Flavia came next week for Saturnalia.

It surprised Alexander, then, to hear a horse in the driveway. The rider turned out to be Senator Marcus Salvius Otho, without his usual retinue but wearing full military regalia... that same crimson and brass that Alexander had learned to hate so long ago in Corinth.

"Take me to your mistress."

"She is resting, sir."

Otho's eyes jeered at Alexander's dirty tunic and the shovel in his hand. Then he turned and headed for the house.

"Excuse me, sir! She does not wish to be disturbed! And she especially does not wish to see you!"

Otho bounded up the stairs and disappeared. Alexander tossed his shovel aside and reached the atrium just as the senator was starting up toward Theodosia's private rooms. Alexander followed.

A few moments later, Otho slammed the door that had stood open since the day Stefan carried Theodosia home from the riverbank.

Alexander hesitated in the hall. His tunic and sandals were muddy, and no slave—not even a high-ranking one—had a right to barge in through a closed door on his betters. But the memory of Theodosia's crumpled body in the fountain—plus that blue glass vial and Marcipor's hunch—made him resolute. For the first time in all his years as a slave in this house, he opened the door of the master suite without permission and walked into the bedroom.

Otho had already removed his helmet. Now he stared angrily at Alexander. The face on the pillow, however, radiated relief.

"What are you doing here, Greek? Get out."

"My mistress has not instructed me to leave, sir."

"Nor did she instruct you to enter."

Alexander made no move.

"Get out!" Otho drew the sword from his scabbard. "By all the gods, Greek, I will kill you if you don't obey me."

"Otho! No!" Theodosia's voice sounded sleepy… and very alarmed.

"Is it your wish that I stay or leave, miss?"

"Stay."

Otho strutted toward Theodosia's bed and surveyed her at length.

"You're in big trouble. I'm the only one who can save you."

"What sort of trouble?"

Otho cast a contemptuous glance over his shoulder.

"Sure you want that Greek to hear?"

"What trouble?"

"You're about to lose a chunk of your property. The emperor plans to confiscate your farm; he may take this villa and the rest of your estate."

"What are you talking about?"

"Nizzo. The things he's saying about you in Rome."

I tried to warn you. Nobody can save you if Nizzo knows that secret.

"What's Nizzo saying?" She was fully awake now. "Lies?"

"Lies? Truth?" Otho shrugged. "Who knows?"

"What does he have to gain from telling lies about me?"

"Your farm. You won't sell it to him, but Claudius will."

"What has Nizzo to do with the emperor? How would he even communicate with him?"

"It seems Nizzo shared some information about you with the emperor's freedmen. They're among the most influential men at court… and his friends. My source tells me that Claudius ordered an investigation as soon as Nizzo's information reached his ears."

"Your source?"

"Nero. The heir to the throne. I introduced you to him in Rome, remember? My best friend."

"I thought Gaius was your best friend."

"Gaius is dead." Otho smiled. "Nero knows everything that goes on in the palace. He grows more influential as the old man totters closer and closer to his well-deserved grave." The smile grew smug. "The prince is all but emperor now, and there's nothing he won't do for me." He paused, looking even smugger. "Nothing. He'll save your property for you, Theodosia… but only if I ask it."

Theodosia clutched at her blanket.

"What do you want from me?"

"Marry me. Seven days from now, at Saturnalia. I'll see to it that you never hear another word about those charges."

"I've already promised to marry Titus."

"Then break that promise. Be smart for once. Aim for the top."

"With you? I can do much better."

Otho snapped his fingers at Alexander.

"Fetch me a chair. Poor little Theodosia... still thinking you're the best catch in the empire?" He sat in the chair that Alexander sullenly set beside the bed. "Face it. You're an aging cripple with a bad reputation."

"I'm also a very rich woman, which seems to be all that's needed to have men competing for my hand. I don't have to marry anyone I don't love, and I definitely don't love you."

"Marriage is about politics, not love. The Flavians want your money for their careers and your name for their next generation. They aren't fooled. They know you're hot for that stable hand."

"They know I've had feelings for Stefan. It doesn't matter to them."

"Don't count on it. Give Titus the chance to be master here and see how fast he sells your hay-seed lover to Camillus for the next games. Tell you what... I'll make a deal with you. Marry me and you can keep your big stud slave. In fact, be a tad more discrete and you can do whatever you want with any of the slaves out here. I certainly won't care."

"What a disgusting thing to say! You think I'm like you and my loathsome brother?"

"Sure you are, just more hypocritical. You start with a stable hand. Pretend to be 'in love' with him. Which slave will strike your fancy next?" Otho jerked his thumb in Alexander's direction. "This bookish Greek, maybe? One of the kitchen boys? How 'bout a shepherd lad?"

"How dare you?"

"Live out here, too, if you want. You'll find me a tolerant master."

Alexander watched Theodosia rally as Otho's words sank in.

Doesn't the stupid bastard realize he's saying all the wrong things?

Theodosia lifted herself on one elbow.

"I've given my word that I'll marry Titus when he completes his training next summer and, by Juno, that's exactly what I'm going to do."

"Poor little Theo. Such a waste." Otho laughed. "Don't you know I can see to it that your soldier-boy husband burns himself out battling dysentery and the Druids in the swamps of northern Britain?"

"Don't belittle Titus. He's the son of one of the greatest generals of this century."

"And the general's the spawn of a tax collector. You'd waste patrician blood on them?"

"So... you admit I'm a patrician? Last time we had a pleasant little chat like this—out by the fountain—you called me a filthy Greek whore."

Otho leaped from his chair, knocked her elbow out from under her, and snapped his hands onto her shoulders, pinning her to the mattress.

"Don't give me that shit!" he shouted into Theodosia's face as she yelped in pain. "You admitted sleeping with a slave. You gloated about it, damn you. Well, a filthy, slave-fucking whore is exactly what you are!"

Alexander sprang to the side of the bed, seized Otho's shoulders, and jerked him back. The senator broke free of his grasp, swirled around, and took a swing at him. Alexander dodged the blow.

"You've laid your hands on me once too often, Greek. Time to learn how a Roman officer deals with an insolent, disobedient slave."

"No one talks to her like that." Alexander was no longer willing to waste his breath calling Otho *sir*.

In the next instant, Otho punched him in the chin with his fist, knocking him off his feet. A flash of fire shot through Alexander's jaw as he staggered.

"Hold your tongue, Greek, or I'll cut it out."

"You aren't my master. You haven't the authority."

Otho yanked his sword out once more.

"I have not only the authority but the weapons."

As Alexander glanced around for something to use to defend himself, Otho lunged at him, flattened him against the wall, and pressed the sharp edge into his gullet. Then—keeping his sword firmly in place—he drew a dagger from his breastplate and began gouging its tip into Alexander's clenched teeth.

Desperate for air and room to maneuver, Alexander put both his hands on the blade of the sword and began pushing back as Otho's dagger sliced across the left corner of his mouth and into his cheek.

Simultaneous with the pain and the red spurt on his hand, Alexander heard a *thump!* against the wall, followed by a clatter on the floor.

Moments later, another *thump!* and another clatter.

Then a third missile hit the back of Otho's head. Hard.

The Roman yelled and turned as a fourth silver-colored missile crashed into the wall nearby.

The distraction gave Alexander the chance he needed. He rammed his palms straight out against the sword, knocked it into Otho's chest, and dashed the blood-covered dagger away from his cheek.

If he comes for me again, I'll grab the dagger.

But that didn't happen.

Instead, Otho turned his eyes to Theodosia, his face a feline mix of curiosity and fury. He replaced his sword in its scabbard and retrieved the four silver objects from the floor.

Ignoring Alexander—who had pressed a towel to his bleeding mouth and cheek and was edging sideways toward Theodosia—Otho deposited the dented cup, pitcher, and small bowl on her bedside table. Then he held out Lucilla's ruby-eating serpent on his palm, showing no surprise that someone had found it.

"You threw this, I believe." Otho tossed the talisman onto the blanket beside Theodosia.

"You're the one who threw it first at me. Last spring, when you gave it to Lucilla."

"Are you going to marry me?"

"No. And I tell you... the coarsest slave on my estate has more chance of marrying me than you do. If you think I'd break my word to Vespasian for the gratification of a foul-mouthed rodent like you—"

"You think Vespasian will let his son marry a penniless whore? Oh, a rich whore offers some benefits, so an ambitious man may overlook certain defects of character. But a penniless whore..." Otho chuckled, but his tone was icy. "If Nizzo's charges hold up, not even the low-born Flavians will have anything to do with you by this time next month."

Theodosia studied the coiled silver serpent, circling a finger over the tiny ruby in its mouth. After a long interval, she raised her eyes to Otho.

"I don't care what charges Nizzo has brought against me. I'd rather lose all my property and rot in the Carcer Tullianum than spend a single night in bed with you."

Otho's expression did not change.

"It's good to know that, because—if you won't have me—that's exactly what's going to happen to you."

Three days before the Ides of December, Theodosia sat by the open south-facing balcony, her legs on a stool, staring at the gulls circling in the gray winter sky. Saturnalia was only five days off, and though she ought to be looking forward to the holiday, she was dreading it.

If it weren't for Flavia's visit and the fact that the slaves expect it, I'd call the whole thing off this year.

The rowdy mid-winter festival had been Theodosia's favorite as a child, when she and Gaius and even their father gleefully participated in the merrymaking.

By ancient tradition, every slave at the villa enjoyed two days of lightened labor and one long, joyous night of make-believe equality with his master. All three Varros would don ragged tunics—artistically torn up for the occasion—and circulate among their impertinent slaves with pitchers of wine and treats. Then they would sing or bestow kisses or join in the wild chain dances or perform whatever other silly feats the slave selected "Lord of Misrule" might order them to do.

Theodosia remembered the laughter...

The delicious shedding of caste roles and rules...

The teasing faces of Gerta, Simi, Arisata, and little Stefan...

The crackling bonfires that burned until dawn beside the rocks overlooking the sea...

And hot tears spilled onto her cheeks.

She had tried to recreate those Saturnalian memories with Lucilla in Rome, but their feasts always paled in comparison. This year, it seemed that Otho, Lucilla, Stefan, and the splints on her legs had conspired to ruin things again.

Stefan continued treating her with the formality of a newly purchased slave. Even the waiters and houseboys were sullen these days, as if they resented the extra demands her injuries made on them.

The only servants whose attitude was unchanged were Marcipor and Alexander.

Lucilla was still confined to a storeroom. Theodosia had decreed that she not be let out for the upcoming frolic, but she knew it would be tough to stand by that edict when the holiday actually arrived.

This morning, Alexander—his facial cuts healing under Timon's care—was crouched beside the physician to help him adjust the splints and rewrap Theodosia's improving right leg. Her left shin, thigh, and knee would need protection for a long time yet and might never support her weight. It was obvious now that—if by some miracle she ever walked again—she would have a severely hobbled gait.

Timon was about to check the left leg when they heard hooves and footfalls in the driveway. Alexander rose and stepped onto the balcony.

"Legionaries. There must be a hundred of them."

Theodosia leaned forward and saw them, too. She had worried for a day after Otho's visit before banishing his threats from her mind. Now the fears returned in a rush.

Waves of armed men were swarming over the grounds as slaves began to pour into the driveway, holding their hands above their heads to defend themselves from the soldiers' spears and swinging wooden clubs. Soon there were scores of them encircled by crimson uniforms.

Etrusca had just left the room with an empty water pitcher. From out in the hallway came the crash of pottery and an anguished cry.

Timon jumped to his feet and moved toward the door, but before he reached it a soldier carrying a club burst through and landed a blow that sent the physician sprawling to the floor.

"Get out!"

Timon picked himself up and bolted through the door. Theodosia heard new shouts, the smack of another club, and the thud of a body hitting the floor. Etrusca screamed again, more distressed than before.

"You the woman who calls herself Theodosia Varra?" A pleased-to-be-the-one-to-find-her smirk spread across the legionary's peasant face.

"By what right do you invade my home?"

The man's expression grew surly as he swaggered forward, weapons in both hands. His rancid body odor engulfed her.

Alexander had already come in from the balcony. Now he stepped in front of Theodosia... a touchingly futile gesture by an unarmed man for whom it was a capital offense to raise a defensive hand against even so raunchy a representative of the emperor's legions.

"You a slave?" The intruder's voice was raspy and loud.

Theodosia peered around Alexander.

"Who authorized you to beat my servants?"

"I asked you a question, fellow. Are you a slave?"

"And I asked *you* a question!" It was unbearable to be so helpless while her home was overrun by rabble.

"My question's the only one that matters. Are you a slave, fellow?"

"Yes, sir."

"Then get outside with the others."

"I'll not leave my mistress, sir."

The soldier brandished his club.

"You'll do as I tell you. Go!"

Theodosia touched Alexander's arm.

"Do as he says, please. I'll be fine."

Alexander turned with an apprehensive glance. Theodosia nodded.

"Please go."

At the door, he lingered longer than she would have expected, looking at her, until at last—his head held high—he stepped into the hall.

Theodosia held her breath, listening for the expected clubbing, but none came. A muffled order and the click of sandals were all she heard.

Soon she saw Timon, Etrusca, and Alexander join the others inside the crimson-and-brass circle.

Stefan must be out there, too.

In another moment, she spotted his huge, shaggy head towering above both slaves and soldiers.

Alexander's words came back to her.

"Have you ever loved someone you were powerless to protect?"

Theodosia swallowed.

Juno, watch over Stefan! I do love him still.

And then she felt guilty for singling Stefan out for special prayer when her entire household was being squeezed into that oppressive circle. She rested her head on the chair, closed her eyes, and begged Jupiter, the father of all mankind, to protect each one of them, since she could not.

A tall, tanned, tough-looking man carrying a red-crested helmet shouldered past the guard, who saluted smartly. Without ceremony, he approached Theodosia.

"I am Centurion Manus."

"What are you doing with my servants?"

"The property is being treated with care."

"Some of them have been beaten."

"They will suffer no long-term effects." The centurion's eyes traveled to Theodosia's splinted legs, propped on the footstool. "You must forgive the abruptness of our intrusion. My orders were to catch this household unawares. The emperor's order."

"Was His Majesty afraid my slaves would escape... or me?"

"Both, I suspect."

"There's very little risk of my escape, as you can see."

Manus sat in another chair and regarded her solemnly.

Theodosia tapped her thumbs together a few times. Then—not wanting to appear nervous—she stifled the motion.

"May I see the emperor's order?"

He took a scroll from beneath his breastplate and handed it to her. Theodosia stared at the purple wax seal. It was genuine. She had seen that same mark on imperial decrees posted in the Forum.

"May I read it?"

Manus nodded, and Theodosia unrolled the document. The scribe's overly ornate writing made it difficult to focus on the message.

TIBERIUS CLAUDIUS DRUSUS NERO GERMANICUS TO
SEPTIMUS ATEIUS MANUS, CENTURION,
FOURTH COHORT, TENTH LEGION.

GREETINGS.

YOU ARE COMMANDED TO LEAD YOUR CENTURY TO THE
VILLA OF THE LATE GAIUS TERENTIUS VARRO,
SON OF AULUS TERENTIUS VARRO, LATE GOVERNOR OF
CORINTH, THEREIN TO ARREST THE WOMAN KNOWN AS
THEODOSIA VARRA.

SUCH ARREST TO BE PERFORMED IMMEDIATELY AND
WITH STEALTH, SO THAT NEITHER THE AFORENAMED PRISONER
NOR THE PROPERTY ON THE ESTATE SHALL
HAVE NOTICE AND SEEK TO ESCAPE.

Otho was telling the truth!
The familiar furnishings and frescoes...
The guard at the door...
The uniformed stranger before her...
All fused into one... a wash of crimson and green and gold and brass and bronze swimming before her eyes in a terrifying blur as she accepted as reality the one thing she feared most.
Beloved gods, they do know about Mother.
"I don't understand this at all," she said, trying to sound confident. "What am I accused of?"
The answer seemed an eternity in coming. Manus cleared his throat, passed his helmet from one hand to another, cleared his throat again, and shifted his weight in the chair before responding.
"Murder. You are accused of the murder of Gaius Terentius Varro."

CHAPTER TWENTY-ONE

"Murder?" Her laugh was real. "That's ridiculous!"

Manus did not smile.

"They're also investigating a separate claim that you are not the legitimate heir to the Terentius Varro properties."

"Not the legitimate heir? That's just as absurd as the other charge."

"The emperor has ordered an investigation."

"I am Theodosia Varra. I was born in this suite. My father gave me his family name, raised me in his house, and presented me to the world as his daughter. His only son is dead. If I'm not the legitimate heir, who is?"

"Unclaimed property passes to the emperor."

Of course. So what incentive has he to find in my favor?

"Centurion, do you know who brought these charges?"

"I am not authorized to discuss the case with you."

"Were you at the palace when the accusations were made?"

No answer.

"I have enemies," Theodosia went on. "I know who they are... or some of them, at least. It's true that my brother was murdered, but I didn't do it, and my right of inheritance is as solid as his was." She leaned forward. "Centurion Manus, please! Give me a chance to defend myself! Tell me who made these accusations!"

Manus looked around her sitting room. As his eyes lingered on the frescoes, the inlaid tables, the antique vases and chests, the mosaic floor, the cushioned chair, and the finely crafted lamps, Theodosia noticed—for the first time in months—just how sumptuously appointed it was.

"You are the obvious beneficiary of the crime."

"Yes, but... I wouldn't have killed Gaius for his property. There can't possibly be any evidence to implicate me."

"If the emperor considers the charges serious enough to arrest you, we must assume he has some evidence. Do you have records of the property that Gaius Terentius Varro owned?"

He's using no honorific, no family relationships, not even my name. Gods, have they already stripped away my status and my possessions? My very freedom?

"I'll search the villa," the centurion went on when Theodosia didn't respond promptly enough. "Question the slaves, if necessary. You do yourself and them no favor by refusing to answer."

"You'll find records for the last eight or nine years in my library."

"Valuables?"

"Also in the library. In the strongbox."

She shuddered inside at the thought of what Manus might have found there... but for Alexander.

"And the key?"

"My steward keeps it. He's dedicated to me," she said, hoping to excuse any resistance on Alexander's part. "He may not cooperate."

"He'll cooperate." Manus stood. "You're confined to this apartment until further notice. The emperor wants you isolated, under guard night and day. No visitors. No servants. No physician."

Theodosia began to protest, but Manus cut her off.

"Be thankful His Majesty is so kind. He could have ordered you held in the Carcer Tullianum while the investigation is carried out."

For the first time, Theodosia realized the full extent of her peril. Years before, in the Subura, she had seen an obdurate slave—jaded by years of abuse—cowed into obedience by the simple threat of being sent to the Carcer Tullianum... the most dreaded of imperial prisons.

"Oh," Manus said, "I'm about to forget. Caesar claims that signet you're wearing. To authenticate certain documents."

They found a duplicate bill of sale.

Trapped in the chair with Manus looming over her, Theodosia could do nothing but acquiesce. She slipped the family ring off her finger, studied it briefly, and deposited it into his open palm.

Theodosia saw only common soldiers for five days. They brought her food, carried her from her bed to the cushioned chair, helped her dress and use her chamber pot. Some turned their heads to give her privacy. Others winked and grinned as they watched.

Her house was obviously the finest any of them had ever seen. A few decorative bedroom items disappeared, but she said nothing, hoping that would dispose them to treat her well. The only thing she made an effort to tuck away was Lucilla's ruby-serpent amulet, which she buried as far under her mattress as she could reach.

It was an illiterate but talkative Sicilian named Cyrus—who reeked of garlic and fish sauce—whom she chose to cast a spell on. He was rude and rough but willing to make a few inquiries for the prisoner who had charmed him.

From Cyrus she learned that Manus had sent the oldest servants —Milo, Jason, and half a dozen others from her father's time—to Rome to be questioned about Theodosia's claim on the estate. She winced at the news. Questioning, for a slave, meant torture. Always.

"They're gonna question 'em 'bout how Aulus Terentius Varro treated that woman he brung with him from Greece."

"'That woman' was my mother!"

"Guess that's the point, ain't it?"

"But slaves can't be forced to testify against their owner. It's the law. Since I'm their owner, how can they be forced to testify against my interests?"

"Guess the emperor's legal advisors found a way 'round it."

Of course.

"Which way around it?"

"Well… best I can figger it, the investigators bought them slaves off you, so now they kin do anything they want to 'em."

"How can they buy slaves from me without my knowledge or consent?"

And how could they pull that off without Lucius Gallio's knowledge or consent? He's Emperor Claudius' main legal advisor, but he's also my friend and Flavia's husband. He'd never let them do that to me.

"Beats me. But don't you go complaining 'bout it to the centurion. Just git me in trouble for telling you."

"Do you know if I got paid in this transaction?"

"I hear they credited some money to the estate."

"Oh, how clever! So… when the emperor winds up with my property, there's no need of payment, and if by some chance they find me innocent, they'll just cancel the credit when they 'sell' them back to me."

"'Course… if them slaves git broke up, they ain't gonna be worth much when the investigators sell 'em back to you. You're gonna lose there, lady, no matter how it turns out."

Stunned by the unfairness of it all, Theodosia wrapped her arms across her chest and rocked in the chair. She knew the elderly slaves would "remember" whatever the torturers wanted them to.

As the week progressed, Cyrus told her of other developments.

One of the Greeks had been reclaimed by his former master, who had ridden out from Rome with an imperial order allowing him to remove the slave. By now, Cyrus added with a wink, the pretty fellow would be cozily restored to his old master's affections.

Remembering her promise that Marcipor would never fall into Otho's hands again, Theodosia clenched her fists and choked back tears of remorse and frustration.

There had been a few problems, Cyrus reported. A couple of houseboys were flogged the first afternoon... mostly as an example to the rest. Cyrus grew even more verbose than usual in describing the scene, as if certain it would amuse Theodosia. Though revolted at the joy he took in every gruesome detail, she still managed to reward him with a smile.

Anything to keep him talking.

Her steward, chuckled Cyrus the next day, had declined to produce the key to the strongbox, but a bit of clubbing on the shoulders had persuaded him. Then he was caught sneaking some sheets of writing out of a cubicle near the back door of the villa. The soldiers couldn't read, so they just tossed the sheets into a campfire. For resisting, the Greek had been confined to the supply tent, chained to the center post. They planned to let him out for Saturnalia, though, the Sicilian assured her.

None of this troubled her smelly guard, and Theodosia tried to keep her distress to herself. The morning of the Ides, however, she could no longer hide it.

Cyrus came in with a report of discontent among the legionaries.

"When we got here, we found only three young female slaves on the whole place. Manus tossed 'em into a tent that first night and let us at 'em. Nobody got enough, of course, long as it's been for most of us, but he said we'd git 'nother chance the next night."

Three young female slaves. Etrusca, Lucilla, and... who else?

Then she remembered.

Rila, the goatherd's daughter.

Theodosia convulsed in horror, but Cyrus didn't seem to notice.

"And then—as if having just three of 'em for a hundred of us wasn't bad enough—yesterday Manus hauls one to Rome for questioning. Big blonde bitch. Real hot duckie, too, and we only got two nights with her. Won't be much left of her once they git done interrogating. That meant we only had a couple of wenches last night... and one of 'em babbling on and on 'bout how she's pregnant."

Oh, Etrusca!

"Then, to top things off, when someone pulled a kid away from the pregnant one—couldn't stand it squalling in the tent, y'know—the crazy thing grabbed his sword and attacked him."

Cyrus turned a leering, yellow-toothed grin on his prisoner.

"Her death means there's only *two* young females left on the whole place."

Theodosia doubled over in her chair, covered her head with her arms, and wept for Lucilla, Etrusca, Rila... and herself.

"Have you ever loved someone you were powerless to protect?"

Alexander's haunting question kept running through Theodosia's head. Although she couldn't imagine what would happen to her, it wasn't hard to guess what the Fates had in store for those who had served her.

Stefan would go to the arena and die.

Alexander, Lycos, Dabini, Selicio, and all her other better-quality servants would be sold to new masters in Rome.

Nicanor would wind up back at the farm, mourning his beloved Etrusca and laboring under Nizzo's whip for whatever was left of his life.

Nizzo would find a way to possess her farm.

Someone else would buy her villa and the land around it.

The old goat in the imperial palace would keep the jewels and the mines and vineyards for himself and pocket the profits from the rest.

Not much I can do to save myself.

She had accepted that now.

But by Juno... I'll find some way to save the ones I love.

It was a dreary Saturnalia. Not a single ray of sunshine pierced the clouds to brighten her mood.

She spent the morning in bed pretending to be asleep, but actually finalizing a scheme to cheat the emperor just a bit. She had thought of little else for two days.

Getting access to papyrus, a reed-pen, and ink—the part she originally thought would be the hardest—had turned out to be easy.

Yesterday morning, she had persuaded Cyrus to bring writing materials from the library… on the pretext that she would teach him to write his name. They spent four hours side by side, bent over a table; by the time his shift ended, the Sicilian could scrawl not only his name but Theodosia's and his mother's as well. And when he departed—excited about his new literacy—he forgot to remove the things he had brought.

Taking advantage of the lull between shifts, Theodosia wrote a message in one corner of a papyrus sheet and blew on the ink to dry it. As the relief guards were coming in, she tore off the corner and dropped it down the front of her tunic. Later, she tucked the scrap under her mattress, alongside Lucilla's ruby-serpent amulet.

Silvanus and Vespillo, the soldiers assigned to the evening shift, always treated her better than the rest, so last night Theodosia had suggested that they bring an additional pair of silver cups and join her in a celebratory toast to Saturn. With Manus gone, his men were more relaxed, and the bored twosome had been delighted to sip good wine from elegant ruby-set goblets at their prisoner's bedside.

So now—as Cyrus and another guard planned their Saturnalian binge in her sitting room—Theodosia feigned sleep. Silver serving pieces from last night's dinner and toasts still sat on the chest beside her bed, with others brought in for her breakfast.

Occasionally, Cyrus came to check on the prisoner.

Whenever she heard his footsteps, Theodosia froze under her covers. Whenever she heard the door close, she went back to work.

Just before noon, she finished. Her fingernails were shredded to the quick, but she grinned with exultation. The long, draping blanket hid the pile of nine defaced silver vessels under the bed. The nine fat rubies that she had pried out of the serpents' mouths lay clustered under her pillow, along with five small ones that she had managed to pop out of their eyes.

Keeping watch on the door, she ripped off a strip of blanket. The rubies clicked as she nestled them into one end and wrapped the fabric around them until it was halfway used. She took Lucilla's twisted-serpent amulet from under the mattress and added it to the rubies. Next, she wrapped the remaining length of the strip around and around and tucked in the end. The bundle seemed too flimsy, so she tore off a second strip of blanket, wound its length snugly around the first, and tied the ends.

Finally, Theodosia tossed the improvised pouch in her hand. There was no tell-tale rattle as she slipped it into her tunic beside the papyrus scrap she had written on yesterday.

The kindly evening guards, Silvanus and Vespillo, came on duty at twilight and carried Theodosia to her chair on the balcony.

"They're building a bonfire beside the sea," Vespillo said. "You'll have a good view from here."

Silvanus returned to the balcony with a large, heavy military blanket. Theodosia thanked him prettily and snuggled under it from toes to chin.

"Won't you join me?" she asked as the men headed to their post by the door. "Why should you be the only ones stuck inside tonight?"

Vespillo glanced at Silvanus, who was older and in charge. Silvanus thought a bit, then shrugged.

"Why not? It's a holiday, after all."

"Too bad the clouds are so heavy," Vespillo said as he stood beside Theodosia. "We'd see everything much better if the moon was out."

"Such a shame!" But she smiled to herself.

As always, Juno is my best ally.

"Do you build bonfires, Vespillo, when you're home for Saturnalia?"

"Sure. We've only got three slaves to work the fields with my father, but tonight they'll be the kings of the harvest. Father and my sisters should be serving 'em dinner about now." He sighed. "I ain't been home for Saturnalia in years."

"Where's home?"

"Arretium. Just this side of the Apennines."

"So... you're an Umbrian! And you, sir?"

"From Tarentum, in the south," Silvanus said. "Too poor to have land or slaves. Me and my oldest son are both in the army. My wife and younger children live off our wages. Ain't much of a life."

"How many children do you have?"

"Seven living. The youngest is just five. Four dead."

"It must be wonderful having children." Theodosia gave a short, sad chuckle. "I've always wanted them, but now it just doesn't seem like..."

She let her words trail off.

There was silence, broken only by the loud crackle of the bonfire as it flared up and the laughter of the men around it. After a while, Theodosia picked up her theme again, letting a catch creep into her voice.

"The closest thing I've ever had to a child of my own is a slave boy here at the villa. Lycos. He's such a sweet little fellow." She raised her eyes, hoping the light from the lamps inside would catch the tears in her eyes. "Have either of you seen him around?"

"Ain't many children here," Silvanus said. "I only seen one, to tell you the truth. Good-looking lad?"

"Beautiful!" She gave him a broad smile.

"Sure, I know him. He's made friends with everyone."

"Lycos would. But I was afraid they wouldn't let him out to play."

"Oh, he plays all right. Runs all over the place. Nobody worries about a lad that age."

"Thank the gods."

Thank the gods!

She sat silently, watching the noisy crowd along the shore.

Poor Nicanor. He must be devastated. And poor Rila... all alone now at the mercy of so many drunken— No! Don't get distracted!

There was too much left to do tonight.

A bit later, she looked at the older guard.

"I was just wondering— Any chance I could—" Breaking off, she shook her head, as if too timid to ask, and dropped her eyes.

"Could do what, lady?" asked Silvanus.

Full of hope, Theodosia raised her eyes again, making sure they were as soft and liquid as possible.

"Oh, you know... just see Lycos for a moment or two. I understand you're not supposed to let anybody in, but... it's Saturnalia... and..."

Vespillo took a step forward.

"I could find the boy, sir, and bring him up for a visit. Everybody's busy celebrating. Nobody's gonna know."

Silvanus shook his head.

"Better not. It's too risky."

"Oh, please, sir! With everything I've got ahead of me..."

The legionary exhaled loudly. Finally, he nodded.

"Well, all right." He turned to his younger colleague. "Be careful. Everyone knows you're supposed to be guarding the prisoner tonight."

Vespillo grinned, saluted, and moved to the door.

"Hope it don't take him too long," Silvanus said. "I could lose my head for disobeying orders."

"The gods will reward you, sir." She raised her right hand to her throat. "Oh, I'm so thirsty. Bet you are, too! How about some more of that wine you liked so much last night?"

Silvanus brightened and headed for the pitcher and cups that sat waiting on a table inside.

Completely enveloped in the blanket, Theodosia reached into the front of her tunic and pulled out the pouch full of rubies. Then, without hesitation, she leaned forward and dropped it through the balcony railing into the acanthus bushes below.

◇ ◇ ◇

Rubbing his wrists and flexing his shoulders, Alexander left the tent where he had been confined for days and joined a group of slaves heading for the bonfire dedicated to Saturn.

"A good night of freedom to you all!" said a passing soldier who was clearly far down the path to oblivion in wine.

The harvest festivities were well under way. Slaves mingled and drank and joked with soldiers inclined by tradition to tolerate their insolence on this topsy-turvy night. Two houseboys were casting verbal abuse on the legionary who had flogged them. Alexander stopped to listen and tried to laugh with the others.

How can they be so unconcerned about their fate?

Glancing around, he spotted Stefan's bulky shape on the opposite side of the fire and elbowed his way toward him.

Stefan broke into a big smile when he saw Alexander.

"We thought you was dead. Lycos cried for hours till someone told us they'd just locked you up."

"Parts of me *are* dead." Alexander gingerly patted his black-and-blue shoulders. "Where is Lycos?"

"Don't know. A soldier came for him."

"What for?"

"You think they'd tell me?"

Alexander glanced toward the house and caught his breath. Theodosia was sitting on her balcony, silhouetted against the brightly lit room behind her. Two legionaries flanked her chair.

"Is she all right?"

Stefan shrugged.

"Nobody's talked to her for almost a week."

"Not even Timon?"

"Timon's gone. Lady Flavia came one day, but the soldiers wouldn't let her in. She begged them to give Timon a chance to check Theodosia's legs once more, but they refused... so she took him home with her."

"Timon's lucky to belong to Vespasian. Looks like the rest of us may soon be at the emperor's disposal."

"You heard about Marcipor?"

Alexander shook his head.

"Otho got him back. I sure wouldn't want to be him right now. Heard about Lucilla and Etrusca?"

Alexander hadn't, so Stefan told him.

"Poor Rila's getting it bad these days. Real shame, too. She was a honey. Won't be fit for nothing but a cheap whorehouse when they're done with her."

It was all too much to learn at once. Alexander knelt on the ground and retched. Had there been anything in his stomach, he would have thrown up.

He was still there—head in his hands and thoroughly miserable—when he heard an excited voice calling his name. He looked around, then swept Lycos into his arms and pressed him tightly.

"I was so afraid they'd kill you!" Lycos sobbed, burying his face in Alexander's neck.

The pressure on his bruised shoulders hurt, but he held Lycos until the tears subsided.

"Where did the soldier take you?"

Lycos pointed to the balcony.

"You saw the mistress?"

"The man said she asked to see me."

"And they let her?"

Alexander and Stefan exchanged amazed looks.

Maybe things aren't so dire, after all.

Alexander lowered his voice.

"I'd been thinking that the three of us should try to escape tonight, but maybe it's not—" He turned to Lycos and switched into Greek. "How did she look?"

More than anything else, he needed to know that Theodosia was not being mistreated.

"All right."

"Did she say anything to you?"

"Not much. She hugged me. She never did that before."

"She was glad to see you."

"She took me on her lap. I was real careful not to kick her legs! And she talked to me in Latin."

"She didn't want the soldiers to think she was telling you secrets."

Lycos nodded soberly, then his eyes brightened.

"I could see the fire from up there. It was pretty! Then, one time when the guards weren't watching, the mistress dropped something down the front of my tunic." He pulled out a folded scrap of papyrus. "I don't think she wanted them to see it."

Alexander closed his hand around the scrap and looked about. Nobody but Stefan was watching him.

"She mentioned you, too," whispered Lycos. "She said, 'Give my regards to Alexander.' Then she patted my chest and said it again. 'My regards to Alexander. To Alexander.' It was weird!"

Alexander stood and lifted Lycos into Stefan's arms.

"Create some distraction," he said in Latin.

Stefan tossed Lycos into the air, then swung him to his shoulders for a lofty gallop through the crowd. The soldiers poked each other and grinned as Lycos squealed in delight.

Alexander sat down on a rock facing the sea and unfolded the scrap close to his body. Shifting sideways to catch some light from the fire, he strained to make out the message.

BAG UNDER BALCONY. SEND L.

LEAVE TONIGHT WITH L. & S.

OBEY ME.

Alexander crumpled the scrap of papyrus and rose to his feet. Without a word, he stepped to the fire and tossed the tiny wad into the center. It popped and flamed and disappeared.

Stefan and Lycos came galloping around.

"Hey," Alexander called. "I heard a good joke."

Together they sat on the rock. Under his breath, Alexander repeated the message. On cue, the others laughed.

"It's a dangerous venture she's proposing for us," Alexander said. "How brave do you two feel?"

"Brave enough," said Stefan.

"Me too," said Lycos.

"Good."

Neither of you has the slightest idea what we're getting into.

"So, now... how do we go about doing this?"

By the time the revelers—soldiers and slaves alike—had polished off their second enormous wineskin, Alexander and Stefan and Dabini and Selicio and a dozen others, their arms linked in drunken camaraderie, had begun snaking through the crowd. Memories of past revelries kicked in. Everybody knew the popular snake-line dance.

Lycos ran back and forth in crazy circles, dashing in and out between the men, shrieking with joy.

From his place at the front of the line, Alexander caught sight of Stefan... merrily waving his arm at the rear of the string and urging others to come and salute the mistress.

"C'mon, ever'body! Godda greed our lady!" Stefan cried. "Godda give 'er Saddurn's comp-lents!"

"Saddurn, hell!" yelled Dabini, who had been drinking heavily. "Godda give 'er *our* comp-lents!"

Dabini stumbled on the uneven ground and cursed, provoking a reproach from the less-tipsy Selicio behind him.

One by one they joined up... until the snake line numbered about sixty, all of them slaves.

Soon afterwards, Alexander led the swaying, singing, staggering group through the garden, where they whooped and mocked the besotted soldiers sprawled around the fountain and in the pergola. Half a dozen sober, heavily armed legionaries on duty near the house closed ranks as the rowdy slaves approached, eyeing them with suspicion.

"What's this all about?" The soldier pointed his spear at Alexander.

Alexander swept his arm in an expansive gesture and swayed on his feet at the movement.

"Godda greed our lady," he mumbled, pointing unsteadily toward the balcony where Theodosia sat between her guards. "Up there. What'sa madder, ossifer? Don'cha see 'er?"

"No one goes near the house! Get back, all of you."

"Aaaaaaaaw! Don'cha know we're free tonight? Saddurnalia! Godda greed our lady!"

With a giddy chortle, Alexander casually knocked the spear aside and lurched toward the balcony, tugging the man behind him to do the same. Lycos skipped on ahead, unobserved in the confusion.

Apparently, the guards decided it would be easier to let the mass of inebriated slaves go ahead and greet their lady than try to contain them, for they offered no resistance and followed the line with their torches.

Alexander pushed ahead until he and the entire group stood squarely in front of Theodosia's balcony. From his spot in the center, he grinned up at her astonished face, raised his hand to his forehead in an intoxicated salute, and bowed with a deep, wobbly flourish.

"Greedings from Saddurn, mis-dress!" he shouted.

Others around him were performing similar noisy obeisance, their incomprehensible shouts mingling with the guffaws of the soldiers.

Meanwhile, Lycos darted in and out of the bushes in the shadows beneath the balcony.

Rising from his exaggerated bow, Alexander lifted his eyes again. The glow from the soldiers' torches illuminated Theodosia's face. Her forehead was furrowed, her eyebrows knitted together, her hands clasped and pressing on her lips... a look of amusement combined with stress.

She leaned toward the railing and grasped the bars with both hands.

"This is forbidden," insisted a guard on the balcony.

Theodosia turned her head and gave him her widest smile.

Alexander stared at her, as amazed as ever at her spirit.

Zeus! Is she manipulating them!

"I know, sir," she said, "but even you must admit... it's funny! Don't worry, I'll make sure they leave right away."

The forced smile vanished from her face as she turned her eyes to the slaves on the ground.

"The gods be with you all."

Lots of tension in her voice.

"Now, you must go." Theodosia stretched one arm toward Alexander and made that familiar flicking gesture with her fingers. "Be gone!"

Alexander bowed, then straightened to look at Theodosia once more.

I'll never see her again.

Through the bars, her eyes bore into his. She gave him another impatient wave.

"Be gone, fellow!"

He held her eyes as long as he dared.

"We will obey you, miss," he said, no longer bothering to sound drunk, "and may all the gracious gods of Greece watch over you."

PART III

A.D. 54 TO 56

CHAPTER TWENTY-TWO

Theodosia opened her eyes in the darkness and—with a curse—lifted herself on one elbow. Rainwater racing its usual course to the Tiber River sloshed into the jagged fissure high above her head. Through the crack, she saw a yellow-white flash of lightning. The earth rumbled as a rush inside the Cloaca Maxima echoed through the solid-rock walls.

As always when she awoke, she gagged at the foul ooze seeping through those walls from the gigantic sewer that hustled its egalitarian mix of patrician, plebeian, foreign, and slave wastes toward the Tiber. Now, with this torrent, the stench from the Cloaca was even worse.

She sat up and pushed back as far as she could from the splashing water. Sharp edges sank into her palms and added another rip to her ragged tunic. The walls dripped steadily, summer and winter, but the floor rose on one side, so it stayed a bit drier. Propped against the wall, she hugged her right knee to her chest, pulled the new blanket around her shoulders, and tossed the old one over her inflexible left leg.

A fine way to start a reign. The gods grant our beloved emperor joy in his moment of glory.

On an ordinary day, a prisoner in the cave cells below the Carcer Tullianum would know nothing about goings-on in Rome, despite the fact that the busiest part of the imperial capital spread out around and above it. But today was no ordinary day. The whole city would turn out this October morning, rain or shine, to watch the new emperor ride in his chariot down the Via Sacra, on his way to address the Senate in the Curia.

"If you're lucky," the guard had remarked yesterday when he tossed in the blanket that was her gift from this latest Caesar, "you'll be able to hear Nero's procession as it moves through the Forum."

"Such luck," she had retorted, "is more than I'd dare hope for."

209

So... old Claudius was gone at last. No doubt the corrupt freedmen who had run his palace for years were scrambling to ingratiate themselves with their new lord. Now Otho would have even more of the power he craved, though Theodosia knew that would do her no good. Her only reasons for hope were Vespasian and Lucius Gallio.

If they're still my friends—if they ever were my friends—this is the time for them to plead my case with Nero.

New emperors generally liked to right the wrongs of their predecessors. It made them look good by comparison.

There were other reasons to hope that Nero might be benevolent. Seneca, his long-time tutor, was one of the most humane men of the century; if anyone could soften the imperial urge to tyranny, it was Seneca. Burrus, prefect of the Praetorian Guards—also respected by the prince—had often spoken out against injustice. And Nero took an interest in artists and musicians, for he fancied himself one of them.

Theodosia prayed he would remember her, too, as one of them.

She closed her eyes and tried to recall the repulsive young man she'd met that September morning in Rome. Thirteen months ago, she had chatted with Nero and promised to perform at his palace.

Instead, she was rotting away in his prison.

The dreadful reputation of the Carcer Tullianum was not exaggerated. Built five hundred years earlier, when Rome was a cluster of villages in the hills, it had become the primary place of interrogation, torture, and patrician execution—by strangulation in Caligula's time—and a dumping ground for anyone the emperor wanted to make disappear.

The prison sat atop and alongside the sewer built to drain water from the once-swampy Forum. Nowadays, in addition to carrying feces and stormwater to the river, the Cloaca served as a convenient disposal system for those who died in the Carcer. Its putrid odor permeated the cell where Theodosia lay.

At first, the stench had made her vomit, which did nothing to improve the quality of her accommodations. She kept almost no food down for weeks, and soon she suffered from dysentery.

Although she felt lucky to have that overhead crack for a modicum of light and fresh air—and a tiny, blessed view of the sky—it was so high and narrow that little but rain reached her.

Eventually, neither the smells nor the tepid mush and abominable water that she received once a day seemed quite as bad as she first thought. A few things actually improved as the months passed. She no longer noticed the stink of her own body. Nor did her scalp itch so badly.

She scarcely remembered her last bath in that steaming pool at home, but at least she had stopped dreaming about it. Her monthly cycle dried up, and she was grateful for that. She had no way to cope with the bleeding.

Below ground that winter, she had battled chills and fever. Dysentery kept her doubled up for days. Memories of home—wildflowers in the meadows, rides in the hills, new leaves in the pergola—tormented her all spring. With summer came new miseries: stifling heat, mosquitoes, fear of plague. Autumn, with its never-ending rains, brought no relief.

Theodosia had now spent ten months in a hopeless, lifeless void.

Seeking relief from the throbbing in her legs, she wadded the old blanket and thrust it under her twisted left knee. Her joints ached from the dampness, but she knew much of her suffering was self-induced.

Determined to *walk* out of the Carcer Tullianum if given the chance, she had counted sunrises through the crack above to calculate the end of her first month of imprisonment. Near the end of January, she removed the splints from both legs. With jaws clenched, she pushed herself to the corner, braced on her palms, and hoisted herself to her feet.

Fire raced through her wasted muscles. She collapsed, rasping her arms and elbows against the walls and landing badly on the stone floor. Screaming in pain and self-pity, she sobbed for an hour.

But she tried again that day and again the next, again and again and again until every surface of her body was scraped and bruised. Each collapse brought rage—at herself, at the world, at the gods—but gradually she found herself growing in strength and muscular control.

Her original goal was simply to stand. That took a month.

Then she began to count the duration of the support her right leg alone gave her. When she reached one hundred, she switched her weight to the left leg. The fall that resulted stripped the skin from an elbow, but she stood up and repeated the right-leg-left-leg drill. Over and over again. Days later—when it seemed she had no more skin to lose—the left leg held to a count of ten. When that count reached one hundred, she set her goal at a single step, then two. When two were steady, she aimed at four.

All told, it had taken four months—and thirty-two painful steps—to round the corners of the cell and make it back to her starting place. Theodosia had never known such pride of accomplishment.

By midsummer, she was up to two trips. By October, she could make three... shaky though the last dozen steps were. She had no idea how long it would take to get to four trips, but time appeared to be sadly abundant.

The effort to walk gave her something to live for.

Someday, I'll walk out of this hellhole!

Crouched now in the corner of her hellhole, she heard a scurrying sound. Without hesitation, she shoved the remains of yesterday's mush toward the mouse. A bit of the dried-up stuff was fair trade for company.

Her hungry companion hadn't always been so welcome. Theodosia remembered that late-December night when the soldiers had carried her to this cell and dumped her on the floor. The icy draft from the cleft in the rock instantly penetrated to her bones, unimpeded by the light tunic she'd been wearing when they hustled her out of her villa earlier that day. The shred of blanket left by a predecessor in the cell provided little warmth, and the stench—far worse than what had sickened her in Nizzo's slave barracks—brought up the remnants of her last breakfast at home.

Panic hit her hard as they slammed the door, leaving her in darkness.

Then she had heard the scurrying. Terrified, she pushed backwards with all her strength until she hit the wall. But the tiny creature left, and came and left again, and gradually she began to welcome his visits.

Take your friends where and as you find them.

Thoughts of friends—or home—led to tormenting questions.

Who's living in my villa now?

Is the family of slaves still mostly intact?

Alexander, Stefan, and Lycos… did they get away?

That last question bedeviled her more than any other. Her rubies could have bought them safe passage out of Italy, helped Alexander find Antibe and Niko, and built new lives in a secure hiding place. But it was just as likely that the jewels had ended up in a legionary's gunny sack and the runaways in the clutches of some corrupt palace freedman. Theodosia feared she'd never learn the answer.

She also knew it was ridiculous to worry about others when she still didn't know what her own status was. Most likely, old Claudius had simply declared her guilty and seized her property.

But…

Was she condemned for Gaius' murder?

For impersonating a Roman?

For false claims of inheritance?

Did they know her mother was a slave?

What were those documents that Centurion Manus had said needed authenticating?

Nobody ever bothered to tell her.

The nine defaced silver vessels had been discovered the day after Saturnalia. Three slaves went missing about the same time. Manus returned from Rome in a foul temper and interrogated Theodosia.

She admitted digging out the rubies, refused to say what she had done with them, and was intimately—and humiliatingly—searched by Manus.

That night, she prayed that Silvanus and Vitello would escape punishment for their laxity with her, but she sought no divine intercession for Cyrus, the lecherous Sicilian.

The next morning, the soldiers deposited her—splints and all—in an army cart and hauled her away to the Carcer Tullianum.

At first, she assumed it was temporary. They'd soon take her out for questioning, for trial, for execution. But nothing happened. Theodosia just lay in her cell, waiting and wondering.

The tongueless slave who came once a day to bring food and remove her waste bucket could say nothing. The guard who unlocked the door was equally unresponsive. Only the death and accession of emperors seemed to make him talk.

Now, huddled under her blanket, she reviewed—again—everything that might have condemned her. It was a game she couldn't stop playing.

Maybe Claudius' freedmen—anxious to please their patron—had discovered new "facts" in Gaius' murder. The old goat wouldn't have troubled himself to dig for the truth if the imperial purse, always short of funds, stood to be fattened so spectacularly. Theodosia wouldn't be the first rich Roman brought down by an emperor's greed.

Maybe Otho—angry at her rejection—had accused her himself. By custom, anyone who contributed to the emperor's enrichment was entitled to a share of the wealth. The benefits of accusing Theodosia might have proven tempting even to someone with more scruples than Otho.

Maybe some of the slaves in Gaius' mansion in Rome—bargaining for their freedom—had turned up "evidence" of the mistress' complicity in their master's death.

Maybe Lucilla and the elderly slaves—desperate to stop the torture in that infamous lower level of the Carcer Tullianum—had flat-out lied.

Maybe... Maybe... Maybe...

Theodosia had plowed this ground for months, always ending with the same cry: "Tell me the charges! Tell me who brought them!"

Shivering, she gritted her teeth and—

Nizzo! Of course! And the bastard even had the gall to warn me!

She had thought of him often since Otho told her he was spreading rumors about her. Now the name hit with the power of summer lightning.

Aloud, she repeated Nizzo's taunting couplet.

"The sad fate of the brother will soon come to the sister."

In an instant, all the pieces of the puzzle fell into place.

Nizzo had everything: motivation, credibility, access to information, and—according to both Otho and Alexander—powerful friends.

Nizzo had motivation.

He was ambitious. He wanted to own that farm.

Nizzo had credibility.

Father freed him, made him a citizen, and gave him his name... plus a good income, responsibility, and respectability. Who would believe that someone could lie about the daughter of such a kind patron?

Nizzo had access to information.

He always acted as if he knew everything about me. Maybe he did!

Nizzo had powerful friends.

All those influential palace freedmen... What was it Alexander told me? "Antagonize Nizzo and you'll have more enemies than you can imagine." Well, he was right. I antagonized Nizzo, and now I can't even begin to imagine who all my enemies are.

Nizzo's words taunted her.

"That's exactly what your brother said a month ago, last time I proposed the deal to him."

That simple statement of fact echoed in Theodosia's head as her fingers dug into her bony arms.

I once guessed that Nizzo had murdered Gaius. Alexander didn't think so, but... Gaius refused to sell to Nizzo, and Gaius died. I refused to sell to Nizzo, and I'm all but dead. Coincidence or cunning?

The more she thought about it, the less coincidental it seemed.

Rain was still splashing onto the floor hours later when Theodosia heard footsteps and jangling keys at the far end of the corridor. Finally, her creaky door swung open.

The guard glanced toward the corner where Theodosia lay, as the mute slave shuffled in with the bowl of mush and chunk of bread that were her daily rations. He dipped a gourd in a bucket of water and held it while she drank.

For months, Theodosia had tried to make one-sided conversation with this slave. But his eyes never rose to her face, and his grunts ultimately discouraged her. Now he picked up the pot of her waste, dumped it into his cart, and tossed it back at her.

"Nero decided to forego the procession this morning," the guard said as he closed the door. "Just too wet. Guess you'll have to wait for the next emperor."

The Greek merchantman *Arsinoe* weighed anchor at dawn on a crisp October morning, oblivious to the money-lust sweeping the port of Itanus, where hucksters of wines and sweets and sex had begun battling for position in the gritty alleyways alongside the waterfront. Their cries floated through the mist and dissolved among the bells of a dozen boats contesting the central channel of the harbor. Equally frenzied were the preparations going on in the bars and brothels near the wharves, where stomping squads of soldiers were already patrolling in preparation for a week of no-holds-barred carousing.

Even the seabirds seemed to screech more exuberantly this morning as they soared and dipped in search of fish.

This was a big day in faraway Rome... and little Itanus intended to be a full partner in the celebration. It wasn't often that the world acquired a new master. Hopes were high for this latest Caesar.

A fleet of Roman warships had sailed into port last night, docking around the merchantman that rode low in the water by the third pier. Their crews—held on board till morning to prevent trouble—swarmed over the decks now, shouting their enthusiasm for five days on shore and scrambling down the rope ladders to the dinghies bobbing below.

It was a good time for a fugitive to leave, although this eastern tip of Crete was a long way—in miles and months and memories—from Rome.

Watching the Roman ruckus from the upper deck of the departing *Arsinoe*, Alexander smoothed his new white wool cloak with the self-confidence of the prosperous merchant he professed to be and wished he could know he was hearing Latin for the last time.

Tempted ashore in hopes of a hot bath and clean clothes, he had just spent two nervous nights in an overcrowded inn three blocks from the water's edge, happy to share a tiny room with a pair of unwashed muleteers if it let him avoid the legionaries in the more spacious quarters.

It was comforting to be back aboard the ship that had brought him from the coast north of Athens. Roman naval commanders were used to Greek ships in these waters. They ignored the *Arsinoe*... to Alexander's great relief.

If I never saw another Roman again, that'd be soon enough.

Such a miracle wasn't likely to happen, of course. There would be as many Romans to elude in Antioch as in Athens or Itanus or any other enslaved city.

The *Arsinoe's* bandy-legged Peloponnese captain began shouting orders to his men as they hoisted the anchors and clambered up the high riggings. Alexander turned to watch as first the square sail, then the triangular topsail, unfurled, flapped with all the joy of a sailor on leave, and snapped, white and crisp, in the wind. Movement was instantaneous.

He leaned on the starboard rail, relishing the roll of the waves and the salt-sting of the bracing air. Sailing this way was a pleasure.

The memory of that other sea voyage he had made a decade earlier—chained to the floor in the stinking bowels of a prison ship bound for Rome—was another advocate of caution. Prisons were closely linked to Romans in his mind. He had to avoid the latter to avoid the former.

Once the *Arsinoe* had cleared the other ships in the harbor, the skipper joined his only passenger at the railing.

"Sorry you're not staying around for the fun?" Captain Andros said in Greek, his brown face crinkling around the eyes. "Every soldier and sailor and strumpet in town will be on the waterfront tonight."

"And miss a ride on the best ship sailing the Aegean? Wouldn't think of it! Besides, my business won't wait. I've come too far to get my hands on those stones to let someone beat me to them."

"Well, if they're half as nice as that ruby you showed me in Eretria, I don't doubt you're onto a good thing."

"They'll be good. My contact in Antioch knows what sells in Rome." Alexander peered into the fog. "Still say we'll make port by next week?"

"Guaranteed. Soon as we clear the islands, the rest of the run's easy. One quick stop in Cyprus and we're there. You do business in Rome?"

"I've spent some time there."

Too much time there.

"Actually, my partner is better at dealing with Romans."

"You're not crazy about Romans?" Captain Andros grinned.

"I prefer to leave them to him. I'm better at sniffing out the gems."

There was a crash in the underdeck of the ship. Andros hurried to the ladder and disappeared into the hold.

Alexander turned to watch the port fade into the mist.

So, it's almost over.

It had been a difficult journey.

First, the winter... an arduous trek on foot for three unarmed, poorly clad, easily identifiable, runaway slaves. They had slipped away that chaotic December night—with nothing but Theodosia's pouch and the clothes they were wearing—and followed the Mignone River past the very spot where Theodosia and her filly had fallen over the cliff, and on through the densely wooded Tolfa Mountains.

For two weeks, they headed across the snow-covered Apennines, skirting the towns and crossing the roads at night to avoid challenge. They became proficient at trapping rabbits for food and fur, but finding dry wood for fires was harder. Exposure took a toll on their strength.

Ten days into the escape, Lycos developed chills and a fever. Alexander and Stefan took turns bundling him under their tunics, holding him close to their chests for warmth. It was a chore neither man resented, but it did slow them down, so it wasn't hard to decide to risk a week in an abandoned mountain cottage, nursing Lycos and their blistered feet.

The hut proved to be a treasure trove of firewood and old blankets, from which they fashioned capes and wraps for their hands, feet, and legs.

When Lycos was better, they reluctantly left the cottage, resisting the temptation to spend the rest of the winter there.

Begging at farms and trading two of Theodosia's little serpent-eye rubies in village markets for food, clothing, and sandals, they reached the northeast coast of Italy by mid March. Just outside Altinum, a brown-spotted hound bit Stefan's left hand when he petted it. In compensation, the dog's owners took in the bedraggled trio and provided food and a dry barn for a second restorative week.

After that—with spring in the air—the trip over the cap of the Adriatic seemed easy. At Pola, they traded the last three little rubies for passages on a south-bound fishing boat to the island of Paxos. Once ashore on the craggy western shore of Epirus—surrounded by clumps of yellow toadflax and delicate white sea squill—Alexander and Lycos wept and danced and shouted for joy. They had made it home to Greece.

Then the summer... on foot across the mountains of Thessaly toward the coast, carefully shunning any place where Romans might spot them.

Near Eretria, drooping from eight months of foot travel, they found shelter in the home of a prosperous farmer who accepted their strange story of shipwreck and pirates and storms at sea without betraying the doubts he must have harbored.

Leios Bryaxis possessed a hundred hectares, twenty head of cattle, seven slaves, one wife, one mother-in-law, and three unmarried daughters... each of whom immediately assigned herself to mother Lycos and fixed on Stefan as the long-awaited man of her dreams.

Alexander leaned again on the railing of the *Arsinoe* and grinned as he contemplated Stefan's plight.

Iocaste was sixteen, taller than Alexander, and robust... with sturdy features, waist-long black hair that she loved to toss, and a lascivious look that sized up the newly arrived colossus as a fair match the instant she spotted him. Hestia and Euterpe were twins, a couple of years younger and smaller than Iocaste, but prettier and equally provocative.

217

Since the sisters had never been to the circus in Rome, never before had they seen a man put together quite like Stefan.

And he—for the first time in his life—didn't have enough arms to hold all the women vying for his eye. Suddenly, there were new problems to be solved. Alexander had said many prayers of thanks to Zeus that they were Stefan's problems, not his.

The two of them had divided eight of Theodosia's large rubies and sold the ninth to Bryaxis for cash to pay for their room and board and Alexander's traveling expenses. Lucilla's silver serpent amulet lay buried beneath an olive tree, with Stefan's four rubies.

Stefan, they had decided, would stay at the Bryaxis farm to help with the harvest. Lycos would stay to be mothered.

Standing now on the deck of the *Arsinoe* as it plowed the eastern waters of the Mediterranean, Alexander remembered the day he had left them to begin his quest alone. Stefan and Lycos had accompanied him to the port at Eretria. All three stood waiting at dockside as Captain Andros took on the last of his cargo.

"Sure you don't want us along?" Stefan asked, probably less in jest than he was trying to sound.

A gull shrieked behind Alexander. He turned toward it, glad for the chance to blink back the emotion welling up in his eyes.

"Hey, old friend," he said after a few moments, "don't lose your nerve now. Separating makes us less vulnerable and guarantees that you and Lycos—and your half of the rubies—will be safe. Besides... it looks like you'll be a slave owner yourself soon. You've just got to decide which daughter you want." He prodded Stefan's biceps. "Bryaxis will be overjoyed to have a hard-working son-in-law with a set of those. Think of the dowry!"

"It sure would make things easier if I could talk with 'em."

Lycos had been staring at Alexander with accusatory eyes. There was nothing new that Alexander could say to explain why he was leaving.

"Well, here's your translator." He ruffled the boy's hair and turned him around to face Stefan. "As perfect a little Cupid as you could want. Besides, you'll soon know enough Greek to get by. You'll do better at that without me around."

"Guess you're right. You always are." Stefan paused, sighed, and shook his head. "I just ain't sure how I'll manage without you after all these years." He reached out and gave Alexander a crushing hug. "Come back safe!"

CHAPTER TWENTY-THREE

"See that mountain?"

Alexander squinted at the purple shadow in the distance and nodded.

"Means your journey's almost over," Captain Andros said. "That's Mount Casius, at the mouth of the Orontes River. We'll make landfall by afternoon. Good thing, too. You'll catch the wind."

"To get us in, you mean?"

"To cool you off."

"In late October?"

"Mornings on the mainland, it's as hot as Rome in August, but the wind picks up around midday and blows clear through the night. Then it dies off till the next noon. Catching the wind will give you a chance to get used to the humidity before the place heats up tomorrow morning."

"Sounds lovely. Is Antioch right on the coast?"

The captain shook his head.

"Seaport is Seleucia Pieria. You'll have to take a barge upriver to the city. A good day's trip. Or rent a camel and make it in half a day."

"Camel?"

"Or a donkey, if you prefer."

"How 'bout a horse?"

"They'll spot you as an outsider right away."

"They'll do that anyway. People start speaking Greek as soon as they see me. Where should I seek lodging?"

"Best bet is to go up to Daphne. Otherwise, if you're staying in the area any time, you'll likely get caught in a donkey drowner."

Alexander frowned.

Donkey drowner?

"Look, I know I'm ignorant of Syrian customs, but…"

"Yeah, they're strange folk, but not that strange." Captain Andros laughed. "I'm talking about the winter rains. Water pours down Mount Silpius into the Orontes, and low parts flood. Everybody who's anybody at all lives up in Daphne."

"Lots of Romans there, I suppose."

"What do you think? Daphne's the most beautiful spot around... woods, villas, gardens, a splendid Temple of Apollo—"

"And more Romans that you can count."

"Of course. It belongs to them, after all. Why are you always so worried about Romans?"

"Not worried. Just curious. Never know where I'll find a buyer for those gems. Might save my partner a long trip to Rome."

Zamaris, a pasty-skinned scribe in a faded green robe and scuffed red sandals, regarded the visitor with disinterest. Two others in the dingy tent hunched over their writing tables once it became obvious that the Greek had nothing that needed transcribing.

"Slave dealers?" Zamaris' jowls jiggled as he discharged a wad of spittle onto the dirt floor. "Sure. There's dozens. They're everywhere."

"Please." Alexander tried not to show his impatience. "I was told you knew everyone in town and might point me in the right direction. I'm looking for a dealer who made at least one trip—maybe lots of trips—to Corinth nine or ten years ago."

"What's his name?"

"I was hoping you could tell me that."

"Then you start at one end of the market, near the bend of the river, and make your way up and down, back and forth, around and about," Zamaris' finger traced random loops in the air, "asking every dealer you come to. Sooner or later—if he's still in town—you'll find him."

"You couldn't suggest anyone who'd know more about it?"

With the scowl of a busy man who has endured one foolish request too many, Zamaris returned to his desk, lifted his reed-pen, and resumed scratching on the papyrus before him.

Recognizing futility when he saw it, Alexander stepped into the street. It was Levi, the Greek-speaking proprietor of the quiet inn deep in the Jewish quarter where Alexander had found lodging last night, who had suggested that he start his search with the Greek-speaking Zamaris. Now it seemed he had no choice but to go door to door, hoping for luck.

It was much too early for that miraculous afternoon wind to bring relief from the Antiochian furnace. Heat radiating from the paving stones blurred the corners of buildings and tents that sprawled along the river.

Despite the torrid air, Antioch was beginning to stir. An aroma of goats and lambs grilling in street-side cook shops had begun to engulf the old city. Boys with lamps jostled with men selling camels, donkeys, tents, and other merchandise. To Alexander's disappointment—for last night he had dreamed of spotting Antibe in the market—there were no women.

He turned into the warren of alleyways, elbowing his way into the throng with a watchful eye for soldiers. The market was a mass of multicolored burnooses; never in his life had he felt so out of place.

Both moved and repulsed by the open sores and empty eye socket of a beggar who plucked at his sleeve, he slipped a couple of coins into the man's grimy, four-fingered hand.

Immediately, he saw his mistake. Out of the crowd came a dozen more—lame, blind, diseased, unwashed, and lice-infested—who clung to his arms and tugged at his tunic... a smelly cloud that pursued him down the street, pleading in loud, incomprehensible whines. It was an ideal situation for one hoping to attract the attention of the Romans on patrol... not so good for a runaway slave desperate to avoid them.

It cost Alexander an hour to lose the malodorous swarm. Shaken, he ducked into a doorway and slumped on the step, willing himself to relax. He felt for the money belt strapped around his waist and let out a long sigh. The belt and his precious quartet of rubies were still there.

More cautious now, he worked his way through the crowd of shoppers and sellers and soldiers to the edge of the market, where the river took a wide turn around a stand of date palms, peering into the faces of all the young vendors he passed. He couldn't tell from their clothing which of them were slaves and which were free.

Would I know my Niko if I saw him?

It was agonizing to think he might be so close and yet not recognize his own son. And at thirteen, Niko couldn't be expected to identify the father he hadn't seen in a decade.

The scene at the riverside end of the commercial district was chaotic, but Alexander resolved to attempt a methodical search. Although Greek was still widely spoken in this former Greek colony, the signs were all in Arabic. Unable to read them, he stuck his head into every entryway... a weaver's shop, a sandal maker's shop, three bakeries, two oil dealers' tents, and a cluster of spice stalls whose aroma of cloves brought back memories he thought he had managed to forget.

Half an hour into his search, he came upon a slave trader's showroom. It was easy to spot, even if one couldn't read the letters overhead. A sentry holding four sharp-pointed spears stood outside... an unmistakable sign of the kind of business conducted within.

Alexander stepped through the door.

Another guard, equally prepared for trouble, waited just inside.

The merchandise to be sold—some forty men, women, and children of varied ages and origins—sprawled on the floor.

In the center of the room, a Syrian wearing a caftan of indigo blue lounged in a chair. In his hand, he held a short, braided-leather whip.

At sight of a customer, he smacked the whip against the arm of his chair. With bored precision, the merchandise rose... each one casting apprehensive glances at Alexander.

Antibe and Niko may have passed through here. And I might wind up someplace like this, too, if the Romans catch me.

The Syrian bestowed on Alexander the eager smile of a man who counts gold coins in his dreams.

"You are looking for a fine strong slave, are you not?" he said in stiff but acceptable Greek.

Despite his uneasiness, Alexander chuckled to himself.

They always do know where I'm from.

"Sabouni sells only the best," continued the dealer, thumping his chest with the stiff handle of his whip.

Alexander forced himself to look around the room.

"I can see that. But I buy only Greeks."

"I have Greeks."

Sabouni snapped his fingers at a stocky fellow. He was shorter than Alexander and younger, with a squarish head, ragged dark hair, and a cautiously resentful look that reminded Alexander of himself when he first arrived in Rome. His heavy-lidded eyes fixed on Alexander's face until he reached the center of the room. Then he blinked and let them fall.

"Pinax here comes from Salamis. Very quiet and obedient." Sabouni poked one of the slave's shoulders with the whip handle and turned him around for inspection. The handle rose again, lifting the long hair to show off a stout neck. "Very strong. Quick to learn, too."

He made a gesture with his hand. Without hesitation, Pinax bent and drew his tunic over his head. Then he stood with his back to Alexander, wearing only a loose cotton loincloth. Without waiting for Sabouni's command, Pinax flexed his muscles to show his strength. It was plain he had been through this before.

"No trace of the whip on this one," said the dealer, running his own whip handle along the slave's spine and into the loincloth, which he pulled down to expose the unscarred buttocks. "You want to see the rest?"

Embarrassed, but trying not to show it, Alexander shook his head. He had already seen more than he cared to, but it was important to look sincere and experienced. Failure to follow through at this point might make Sabouni suspicious, so he moved around for a frontal check, pushing up Pinax's lips to see his teeth and gums and pinching his skin... things he had seen Gaius do in the slave market in Rome. Of course, Gaius always insisted on seeing "the rest" before he bought.

"Quite nice, but... I was hoping to find a dealer who imports directly from Greece. I plan to buy several Greeks for my new household up in Daphne."

"I have others. Let me show you. Greeks!"

Half a dozen adults and three children came forward to form a scraggly row beside Pinax. Alexander found himself facing ten of his countrymen, forced to see more of them than he cared to and listen for an hour as the Syrian recited the virtues and skills and possible—though highly unlikely!—defects of each of the Greeks in his possession.

The irony of a runaway slave's being the target of such fervent salesmanship in a slave shop could have been amusing, but Alexander's growing frustration overwhelmed whatever perverse pleasure the situation might otherwise have given him.

At this pace, it'll take me a month to visit every slave shop in Antioch.

"They are all outstanding," he said when Sabouni finished praising the fertility of the woman at the end of the line.

How do I get out of this without giving myself away?

"I'm interested in those two." He pointed to Pinax and a taller man in the middle of the line. "I'll be making my final selection in a day or so, but first I want to see what else is available in town."

He turned toward the door, knowing Sabouni would follow.

"You will find none better!"

"In that case, I'll be back for sure. By the way," he said with a smile when they reached the street, "how long have you been traveling to Greece?"

"Oh, I pick up Greeks wherever I can. Lots of them come on the market when the Romans die or get transferred."

"Where in Greece do you go?"

"Oh, I never go to Greece myself. Too much bother."

"Doesn't anyone in Antioch bring them in directly?"

"Not that I know of. Most quality Greeks are taken straight to Rome." Sabouni scratched his nose. "There's only one local dealer who's ever gone to Greece, but that was years ago."

"What's his name?"

"Solteris. But he doesn't go there now."

"Where would I find him?"

"A few blocks up the street. But he won't have anything better than what I've just shown you."

"Then I'll be back." Alexander's smile was wider now, and genuine.

Maybe the hour wasn't wasted, after all.

Solteris was out of town.

"Know when he'll be back?" Alexander asked the guard at the door.

"You'll have to ask Xantho." The man gestured past dozens of slaves —lying or standing behind bars on one side of the windowless room—to a door in the rear. "Go on in if you're looking to buy."

White-haired and nearly toothless, with an enormous nose and two long black hairs sprouting from a mole on his forehead, Xantho was a retired camel dealer who minded the store when Solteris was out of town.

Alexander liked him immediately.

This is a decent fellow. A man I can trust. Maybe it's best to be honest from the start.

"I seek information, not to buy. I heard that Solteris goes to Greece."

"Used to. Have a seat."

Alexander hesitated before lowering himself into a chair.

How long before I feel comfortable doing this?

It had been hard to break the habits of freedom when he was first enslaved; now he was finding it hard to get them back. A decade since he had sat in the presence of free men... or spoken to them as an equal... or called them by name... He could manage it now with Greeks or Syrians or Jews, but what would happen if—when—he had to engage socially with a Roman? Would the emotional residue of slavery betray him?

Xantho offered his guest bowls of figs and soft white cheese, an odd round of flat Syrian bread, and a cup of date wine.

"Thanks." Alexander bit into a fig, savoring the burst of sweetness in his mouth. "I've heard Solteris is the only slave dealer in Antioch who's ever personally gone to Greece."

"Probably so."

"Any chance he got to Corinth?"

"Why're you interested in Corinth?"

"I'm from Corinth."

"You're looking for someone in particular?"

Xantho scooped a bit of cheese and worked it in his mouth for a few moments. Alexander watched his gray eyes as they watched him.

He'll help me if I tell him the truth.

"My wife and my son."

The gray eyes revealed no surprise.

"We were separated almost ten years ago. I recently learned that they were brought here."

"As slaves?"

"Bought from the Romans in Corinth by a slave dealer bound for Antioch-near-Daphne. That's all I know."

Xantho regarded him levelly.

"You were sold as a slave, too, I think."

Shrewd old man.

"And sent to Rome."

"Free now?" The gray eyes bore into his.

"Free enough."

"So… you ran away. When?"

"Last year."

"Who was your master?" There was no malice in the eyes.

"Mistress." Alexander smiled. "A young woman—very rich, unmarried at that time—who lives on the coast north of Rome. She had some legal troubles last year, and at that point she helped me escape."

"Why didn't she just free you?"

"Not old enough." Alexander chuckled. "I really don't think of myself as a runaway since I had her permission to run."

"What sort of trouble was she in?"

"Truth is, I never learned exactly what the charges were, but with all her well-connected friends, I'm sure everything was straightened out long ago. Fact is, she should be married by now."

I hope Titus Flavius Sabinus Vespasianus the Younger appreciates how lucky he is.

"Any chance they've sent men looking for you?"

Alexander shook his head; then his heart almost stopped.

Theodosia wouldn't, but Titus— If they're married now, that makes me his runaway, too, not just hers.

225

Beads of sweat popped out on his forehead. Titus might be a fine young man, but he was also a Roman through and through.

Immortal Zeus! Theodosia would know exactly where I was headed. If she told Titus, there could be notices about me all over Antioch.

"Solteris was going to Corinth regularly a decade ago," Xantho said.

"Are you thinking of turning me in?"

"There are no records of slave purchases that far back, but—"

"I'm a fool for confiding in anyone. I just felt I could trust you."

"Solteris has a wonderful memory. If he bought your wife and son in Corinth, he'll remember them."

"The Romans pay a generous bounty for recaptured slaves."

Xantho shook his head at that.

"I'm an old man, my son, with no family... and no need of Roman gold. Right now, I'm much more concerned with the state of my soul. Your secret is safe with me."

The tension in Alexander's muscles vanished.

"Thank you."

Safe for now, but I've got to be more careful. Someone may be on the watch for me.

After an interval, he leaned over and laid his hand on Xantho's arm.

"Tell me where to find Solteris."

"He left two weeks ago on his annual buying expedition."

"Could I write to him?"

"Useless. That young lunatic never knows where he'll go when he sets out. Palmyra, Damascus, Jerusalem, Caesarea, Memphis, Tyre... He takes an army of men along. They bring back batches of the slaves he purchases for us to sell here, while he goes on to the next city."

"Could I catch up with him?"

"You'd have a better chance of catching up with a shooting star."

"I could ask around for slaves with the names of my wife and son."

"They've probably been given other names, two or three times perhaps, depending on how many masters they've had. Unless you're anxious for some long, cozy conversations with a series of Romans—and they do make up the majority of slave owners in and around Antioch—I wouldn't recommend it. Start asking questions and you're likely to find yourself answering others before the governor... surrounded by men who turned you in for that bounty you mentioned."

"How long do you think Solteris will be gone?"

"Let's see. It'll soon be November. Four, five more months, at least. I don't expect him back till spring."

<> <> <>

There was no change in Theodosia's condition. No friends came forward to champion her release. No commission reopened her case. And by the time the second winter began dumping its freezing rain into her cell, she had lost all hope.

It no longer seemed to matter that she had learned to walk again and built up the strength of her legs. Her hair hung long and shapeless around her shoulders and came out in handfuls if she tried to comb it with her fingers. She hadn't heard a human voice—or used her own for anything but babbling to herself—since the day Nero became emperor.

Half mad with loneliness, she began inventing fantasies that reawakened dormant emotions and their corresponding erotic responses.

Stefan was a young knight (or a silk merchant, or a war-weary centurion) come to court her at the villa (or to sell fabrics, or in search of a brigand).

He kissed her in the pergola (or in the garden, or in the cove), fell in love with her, and gave up his house in Rome (or his shop, or his legion).

They rode their horses over the hills (or along the shore, or through the woods), entertained at opulent banquets, made love under the pines (or in the pool, or in her bed), and produced a dozen children... each the result of a frenzied night of passion.

For weeks, it was colossal, azure-eyed Stefan who played the lead role, and Theodosia thought nothing of it. Who else but Stefan?

But gradually, imperceptibly, another figure began to intrude.

Deep-set eyes penetrated her dreams.

Ink-stained fantasy fingers touched her lips, caressed her breasts.

A half-forgotten foreign inflection echoed in her head, read poems to her, spoke her name as in a faded memory.

It was a month before she let herself admit that the eyes and hands and voice in her most recent daydreams belonged to Alexander.

She dug her fingers into her filthy hair, trembling and sobbing, the first time she realized what she had been imagining. She remembered the warmth of Stefan's body, his calloused hands on her body, his kisses... but there had been no such sensual contact between her and Alexander.

It was Alexander's mind, his companionship, his loyalty that I loved. There was never any physical attraction. He has a wife. He loves Antibe.

Despite her denials, her mind called up—endlessly and out of sequence—a series of memories that spoke of a love she had never acknowledged before.

Alexander's voice whispering her name as she lay by the river...

His arm holding her close when she told him she was pregnant with Stefan's baby...

His exuberance in the days after the big storm and throughout that summer...

His determination to burn the document that would have cast her into slavery...

His joy as he took her hand the night she regained consciousness...

His courage against Otho, against the legionary, against Titus and Vespasian when they wanted to take her to Caere...

The poems he brought to her the night of the big storm and countless other nights...

The intimacy that flowed between them whenever she set his verses to music...

The chill—the odd, abrupt shift from warmth and friendship to frigid formality—during Theodosia's brief romance with Stefan...

That shift!

Theodosia had paid little attention to it when it happened. Now she understood. Alexander was jealous.

Jealous! But why? Wasn't he the one who told me to go out to Stefan in the garden? Who encouraged me to marry Titus?

She shook her head, disbelieving.

Alexander isn't shy, and we had torn down almost all the barriers before that night when Stefan and I made love in the woods. If Alexander loved me then, wouldn't he just have said so?

Gradually that winter, as she slipped with increasing frequency from icy reality into the warmer world of her fantasies, another question began to take shape in her head, where it lingered and would not go away.

Could it be... it wasn't Stefan I really loved... but Alexander?

At some point that January—on a date marked only by the frozen crust on the floor of her cell—Theodosia Varra passed her twenty-first birthday.

She didn't even know the day when it arrived.

Levi's Inn stood on a narrow, twisting street in the heart of the Jewish quarter. It was a pleasant place with a small garden, a bathhouse, a stable with horses and donkeys to rent, ten guest rooms, and a kitchen. Its clients were mostly Jews come to Antioch on business.

Active in street warfare against the Romans as a youth in Jerusalem, Joshua Levi was law-abiding now and disinclined to quarrel with the authorities. His inn was a family operation. Two sons ran the stable. Every day but the Sabbath—when guests were expected to fast or eat elsewhere—Levi's wife and daughters cleaned the rooms and the bath, cooked and served the meals. There were no slaves.

Few Romans found their way to such a modest inn, so it had proven to be an ideal hideaway.

In his snug little room behind the kitchen, Alexander had discovered a loose floor plank under the bed and hidden Theodosia's rubies in the crevice below. Now, if he were arrested on the street and searched, at least the soldiers wouldn't find any "stolen" rubies to identify him by.

After breakfast this morning, Alexander donned his cloak against the January chill and set out for work. Three months ago—unwilling to waste on living expenses the gems that could buy freedom for Antibe and Niko—he had persuaded the taciturn Zamaris to give him employment as a bookkeeper and Latin-Greek translator.

The job was tedious, but it paid a bit more than his room and board. Over the winter, his stash of coins under the plank grew. It was Alexander's first paid labor in a decade. Each evening, as he accepted the five sesterces that Zamaris handed him, he said a silent prayer to Zeus for his continued freedom.

It was to pray, too, that he walked once a week up to woodsy Daphne, to the temple of Apollo, Greek god of music, medicine, and prophecy. "Better be a worm and feed on the mulberries of Daphne than a king's guest," the locals said. Alexander quickly decided they were right.

The temple—with its sacred cypress grove and the ever-flowing springs channeled around it—was a reminder that Antioch owed its founding to Seleucus, the restless Greek who had conquered Syria four hundred years before the Romans arrived.

Going "up to Daphne" was a trek on foot, but Alexander refused to waste precious coins renting a horse from Levi. That would be too dangerous, anyway. Galloping up the mountain was for Romans; the lords of the earth ignored the trudging pedestrians, who were mostly slaves. Alexander's last face-to-face with a Roman had been many months ago. He was more than willing to walk to keep it that way.

Besides, the walk was pleasant, and the views evoked his poetic instincts. Antioch sprawled along the valley like an old dog in the sun. The Orontes bent at the marketplace and split—like a sinuous dancer's upraised arms around her head—to form an island. The wharves jutted into the river like fingers against glass. The walls and bridges and buildings constructed by Seleucus, Herod, and Tiberius gleamed... polished by the years. The governor's gray palace lorded it over the city.

A fine metaphor for Rome's view of the world.

Needing a rest after his first climb, one bright afternoon at the end of October, Alexander had stretched out near the gate in Apollo's thyme-scented garden. As he lay there, a solemn-faced Greek with four solemn-faced children passed, leading a white goat into the temple. Some time later, they came out... without the goat but with radiant faces.

Curious, Alexander rose and asked the reason for the transformation.

"It's the power of Apollo." The other man was about his age. "Pray at the god's feet and those you love will be made well."

"The tumor in our mother's side is smaller," said his son, a youth about twelve, "since we started coming here."

"We live in Laodicea-by-the-Sea," said a much younger daughter. "It's a long journey!"

Alexander smiled at her.

"But a worthwhile one, it seems."

This could have been my family had things gone differently.

"Our physician believes she will recover completely," said the father. "We came today to offer a sacrifice of thanks to Apollo."

Perhaps if Apollo can heal the sick, he can restore the lost.

Alexander wished them well and strode into the temple. There were no other visitors, but a handful of priestesses bowed in greeting.

Behind the bloody sacrificial altar, a fire crackled in a gigantic golden urn, wafting its plume of smoke to the peak of the rotunda and filling the vast space with the aroma of roasting goat. Having brought nothing to sacrifice, Alexander deposited a silver coin in the altar box and turned his attention to the temple's divine resident... a massive figure standing directly under the gilded dome.

Apollo's arms, legs, and head were brown-veined marble. Amethyst eyes stared out under a laurel crown of gleaming gold. His wooden torso was draped with a silver fabric that glinted in the sunlight reflected off the marble floor. In one hand, Apollo held a golden lyre. His mouth was open. Clearly, he was singing.

It was the lyre that caught Alexander's attention.

Alone in the shrine, he stared at the instrument, then at the face above it. After a while, he stepped closer... no longer seeing amethyst eyes in a face of hard marble, but gold-flecked pupils in a soft frame of back-lit curls.

Transfixed by the vision, Alexander half expected the lips to move and the slender fingers to sweep across the golden lyre-turned-cithara.

Standing there without awareness of time—his breath constricted, his misty eyes switching between the lyre and the mouth open in song—he found himself praying—not for information about his wife and son—but for the safety and survival of Theodosia Varra.

"I abandoned her!" he whispered to the marble god. "I convinced myself that she'd survive, that someone else would save her, that everything would turn out right. All this time, I let myself believe... I counted on her marriage to Titus."

For months, a tiny, nagging voice inside his head had been struggling to be heard, but he had always quieted it.

The voice was shouting now.

But you knew that would not happen! She was destroyed that week! You knew it! You knew it... and you abandoned her!

He took a few more steps forward and fingered the hem of the god's silver robe.

"Send me word of her, O Apollo, I pray you. If she is still alive... help me find some way to save her."

The next day, Alexander bought writing materials and a scroll ring from his employer. That night, he battled his fears and his judgment into silence and wrote a cautious letter to the only pure-bred Roman in whom he had even the tiniest bit of trust.

ESTEEMED LADY: ONE WHO PLACES CONFIDENCE IN YOU ABOVE ALL OTHERS SEEKS WORD OF A MUTUAL ACQUAINTANCE WHOSE FATE I DO NOT KNOW.

OFTEN IN THE PAST, IN THAT LOVELY LOOKOUT BY THE SEA, YOU TEASED ME FOR MORE INFORMATION THAN I COULD RIGHTLY SHARE WITH YOU. NOW I MUST BEG THE SAME OF YOU AND HOPE FOR BETTER RESULTS THAN YOU OBTAINED FROM ME.

IF YOU ARE INDEED THE TRUE FRIEND SHE BELIEVED YOU TO BE, PLEASE SEND ME WORD OF HER.

WITH GREATEST DEFERENCE AND A PLEA FOR DISCRETION, RESPECTFULLY, A.

He reread the letter, rolled the parchment, sealed it, and addressed the scroll ring to Flavia Domitilla at the villa of Lucius Gallio in Rome. For the return address, he put that of Xantho, the only Antiochian he trusted. The next morning, he gave a special tip to the courier who carried mail from Zamaris' tent downriver to the ships at Seleucia Pieria.

And every week since then—October through January—Alexander had gone up to Daphne to beg Apollo for news of Antibe, Niko, and Theodosia Varra.

CHAPTER TWENTY-FOUR

It was the third week in April. Pale-yellow native crocuses had bloomed around the temple of Apollo and in the gardens of Daphne, followed by acres of early roses. Even Antioch was redolent of spring as the almond and pear trees swelled with buds, the larks with song.

Alexander left Zamaris' tent when his work was done and hastened to the shop of Solteris.

"Come tonight," the note had read. "You have a letter."

Without a word, Xantho led him to the back room. Alexander took the scroll and inspected the tag hanging from its sealed ring.

"For Alexander," wrote a delicate hand, "care of Xantho, at the shop of Solteris, Antioch-near-Daphne, Syria." There was no return address, no identifying mark stamped into the wax.

He slit the seal, unrolled the scroll, and held it up so his friend—who now knew all about Flavia and Otho and Titus and Gaius and Antibe and Niko and Stefan and Lycos and Theodosia—could read along.

Flavia's letter was more succinct than his own had been, and there was no signature.

ALEXANDER: SHE IS IN A CAVE CELL BELOW THE CARCER
TULLIANUM, STILL ALIVE AT LAST REPORT. NO ONE IS
ALLOWED TO SEE HER. ALL EFFORTS TO FREE HER PROVE
FUTILE. WE HAVE BOUGHT HER VILLA. WRITE TO ME
THERE IF NEED BE. GLAD YOU ARE SAFE.

Xantho turned his ever-curious eyes to Alexander's.

"What's this Carcer Tullianum?"

It was a while before Alexander could answer. His eyes burned. His ears rang. There was a pounding in his throat. He dropped into a chair, bowed his head, and rubbed his fingers hard into his temples.

"The Carcer Tullianum," he said at last, half choking, "is the dankest, dirtiest, deadliest prison in the whole rotten Roman Empire. A place of torture, sickness, and death."

"How long do you suppose your lady's been there?"

Alexander made the calculation.

"Must be sixteen months, if they took her right away. I wouldn't have thought she'd survive six."

"Maybe she's stronger than you think."

"She *is* strong, but not *that* strong! So, all this time, as I was sailing off in search of my own happiness... breathing the clean air of Greece and Syria... rejoicing in my freedom... Damn them! And damn me, too, for leaving her to that fate."

"What else could you have done? If those patrician friends of hers can't save her—can't even get in to see her!—what could a slave hope to accomplish?"

"I only know I abandoned her to her enemies. I've got to do something to make amends for that. I don't know what, but... I will do something. And in the meantime, I've a wife and a son to find, if your wandering friend ever decides to come home."

Solteris returned to Antioch the second day of May.

At dawn the next morning, a message came to Alexander as he was eating breakfast in Levi's kitchen. He gulped his bread and figs and set out in the thin pink light. After some wrangling—and Alexander's offer to work tomorrow without pay—Zamaris agreed to give him today off.

For two hours, he sat in Solteris' shop, concentrating on keeping his nerves and his anger under control as he listened to the man he was sure had carried Antibe and Niko into slavery ten years ago this spring.

Much as Alexander liked Xantho, he found it hard to like Xantho's friend. Solteris exhibited all the swagger of a man accustomed to absolute power over powerless people. Alexander's long-ago memories of a similar slave trader—not to mention more recent experiences with Gaius Terentius Varro and Marcus Salvius Otho—were still too brutally vivid.

Yani Solteris was handsome, urbane, and younger than Alexander had expected... only four or five years older than Alexander himself.

He couldn't have been more than twenty-five when he made that trip to Corinth. Antibe was eighteen… and he held her on his ship for weeks.

Watching Solteris' animated face as he recalled recent forays across Africa, reminisced about his trips to Greece, and told derisive anecdotes about his captives, Alexander struggled against indignation and suspicion.

He's my only chance to find them. Don't antagonize him!

As Alexander described the slaves he hoped to find—"for my employer in Corinth"—Solteris picked at his teeth and searched his memory. After a time, he gave a dry chuckle.

"I remember her. Just forgot the name." He chuckled again. "Antibe. What a tempting little package she was. So… someone sent you all this way for that one slave?"

"Two. My employer wants both the woman and the boy back."

"Must be his son. I can't picture the boy, but I sure do remember the wench. Slender, pretty, olive-skinned thing. Difficult at first, but pliant enough once it sank in I had her child, too. Your employer certainly hasn't been in any big rush, has he? Waiting so many years. Let's hope he's not disappointed. She'll not be so delicate as he remembers."

Alexander clenched his fists under the table and avoided the eyes of Xantho, his co-conspirator in this perilous venture.

"Will you help me find them?"

"For a consideration. I'm a businessman, after all."

"Of course." Alexander wanted to wring his neck. "How much?"

"One hundred sesterces."

Alexander exhaled sharply. By saving his wages for six months, he had put aside almost ninety sesterces to pay for three passages to Greece. It had never occurred to him that just finding out who had bought his family would wipe him out. All four rubies might be needed to buy them. He couldn't afford to sell even one to bribe a greedy trader.

"Twenty."

Solteris shook his head.

"Your employer is rich, is he not? He's already spent a fortune getting you here and keeping you here all winter. No doubt he provided a bagful of gold to buy those slaves he wants so badly. Don't tell me he won't pay good money to locate them."

"Twenty-five, then. I can go no higher."

"Fifty… or you will have no information from me."

Xantho threw an arm around Solteris and gave him a teasing shake.

"Come now, old man! Alexander's been a friend to me all winter, as you were jaunting around the world piling up the wealth of Croesus and warming your nights with those little packages, as you call them. Don't be so stubborn with him."

"I'm not being stubborn with him, just with his employer. What are fifty sesterces to a rich Greek?"

"Ah, but you've got it all wrong! See, Yani, the rich Greek gave Alexander a certain amount of money for this project, leaving him to budget his own expenses." The gray eyes twinkled as the lies tumbled out. "Alexander's pay is what he manages to save. Nothing more. Those fifty sesterces you're demanding will come right out of his pocket."

Alexander smiled in appreciation of this skillful weaving of fact and fiction.

"And waiting for you all winter," he said, "has almost wiped me out. If I pay you fifty sesterces, I won't have enough to buy the two slaves and take them to Greece."

"You will pay me twenty-five then?"

"I'd prefer to pay you with my gratitude." Alexander looked into the dealer's cold eyes. "You made a fine profit selling those two once. Most men would be content with that."

"I am not most men, nor do I make my money by being a fool. And I cannot eat gratitude. Twenty-five sesterces."

Alexander slid the coins across the table.

"Excellent. Well… I sold the woman and her son to a spice merchant who lives up in Daphne, name of Lero Heiron."

"A Syrian?" Xantho glanced at Alexander. "Not a Roman?"

A wave of relief washed over Alexander.

"A Syrian," Solteris said. "His wife's Roman though. She will have only Greek slaves around her, so I used to do a lot of business with Lero Heiron. Not too much since I stopped going to Greece." He paused. "Come to think of it, I haven't seen him around for quite some time."

"Tell me how to find his house."

"Be easier for me to take you than to tell you."

"All for twenty-five sesterces?"

"All for Xantho's friendship."

Good enough.

They left in the trader's wagon, sitting in the rear as Solteris gave directions to his driver in the front seat. It was Alexander's first ride ever in a slave-driven conveyance. Solteris chattered on and on about the aggravations of his trade. Alexander found it difficult to sympathize.

"It's mostly the people you've got to deal with," Solteris said as they turned into the noisy mass of litters, carts, chariots, horses, mules, camels, and pedestrians jostling one another in the broad street named jointly after Herod and Tiberius. It was a long boulevard lined with buildings that rivaled many in Rome.

"You wouldn't believe what they'll do to cheat me," Solteris went on, raising his voice to be heard over a group of angry muleteers arguing in the middle of the road, where there had been a collision. "They'll take me to their camp—way out in the desert maybe—saying they've got such and such an assortment of merchandise. But when I get there, they've stashed the slaves somewhere else and are demanding an exorbitant sum for the privilege of laying eyes on them."

Like demanding an exorbitant sum for simple information?

"By then, you've got so much time invested in the process," Alexander said to be sociable, "you don't have much choice."

I can understand that.

"Exactly, and they know it. Pull right!" Solteris yelled at his driver.

When the man didn't respond, Solteris took a stick from the floor and jabbed it into his back. Then he motioned for him to pull onto the shoulder to get around the tangle of carts.

"Then, of course, when I do get a coffle together, the damned fools go out of their way to be annoying. They slow down, get sick and listless, whine and complain. Sometimes it takes a heavy hand to shut 'em up."

"Why stay in the business then, if you dislike it so?"

"Money. And excitement. I'm not a man to stay home. Rather be on expedition, even with the problems, than spend my life in Antioch with a fat wife and a flock of squalling brats." Solteris chuckled in that dry way that was beginning to annoy Alexander tremendously. "There are better ways for a man to take his pleasure."

The wagon lumbered along the dirt shoulder for a while.

"So, you find some of the women you buy… inviting?"

Solteris grinned and eyed Alexander sideways.

"Don't you ever see a slave gal you'd like to screw?"

"Of course."

"Well, so do I. That's a plus to the business." Another dry chuckle. "All those tempting little packages that can't say no… never enough time to get bored with any of 'em. Who wouldn't take advantage of that?"

"Don't their men put up a fight?"

"Their men? Pfffffh! Slaves aren't men." Solteris looked smugly at Alexander. "It's real fun to take their women in front of their eyes—or hand somebody's daughter over to my lads—and watch the explosion in their dumb heads when they realize they can't do a damn thing about it."

Alexander fell back on the training of slavery as he swallowed every visible sign of anger.

He'll turn me in for the reward—in an instant—if he finds out.

He averted his face, pretending an interest in another collision, aware that if he said anything at all right now, he'd give himself away.

He had her on that ship. Antibe would've been just another "tempting package" to break up a dull voyage. Wonder how many other men have had her since?

He bit his tongue and silently cursed every god he knew of.

Antibe and Niko... they've been through so much. Will they blame me? Will they even want to see me? Can our lives ever be the same?

"Lero Heiron died two years ago."

The Greek porter watched a squad of legionaries passing on patrol, then shifted his eyes to the strangers standing on the cobblestones of the most exclusive residential street in Daphne.

Solteris chuckled.

"Guess that's why I haven't seen him lately. Who lives here now?"

Beyond the cool atrium, Alexander could see the yellows and reds of a flower-filled peristyle.

A Roman house.

He braced himself for bad news.

"My master is the most noble Tribune Sextus Valerius, first deputy to the imperial governor of Antioch."

Alexander felt as if his heart would fall and smash against the floor, and for a time he had no voice.

It was Solteris who asked the questions that Alexander could not.

"Did your new master buy the entire household staff?"

"Yes, sir, except some maids the old mistress took with her when she went back to Rome."

May it please the gods... let them still be here!

The idea of returning to Rome—even for Antibe—was unnerving.

The porter peered cautiously over his shoulder.

"I should not talk about such matters to strangers."

"Is your master at home?"

"He's lunching with the governor today, sir."

"Is his steward available?"

"He is. Who is it that seeks to speak with him?"

Solteris turned toward Alexander, who rallied.

"My name is Alexander Demodocus. I am from Corinth."

The porter waved them into the atrium, then slipped away.

It was a classic Roman house. Apparently, the deceased Syrian had reconstructed a piece of Rome for his wife. A murmur of Greek wafted out from an unseen room, competing with the splash of the fountain.

Beloved Apollo, grant me the strength to look on Antibe as a stranger, and give her the wits not to show she knows me.

The steward—an elderly Greek, obviously a slave by his clothing and demeanor—approached and bowed.

The very image of what I would have become in time.

"My name is Decimus. How may I serve you?"

"I've come from Corinth in search of two slaves who were sold from the household of my employer many years ago." Alexander turned and gestured to Solteris. "This gentleman is a dealer here in Antioch. He recalls bringing the two from Corinth a decade ago and selling them to Lero Heiron. I have hopes of buying them back for my employer."

"You must speak with my master, sir. Come tomorrow morning."

"May I ask—" Alexander found it difficult, after waiting months for this moment, to phrase the hardest question of his life. "Is there in this household a woman named Antibe... and a boy of thirteen named Niko?"

The steward studied Alexander's face at length. Too long.

Dear gods, have I given myself away? Too much emotion?

"There is a boy named Niko about that age."

Alexander tried to return the man's gaze casually.

"And his mother, the woman Antibe?"

"She died in childbirth, sir. About five years ago."

"My master will see you, sir," said Decimus to the fellow Greek waiting in the atrium.

Solteris had offered to drive him up to Daphne again, but Alexander declined. He didn't know how much longer he could bite his tongue, so he had made the two-hour walk alone.

Zamaris was expecting him at work today, but Alexander had no intention of returning. He paid Levi as he left the inn, carrying his four rubies and what was left of his savings, wearing his good tunic and cloak.

The night had been endless, sleepless, filled with rage and grief and guilt... and the ordeal wasn't over yet.

Now... all I have to do is face down this Roman, buy my son, and get out of town before I'm caught.

"I told my master about your mission," Decimus said as he stopped at a closed wooden door and knocked.

Alexander found himself standing before the first deputy to the imperial governor of Antioch. Sextus Valerius was about forty, with a high-bridged nose, graying hair that still waved above his forehead, and the elegant, purple-bordered toga of the senatorial class. It was easy to picture him strolling through the Forum with General Vespasian, Gaius Terentius Varro, or Senator Marcus Salvius Otho.

Courage and caution! All the anger in the world won't bring Antibe back, but if I slip up the Romans will have another runaway slave for their sport.

He had to stay alive for Niko... though in his darkest hour last night, he had wondered if anything really mattered, now that Antibe was gone.

The Roman rose from his desk and came forward.

"Decimus says you are searching for two slaves that were sold into this household."

"Yes, sir, although I understand one of them has died."

He made it a point to meet the deputy governor's eyes.

This isn't the man who raped her. Not the one whose baby killed her. He wasn't even here then... but now he holds my Niko's life in his hands.

"Unfortunately, yes. I can tell you nothing more about her."

Valerius moved to a table, poured two cups of wine from a pitcher, and offered one to his guest. The gesture took Alexander by surprise.

"Please have a seat."

This was the moment that Alexander had been dreading most.

You're a free man in his eyes. Play the part!

He sat, trying not to look too out of place.

Pretend it's Theodosia Varra you're sitting with.

"Leave us," the tribune said to his steward.

The old man bowed and departed as Alexander sipped from his cup.

"Decimus said something about your employer."

"Yes, sir. Timaius of Corinth, who had a son years ago by a young slave woman in his household. He hopes to get both of them back."

"How did he happen to sell them in the first place?"

"He was traveling when his wife had the woman and her child sold."

"Jealous, I suppose."

"I suppose."

"It happens a lot."

Valerius took a leisurely drink and lounged in his chair.

"Now... tell me the real story."

"Sir?"

"There's not a word of truth in anything you just said."

Alexander leaped to his feet.

"I may not be a Roman, sir, but that does not make me a liar! Perhaps I should go."

"Calm down, fellow." Valerius was maddeningly calm himself. "And sit down."

Alexander remembered the legionaries he had seen all over Daphne.

If I run, he'll have me arrested before I get to the end of the street.

He sat again.

"What makes you think I've kept the truth from you, sir?"

"Two things. Decimus remembers that when the woman Antibe was brought to this house, she claimed all sorts of things... that her husband was falsely accused of some trumped-up offense, that the Romans had no right to enslave her and her child, that she would never be a slave. It required a couple of encounters with the whip to convince her otherwise."

Alexander gripped the arms of his chair and turned his face away, although he was sure it had already betrayed him. Whatever answer he might have found died in his throat.

My beloved Antibe... not just raped but also whipped?

Valerius said nothing, but Alexander knew he was watching him.

I've got to answer him somehow.

"You said there were two things, sir."

"So I did."

Valerius clapped his hands. When Decimus appeared in the doorway, the Roman nodded, as in a pre-arranged signal. A moment later, a slim youth stepped in, bowed, and stood with his hands at his sides, eyes on the floor... the classic pose of slavery.

"Come here, Niko," commanded the Roman.

The boy walked forward until he stood a few paces from his master and bowed again, formally.

Alexander watched his stiff moves with horror. Whatever had happened to the giggly toddler who loved to run downhill as fast as his legs could carry him... loved to be tossed in the air... loved to gallop around the house on Alexander's shoulders? There was no trace here of that child, yet so many aspects of the boy's face reminded Alexander of Antibe... the curly hair, the olive skin, the round mouth and chin.

"Look at my guest."

The boy raised his eyes, and in that instant Alexander knew what had given him away. There—in Antibe's gentle face—his own deep-set eyes stared back at him.

Valerius watched as Alexander and his son regarded each other for the first time in ten years.

Does he have any idea who I am?

"You may go, boy." The order was abrupt.

Niko stood still, his eyes fixed on Alexander's, curiosity written on his face. Alexander feared his disobedience would anger Valerius.

"Go!" the Roman barked.

Finally, Niko bowed and left. There was a long silence.

"Why have you let me see him?"

"You came to see him, didn't you?"

"I came to buy him."

"That may not be possible."

Alexander blinked a couple of times. It had never occurred to him that he might find Niko and still be unable to take him away.

"Why not, sir?"

"He's well trained, gives good service. Handsome. Intelligent. Honest. Obedient... usually. A valuable slave. He's worth a lot to me."

"He is also worth a lot to me." There was no reason to continue the pretense of the Corinthian employer. "I am his father."

"I know. But that gives you no special right to him. He may be your son, but he is also my slave."

"Yes, of course. Sir, I am prepared to pay you well for him."

"I see no reason to part with a good slave just to satisfy the wishes of a man who shows up at my door and doesn't even have the decency to come forward with his own story, but resorts instead to subterfuge."

How do I respond to that? The truth might be deadly.

"Besides," Valerius went on, "I'm responsible for him. How do I know you will treat him as your son? What proof do I have that you will not abuse him? Misuse him? Sell him to someone else?"

"My lord, at least let me respond to the first issue before you assault me with accusations!"

"Very well." A hint of amusement crossed the Roman's face.

"You have said it already, sir. You said that the boy's mother—my wife, Antibe—claimed that her husband was falsely accused. I was born free and worked for my father before I was accused—falsely, as Antibe said—of corruption by the very Romans who were our competitors. Accused by Romans and convicted by Romans when I was twenty years old. I spent ten years in prison—*perhaps one little lie will pass*—living for the day I'd be reunited with my family. When they finally released me last fall, I found out that the Romans had sold my wife and son—who were accused of no crime—into slavery." He paused and looked Valerius straight in the eye. "Can you give me any reason, sir, why I should trust a Roman now?"

"If you're so distrustful of Romans," said the Roman, "why are you telling me all this? Admitting you're a prison rat doesn't do much to enhance your case."

"You seem like an honorable man, sir." Alexander hoped it was true. "And I believe that an honorable man—of any class or nationality—will respect the love of a father who has traveled so far to find his son. I had hoped to find my wife, too. Please allow me to buy Niko's freedom."

Valerius stood. Alexander followed.

"How much are you prepared to pay?"

"How much is he worth to you, sir?"

The Roman shrugged.

"I've given it no thought. Wasn't planning to sell him. Been training him for a secretary." Valerius went to the window. "If you want the boy, you'll have to make an offer."

"I haven't much money, sir. I've been in Antioch since fall, working for a scribe in the market, saving my wages. The slave dealer who brought me here yesterday demanded a third of what I'd saved. What's left wouldn't buy a baby, let alone an educated youth. But I do have this."

Alexander reached into his tunic and pulled out a small cloth pouch containing one of his four large rubies. The others were in a leather bag, still safely tucked away.

"I didn't steal this, sir. Let me say that to you plainly. It was a gift."

"A gift? From whom?"

"From a friend, sir. A wealthy, generous woman who knew how much my family meant to me." He handed the stone to Valerius. "She gave me that ruby to ensure I could find them and take them home."

A shaft of brilliant red fell across Valerius' palm as he held the gem up to the light and studied it.

"It's beautiful." A new tone appeared in his voice. "You know... it's odd that your generous friend would give you just one stone. Sure you don't have another stashed away somewhere... to sweeten the deal?"

Alexander hesitated. The three other rubies would guarantee him and Niko a good future in Greece. He couldn't afford to trade them now.

"Surely one fine ruby is enough for a young boy."

Valerius raised one eyebrow and pursed his lips.

"You may not know... I came here from Rome about a year ago. There had been gossip before then about a wealthy young woman who was accused of terrible crimes. When her property was confiscated, they found she had pried a number of large rubies out of her serving pieces. Those rubies were never found, despite an exhaustive search... nor did they ever catch three slaves who ran away from her villa at the same time. It seemed there might be a connection between the vanished rubies and the vanished slaves, so word went out to government offices throughout the empire to be on the watch for large, unset, deep-red rubies." Valerius continued watching Alexander. "The escaped slaves were described in considerable detail, too."

Alexander turned his eyes to the window, forcing himself to keep his hand away from the tell-tale scars left on his jaw and cheek by Gaius' ring and Otho's dagger. His mind was blank except for one dreadful thought.

He knows.

"What have old rumors to do with me, sir?"

Valerius tossed the ruby in his palm.

"This is indeed a fine stone. My wife would love to have it set into earrings, but that requires a pair. Should you perhaps have another ruby of equal size and quality... I could forget to inquire the name of the prison where they held you all those years or why they kept you in prison at all, since the normal penalty for a non-citizen convicted of corruption is slavery. I'm sure my good friend the governor would be most interested in your answers."

Alexander opened his mouth, but the tribune hadn't finished.

"Two fine rubies for one fine son, Greek."

That derogatory "Greek" on a Roman tongue brought a surge of stinging memories.

I will not have my Niko submit to that for the rest of his life.

"I have your word, sir?"

Alexander knew Valerius would honor his word. If his superiors got wind of this, he himself would be in trouble for corruption.

"My word."

Alexander reached into his tunic once more, pulled out the leather bag, and laid another big ruby on the table.

Valerius took it and examined it as he had the first one, then held them both against the light, side by side. His lips curled into a smile.

"The slave is yours."

He clapped his hands again, and Decimus opened the door.

"Bring the boy back."

"I do not want a slave, sir. I insist on a certificate of manumission for him, properly witnessed... so it can stand up in any court."

At least Niko will be free, even if I am caught.

"Of course."

Valerius pulled a sheet of parchment, a reed-pen, and ink from his desk and wrote rapidly. Then he stamped it with wax and his signet ring.

"Find my wife and son," he said when the steward reappeared, "and tell them I want their signatures on this."

Neither Valerius nor Alexander said anything to Niko, who stood waiting in that same subservient posture, just inside the door. When Decimus returned with the document, Valerius showed it to Alexander. He was satisfied, so the tribune rolled it, thrust it into a scroll ring, and handed it over. Alexander stashed it in the breast of his tunic.

"You are to go with this man now," Valerius said to Niko. "You no longer belong to me."

The Roman scooped up the two rubies and departed without another word, leaving Decimus to escort Alexander and the stranger who was his son to the street. There was to be no explanation for the boy, no farewell from master to servant, no chance for Niko to say good-bye to the other slaves who had been his friends and family for most of his life.

Alexander watched his son's perplexed face as they stepped onto the cobblestones and the bronze door closed behind them.

Niko looked at the walls that kept the world out of the only home he could possibly remember. His eyes lingered on the red roses spilling over the top, then ran the length of the wall to a pear tree lifting its fragrant white flowers above the corner of the garden. Voices and a childish song floated out from inside. Alexander was sure he knew what the boy was thinking. His mother had died somewhere within those walls.

"Come," he said in Greek. "We must go quickly."

Niko raised questioning eyes, then dropped them.

"Yes, my lord."

"I am not your lord, my son. I'm your father." Alexander put his arm around the boy's shoulders and smiled into the bewildered olive-toned oval. "And I hope that someday you will wish to call me that."

CHAPTER TWENTY-FIVE

At dusk, four days past the Ides of June—after weeks of catching free boat rides from Syria to Crete and on through the Cyclades—Alexander and his son debarked at Piraeus, just southwest of Athens.

They spent the night at a quiet inn on a dead-end street a mile from the crowded waterfront taverns where Roman soldiers would be lording it over Greek sailors, longshoremen, and harlots.

At dawn, carrying bread, goat-milk cheese, and a wineskin filled with water, they set out on foot, skirting around Roman-infested Athens and heading north through pockets of poppies across the rocky peninsula toward the gulf of Eretria.

"Are Stefan and Lycos expecting us?" Niko asked over breakfast the third morning out.

They were sitting on the raised roots of an ancient cypress, savoring the washes of pink and orange that swept the sky.

Alexander finished his cheese, shaking his head as he swallowed.

"I've been gone so long, they probably think I'm dead."

"That's what Mother thought."

Alexander looked at the boy. This was the first time since their reunion that Niko had mentioned Antibe.

"She thought I was dead?"

"That's what she said. She said you'd have come for us if you were alive. When you never showed up, she said the Romans had killed you. So—since they didn't kill you—why didn't you come for us?"

Alexander dropped his eyes. He had told Niko about Rome, about the villa, about Stefan and Lycos. Even about Theodosia. Until now, Niko had revealed no curiosity about Alexander's past, no interest in personal conversation. This was a good first step, but...

"That's a difficult question. I did write to your mother several times. I tried to get information about both of you, but by then you were gone from Corinth. I didn't know where they'd taken you. And I was a slave all those years, too, as you were, so I couldn't just leave and look for you."

"Did they whip you like they whipped Mother?"

Alexander's jaw tightened as he shook his head.

"I was luckier than most."

"But they wouldn't let you come for us?"

"No. But remember... I *did* come for you, soon as I could. And I'd have bought your mother out, too, if—" He traded a shrug for the words.

Niko nodded and reached into the sack for more cheese.

"Tell me more about Lycos."

"Well, he always reminded me of you. I especially liked to read with him, because I could pretend I was reading with you. You'll like him."

"Will I like Stefan, too?"

"I think so. Just don't be intimidated by him. He's probably the biggest human you'll ever see in your life."

"Will he like me?" The deep-set eyes peered anxiously out of that eerie oval replica of Antibe's face.

Alexander smiled and a swell of love flowed through him. Lots of walls had come down since that morning in Daphne. Niko had dropped the stiff "my lord" right away, but he hadn't yet said "Father," much less "Papa," as he once did. But Alexander was willing to wait. It was enough that he had his son again.

"Oh, yes. He will like you as much as I do."

Two days later, they made their way in a steady drizzle through a mountain pass and caught the road heading south toward the ancient town of Eretria. The sun was out by late afternoon when Alexander spotted the rutted path leading to the farmhouse of Leios Bryaxis. About sundown, they opened the gate near the barn of native stone. Wolf, the gray dog that guarded the yard, began to bark.

Alexander silenced the dog with a friendly pat. When he stuck his head through the open barn door, expecting to find nothing but tired mules and oxen, he caught sight of Stefan and Iocaste—her thick black hair spilling around the post behind her—locked in a prolonged kiss. So surprised was Alexander that he laughed. Stefan drew back angrily, still clutching Iocaste's shoulders; then his face buckled with joy.

"Alexander!"

Almost immediately, Stefan wrapped his arms around his friend and lifted him off the ground in a boisterous hug.

"By all the gods, man! You still alive!"

Stefan is learning Greek.

"Alive, temporarily, till you squeeze me to death."

Stefan set him down but kept both hands on his shoulders.

"Alive! Safe!" The big man's eyes filled with tears… an incongruous sight. "I give back hope for you months ago."

Stefan's Greek was garbled, but the meaning was clear.

"Yes," Alexander said with a grin for the beaming Iocaste, "I can tell you've been grieving. But come, both of you. See what I found in Syria."

Niko had remained outside the barn. Alexander put his arm around him and drew him close.

"Niko, my son, this is Stefan."

Niko gaped at the hairy giant emerging from the barn.

Stefan's face, on the other hand, softened even more. In the next moment, he was on one knee, clutching the boy to his chest.

"It like meeting my personal son."

If Niko was confused by the botched Greek, he didn't show it.

"I never happier in my life," Stefan said, his eyes welling with tears again as he lifted Niko in his arms and rose to his feet.

Leios Bryaxis, his wife, his mother-in-law, his younger daughters, and his slaves began emerging from the house… all of them calling Alexander's name in wonder.

Lycos raced across the driveway, leaped into Alexander's arms, and planted a teary kiss on his cheek.

"Where you mother?" Stefan asked Niko.

Still holding Lycos, Alexander took one of Niko's hands.

"Antibe is dead." The words—spoken aloud for the first time—tore at his heart. "But at least our son survives."

"I'm going back to Rome."

"You're crazy, man. You're absolutely crazy."

They were walking in the dappled sunlight beneath the well-pruned, aromatic trees of Leios Bryaxis' apple orchard, speaking Latin again.

"Maybe, but I have to do something. It'd be different if Antibe were alive. I'd owe it to her to stay. But—"

"Your boy's alive. Don't you owe something to him?"

"That's different. It really is. Besides… I can't just forget. I can't just settle down here with Niko and Lycos and Iocaste and you as some odd sort of family and forget that a woman I—"

He caught his breath.

A woman I love as dearly as I once loved Antibe… but how can I say that to you? You're the one Theodosia loves, even if you have forgotten about her.

"I can't forget that a woman who's done so much for us is starving to death or dying of fever in that stinking pit."

"They'll kill you. Too many Romans know you… and there ain't one of them wouldn't love to make an example of you."

"I'll be careful."

"Oh, right! Just because you had one lucky run-in with a bureaucrat who turned out to be more greedy than patriotic, don't assume you're always gonna be that lucky."

"There *is* one Roman who'll help me." Alexander patted Flavia's letter, which he had read to Stefan and replaced inside his tunic. "I trust Flavia Domitilla. Wasn't sure if I should, at first, but if she wanted me arrested, it would've been easy to do while I was in Antioch."

"Well… not having you arrested in Antioch ain't the same as risking her own neck to help you in Rome."

"It's not me she'll be helping, but Theodosia."

"You need to think about your son." Stefan bent to pick up a stick. "He's just learned he's got a father. What's it going to do to him if you go and get yourself crucified?"

"You'd take care of him, wouldn't you? You and Iocaste?"

"She's only four years older than Niko. What kind of mother do you think she'd make to him?"

"Better than no mother at all, which is what he's had for years. Iocaste has all but adopted Lycos already, and you saw her take Niko under her wing last night. Lycos and Niko will be like brothers in no time. And I trust you to be a father to my son."

"No talking you out of it?"

Alexander shook his head.

"I'm going to write to the lady Flavia again and—"

"From here? You'll have the garrison from Eretria swarming all over Bryaxis' farm. By all the gods, man, you really *are* crazy!"

"I'll find some scribe in Eretria who'll let me use his address and just see what happens. It may take as long as a year. Have to develop a plan."

"If that 'stinking pit' is as bad as you say, you can't really believe Theodosia will last another year."

"I've got to think she'll make it. There's no other way for me to live." He glanced at his friend. "Don't worry. I'll keep the Romans away from here... for everyone's sake."

Stefan was peeling the stick, leaving it greenish and shiny. After a long interval, he shook his head and sighed.

"I can't let you go back there alone. Not after all we've been through together." He tossed the stick away and grasped a branch overhead. "Life is good here. Freedom's every bit as sweet as I thought it would be. I finally got paid work and a woman who ain't so complicated. But—"

"Stefan, you mustn't think of—"

"When you go to Rome, I'm—"

"You've got a good future here if you—"

"I'm going back with you!"

"What for?"

"I can't sit and watch you get crucified. I can take care of you."

"It would help more knowing you're here taking care of those boys."

"Damn you, Alexander, don't argue!" Stefan gave a soft, bitter laugh. "Damn me, too, for a fool, but I can't help it. Iocaste's warm and lots of fun, but Theodosia's still the only woman... After all that's happened, wouldn't you think I'd finally stop loving her?"

Theodosia marked her twenty-second birthday the same way she had marked her twentieth and her twenty-first... sick and cold and hungry, but still alive and mostly sane, although she often wondered how long either would last. Then, a couple of months later, came new reason to hope.

Heightened bird noises and warmer air from the fissure overhead said it was spring... her third spring in the Carcer Tullianum.

She was exercising her stiff legs one morning, continuing her paces around the cell. Her meal had been delivered; there would be no more interruptions today.

All of a sudden, she heard activity in the hall. Feet stamping to a halt. The smell of pitch. The rasp of a bolt. The door swung open, and into her cell strode a guard. In one hand he carried a torch, in the other a cithara.

"You're Theodosia, daughter of Aulus Terentius Varro?"

Theodosia blinked. It was the first time anyone had spoken to her in almost two years.

"I used to be."

"I'm to give this to you. You're to practice."

He shoved the instrument into her hand and was gone.

Theodosia leaned against the wall, pressing the cithara to her breast. Slowly, she turned it over. Her fingers moved to the lower curve and —disbelieving—ran back and forth in the long gouge she'd made as a girl when she dropped it against a bench.

My own!

She slid down the wall, cradling the beloved piece of wood, and plucked the strings as tears overflowed her eyes.

Practice? I'll play all day! Every day!

Unaccustomed to new thoughts, her mind strained at the questions racing through it like water in a mountain stream.

Who found my cithara?

Where was it?

How would they know it was mine?

Who could have enough influence to smuggle it in?

Who would take the risk?

And finally, the question that kept rising to the surface when all the others had washed away.

Why?

Theodosia couldn't tell if it was the same guard who came to fetch her out, and she didn't care. It was June. The morning sun shone warm on her face. Sweet spring air filled her lungs. And she *walked* out of the Carcer Tullianum.

The soldiers who accompanied her refused to adjust to her lopsided, barefoot gait; she struggled to keep up. But still, it was a joyful journey that she made through the streets of Rome, swinging her rigid left leg to the outside and clutching her cithara with both hands.

People stared as she passed. Theodosia just smiled back. She knew she was a strange sight… grimy, gaunt, ragged, stiff, and smiling.

Even before they rounded the last bend of the road that ascended the Palatine Hill, she knew they were taking her to Nero's palace.

Haven or hell for me?

The question came and went, replaced by an overwhelming thought.

I'm free!

The overseer looked her up and down with distaste and passed her on to a trio of silent, sullen women. The bath they gave her bore no resemblance to any she had ever taken before. They stripped her and immediately burned her tattered tunic; then they submerged her in a tub of strong, acrid liquid and scrubbed her scalp with pitiless fingers. When she surfaced, she saw hundreds of lice and other creatures floating around her.

Finally—after another submersion in a fresh tub of the acrid liquid, another rough scrubbing, and a soak in a tub filled with hot water—the women oiled, scraped, and dried her, cut her hair, and handed her a plain off-white tunic, sandals, and a shawl. After she had dressed, they led her —still not speaking—through a maze of corridors to the kitchen.

It was a vast room with huge beams and enough tables and stools for hundreds of people. Theodosia sat where she was told, trembling at the thought of food. She was watching—and being watched by—slaves at other tables when she caught the flash of a green tunic approaching her.

"Hello, miss."

Amazed at the honorific, Theodosia looked up. It was Marcipor.

"You're an imperial slave, but they finally decided you weren't guilty of murder."

Marcipor sat across the table as Theodosia gulped the hard-cooked eggs, greasy sausage, and brown bread that a cook had set before her. It was a slave's meal, but still…

She no longer itched.

She smelled something other than sewer gases.

She was sitting at a real table, eating real food with a real spoon, wearing sandals and a clean, untorn tunic.

If this is a slave's life, I'll take it.

"It all tastes so good!"

Her hand shook as she reached for the cup of vinegary wine.

"I imagine it does. You've been in the Tullianum all this time?"

Theodosia nodded.

"Tell me," she whispered, glancing cautiously around the room, "did anyone get away from the villa?"

"My lord Otho hauled me off the day the soldiers arrived. Alexander, Stefan, and Lycos ran away at Saturnalia. I never heard if they were caught." He lowered his voice. "I knew I was in trouble even before the senator got there. The moment I saw Centurion Manus, I knew it."

"You knew Manus before then?"

"His family lives next door to my lord Otho's. They were friends as boys. I used to wish I belonged to him. He's a better sort."

"Wish I had such fond memories of him. What're you doing here?"

"My master's visiting the emperor. He always brings a horde of us along so people in the street can see how important he is."

"How've things been for you?"

Marcipor's shrug was noncommittal.

"I'm sorry," Theodosia said. "I promised you were safe from him. Has Otho forgiven you for refusing to spy on me?"

"He'll never forgive me for that."

Neither spoke for a time.

"Whatever happened to Lucilla?"

"She died. Under torture. My lord Otho told me. He knew I was sweet on her, so he made it into a big joke."

Theodosia wanted to feel sorrow for Lucilla, but after so long she found herself incapable of it.

"Do you know what's in store for me? Why they let me out?"

Marcipor shook his head and shrugged again.

"What happened to my villa?"

"You didn't hear? The lady Flavia lives there now."

"Flavia?"

"Her husband bought it a couple of months after they married. She's there a lot, I understand, although I see her around here quite often. Not sure if she recognizes me. She never acknowledges me."

Flavia in my villa? That so-called "friend" always wanted my villa. Made no secret of it. Talked about it all the time.

Theodosia experienced a rush of hatred as powerful as any emotion she had ever known.

So... Lucius Gallio did help Claudius figure out how to get his hands on my older servants. Forcing them to testify was the key to giving his precious Flavia her heart's desire.

"It's a shame, you know," Marcipor went on. "After being married for several years, the lady Flavia still has no children. And I hear she wants them badly."

So... all this time—while I was praying my friends would save me— they've been merrily helping themselves to what was mine. And there's no way to get back at them except...

Theodosia's hatred changed instantly to delicious, malicious joy.

Praise Juno, who found a way to avenge me! Flavia is barren!

253

◇ ◇ ◇

Novelty. Variety. That was what they wanted. Nero was tired of his musicians, said Scopan, the pompous freedman who scheduled entertainment for the palace. Somehow, the master of the world had remembered a young singer he'd met long ago, learned she was in prison, and ordered her released to serve at his pleasure.

Theodosia stood before Scopan's desk, chafing under his condescension but grateful to have been remembered by someone. Right now, she would cheerfully sing and play and scrub floors and serve Nero's table and do almost anything else that would keep her out of the Carcer Tullianum.

"You're to perform tonight," Scopan said. "A small party... just His Majesty and a few friends. Meanwhile, Senator Marcus Salvius Otho commands your presence in the emperor's salon. The page outside will take you there. Don't keep the senator waiting."

◇ ◇ ◇

Theodosia followed the liveried slave through a network of passageways to the most elegant chamber she had ever seen. Frescoed walls of purple and gold soared into a gilded dome. Fine Greek statues stood guard around the perimeter, and in the center an enormous fish of hammered gold spouted purple-tinted water into a golden pond. The white marble furniture was draped and cushioned with such opulence that someone raised with ordinary wealth would feel out of place. Even if Theodosia hadn't spent the last thirty months in a cave cell, the splendor of this room would have overwhelmed her.

"Theodosia."

Her eyes followed the voice to her right, where Otho lay sprawled on a couch beside a statue of Zeus. He had put on weight, and though he wore the toga of a senator, his face had the look of a sated cat.

Same old Otho. Lounging around the emperor's house as he once lounged around mine.

"I see you're walking again," he said.

"Yes."

I'll be as civil as he gives me cause to be. Maybe he played some part in getting me out of the Tullianum.

"You look every bit as bad as I expected."

Theodosia felt herself blush and hated it.

"This is outstanding wine." Otho lifted his golden goblet. "The finest product of the emperor's vineyards. Formerly, your vineyards."

For a moment, Theodosia thought she would knock the cup from his manicured hand and the smile from his smooth, smug face.

"Lucius Gallio," Otho went on, "bought your villa and household slaves. Someone else owns your hovel in the Subura. Gaius' mansion sold fast, too, once the question of your identity was resolved."

"Who did they decide I am?"

"The bastard daughter of Aulus Terentius Varro by his Greek slave girl. Just as Nizzo said."

I was right. It was Nizzo who destroyed me.

"Since Gaius' death ended the Terentius Varro line, everything he owned reverted to the state... including you. Came at a good time, too, not long before the start of Nero's reign. Selling off the residential properties gave him quick cash, not to mention that amazing pile of gems and gold they found in Gaius' strongbox."

My strongbox.

"Nero had great fun selecting the jewels he'd keep for himself. And, of course, income from the farm, mines, and quarries provides steady funding for the circuses that make him so popular."

"And the slaves at the villa?"

"Still there. All but Marcipor and those who died or got away."

Otho looked up abruptly—as if hoping to catch a betraying reaction —but Theodosia held her face steady.

They got away! He would have expressed it differently if they were captured later.

"Who got away?"

"That arrogant Greek. What was his name?"

"Alexander."

So... it worked!

"That's it. Well, the coward ran away. Somehow, he managed to steal a bunch of rubies from the silverware; then he made off with a child and that stable hand you liked to fuck."

Gloating inside, Theodosia refused to flinch.

"I'm glad they got away."

"I bet you are."

She smiled at that.

Let him wonder if I helped them.

"You said somebody bought my house in the Subura?"

"Nizzo. Of course, what he really wanted was your farm."

"I knew that. How did you?"

Otho took another swallow of wine.

"I bet you're wondering how you happened to get out of your cozy little hole by the sewer."

Theodosia was curious about that but refused to ask. She was more interested in Nizzo, anyway.

"How did you know Nizzo wanted my farm?"

Otho rose and looked into her eyes, bringing memories of that same conceited face glowering over her as she lay in bed, with Alexander fuming a few steps away.

"I'll tell you how you got out. It started a while ago at a little dinner party for Nero's friends. He's quite an artist, you know—even entertains us himself sometimes—but he gets bored fast and needs lots of variety. Always has. So, lately Scopan's been beating the bushes, finding dancers, poets, and musicians under all sorts of odd rocks."

"Such as the Carcer Tullianum?"

The sardonic lips curled up.

"Someone mentioned your name at the dinner that night. Quite out of the blue. Remembered your curious knack for setting poems to music, even ones you'd never seen before."

"Who?"

"We decided it might be fun to set up a competition, to see how you and a few others could handle the pressure when there was something really desirable at stake."

"Who mentioned me?"

"Nero was interested, but not quite ready to let a convicted murderer out of prison."

"Tell me who mentioned me to the emperor!"

Otho smiled indulgently and sipped his wine.

"Your old friend Flavia Domitilla, I think it was."

Fury flashed through Theodosia's body once more.

Of course! She's got my house and my servants. My pergola. What's left for her to enjoy but my total humiliation?

"Well," Otho's too-jolly voice went on, "Nero couldn't just let a murderer go free, could he? So I—out of love for my emperor—set out to prove you innocent of Gaius' death."

"I *am* innocent!"

"So we all know now."

"You knew it all along. Why didn't you prove it thirty months ago?"

Otho smiled again, drained his cup, and snapped his fingers.

A serving boy came running from behind a curtain, refilled the cup from a pitcher on the table, and returned to his hiding place.

"Who provided the evidence against me in the first place?" Theodosia demanded in a whisper, aware that there might be someone else besides the slave boy behind the curtain.

"The same clever fellow who discovered new evidence last week."

"Who?"

"Who discovered the new evidence? Or the old?"

"Both, damn you!"

"Why, I did, of course!" A laugh gurgled up from Otho's throat. "Don't believe me? Poor little Theo... always so gullible before. Now she doesn't know what to believe."

"What—exactly!—was this 'evidence' you found to implicate me in Gaius' murder?"

"Ho! Such a lofty tone! I would have thought you learned something about humility in the famous pleasure halls of the Carcer Tullianum."

"Well, it's clear you want to tell me. Otherwise you wouldn't have mentioned it."

"Oh, it wasn't hard to come up with evidence. Not when the feeble emperor's heir is your best friend. Not when the Senate is clamoring to solve the murder of a fellow patrician. Not when your prime suspect is a Greek-whore slave masquerading as a Roman heiress."

"Not when you've spent the better part of a year bribing the heiress' maidservant."

"Just turn up a bit of evidence, some damning testimony, and you've got the matter settled."

"So... what was this 'evidence' you turned up?"

Otho strolled back to his couch and stretched out again.

"A slave of mine. Nervous fellow named Calchas. You may remember him. He was always with me whenever I visited your... what was then believed to be your villa. One day, he came to me with a strange story. Right after we'd been there that last time. When you were lying in bed, remember? Calchas said he'd heard something I should know about. A slave... your maid, I believe—"

"Lucilla? The one you bribed?"

"Calchas said she told him you forced her to recruit street thugs to murder your brother. Said you threatened to kill her if she told anyone."

Theodosia stared at the smug figure sprawled on the couch and wondered if she wasn't still in the Carcer Tullianum, sleeping on that slimy rock, dreaming all of this.

"That's ludicrous. A totally ludicrous, made-up story. But even if it were true," she said, recalling the sequence of events, "Lucilla couldn't have talked with Calchas or anyone else at that time. I had her locked in a storage room for trying to poison Titus. On your behalf," she added emphatically. "I could have proved my innocence back then, if I'd ever been given a chance."

"But your girl later confessed—gave all sorts of convincing details—and when my Calchas corroborated everything she said—"

"Under torture? Both of them?"

"Of course."

"You had your own slave tortured?"

Otho's eyebrows rose in a display of offended integrity.

"I've never been squeamish when it came to justice."

"There's no justice in torturing a slave. You just keep it up till you get the confession you want or whatever other twisted information you're looking for."

"You question the emperor's justice?" A heavy pause. "Be glad *you* were never questioned, Theodosia. It could have happened. Anyway, Septimus Manus supervised the interrogations. He's good at it, and thorough. Even Emperor Claudius was satisfied."

Theodosia decided to try another approach.

"Marcipor said you grew up with Manus, so you must know—"

"When have you spoken with Marcipor?"

"A bit earlier. In the kitchen."

Otho slammed his palm on the arm of his couch.

"That boy talks too much. I'll put a stop to it."

Oh, Marcipor… forgive me!

"What did he say about Manus and me?"

"Just that you were friends as children. Nothing else. You've no cause to punish Marcipor for that!"

"That's for me to decide, isn't it? He's my boy now, not yours." Otho gave her a malevolent smile and took another drink. "I didn't see much of Manus for a while. He was stationed in Greece for five years."

"What part of Greece?" For some reason, she knew the answer.

"Corinth. He used to be first deputy to Marcus Viticus, the governor. It never hurts to have an important father, you know. Gets you special posts and privileges."

"Does this have anything to do with my case?"

"Why… I guess it does. Seems the governor decided to check on you, so he contacted his former subordinate, Septimus Manus, in Rome."

"Why?" For some reason, she knew the answer.

"You wrote and asked questions about an old criminal case. Something about that Greek who later ran away."

So, that's it. Trying to help Alexander, I ruined myself.

"Your claim of relationship to the previous governor made the current governor curious, because when he'd served under your father, Aulus Terentius Varro only had a son, and his wife had recently died. It didn't take long for some elderly clerk to remember that—shortly after his wife's death—Governor Terentius Varro bought a female slave who'd caught his eye in the market."

"There's no reason to assume that slave had anything to do with me."

"He bought her ten months before you were born."

Otho's voice faded as Centurion Manus' words slipped into Theodosia's memory.

"It may help to authenticate certain documents." Gods, did my own ring condemn me?

"You're saying they found a bill of sale?"

She held her breath and waited for Otho's answer.

"No... although they searched hard enough for one. But the staffer in Corinth was sure of his facts, and his description of the woman Varro bought in March matched the description of the woman he took to his villa that summer... who gave birth to you the next January."

"But no written evidence from Greece?"

"Nothing. I understand they read every document in the family strongbox, hunting for that bill of sale."

Beloved Juno, smile on Alexander and his family, wherever they are.

"But even if that woman was my mother, how could they be sure she was a slave when I was born? Maybe Father freed her before that."

"They turned up plenty of testimony that he treated her as a slave from the moment she arrived at his villa to the hour of her death."

"Who testified to that?"

"You can't expect me to remember minute details from so long ago."

"You remember everything else."

Otho grinned, taunting her.

"Tell me, damn you!"

"Well, Nizzo for one."

I knew I was right.

"Nizzo was most helpful throughout the investigation. And those old slaves they questioned after your arrest... they all agreed with him."

"When did this begin to come out?"

"Early that December. Manus first told me what Nizzo was saying about you a couple of weeks before Saturnalia."

"Before you made that last trip to my villa?"

"I warned you that day, remember?"

"You threatened me."

"I told you I could save you."

"You tried to force me to marry you."

"Yes, I did, although—looking at you now—it's hard to remember why."

Theodosia turned her back then... wishing she didn't hate Otho and Nizzo and Flavia and Lucius Gallio so much. That would make it easier to think clearly.

"What was this 'evidence' you turned up that proved I didn't murder Gaius?"

"Well, after Flavia convinced the emperor that you would provide amusing entertainment, I had to make Calchas confess he had lied that December."

Theodosia's mouth fell open.

"You had him tortured again?"

"Oh, it didn't last long. He readily admitted he invented the whole thing about your hiring thugs to kill Gaius. Said your girl never made any such statement."

"And that single slave's recantation was enough to get me out?"

"It happened to coincide with His Majesty's wishes."

"You are despicable. I remember telling you I'd rather rot in prison than spend a single night in bed with you. Even now—knowing full well what that means—I would make exactly the same choice."

She heard Otho rise. He strutted around, leering at her.

"Unfortunately, little Theo, you no longer have that option. You will sleep with me whenever I wish it. And I can hardly wait to hear you play for us this evening."

CHAPTER TWENTY-SIX

Theodosia shivered as Scopan led her into Nero's private dining room. The one-shouldered, radish-red tunic they had forced her to wear was uncomfortable and only emphasized her pallor and gauntness. She clutched her cithara for moral support, wondering if she could manage to play anything at all.

The sight of another gilded room no longer impressed her, but the ostentatious number of servants in attendance on nine people made her jaw drop. Behind the three couches stood a waiter for every diner. Others moved about the room with enormous gold salvers, bowls, and pitchers. Still others stood at attention against the side walls... as if waiting to do something that someone else might somehow have forgotten.

The enormous, purple-clad figure of Nero shared the center couch with two women, one of whom Theodosia identified as the Empress Octavia. Six other guests lounged on cushions that sculpted a purple arc around the table. In front of them, a troop of nearly naked dancers had reached the climax of an erotic dance.

Theodosia was trying to steady her nerves when the emperor gestured in her direction.

"Look what's flown in to amuse us!" It was the over-enunciated effort of a man trying to sound sober. "Our little songbird from the Carcer Tullianum!"

Scopan propelled Theodosia into the clearing as the dancers swept around them toward the door.

"Bow before His Majesty," the freedman said.

Theodosia gripped Scopan's arm and managed a wobbly obeisance.

Otho was lying at the upper end of the right couch. Theodosia couldn't focus her eyes; all she saw in the blur was his smirking face.

Only after she had lowered herself to the cushion that a slave had set on the floor—with her inflexible left leg sticking out to the side—did she take in the complete scene on the center couch.

Dressed all in white, the Empress Octavia was toying with the remnants of her dinner, looking bored. Theodosia's eyes shifted to the other woman sharing the emperor's couch.

There—between Nero and Otho—lay the loveliest human being she had ever seen. The young woman was fair, with delicate eyebrows and spidery hair spilling over the intricately beaded gold bands wrapped around her head. Dangling from her ears were enormous pearls encased in gold filament. The diaphanous yellow silk of her stola drifted about her as she lay on the purple cushion. It was a while before Theodosia recognized Poppaea Sabina, whose curiosity about Stefan had caused so much trouble at that ladies-only dinner party years earlier.

What was it Marcipor once said? That Otho was—what word did he use?—"smitten" with Poppaea Sabina.

So, here she was… a yellow flower set in an imperial purple vase.

Poppaea had been eyeing Theodosia. Now she reached over to caress Otho's arm.

"This is the one you're sponsoring in the competition?"

Otho nodded and lifted her hand to his lips.

"She looks dreadful!" Poppaea's silk fluttered as she stroked his cheek. "Does she play well?"

"That's for you ladies to decide," Nero mumbled. "If you like her, we'll have to…" His words faded into incomprehensibility.

"What if we don't like her?" Poppaea said.

"Ooooooh, you will! She does things nobody else can do."

Theodosia's head jerked around as her throat contracted.

This is more than I can bear!

For there lay Flavia—a fluff of pink on the left couch—between Lucius Gallio and a man Theodosia didn't know.

"But suppose we don't?" Poppaea sounded petulant.

Nero shifted his bulky body to address her.

"Then we'll have to decide what else to do with her."

"Singing's all she's good for," Otho said, "unless you call warming a stable hand's straw a useful occupation." He snapped his fingers in Theodosia's direction. "Come on, girl. What are you waiting for?"

At first, it was terrible. Hot with humiliation, Theodosia kept her eyes lowered, not wanting to see how her audience responded. She began with the old Greek ballads, added some lyric verses, and ended with her interpretation of an ode that had been popular in Emperor Claudius' court right before she went to prison. Silently thanking the gods for music—which always had the power to erase her surroundings—she soon felt as if she were playing and singing for herself alone.

"Is that really the imposter?" Poppaea asked when Theodosia had finished. "I met her once, but this woman looks so much older!"

"She does have talent," said the man beside Flavia. "Those Greeks are something else, aren't they?"

"Come here, girl," said a woman in pale blue lying beside Otho.

Theodosia laid her cithara on the floor, rose with difficulty, and made her way to the right couch. Only up close did the obvious falseness of the woman's wig identify her as Annia, the wife of Sullus.

"Oh, my... I hardly recognized her." Annia's voice was syrupy. "What an immense come down!"

Meanwhile Sullus, on the other side of his wife, lifted the hem of Theodosia's tunic to inspect her twisted left leg.

"However did the poor thing learn to walk again?"

Why don't you just ask me?

But she knew it would never occur to an old-guard patrician to ask such a human question of a slave.

Just when she thought the emperor was going to dismiss her, Theodosia heard Flavia's voice once more. For the first time, she looked at her former friend. Flavia held her glance briefly... an odd expression in her eyes. Then she turned to Nero.

"But that's not enough, Sire! You promised you'd select a poem."

Theodosia wanted to bash Flavia's nose, bloody her pretty pink stola.

Gods, how I hate her! I hate them all!

"Yes, yes, select a poem."

Nero waggled a finger at the slave standing behind him. The man hurried out of the room.

"Poor little Theo." It was Otho, oozing false sympathy. "She must be worn out by now."

"You would have her stop?" the emperor asked.

"Oh, no!" Poppaea rubbed a hand up and down Nero's arm. "We must decide if she's worthy of the big competition."

So, Theodosia returned to her place on the floor. Soon the slave arrived with an armload of scrolls. Nero made a show of shutting his eyes and blindly selected a scroll. Then he unrolled the parchment and randomly pointed to a spot on the page. The slave delivered it to Theodosia, his finger carefully fixed at the same location.

It was a Latin ode by Horace... one she had never seen before. She skimmed the poem, then raised her eyes to Nero and announced the title before she began to sing. The melody came with surprising ease, the notes bubbling up from some fountain deep within her. This was what she always did best—although it had been years since she'd tried it—and suddenly she relaxed.

She found a pair of lines with which to construct a chorus and spun out an intricate pattern around them, harking back in increasingly elaborate echoes to the rhythm of her chorus. And by the time she drew out the last note and strummed her final chord, Theodosia was sure she had won a chance to compete at Nero's banquet.

The only thing she didn't know was whether that was a reason to laugh or cry.

"Theodosia."

She was making her way to the kitchen when the whisper spun her around. A fluff of pink slipped into the circle of light under a wall sconce.

She's beautiful, damn her. And she's got it all now.

Married to a rich and influential man...

Savoring her position in the emperor's court...

Living in Theodosia's home...

Conversation with Flavia was the last thing Theodosia wanted. Without a word, she resumed her lopsided walk down the passageway.

"Theodosia!"

Theodosia stopped and turned around again.

"Why don't you just snap your fingers? Little Theo always obeys."

"My dear, don't talk to me that way!" Flavia hurried forward, took her hand, and pulled her into an alcove. "Gods, they've hurt you so! Listen... I'm trying to help you."

"Sure, you'll help me, won't you?" Theodosia could barely speak for the rage she felt. "Just like you helped yourself to my villa."

"Oh, no... you don't understand! I wouldn't have—"

"You would! You'd have done anything to live there. You said so over and over. Don't think I don't remember."

"I wouldn't expect you to understa—"

"Well, it's yours now, so what more do you want of me? Haven't I lost enough? Suffered enough? Been humiliated enough? Do you have to rub my nose in it?"

"Oh, my dear, you've got to listen! They'll come looking for me any moment now. This competition is your chance." Flavia's voice was low already, but she dropped it to a bare whisper. "Someone's going to be there! It's too dangerous to say the name, but—"

"I don't care who's going to be there." Theodosia was determined not to let Flavia hurt her further. "And I don't know why you're doing this to me." Then—stunned as a couple of pieces of the puzzle came together—she raised her cithara. "You found this in my villa and had it smuggled into the Tullianum, didn't you?"

Flavia nodded... so round and soft and refined in her pink silk stola. Theodosia felt so scrawny and coarse and cheap in her radish-red tunic.

"Can't you see why?" Flavia asked. "Don't you understand now?"

"Of course!"

I'll find a way to get my villa back from you.

"Go ahead and enjoy my humiliation, Flavia, but don't expect me to contribute any more to your amusement than I have to."

Flavia's forehead wrinkled, but before she could respond, Theodosia turned and walked out on her.

The sun's first rays penetrated a crack at the edge of the tiled roof. Theodosia stretched one arm up to touch the cheery finger of light on the wall above her head.

She had lain awake all night—her first night out of the Carcer Tullianum—listening with amazed pleasure to the grunts and snores of the two hundred-odd slave women in the stuffy attic. It was a relief to be surrounded by other human beings, whatever their social status or degree of cordiality.

And they definitely had not been cordial last night when the sharp-spoken freedwoman who ruled the women's barracks led Theodosia to the bed assigned to her. The pockmarked scullery maid in the next bunk stared with open hostility and turned her back when Theodosia smiled at her. She had expected curiosity—they were bound to know who she was—but this antagonism baffled her. Eyes followed each clumsy step she took, yet no one said a word to her. They held themselves apart as if Theodosia still belonged to the master caste.

But none of that mattered. She stretched again, relishing the straw mattress and the sense of freedom. Never mind that technically she was a slave. Release from prison was the first step toward true liberty.

According to Scopan, the emperor would dine elsewhere tonight, so Theodosia would not be called this evening. She had been told to practice all day and tomorrow, too, for tomorrow night's competition. But she had other plans for some of that precious time. For a couple of days, at least, she would be relatively free of constraint.

Who knows how long that will last? Better take full advantage of the time I have.

During the night, she had set a series of goals for herself.

Uncover the rest of the Otho-Nizzo plot.

Prove her innocence.

Regain her freedom and her name.

Get revenge on those who had set her up.

Take her villa back from Flavia.

Soon the freedwoman rang the bell to summon the women from their sleep. Theodosia stood in line to splash her face in a bowl of cold water. Then she smoothed her hair with one of the thick wooden combs hanging from ropes attached to the wall and bound it behind her head, as she had been instructed.

After the others had hurried out, she hobbled downstairs with her cithara, ate breakfast, and made her way to Scopan's desk.

"Is there any chance I could have writing materials while I practice?" she asked when he glanced up.

"What for?"

"To make notes when I do something I like."

Scopan provided what she wanted, then pointed to a cubicle whose only door opened directly into his office.

"Practice in there. I want to hear what you can do."

And practice she did, all morning and well into the afternoon... so steadily that Scopan had to tell her to get something to eat. She obeyed, but then—instead of returning after lunch—she wandered around the service halls, looking for an inconspicuous route out of the palace.

In the center of a labyrinth of corridors—separated from an immense banquet hall by a bank of purple curtains—she came to a storage room where men were hauling in wine from a rear alley through a stone-arched doorway.

Falernian. The aroma generated memories that Theodosia quickly shrugged off. *I will drink Falernian again, and at home. But for now... too many other things to think about.*

She slipped into the alley, carrying Scopan's reed-pen, a vial of ink, and a folded sheet of papyrus tied securely to her belt.

From the top of the Palatine Hill, the city glowed as the afternoon sun lit up its multi-colored walls. Theodosia gazed at the flowery masses of crimson and violet in the imperial gardens that surrounded her.

How beautiful my villa must be right now.

"Juno, hear me," she said aloud. "By this time next year, I'll be living at home again. Nothing else matters to me. No one will stop me. Hear me, blessed Juno, for I swear it."

So much was different in the Subura that Theodosia lost time finding her street, and once she did, she hardly recognized it. Scores of new tenements had gone up, bringing the slums even closer to her old house. Where perhaps a handful of children had played in the street, now there were dozens. Corners were blocked with piles of garbage. Dogs roamed in packs. The taverns had always been there, but now it seemed the entire male population of the Subura was soggy with cheap wine. She had never seen so many drunken men in the streets.

At this hour, respectable women were home preparing dinner or—if they were lucky—supervising the slave or two at their disposal. Theodosia had always made sure she was safely inside by midafternoon.

It was dangerous then... but nothing compared to now.

Dodging drunks who urinated on the walls and muttered obscenities, she picked her way through the garbage, the dogs, and the offal, grateful to make it without incident to the block where she had lived.

At the last street corner before her destination, two men stepped up and obstructed her path.

"Wha's'is?" said a stout fellow as he wiped the back of a dirty hand across his mouth. His tongue lolled outside his lips for a moment. "Lil' duckie fall outta th' nest?"

"Co'mon in, gal," said the other, reaching out to snag Theodosia's shawl. He was taller and even heavier, and he smelled of cheap wine and old grease. "Buy ya a drink!"

Theodosia retreated a step as his fingers closed on her shawl. It slipped away from her face.

"Puny lil' thing, ain't she? Gotta funny walk, too." said the first man, clamping his fingers around her wrist. "What'sa matter, honey? Whad'cha do t'get so hurt?"

Theodosia tried to pull away, but the taller man threw his arms around her from behind.

"Bet'cha some ol' master beat 'er!" he chortled as his left hand crossed her chest and grabbed her right breast. Theodosia gagged at the smell of his armpit. "Caught 'er in the stable wi' one of th' hands!"

"Bet'cha she ain't had a goo' man since!" said the first as he pinned her between himself and his smelly companion. "Ain't that right, honey?"

Jerkily, he bent and pressed a rancid, vinegar-wine kiss on her lips.

Theodosia heard the man behind her laugh. Wide-eyed and squirming, she was trying to free herself when she saw a third pair of hands encircle the forehead of the man who was kissing her. An instant later, her assailant's head flew back; he released her wrists. The hand at her breast eased its grip, and Theodosia stumbled free of the drunken pair.

Chest heaving, she rubbed her mouth, straightened her tunic, and pulled the shawl over her head.

"Go back to your wine," a quiet voice said. "I know this lady."

"Lady? This here's a slave duckie. Don'cha know nothin'?"

"More'n you. Get away from her."

Theodosia stared at the tall, stooped figure who had rescued her, then gasped in recognition and relief. It was Rubol, the sandal maker's slave.

"Come with me, lady."

For a few moments, she hesitated... smelling wine on his breath, too.

Since when does stingy old Dinos let him visit a tavern?

Then she looked at the crowd of men gathered on the corner, all of them leering at her. Rubol didn't seem nearly so threatening as the rest.

He opened the door to the shop attached to her old house.

"What're you doing here at this hour, lady? Those men would've raped you right in the street."

Theodosia nodded and stepped into the shop. She caught her breath for a few moments, then looked around and shook her head in wonder.

"Even this place is different. I feel like I've been gone a century." She lifted some of the sandals on display near the door. "These are wonderful, Rubol. Much nicer than what you two made before."

"My master refused to do the newer styles. Always said the old ones was good enough."

"Refused? Said? Past tense?"

"He died two years ago."

"Oh, how sad!" But as Theodosia spoke, she saw a rare smile cross Rubol's gaunt face and knew he was anything but sad. "So, you're... That's why you were in the tavern."

"Freed by his will. And now the owner of the shop."

"I'm happy for you, Rubol," she said as he offered her a chair.

"You don't look too good, lady. What happened to your leg?"

"It's a long story. I'll tell you some other time."

She spotted a boy about twelve coming in from the rear.

"Gotta couple slaves of my own now." There was pride in Rubol's voice. "Doing better than my master ever did."

Another man came out to gape beside the boy. Rubol ordered them both to return to the room behind the curtain.

"You deserve to be successful," Theodosia said, thinking of his life spent hunched over a workbench in that sunless back room.

"I owe you a lot, and I haven't forgotten it. Like to know how I can repay you."

Theodosia cocked her head, puzzled.

"All those months," Rubol explained, "you let Dinos stay on without paying rent. Otherwise—hard as times was—he might have had to sell me to pay it. All the days you slipped food to me, remember? And when you came for a visit that summer... those hundred sesterces you gave Dinos to buy us a good meal. Well, he didn't. I knew he wouldn't. He buried them under his bed with a few coins he'd hoarded over the years. Your money more than quadrupled his savings, so when he died and left this place to me, I soon had enough to buy an experienced man and a boy to train."

"Do you pay rent to the new owner of the house?" Theodosia asked. "A crude fellow called Nizzo?"

"Yes. You know him?"

"He was my father's freedman. The bailiff on my farm."

"How'd he get your house?"

"That's something I plan to find out." She drew her shawl over her head and made ready to leave.

Rubol was rearranging the sandals on the table.

"What makes you think he'll want to talk to you?"

"I don't expect he will." She moved to the door. "You've repaid any debt by saving me from those drunks. Thank you."

Theodosia was crossing the threshold when Rubol caught her arm.

"When you're ready to leave, knock on my door. I'll see you safely out of the Subura."

CHAPTER TWENTY-SEVEN

The plump, pale-skinned, red-haired woman Theodosia remembered as Persa opened the door and stared at the skeletal figure in the street.

"I've come to see Nizzo."

"He's eating."

"Tell him Theodosia Varra wants to see him."

Persa looked stunned. She glanced toward the kitchen as Theodosia pushed past her into the low-ceilinged atrium.

"Tell him!"

As Persa scurried off, Theodosia entered the tiny peristyle. Weeds choked the garden and smothered the bench. There were no flowers.

Nizzo emerged, looking cleaner than she remembered but otherwise unchanged. As usual, his face revealed no emotion.

"You're supposed to be in prison."

"I was released yesterday. Does that worry you?"

"How'd you get out?"

Theodosia took a deep breath and prepared to tell the lie of her life.

"I have a powerful friend, Nizzo."

She paused for effect… and then a new thought occurred to her.

That might actually be true. Nero was Gaius' friend, so shouldn't he be glad to see the real murderer exposed at last?

"A very powerful friend," she repeated.

"You got no friends. They all turned their backs on you years ago."

"Then what am I doing here? Why am I not still in the Tullianum?"

"If you've come to play guessing games, I got better things to do."

He returned to the kitchen. Theodosia followed.

Nothing there had changed. The same pot hung over the fire pit; the same poker stood against the wall.

270

Nizzo sat down to his bowl of pottage and loaf of bread.

Theodosia dropped to a stool as Persa stood by... eyes wide, fingers fidgeting with her thread-bare tunic.

"Tell her to leave," Theodosia said.

Nizzo appeared to think it over, then jerked his head at Persa.

"Go to the bedroom and close the door."

Persa glanced suspiciously at Theodosia as she hurried out. Soon a door banged. Theodosia hoped the woman had obeyed and wouldn't double back to eavesdrop.

Nizzo took a chunk of bread, sopped it in the pottage, and finished it in several large bites.

"This ain't a social call, I bet. What're you here for?"

"The truth."

Theodosia's eyes explored the brick wall behind his chair.

Nothing is changed.

"I want to know what you told the emperor's freedmen before I was arrested."

"What I told the emperor's freedmen?" Nizzo shoved the bowl aside and laughed. "How would I know the emperor's freedmen?"

"Marcus Salvius Otho told me years ago that some of them were friends of yours."

"You should know better than to believe anything Otho says."

"I want to know what lies you told them about me."

"I told no lies about you."

"You did... and you're lying still."

"What would I hope to gain by telling lies about you?"

The calm in his voice was infuriating.

"My farm. You wanted it more than anything else in the world. Tried to intimidate me into selling it. You even threatened to kill me."

"When did I threaten to kill you?"

"That summer after I refused to sell the farm to you. You left a note in my library... that pathetic excuse for a poem I found in the scroll I was reading. 'The sad fate of the brother will soon come to the sister.' You wanted me to think Alexander wrote it, but it didn't fool me. I knew it was your doing."

"I don't know nothing 'bout no poem." Another laugh. "I don't write poetry, lady."

"Well, it wasn't much of a poem." Theodosia pushed herself to her feet. "So, when that trick didn't work, you started lying about me."

"When did I do that?"

"Before they arrested me, and afterwards, too. You spread malicious rumors about my mother. You destroyed me with lies, because you thought that would encourage the emperor to sell you my farm."

"I didn't have to lie to do that. They had plenty of evidence against you. But I did almost buy the farm straight out, same way Lucius Gallio bought your villa."

"Gallio conspired against me. So did you."

"Didn't have to conspire. I could've paid for what I wanted... just like he did."

"Gallio is rich. You're not."

"I had backers."

"Who?"

"That ain't your business. Don't matter now anyway."

Theodosia turned toward the fire pit, took the poker, and jabbed the fire until it began to crackle. Nizzo was watching her. When she dropped the poker into its niche, he relaxed and went back to his bread.

She let her tone soften as she strolled behind Nizzo's chair. He was chewing steadily, talking with his mouth full.

"Otho was one of your backers, wasn't he?" she asked.

"He tell you that?"

"What was he asking in return?"

"Just a small share of the profits."

"I don't believe that. A man as rich as Otho doesn't need a small share of anything."

"He said he'd do it as a favor."

"Otho never did anyone a favor in his life."

Nizzo shrugged and continued chewing his crusty bread, as the fire popped loudly behind him. Casting her eyes back and forth from Nizzo to the wall beside her, Theodosia slipped the loose brick out with her left hand and removed Phoebe's long-hidden knife with her right.

"I can't imagine," Nizzo was saying through a mouthful, "what you think someone like Otho would want from someone like me."

"Lies." Holding the brick behind her and the knife in a fold of her tunic, Theodosia stepped to Nizzo's side. "He wanted lies about me."

In the next moment, she flashed the knife up and pressed its keen edge above the ring of tough skin on the freedman's throat.

"Flatten your hands on the table!"

Nizzo obeyed instantly. Through the blade, Theodosia felt him swallow. She tossed the brick into a corner.

"Now, you're going to tell me everything you told the investigators."

"I only said what Otho wanted me to say."

"And that was…?"

"He'll kill me if I tell you."

"And I'll kill you if you don't. So… let's take it step by step. You murdered my brother, didn't you?"

"No."

"You took a slave from the farm. Then—after you killed Gaius—you killed the slave, too." She paused. "Confess."

Sweat was glistening on Nizzo's forehead.

"I can't confess to what ain't true."

"Don't lie to me."

"Ain't lying! I swear it!"

"Then tell me who did kill Gaius."

"You don't want to know."

"Now who's playing games?" She pressed the knife deeper into his throat. "You ruined my life. I lost everything because of your greed. So… I think it'd be a real pleasure to watch you die."

"I'll die anyway if I tell you."

"Who killed my brother?"

Nizzo muttered something that Theodosia couldn't understand.

"Speak up!"

"It was Marcus Salvius Otho that murdered Gaius Terentius Varro." Nizzo sounded as if he were testifying before an official investigator.

"How do you know that?"

"He told me."

Marcipor was right!

"Why would Otho say something like that to you?"

"I dunno, but he invited me to his house one night, gave me lots of good wine, and told me that. Must have been trying to convince me he was serious. Said he knew I hated Gaius as much as he did… and that I'd never tell on him if he helped me get what I wanted."

"Our farm?"

Nizzo nodded gingerly and drew a thin breath.

"Said he'd make sure I got it if I did one thing for him."

"And that was…?"

No answer.

"Come on, Nizzo. You've been doing so well. I was beginning to think you might actually survive this." She kept her voice soft. "What did Otho want you to do?"

"Swear your mother was a slave."

"Why would something that absurd even occur to him?"

"I guess your brother said something when Otho told him he wanted to marry you. Something about how you was a bastard, since the old man never married that whore he brung with him from Greece."

"So... the only thing Gaius thought was that I was Father's bastard child?"

"I guess. It was Otho's idea to prove your mother was a slave. He said there'd been talk about her in Greece, but it was just some Greek clerk saying it. But if a Roman citizen like me would swear it was true..."

Of course. Since there were no documents to prove it.

"And did you swear it?"

Silence.

Pleased by the sweat running down Nizzo's temples, Theodosia increased the pressure on his throat to the point where she thought she might actually cut him. After another moment, he nodded.

"What lies did you invent to convince the investigators that my mother was a slave?"

"I said your father bragged about the duckie he'd bought cheap at a country market in Greece."

Theodosia laughed at that.

"Didn't it occur to anybody that my father would never refer to any woman—slave or free—as a 'duckie'? That's how a slave talks... or a coarse freedman. Not the grandson of one of Rome's most learned men. Not someone who had such a fine way with words... who took such delight in language and literature. Besides... how could they think a patrician like my father would even get into a conversation about personal matters with the bailiff on his farm?"

"Well, they believed it."

"No doubt."

Otho saw to that.

"What other lies did you tell them?"

"I said my former master told me there wasn't no Roman lady could screw as good as a Greek slave whore, and that he was a fool for waiting so long to get one for himself. And then I told them something your father really did say—I didn't invent it!—right after your mother died."

"What?"

"Said he shouldn't have forced her to have a child, because she was so delicate and ended up dead."

"He might have said that about a wife."

"That ain't how the investigators understood it."

Of course not.

"I heard the old slaves that belonged to your father remembered something similar."

"Well, after you made the original accusations, it's not surprising they managed to recall it. Torture must have a strange effect on the memory." Theodosia paused again, but kept the pressure on his gullet. "I have two more questions, and if you don't lie, I'll let you go. Why did Otho kill my brother? And... who was his accomplice?"

"How should I know? I wasn't there. Immortal gods, I'm telling you the truth! You gotta trust me now, lady."

"Give me one good reason to trust you."

"Because that damned sonofabitch betrayed me, too."

"What do you mean?"

"After all I done for him, Otho backed out on his part of the deal. Refused to lift a finger to help me get that farm. When the emperor decided to keep it and put somebody else in charge, Otho didn't do nothing to stop it. Now I'm stuck here with only my savings and that dumpy woman I bought years ago. No real money coming in, just dribbles of rent from them two shops outside."

"How did you end up with my house?"

"Otho bought it cheap and gave it to me."

"Why?"

"To shut me up, I guess."

For some reason, Theodosia believed him.

"Couldn't you have told the investigators the truth and exposed his scheming? That might have saved me a few years in prison, not to mention my name and property. I would've given you a much larger share of the farm income out of gratitude."

"Only a fool of a freedman would admit he lied to the emperor's men and accuse a powerful senator of murder."

"So, you took what you could get and kept your mouth shut."

Makes sense.

"I have to admit," she said, easing the knife away from his throat, "in your situation, I might have done the same."

Nizzo inhaled and exhaled slowly; then he straightened in the chair.

In the next instant, he slammed his hand on hers, pinning the blade against the table. Theodosia yelped as her knuckles hit the wood.

"Sit down," Nizzo ordered, and she did.

They studied each other across the table. His heavy hand still pressed the knife—and her hand—against the boards.

275

"I should kill you for that," he said.

"Go ahead. I don't care."

What a fool! I'll never get a signed statement from him now.

"I might as well be dead," she added, "for all my life's worth, for all it's been worth these past years."

"You ain't the only one whose life ain't worth shit nowadays. Think I've been happy away from everything I know how to do... everything I worked hard to get... everything I ever built up in my life? I had some pride and power at that farm, and something to aim for."

He stared at her, but Theodosia said nothing.

"I worked hard for your family, lady, my whole life. Thought that sooner or later one of you would appreciate it enough to reward me. But except for your father setting me free after I ran his farm for years as a slave, that never happened. Then, when you started meddling and—even worse—after you refused to see me anymore... Can you blame me for thinking that maybe Otho was the one who'd finally help me get what I deserved? But that bastard double-crossed me."

Nizzo released her hand and wrapped his fingers around the handle of Phoebe's knife.

"You don't know," he went on, "how much I despise that man. I hate him. I'd kill him right now if I thought I could get away with it."

Surprisingly moved by Nizzo's rant, Theodosia leaned forward and put her hand on his.

"I hate him, too. So, let's help each other." She untied the papyrus, ink, and pen on her belt. "Give me a statement to take to my powerful friend in the palace. I'll write down whatever you say, and you can sign it. I promise... if we work together, we can both get revenge for what Otho did to us."

"I ain't signing nothing. Don't care how powerful your friend is. I ain't crazy."

"All right. You don't have to put anything in writing. Just give me the information I need to clear my name and win my freedom."

"After you almost slit my throat? Next thing, you'll have me up in front of the emperor, explaining why I lied. Next thing after that, I'll be back in chains. Back in hell." He gestured around the shabby kitchen. "This place ain't much, but... Shit, lady. Life and freedom and citizenship is all I got. Why should I risk all that to help you?"

"Because you owe all that to my father. Without him, you'd still be a slave chained to a bunch of other men, laboring under some overseer's whip. For his sake, Nizzo... please help me!"

Nizzo sat still, with the knife resting under his fingers, which rested under hers. It was a while before Theodosia went on.

"Someone told me long ago that Otho was the one who had killed Gaius, but I couldn't believe a man from a distinguished family would do such a thing. From the start of my relationship with Otho—when he first came to this house to offer his condolences—I accepted his story that he and my brother had been close friends. I guess I was too trusting. Or maybe I didn't want to think that a patrician could do something so wrong to a friend. Maybe it was just easier—and safer—to figure out *your* motivation and blame *you*."

She lifted her hand from his.

"Nizzo, that same person told me that Otho was afraid his father would find out how dissolute he was. Then the old man would disinherit him, for sure. I know Gaius was blackmailing him. Otho gave Gaius a valuable slave and a set of silver serving pieces inlaid with gigantic rubies. It had to be to keep him quiet about something. So, I think Otho killed Gaius to stop the blackmail."

"Maybe. But lots of people knew Senator Salvius Otho would have disowned his precious son if he found out half the things he was doing. No telling how many people were blackmailing Otho. His father could have learned those secrets—and disowned him—at any time... and Otho would have been out on the street with no money."

Nizzo dug the point of the knife into a crack between the boards of the tabletop and began gouging out years of accumulated sediment. After a long wait, he looked straight into Theodosia's eyes.

"Here's my suggestion, lady. If you're looking for motivation for the murder—and the key to proving your innocence—forget about your brother's blackmail. Start with the Terentius Varro fortune. If Otho had gotten his hands on your money, that would've stopped all further attempts at blackmail from anybody else in his slimy circle of friends."

"You're saying... our money was the one thing that would have protected Otho from the risk of disinheritance, no matter who might decide to rat him out to his father. That makes sense to me. But what gave him such confidence that he could get his hands on it?"

"He almost did."

"By marrying me, of course. But what made him so sure he could pull off such a thing?"

"He figgered a young, inexperienced girl would be an easy conquest. More than anything else, Otho's arrogant. He just assumed you'd fall all over yourself the instant he showed an interest in you."

"Well, yes, and it worked at first."

Juno, it's all so obvious!

"I see the scheme now. That's why Otho started bribing my maid months before he killed Gaius. Why he got to me so fast the morning after the murder and made sure he was the one I'd turn to for advice. That's why he had me so afraid of Alexander before I even got back to my villa, and why he kept hammering on that theme all summer. And then—when he saw how well we were getting along—that's why he hated Alexander so much. I bet he even wrote that stupid poem and got Lucilla to plant it in the scroll I was reading... to make me afraid of Alexander again, after I had become too comfortable with him."

Nizzo continued his tabletop excavations in silence.

Theodosia walked to the fire pit and stared into the glowing embers.

"That's why he was so determined that I not marry Titus. Why he tried to poison him. Why he preferred to destroy me, rather than see—"

She turned back to Nizzo, marveling at her own discoveries.

"Of course! My money and my Terentius Varro bloodline would've made Titus a threat to Otho's ambitions. And so... after everything he had done —after blackmail and bribery and murder—Otho couldn't bear to see a rival reap the rewards of marrying me!"

An hour later, in the doorway of the house that had once been hers, Theodosia shook the hand of the man she had hated and feared and threatened to kill.

"I'm grateful for the insights you gave me. You have my word that I won't mention your name until I've got every piece of evidence I need to prove the truth to Nero. And also my word on this, Nizzo... when I regain my name and my estate, I'll welcome you back to the farm as a full and equal partner."

"That's good enough for me, lady. Just be careful who you talk to. And keep your hand on that weapon tonight."

Theodosia fingered the knife that was now tucked into her belt, pulled the shawl over her head, and stepped into the dark street.

She had planned to accept Rubol's offer to escort her out of the Subura, but it was very late. He and his slaves were probably sound asleep by now.

Besides, the streets were beginning to fill with night traffic. Soon the city would be bustling with the carts of construction and market suppliers, who were forbidden to haul in goods by day. Surely the honest workers would protect her from any drunks that might be out at this hour.

Sticking to the main thoroughfares, she made her way out of the Subura to the area bordering the Forum. Wheeled traffic had not yet reached this far into the city. There was no moonlight, but still... it was unlikely she would be accosted in the commercial district. A bit further along the Via Sacra and she would be at the foot of the Palatine Hill.

She turned a corner at the far end of the deserted street of the potters and was halfway down the block when she heard scuffling sounds.

She froze.

At the end of the street, she could make out four hooded thugs who had attacked a man and were beating him with their fists. She ducked into the closed doorway of a shop and drew her shawl to her face, almost certain they had seen her. The next instant, she heard shouts and the smack of sandals on cobblestones.

Before she could get to her knife, three of the men surrounded her, grabbed her arms, and ripped the shawl off her head. The hoods they wore muffled their words, but they smelled of wine... a quality wine this time.

Trapped in the doorway, Theodosia did the only thing she could. She screamed.

A skinny-legged tough in a gray hood and tunic clapped his right hand over her mouth. Desperate to fight him off, Theodosia sank her teeth into his palm, feeling a simultaneous rush of blood on her tongue. The man cursed and yanked his bleeding hand away; then he slapped her hard on the mouth, splitting her lip with his ring.

"Bitch!"

He grabbed her by the hair, jerked her to the paving stones, and was fumbling with the hem of her tunic when the fourth thug ran up.

"Wagon coming!" he shouted.

Without hesitation, the men took off along the deserted street.

Theodosia raised one hand to wipe the blood from her lips as she lifted herself on her other hand and stared at the fleeing gang.

And then she began to tremble... for the voice that had shouted the warning was Otho's, and the ring on the pudgy hand she had bitten bore an enormous ruby set into a twisted-serpent design.

CHAPTER TWENTY-EIGHT

The narrow, winding street of the goldsmiths was one of many in the commercial district between the Palatine, Caelian, and Esquiline hills. Despite the early hour and the threatening sky, the area hummed with life. Slaves unfurled awnings and hauled displays into the street as their masters looked on. Children racing each other to their pedagogue's house hurtled down the cobblestones and careened around corners. Beggars plied their trade with the zeal of mosquitoes after a big rain. Litters clogged traffic near the best shops as teams of bearers crouched beside their poles... complicating the situation for a lame pedestrian who had slipped out of the emperor's palace on an urgent mission.

"Odd walk for a cute little duckie," cackled one litter slave as Theodosia approached. "Musta got its leg run over by a cart."

"What'sa matter with you?" said his pole-mate, a blond, brawny Gaul. "Never seen a gimp whore before? Man, they's lotsa ducks like that'n down by the river."

"Ain't never seen no duckie walk like that."

"Hell, man, you don't know nothin'. Cheapest ducks in town, they all walk just like that. One bad night, y'know, and the duckie's banged up for life. Then nobody but a dreg like you'd want 'er. Hey there, duckie!"

The Gaul reached out and tugged at Theodosia's tunic.

"Tell me where they keep you. I'll come give you a real good time tonight!"

"You would, wouldn't you?" said a third man as Theodosia stepped back and pulled her shawl more snugly around her face before picking another route around them. "You spend every sesterce you can steal in them duck nests."

"Beats chasin' girls that see you haulin' a litter."

Without warning, the Gaul stuck his foot out and laughed heartily when Theodosia stumbled over it, dropping her shawl.

"Weedy thing, ain't she?" said the Gaul. "Not so cute up close. Got yourself cut up some, eh, duckie?" He turned as he lost interest in Theodosia. "Down by the wharf, any man's a king who's got three sesterces. Pay the fellow at the door—or the slut-lady at the door—and you got a little duckie all to yourself for the night. Do anything you want. Nobody's gonna say nothin' 'less you kill 'er outright."

Burning with humiliation, Theodosia continued along the street. She couldn't recall the name of the goldsmith who had come to her villa to size the signet ring, but most merchants displayed their names on awnings above their doors. She searched two dozen shops before she spotted a familiar name and knew she had found him.

"Get out, slave. We have nothing for the likes of you."

"Please... may I speak with Reuben ben Judah?"

"He's busy."

"But he knows me."

The clerk looked amused.

"You must go."

"It's important!"

Theodosia slipped past him, heading for the rear of the shop as fast as her stiff gait would take her. Reuben ben Judah and two others working at a long table looked up as she barged in, followed by the clerk.

"I'm sorry, Reuben. She got away from me."

Theodosia dropped the shawl from her head. Ben Judah stared at her, obviously searching his memory. The next moment, he rose, frowning.

"Leave us, please," he said to the other three. When they were gone, he closed the door. "What are you doing here?"

The man's Semitic accent revived bittersweet memories of that long-ago day when Theodosia had felt as beautiful and pampered as Cleopatra.

"You know who I am?"

"I know all about you."

"Then you know I was falsely accused and have been released—"

"What do you want from me?"

"Just some information, then I'll leave. I won't scare off your customers, and you'll never see me again." She sighed. "You once told me you had made a very special ring for my brother. Do you remember?"

"I remember."

"You said he picked that ring up from you just a few hours before he was murdered. Remember that, too?"

"I do."

"You said you hoped the ring had made it into my hands, but I think you knew I'd never seen it. I believe you told me that for a reason."

Theodosia waited for a response, but none came.

"Can you tell me what that ring looked like?"

"Why?"

"It may help solve the mystery of my brother's murder."

"That murder was solved years ago."

"They found a scapegoat—me—but they solved nothing."

"Why should I get involved with a murder?"

"You're not! Nobody's going to think you had anything to do with my brother's murder. But the information you have about that ring may help me prove who did and restore some sanity to my life."

"Look, slave or lady or whatever you are... I'm not a Roman citizen, just a foreigner trying to make a living in Rome. A Jew with a little talent who likes his head attached to the rest of him. I've got a wife and six children. I can't afford to get involved with you."

Theodosia laid her hand on his sleeve.

"My brother gave you a lot of business. His money must have bought plenty of meat and sandals for those children. Reuben ben Judah, please. Help me identify his real murderer and clear my name!"

The goldsmith stared at her bony hand; then he shook it off his arm, moved away, and opened the door.

"Joseph," he called, and the clerk entered quickly. "Show this woman to the street."

Fighting tears—barely able to see where she was going—Theodosia brushed past the obnoxious litter slaves and joined the flow of people moving toward the Forum. After a while, exhausted from trying to keep up, she collapsed against a wall on the southwest side of the Via Sacra.

It's hopeless. Nobody will ever give me the proof I need.

Glancing around, she identified the building as the Temple of Jupiter Stator... built four centuries earlier in fulfillment of a vow made by Romulus at a moment of apparent defeat by the Sabines. Romulus had managed to turn that defeat into victory, but Theodosia saw little chance of such a turnabout for herself.

Desperate for a place to rest, she stood and sidled along the perimeter wall to a gate that led to a quiet garden at the rear of the temple. Well-tended roses in orange and yellow raised their heads as if to defy the increasingly dark sky, but they did nothing to cheer the woman who limped past them. Theodosia lowered herself onto a long bench in a secluded spot behind the flowerbeds and gave in to her tears.

All last night—her second sleepless night in a row—she had thought of nothing but meeting with ben Judah. Nothing else had mattered as she lay awake in the women's attic. Not being attacked twice on the street. Not her cut and swollen lip. Not the scolding she received when she came in late. Not even the prospect of the competition that would take place tonight. Nothing mattered now except identifying the owner of that ruby-serpent ring and the plump hand she had bitten. Surely that was all she would need to expose Otho and his fellow thugs.

She sat in the garden as the morning sky grew black.

Better get back before the downpour.

But still she stayed. Fat drops began to shake the roses and spatter on the ground around her. Savoring the unaccustomed freedom, Theodosia stretched out on the bench, closed her eyes, and lifted her face to the warm spring rain as her hair and tunic went from damp to wet to soaked.

Finally, she turned on her side, cradled her head in her arms, and—as if blessed by a magical temple spirit—fell into a deep, restorative sleep.

She awoke to footsteps on the gravel walk.

"I've been looking everywhere for you. For hours."

Theodosia opened her eyes and saw Joseph, the goldsmith's young clerk. It was still raining, and he was as drenched as she.

"Reuben will tell you what you want to know."

Reuben ben Judah nodded as Theodosia stood dripping just inside the door of his shop. Another clerk offered towels to her and Joseph.

"This is undoubtedly the most foolish thing I've ever done," ben Judah said as Theodosia blotted water from her tunic and hair, "but I fear God too much to refuse to help you."

He led her to his workroom, where a series of parchment sheets lay on the table.

Theodosia stared at the drawings in silence. There were sketches of those serving pieces at her villa—each one with that familiar ruby-serpent motif—as well as a ring with the same design. She took the drawing of the ring and studied it at length.

Unlike the other sketches, the only specification here was that the ring was to be of gold. No notation as to the sort of stone to be set into the serpent's mouth.

Even so, Theodosia's skin began to crawl as she read the writing at the bottom of the page: "Ring commissioned and paid in advance by Marcus Salvius Otho. Deliver when completed to Gaius Terentius Varro."

The page bore two seals. The upper one was Otho's, the lower one the Varro seal acknowledging receipt of goods. Alongside it was the date of Gaius' death.

"May I have this?"

"To take to the Praetorians?"

"No! I mean to present my case to the emperor himself."

Ben Judah ran his fingers through his hair.

"It's too dangerous. We'll both be put to death."

"I don't think so. See—" She groped for convincing words. "I know Nero. He's a fair man, and Gaius was his friend. The emperor knows now that I'm innocent. It's because of him that I'm out of the Carcer Tullianum. I believe he'll do whatever he can to see the real murderers brought to justice."

"And you can prove who they are?"

"With this and some testimony that's pledged to me... yes. But I need to document the gem you set into that ring. Do you remember?"

"Oh, I'll never forget that." Ben Judah took the sketch, jotted a notation on it, and returned it to her. "It was the stone that held things up. Must have taken me eight months to get it."

"Why? What was so special about it?"

"The color—blood red—and the size. Your brother refused three or four others before my suppliers found the one he finally accepted. Tribune Otho was disgusted when he discovered he'd have to pay so much more. He said his father would disinherit him if he ever learned how much money he'd wasted on gifts to Gaius Terentius Varro."

Ben Judah shook his head, as if it still amazed him.

"I set the biggest ruby I've ever seen in my life into that ring!"

The banquet hall glowed with hundreds of lamps, but the perfumed oil that fueled their flames had long since lost its duel with the aromatic

dishes on their golden platters. Gigantic vases of cobalt-blue glass—
overflowing with purple and gold lilies—set off the ten trios of couches
where the emperor and his eighty-nine guests had been lounging for over
three hours.

Playing in one corner, the palace musicians were occasionally
drowned out by thunder. An aggressive squadron of belly dancers had left
the open area in the center. Around the room, restless guests stirred to
ease their overburdened stomachs... or maybe just impatient for the next
phase of the entertainment.

Uncomfortable in the mass of slaves awaiting their masters in the
servants' kitchen, Theodosia had wandered past the men hauling kegs of
wine out of storage cubicles and made her way to one end of the banquet
hall, where she was now standing in front of the purple draperies.

Her discussions with Nizzo and ben Judah, that restful sleep in the
temple garden, a warm-up hour on her cithara, and a cup of wine had
combined to relax her and build her confidence. She would play and sing
like a demon tonight, win the newly announced prize of freedom, and
then, in her moment of triumph, present her case to Nero.

Surely she could convince him, given Nizzo's promise to tell the
truth and ben Judah's ring sketch, which was now folded and waiting
inside her tunic. Somewhere out there—on one of those overfed patrician
fingers—was an equally oversize ruby-serpent ring that would incriminate
its unwary owner. And even if no one were wearing that particular ring
tonight, others would remember seeing it.

A few well-put questions to Otho—Theodosia already had them
worked out in her head—and the truth would be plain to everyone in the
hall. Nero would have no choice but to restore her name and property.

I'll make Flavia regret she dreamed up this competition!

Hope for justice had done a great deal to restore Theodosia's spirits.
Scopan had insisted that she put on that hideous radish-red tunic again,
but the freedwoman had provided a finer comb, so now her hair looked as
good as it could after years of sickness and neglect. Even her cut lip felt
better tonight. She had worried that the swelling might interfere with her
singing, but that hour of practice had eased her mind.

And right before she left the attic—following some compulsion she
did not understand but knew she had to obey—she had torn a strip from
her shawl, wrapped it around her right thigh to create a smooth, wide
band, and slipped Phoebe's knife up into it, on the inside of her leg.

The weapon lay there now, snug and invisible under her tunic... a
comforting presence in this risky venture she was about to undertake.

Occasionally, looking into the banquet hall, she recognized one or other of the guests heading for the toilet. She spotted Lucius Gallio that way, and by watching his return, picked out Flavia near the center of the room. Primus Sullus was there with his wife, Annia. So was Marcia, the woman who had tried to buy Stefan four summers ago.

Theodosia's heart almost stopped when she saw Titus, wearing a scarlet uniform that looked splendidly out of place among the togas of the other men. He entered the hall on the opposite side and waved to someone across the room. Theodosia pulled her eyes away from him in time to see Vespasian wave back.

Juno, every Roman I know is here tonight. What a chance to present my evidence!

Just as at the dinner two nights earlier, Otho was positioned next to the head table, with only the gold-and-pearl-wrapped Poppaea Sabina between him and Nero. The Empress Octavia, on her husband's other side, looked every bit as bored as before.

Scopan bounded into the center of the hall and bowed with an exaggerated flourish. Theodosia cocked her head to listen.

"Illustrious Romans... our featured entertainment will be among the most memorable ever presented in this imperial capital. Perhaps even worthy," Scopan made another obeisance to Nero, "to be heard by the greatest poet and musician the world has ever known."

He paused for dramatic effect.

"Exalted nobles... it is my pleasure to present a competition of outstanding talent: four superb musicians and an equal number of poets divinely inspired by the muse. The poets are all Greeks, of course... free men who will be generously rewarded for their participation, as will those who discovered them and brought them here for your enjoyment. But the musicians come from your own great households. I beg your assistance in selecting for freedom the one talented slave who comes closest to exemplifying the sublime gifts of our beloved emperor."

The hyperbole was continuing, but Theodosia ducked behind the curtain, pressing her hand across her mouth to restrain the laughter that would destroy any hope of carrying out her plan. A few moments later, she made her way through the labyrinthine corridors to the kitchen.

But, try as she might, she couldn't rid her mind of Scopan's excessive adjectives.

Who are the other superb musicians? The divinely inspired poets?

All Scopan had said was that they were sponsored by Nero's friends, which had the potential to make the evening explode with court rivalry.

No doubt that's part of the appeal of this event.

According to Otho, the idea of a competition had been Flavia's.

That little social climber would do anything to ingratiate herself with Nero.

But Theodosia smiled to herself. For some reason that she didn't understand, she had ended up under Otho's sponsorship, which would make exposing him doubly satisfying.

And I bet Flavia's having a fit right now, since there's a chance I might go free. She's got to know I'll fight to get my home back.

In the kitchen, Scopan's assistant was calling for the musicians, and Theodosia presented herself.

After they entered the great hall, Scopan began explaining the rules of the competition. First, the musicians would perform numbers of their own choosing, to let the emperor's guests hear how they sounded when familiar with their material. Then each one would be given eight poems —two by each poet—from which they were to select four that would serve as the bases for their improvisations. Finally, each couch of three guests would make its choice.

The musician with the most of the thirty votes, Scopan announced with drama, would be set free by the grace of His Majesty. Whoever sponsored the winner would be granted a special imperial favor of his choosing.

So, that's why Otho's sponsoring me. To put Nero on the spot and win some favor that he wouldn't be able to get otherwise. What fun it's going to be to turn the tables on him. Otho and his fellow thugs will be the ones on the spot tonight, not Nero.

Theodosia watched as the poets were introduced.

A rumble of admiration swept the room as Marcia presented the handsome, athletic-looking Greek at her side.

An elderly senator announced the name of the bearded Greek who accompanied him. Both had the wizened look of philosophers.

Another sponsor was a woman whom Theodosia didn't know. Her Greek was younger than the others and taller, too, though not so good looking as Marcia's.

And—*of course!*—Flavia had her own Greek to show off... a shy-looking fellow with a beard who kept his eyes lowered and, when introduced, only rose half-way from his place beside her on the couch.

It was a given that the poets were Greeks. Even the proudest Romans readily admitted they had yet to produce a poet the equal of a moderately gifted Greek... Scopan's effusive praise of Nero notwithstanding.

Next came introductions of the slave musicians. There were two men and two women, so Scopan had paired them as couples for the procession.

The other woman, who carried no instrument, was a tall, willowy German with a radiant smile and waist-long yellow hair that caught the glow of every lamp. Her escort, a brawny Numibian with a drum strapped to his bare ebony torso, made for the sort of amusing color contrast that the Romans always enjoyed.

Theodosia knew that she—with her old-fashioned cithara and stiff, side-swinging gait—and the hollow-chested Greek pipe player she was standing beside would look pathetic in comparison.

Scopan announced their names as each pair entered. The crowd roared its approval of the German and the Numibian, but at Theodosia's name the roar subsided, replaced by a wave of murmurs. She held her head high as ninety necks stretched to look at her... and managed to avoid Titus' eyes as she passed his couch near the door.

They went to the center clearing, where they sat on large white cushions. An armless x-chair stood in the middle, a blessedly long way from the purple mass that was Nero. Their order of performance was established as the German, the Numibian, Theodosia, and the Greek.

The blonde Venus bowed in every direction and, spurning the chair, sauntered sensuously toward Nero's table. Her voice had a wild, barbaric edge as she sang a haunting ballad in her native tongue. Although few of the Romans could have understood it, they responded with such vigorous applause that Theodosia's confidence quickly began to fade.

The Numibian took the chair, unstrapped his drum, bent over it, and began a soft beat, steady and lovely, which rose to a loud pounding that rivaled the thunder outside. Abruptly, it stopped. Then his song began... with an identical soft, sobbing rhythm in his voice that swelled until it, too, threatened to shake loose the roof tiles.

There was an uncertain silence when the Numibian finished. But soon the applause came, even more appreciative than for the German. Theodosia took a deep breath, closed her eyes, and said a quick prayer to Juno.

Unable to rise easily from the low cushion, she laid the cithara down, braced herself on her hands and slowly stood, supported only by her right leg. The Greek piper kindly handed her the instrument, and she accepted it with gratitude... conscious of the whispers all around.

Making an effort to swing her left leg as little as possible, she moved to the chair. She bowed to Nero, sat as gracefully as she could, and cradled her cithara in her lap, trying not to think of the once-friendly eyes now reveling in her shame.

She had planned to play one of the traditional Greek hymns that Phoebe had taught her, but after hearing her competitors, she knew that wouldn't be exciting enough. She made a quick decision to change to a bawdy popular tune, "My Faithless Sailor from Ostia," which everyone would know and could join her in singing.

But almost as soon as she began, she knew the switch was a mistake. She had never liked that song, so she hadn't practiced it much in the Carcer Tullianum. Her fingers missed some notes. Her voice sounded thin. She felt her face turning the same ugly red as her tunic. When at last she finished, half-hearted clapping and louder murmurs accompanied her back to her cushion.

Theodosia hardly heard the Greek piper as she slumped over her cithara, eyes squeezed shut.

It's lost. Hopeless. No chance now to win my freedom or present the evidence I struggled so hard to get.

She would lose the competition and disappear into Nero's kitchens or laundry until someday, in a fit of economy, they'd sell her to someone else. As she raised her hands to applaud the piper's performance, a corner of ben Judah's document—tucked into the front of her tunic—pricked her breast... as if to taunt her.

Beloved Juno, let this be finished soon!

Scopan came forward and, with all the manners of a courtier, ushered the luminous German to the center. The poets had been dining with their sponsors along both sides of the clearing. Scopan collected two sheets from each and handed them to the blonde with instructions to improvise a performance of four of the eight poems. But she hesitated so long—stared at the pages so long—that Nero rolled onto his stomach and glared at her.

"What's the matter?"

The woman looked at him with a stricken expression.

"Sire, I not—" she said in broken Latin, "I not read this."

"Jupiter's shit! Who sponsored this woman?"

A doughy-faced patrician rose from a nearby table.

"I did, Sire. The girl is mine."

"The rules were announced in advance," Nero said. "The contestants must be able to read the poems they are given."

"I only knew the palace desired superlative talent, Sire."

"You only knew that I would grant a favor to whomever sponsored the winner. Do you deny it, Septimus Terentius?"

"No, Sire, but… your freedman made her perform when I brought her in. He said he found her acceptable, so I assumed she fulfilled the requirements."

Scopan—all defensively raised shoulders, palms, and elbows—came forward to explain.

"The girl sings wonderfully well, Sire, as Your Majesty has heard. It is not her fault she does not read Greek."

"Nonsense. You knew we were using Greek poets. You should have made sure she could read what those poets had written."

"Perhaps the girl reads Latin," Scopan said. "There are among this illustrious group any number of fine poets. Your Majesty included, of course. We could certainly find a few poems in Latin for her to interpret."

"Do you read Latin, girl?" Nero's tone was sharp.

"I not read at all, Sire."

"She is disqualified. Take her away."

Nero drank deeply of his wine as Scopan led the weeping German to the door. When the room was still again, Nero nodded toward the bare-chested Numibian.

"Who sponsored that fellow?"

"Niger is mine, Sire," said a senator sharing a table with Titus, "and I'm happy to say that he does read Greek. He's an educated man as well as my valet. He was with me in Athens for many years. I can assure Your Majesty that he is an accomplished interpreter."

"Excellent! And the other two?"

"My slave, Pylades, is a native Greek, Sire." This time the speaker was a woman on a couch behind Theodosia. "He is a poet, too, and an actor. We have tested him with poetry he has never seen before. I think Your Majesty will be pleased."

Otho rose now. One corner of his mouth curled upward as he pointed to Theodosia.

"Sire, the girl I am sponsoring speaks, reads, writes, and sings in both Greek and Latin. She is a half-breed, as you know."

Theodosia winced, but Nero looked satisfied.

"We still have three fine contenders. Proceed with the competition."

Scopan passed the German woman's poems to the Numibian, who took a few moments to read the one on the top of the stack, then handed the sheet to a page assigned to hold it before him, and—almost without hesitation—began to beat his drum.

The rhythm was gentle now, for Niger had picked a love poem. Theodosia listened with interest. This combination of voice and drum was something she had never heard before. Despite her growing despair, she found herself tapping her fingers to the unusual rhythm that Niger had created. He did equally well with the other three poems. All were different in subject and style, which showed he was picking one from each poet. There was something of the jungle in his music, something free-spirited and soaring that seemed incongruous in such a setting.

The audience erupted in applause after his fourth song.

It was supposed to be Theodosia's turn next, but when Scopan came to get her, she asked if she might go last.

"That is impossible," he said.

"Please! I can't play just now."

Scopan sighed and turned to face the head table.

"The slave Theodosia has asked to perform last, Sire," he said. "Is that permissible?"

Nero glanced at Otho.

"Do you suppose your girl is afraid?"

"Timid, Sire," Otho said, his voice sticky with condescension. "She has been in prison a long time. I beg your indulgence for her."

Nero shrugged and nodded, so Scopan moved on to Pylades, who stepped eagerly to the chair.

His performance was dramatic and confident, as befit an actor and a Greek. Somehow, he managed to convert each poem he was given into a sort of dialogue, with unique characters. He alternately explicated the poem, spoke the various characters' lines, and played his instrument, changing to a different pipe theme whenever he changed the speaker. Theodosia found it less appealing than the Numibian's interpretations, but it was clear the audience was delighted. They laughed often and applauded loudly when he finished.

There was no escape now. Theodosia limped to the chair as Scopan made the round of the poets. She accepted the eight poems he handed her and flipped through them nervously, barely able to focus her eyes.

The one she chose first was the most legibly written of the batch and contained a repeated verse at the end of each stanza that she could use as a chorus, as she had always liked to do.

Then, her head bowed over the cithara, she concentrated on picking out a tune to fit. As soon as she began to sing, she relaxed. Improvising was easy if she liked the poem, and this was no frivolous ditty about a lovesick girl and a philandering sailor.

This poem was a work of art, as right for her voice as if it had been written just for her. The words felt soft on her tongue; the intricate pattern was structured in a way that made it easy to sing. The final interlocking rhyme of every other line echoed the intermediate rhyme of the line before it. The meter was perfect, so once she found her melody, it was almost as if the cithara were playing by itself.

But what Theodosia liked most about this poem was its story... the poignant tale of a mythic hero and his lady—separated by years and ruthless, god-like forces—reunited at midnight in some secret hiding place known only to them.

It was the repeating verse—"And she met her lover where the dead heroes lay"—that she found most moving. She closed her eyes each time she came to that line, and when her voice trailed off at the end, the wave of applause that washed over her assured her that others had been moved, too.

I have a chance!

Reanimated, she selected two other poems in different styles; they, too, came easily to her lips and her cithara. The spunk was back in her spirit. The fire returned to her fingers.

Pausing at the end of her third song, she glanced at the nine people around the head table. Otho, she noted, was beaming.

He's winning, too. Wonder what favor he intends to ask of Nero?

For her last song, she pulled out the other sheet in the same clear handwriting as the first poem. There was something familiar about this one, but she couldn't take time to decide what it was.

Four lines into the song, however, her heart began to pound.

I know this poem!

A tingle crept up from the base of her spine.

I've sung it before!

Lightly fingering a simple cadence that would allow her to stall between stanzas, she raised her eyes and let them roam the room.

Let them pick out faces in the crowd.

Let them settle for a moment on the bearded poet lounging between Flavia Domitilla and Lucius Gallio.

The deep-set eyes met hers then, and though there was no expression on the Greek's face, a silent surge of energy and emotion swept between them.

Theodosia's eyes dropped to the cithara, but her heart picked up the rhythm of her song, and she finished the remaining stanzas with the wildest burst of joy she had ever known in her life.

CHAPTER TWENTY-NINE

Theodosia hadn't recognized him yet.

That's good. Don't want to rattle her.

Later, of course, she would have to realize he was there or the plan wouldn't work.

As for Alexander, if they hadn't announced Theodosia's name, he might not have known who she was. A while ago, he'd caught a glimpse of that same haggard woman in red standing in the corner, half hidden by the curtains... and didn't identify her.

Sweet gods of Greece, was that Theodosia?

Emaciated and colorless except for a red welt on her lip and the deep shadows that ringed her eyes, she had aged twenty years. But Alexander remembered his own three miserable months in a Roman prison.

What would I have looked like after thirty months?

His memory had harbored other images of Theodosia Varra.

Studying his records that first morning in the library, her radiance in the pool of sunlight undermining her efforts to look stern...

Flirting on the stairs as her emeralds sparkled in the lamplight...

Dashing in from the storm later that night, barefoot, soaked, wearing Alexander's muddy cloak, with a slave child clinging to her neck...

Racing her filly through the hills, laughing a challenge to the two grown-up slaves who loved her...

Flavia Domitilla had tried to warn him earlier, but sometimes the mind refuses to believe. Now—as Theodosia limped into the hall behind a flamboyant blonde—Flavia shot him a look that urged self-control. It wasn't necessary. Years of slavery had taught him that.

Hoping to appear disinterested, he pulled his eyes away from Theodosia and gazed around the room for the first time.

He had been nervous all evening—keeping his head down and avoiding eye contact with anyone—but now the enormity of the risk he was running crashed into his consciousness. On these thirty couches, surrounded by scores of armed Praetorians, lay the master of the Roman Empire, eighty-five patricians, three free Greek poets, and one runaway slave. Without rising, he spotted a dozen men who could expose him. It wasn't hard to imagine what the lords of the world would do to a slave who had the temerity to thumb his nose at them this way.

Would I have written that first letter to Flavia if I'd known it would lead to this?

Fortunately, nobody was paying attention to him. Flavia had already introduced "her poet" to her friends and family, though she carefully avoided presenting him to Otho. Titus and Vespasian politely shook the hand that so often in the past had poured their wine, then went to seek out their friends, leaving Alexander queasy with relief at their lack of interest.

He had no idea how much Lucius Gallio knew. Ostensibly, they hadn't met until tonight, and still—after hours of dining side by side—Gallio showed no sign of recognizing the Greek he had helped Gaius buy in the slave market eleven years before. In this case, the lack of recognition left Alexander more curious than anything else.

Could Flavia possibly pull this off without his knowledge?

The anxiety was the worst of it. At any moment, this masquerade might fall apart, exposing him for what he was and putting both Flavia and her husband—the emperor's own legal counselor—at great risk. Alexander couldn't help thinking about what discovery would mean.

Prison, probably, for them. And for me...?

He shut his eyes for a couple of heartbeats.

Still, all was going well. Flavia had done her part flawlessly, planned everything to the smallest detail—even bribing a Carcer Tullianum guard several months ago, so Theodosia would have enough time to reacquaint herself with her cithara—and laid the foundation for this night so subtly that neither Nero nor Otho suspected he was being manipulated.

The plan seemed sound. If Theodosia won the competition, as Flavia expected, she would win her freedom, too. Flavia had had to convince Nero of the necessity of providing that incentive for the musicians, but now... success meant that Theodosia could leave Rome openly, without being pursued. Accomplishing Flavia's goal—to get Theodosia legally free—depended on Theodosia's winning tonight.

It was just as important that Alexander not be around later when Nero presented honoraria to the poets. So, he and Flavia would leave as soon as the competition ended—the excuse was already arranged—and be at the villa by midnight, if the storm didn't cause too much delay.

Somebody else—Flavia wouldn't tell Alexander who it was—had agreed to accompany Theodosia to the necropolis near Caere, where Alexander and Stefan had been hiding for weeks. Stefan was still there, impatient to spirit his beloved Theodosia out of Italy.

Of all Flavia's servants, only Nicanor knew what was happening, and he would gladly lie and kill—or be killed—for Theodosia.

The one thing Flavia hadn't counted on was Theodosia's hostility, which had hindered communication. But maybe it was better that she didn't realize exactly how much was riding on her performance this evening.

Things would be more difficult if Theodosia lost the competition, but some parts of the plan might still work. She would just have to run away, despite Flavia's efforts to work it out otherwise.

Alexander had buried clues in one of his poems and tried to ensure by the way he wrote it that she would pick that particular poem. When she recognized him, she would understand those clues. He deliberately had included a poem she had sung many times before, to guarantee that she would recognize him.

Nevertheless, it was chancy. If she lost, Theodosia would have to find her way to the necropolis on her own... tough enough even without such bad weather. Not even Flavia had the nerve to help the emperor's slave run away.

The boat and rowers hired for their escape had to leave the cove at the villa by dawn, when the household slaves would arise and begin their day's work. There was no time to spare.

Alexander's hope disintegrated as Theodosia sang her first song. She sounded frail and flat. Her voice quivered. Her fingers fumbled on the strings. She knew dozens of lovely ballads. Why choose something as insipid as "My Faithless Sailor from Ostia"?

He risked a glance at Otho, whose face was stony, then at Flavia. Her expression said it all... the easy route was lost. If Theodosia was going to leave with Stefan and Alexander on that boat tomorrow morning, she'd have to get there by herself.

But then came the German woman's embarrassment, and the favorite of the crowd was removed. Alexander shook his head and murmured in disappointment along with everyone else.

Down to three.

The Numibian and the Greek both extemporized well.

But not so well they can't be beaten.

Then, when Theodosia selected Alexander's encoded poem first —and rallied—he began to hope again.

She was singing superbly now, improvising with spirit and flair, even before that moment when she looked straight at him and *knew!*

And after that... it seemed Apollo himself seized control of Theodosia's voice and gave it wings.

Strutting like one of the peacocks in his master's gardens, Scopan returned to the center of the great hall to supervise the voting of the thirty couches. Acrobats swung into action as the guests began arguing for their favorites. Gradually, one couch after another sent their purple ballots to Scopan; then they settled back to enjoy the Falernian, the more traditional entertainment, and the unexpected drama of freedom for a slave.

Stomach knotted, teeth clenched, body all but paralyzed... Theodosia huddled on her cushion and peered around the room. Her eyes drifted to Lucius Gallio's couch, almost expecting to find that Alexander had disappeared or been an illusion, just another prison fantasy.

What are you doing here? They'll crucify you!

Her gaze lingered on his face as he chatted with Flavia. As if sensing her eyes on him, Alexander suddenly shifted his glance to Theodosia for a moment that felt like eternity. Then he turned away, as from a stranger.

Theodosia looked away, too, though she wanted to leap up, shout "Alexander came back!" at the top of her lungs, and join the acrobats in their cartwheels.

What an incredibly brave thing to do!

It was her delighted inner voice.

He got away... was safe and free... and he came back!

But why?

It was the voice of her more-cautious self.

Why on earth?

For me! Maybe he didn't find his family...

No. Pray Juno that he did. Antibe and Niko mean the world to him.

But I love him!

And he loves Antibe.

And yet, if he didn't find her...

Theodosia shut off the dialogue in her head, refusing to entertain foolish hopes. All she should be thinking about was the terrible risk

Alexander was running. There was nothing Otho would enjoy more than exposing a runaway slave... especially that one. And he'd expose Flavia, too, for what was clearly a conspiracy. Flavia could lose her head, and Lucius Gallio, too, and—

Flavia!

Theodosia's hand flew to her face as fire raced up from her neck.

Oh, my dear, marvelous friend! She planned all this to get me free!

The cithara smuggled in to me...

The pressure on Otho to find new testimony to exonerate me...

The competition tonight...

The promise of freedom for the winner...

Blessed Juno, why didn't I see what she was up to? Why couldn't I have been more grateful?

She glanced over, desperate to catch Flavia's eye, but Flavia and Alexander were both watching Scopan.

Theodosia held her breath as Scopan announced the early votes.

Six of the first ten couches had gone for the Numibian, three for Theodosia, and one for the Greek. The agony went on as some couches broke evenly and squabbled over their decision.

By the time twenty couches were tallied, she had gained five, for a total of eight. But the Numibian had gained five, too, and was up to eleven. There were no new votes for the Greek.

Sweat coursed between Theodosia's breasts. She tried to breathe, but the room was too close.

Alexander took such risks, came back for me, and now I'm going to lose!

She laid the cithara on the floor, fanned her tunic in and out at the neck, and glanced at her competitors. Both looked anguished. They had obviously been slaves far longer than she.

If I want my liberty, how much more must they?

The final ten votes remained to be tallied before the winner was announced, which consumed more time. The acrobats kept performing until, at Scopan's signal, they cartwheeled from the room.

Theodosia braced herself for disaster.

Scopan eloquently and lengthily thanked the poets and their sponsors, the musicians and their masters, the noble Romans whose deliberations had made possible the selection of a winner, and, of course, the brilliant mind of the emperor, whose genius had conceived the idea of such a competition in the first place. Then he humbly presented the tally sheet so that Nero himself could announce the results to his guests.

Nero glanced at the sheet and showed it to Poppaea, who responded with a wan smile. The process of making a simple announcement threatened to last all night. Finally, he rose from his couch. The entire assembly stood, including the three jittery musicians in the center.

"Be at ease, my friends," said Nero with a broad, inebriated sweep of his hands. He waited until everyone was seated. "We have a winner. Here are the totals of all thirty tables."

Theodosia bowed her head.

"For the Greek: two votes."

There was polite applause from the Romans and a groan from Pylades.

"For the Numibian: thirteen votes." A slight pause. "And for the half-breed: fifteen votes. We shall have a certificate of manumission prepared for her immediately!"

Stunned, Theodosia lifted her eyes to Niger, who touched her arm in congratulations... even as his own eyes filled with tears.

Her gaze swept the room—full of men and women who had answered her prayers and given back her life—and lingered for a moment on the jubilant faces of Flavia and Alexander. Without them, she would still be lying on the wet rock of the Carcer Tullianum.

Juno, hear me! I'll find a way to repay them both... many times over. I swear it!

"Sire," called a man at the edge of the hall as the applause subsided, "we request that the winner interpret the unused poems as a final condition for winning her freedom."

"Aye!" The cry reverberated around the room.

Theodosia returned to the chair in the center of the room and began to sing, feeling life and strength enter her voice and her instrument once more. The performance that followed was—she knew as it was happening —her finest ever.

During the second song, a slave hurried into the hall, approached the emperor, and whispered in his ear. Nero nodded. The man stepped over to Lucius Gallio; his message caused a stir among those sharing the couch.

Theodosia stopped singing.

Lucius Gallio rose and turned to face the emperor as Flavia and her poet swung their feet to the floor.

"What's happening?" asked Nero.

"Sire," Gallio said, "we have just received word that the wife of the poet Demodocus has fallen ill. Flavia Domitilla requests leave to take him to his wife."

The wife of the poet.

Theodosia heard nothing more. Saw nothing more.

He found Antibe.

The selfish hope that had revitalized her dissolved in an instant.

He came back out of honor. To repay a debt.

When she looked up, Flavia and Alexander were gone... without a word for the woman who would have died to speak to them.

She played two more songs, but the muse had abandoned her. The victory she had just won seemed empty in the face of her loneliness and exhaustion.

Nothing is left but to seek vengeance.

When her performance ended, Theodosia stood in the center of the banquet hall, listening almost without interest as Nero praised her talent and pronounced her free. Scopan gave her a parchment covered with seals and propelled her toward the door. The other two contestants had already left... returned to their slavery.

"I have something to say to the emperor." Theodosia pulled back.

Scopan increased the pressure on her arm.

"His Majesty has other concerns. He must reward the poets and those who brought them, then he will grant my lord Otho an imperial favor for having sponsored you."

"But that's— No, I must be there when he does!"

Scopan hustled her into the hallway and left her.

Theodosia stared at the ornate document that restored her freedom; then she folded it and stuffed it into the breast of her tunic alongside Reuben ben Judah's sheet.

One more challenge tonight. Then I can rest.

In the next moment, there was a hand on her shoulder. She turned and found herself standing beside Centurion Titus Flavius Sabinus Vespasianus. They hadn't seen each other since the day she promised to marry him, which had long since become impossible. The wave of fire that always tormented her at such moments swept over her cheeks. She tried to step away, but his grip was firm.

"You sang beautifully. Congratulations on your victory."

Feeling old and ungainly beside him, Theodosia wanted to hide. Time and anger had erased her affection for Titus.

"Thank you."

If only this were Alexander. But he's gone back to his wife.

"Come with me," Titus said. "I'm taking you—"

"No!" Theodosia could think of one thing only. "I'm going in there."

"Listen to me!" It was the tone a Roman would use to address a slave. "You're to ride with me to Caere, then—"

"But I don't want to leave. I've got something to tell the emperor."

"No. You'll ruin everything." Titus' voice was low but urgent. "Look, I promised Flavia. You'll escape with the others and—"

"I don't have to escape. I'm free! And I'm not leaving until I tell the emperor what I know about Gaius' murder. I can clear my name tonight, don't you see?" She paused and looked into Titus' face. "Please... tell Flavia I'll join them tomorrow at my—at her—villa."

Oh, gods... now it always will be her villa! There's no way I can try to reclaim it after what she's done to free me.

Without another word, she extricated herself from Titus' grasp and headed to the banquet hall, certain that he could not force her to leave with so many others looking on.

"Tomorrow," he called behind her, "will be too late!"

But Theodosia—thinking only of revenge—ignored him. She made her way along the back wall until she stood opposite Nero's couch.

Otho was speaking... laying the groundwork for the personal reward that Nero had promised to the sponsor of the winning musician by praising the emperor's generosity and genius for government.

The object of this acclaim looked drowsy as Otho droned on. The bored empress had already left. Poppaea Sabina toyed with the pearls at her throat, wearing the smile of a cat after a kill.

Then Otho made the request that everyone was waiting for and nobody expected.

"My request, Sire, is simple: a public declaration of your oft-stated pledge to me... that should our most-beloved Empress Octavia—for whose fertility we all pray each day—that should she by some terrible fate —may the immortal gods prevent it!—fail to produce an heir... that those present should bear witness that Your Majesty tonight appoints your life-long friend and most faithful servant," Otho thumped his own chest, "to succeed you."

Whispers and snickers rippling throughout the hall abruptly ceased.

Two hundred eyes turned to Nero, who was at that moment pouring the contents of an enormous goblet down his throat. He burped, wiped his mouth with the side of his heavily jeweled hand, and stared expressionless at Otho.

And then—when the atmosphere inside the hall had grown as ominous as the storm outside—the emperor's mouth opened wide, sending volleys of laughter blasting against the ceiling.

The guests—apparently unsure how to react to such a vigorous display of imperial mirth—regarded one other in cautious silence.

Slaves and Praetorian Guards froze in action.

Poppaea released her pearls and shifted her astonished eyes back and forth between the two men who flanked her. Theodosia wondered, briefly, what she had been expecting Otho to ask for.

Otho stood beside the couch—his face rigid, his chin tilted upward—until Nero's guffaws subsided.

"So," said the emperor of Rome, "you aspire to be my successor."

"In private, Your Majesty has encouraged that ambition."

"In private, one says many things."

"And in public, one honors one's promise to grant a favor."

There was another long silence.

Theodosia pressed her back to the wall, as awestruck by the scene as everyone else in the room.

"Very well," said Nero at last. "We shall refer this matter to our noble guests. Another issue of profound importance for them to decide this evening." The emperor's words rang with the most delicious, mocking irony that Theodosia could have imagined from such an inebriated source. "Illustrious Romans, most worthy descendants of your proud forebears, fearless conquerors of the world... I beg you, speak your minds on the direction of our ship of state."

Not a single senator, knight, tribune, general, consul, quaestor, or praetor raised his voice in comment.

Nero looked at Otho and expanded his naval metaphor.

"You have little backing, it seems, from our loyal sailors."

"They are frightened, Sire. They fear that supporting me will be interpreted as mutiny."

"So... they would support you but for fear of their captain? Very well, let's sail the opposite tack." Nero lifted himself from his elbow and propped his weight on one hand. "Does anyone in this hall have a reason to offer why we should *not* designate Senator Marcus Salvius Otho as our successor and the next emperor of Rome?"

Theodosia laid her cithara on the floor, held her breath, and waited for the inevitable uproar of objections. Otho's reputation was as unsavory as a patrician's could get. No one could possibly want to see him named as Nero's successor.

From her place at the edge of the room, she watched the crowd.

Suddenly—as if choreographed—faces buried themselves in golden cups. Women laden with gems caressed their husbands' arms in subtle

301

restraint. Men famed for battlefield heroics rolled onto their stomachs and smiled sheepishly at their neighbors.

Otho was still standing. The subtle smirk that had been playing across his lips grew blatant. Now he bowed to Nero.

"You see how well received is Your Majesty's choice! Of this vast assembly of highborn Romans, not one opposes me!"

In that instant—as if prodded by some malevolent force—Theodosia began to move forward. She was halfway across the room when she heard a voice she barely recognized as her own.

"I have a reason, Sire."

Throughout the hall came an echo of the silence that had followed Otho's brash request. Theodosia kept her eyes on her enemy as she approached. His smirk faded fast... replaced by a look of homicidal fury.

"This is unacceptable, Sire!" Otho shouted.

"Marcus Salvius Otho is not fit to be a senator," Theodosia said as she neared the head table, "much less emperor of Rome."

Otho's face had turned as purple as the robe he longed to wear.

"That is a decision for Romans, not slaves convicted of murder."

"I never was a murderer. I should never have been declared a slave. And I am now freed by the emperor's own hand." Theodosia's voice rose, increasingly strong and confident. She knew that everyone in the room could hear her. "In the name of my patrician father, Aulus Terentius Varro, whom many of you still remember with affection... I tell you that Marcus Salvius Otho not only instigated but also—with the help of a man who can be identified here tonight—carried out the murder of my brother, an act he later managed to blame on me."

"Ridiculous!" Otho's laugh was just a bit too loud. "Gaius was my friend. Why would I want to kill him?"

"To possess the Terentius Varro fortune by marrying me."

"What nonsense. Sire, this woman is insane."

Otho's stare was chilling. It was dangerous to accuse him, but she was sure that making the accusation in public kept her safe. The presence of other Romans—many of whom no doubt despised Otho as much as she and probably did remember her father with affection—would force the emperor to investigate her charges and prevent Otho from harming her.

"I offer this document and other evidence... in hopes of getting the justice that my family was denied years ago."

She walked toward the emperor's couch, taking out ben Judah's parchment as she went, increasingly conscious of Nero's raspy breathing, of Poppaea's perfume, of Otho's eyes boring into her.

302

"Sire, there is a Roman citizen who will testify that Marcus Salvius Otho admitted killing my brother and then bribed the citizen to lie about my mother's legal status. And this parchment contains a drawing of a ring that my brother was wearing the night of the crime... a ring that Otho and his accomplice stole from him as they were slaughtering him. Find the man who wears the ring described here, Sire, and you will have found Otho's accomplice in murder."

Theodosia stopped directly in front of Nero, bent her right knee before him, and stretched the document out to him.

"I ask only for justice, Sire," she said, looking confidently into the emperor's eyes.

Nero glanced at Otho. Then he rose on unsteady feet and reached for the parchment.

As in a nightmare, Theodosia saw the spindly legs under the corpulent torso.

The fat hand coming closer...

The fingers heavy with rings...

The flash of an enormous ruby in the mouth of a golden serpent...

The marks of her teeth in the fleshy palm...

Reacting instinctively, she pulled back, her eyes frozen in horror under the icy glare of the emperor's own.

"Sire... I am... ill!" She crumpled the parchment with both hands and clutched it to her stomach as she stumbled toward the curtain at the rear of the room. "Forgive me!"

Without looking back, she dashed as quickly as she could toward the spot where she had stood a few hours earlier and lurched into the labyrinth of service corridors behind the dining hall.

"Catch her!" screamed Otho.

Theodosia pushed open the first door and escaped into another corridor. There was no light, but she knew from the aroma of Falernian that the wine cellars were nearby. Dropping ben Judah's parchment into her tunic to free her hands, she groped along the walls until she came to another door, which she opened and quickly shut behind her.

Still blinded by the darkness, she picked a zigzag route through a maze of kegs. Whenever she hit a wall, she followed it to the left... hoping that she wasn't somehow taking herself straight to Otho and the Praetorian Guards and the spindly legged emperor with the bitten, bejeweled hand.

She followed a sliver of light to the stone-arched door where just yesterday she had slipped out past the men unloading wine. She heard voices and heavy footfalls in the passageway. In desperation, she pounded her palms up half a dozen bone-jarring times, until the bolt gave way.

Blessing Juno once more for the strength of her arms, she yanked the bar and plunged out into a torrential downpour.

The service alley behind the palace was empty, but over the thunder Theodosia could hear soldiers and horses around the corner. Guided by the lightning, she fled down the rain-slick Palatine Hill, heading for the treacherous streets of the Subura.

An hour later, soaked and exhausted, Theodosia rapped on the door of Rubol's shop. The younger of his slaves opened the door and stared sleepily at the caller.

"May I come in?"

"Who is it, boy?"

It was Rubol's voice, but Theodosia couldn't see him. There was a rustle in the back; the sandal maker emerged, looking as sleepy as his apprentice. He held up a lamp to see her face, clearly surprised by who was there. Then he drew her into his shop, out of the rain.

"You in trouble, lady?"

"I need a horse, Rubol, and a change of clothes. Urgently."

"I'll go get a horse."

He fetched a stool for her, and she collapsed onto it, too spent to care that she was dripping all over his floor.

"I've no money to pay."

"I got money."

Rubol donned a long, hooded cloak and disappeared into the night. The boy stood gaping, but the older slave poured a cup of wine from a black-clay pitcher and handed it to Theodosia. The wine was cheap and vinegary, but she swallowed it gratefully and smiled at him as she returned the cup.

"What happened to you, lady?" the man asked. "Where've you been? Where're you going?"

"You'll be in danger if you know. Both of you... say nothing about my visit to anyone."

Rubol returned before she had completely caught her breath. He gave her a pair of sandals and led her to the workroom, where he dug into a chest and brought out a heavy tunic and a rope to tie around her waist.

"Change into these."

When she stepped back into the front room, Rubol held out the wet cloak he had taken off just a few moments ago.

"This is wool, so the rain rolls right off."

He draped the cloak around her shoulders, pulled the hood over her head, and tied the cords securely under her chin and across her chest. It dragged on the floor, but she could walk by carrying it. Then he opened the door again and led her to a dray horse waiting in the rain.

"Where'd you get the horse?"

"Belongs to my friend down the street." He lifted her onto the animal's bare back. "I'll pay him in the morning."

"I won't be able to repay you for any of this."

"It's a small part of what you gave me over the years."

Theodosia pulled the hem of the cloak forward and sat on it, glad it was dry on the inside and long enough to cover her limbs. Her deformed left leg could no longer hug a horse's ribs; riding with only a single functioning knee would require all her skill and strength.

Rubol gathered the reins and placed them in her hands.

She looked into his gaunt face.

"May the gods bless you, Rubol."

She was about to tug the horse away when she remembered.

Reaching through the ties of the cloak and into the tunic, she pulled out ben Judah's crumpled drawing. She would carry only her certificate of manumission and her knife... which she had moved to the outside of her right thigh for greater comfort and accessibility.

"Burn this." She handed the parchment to Rubol. "Right now! Don't look at it. Don't let your workers even catch sight of it. Burn that red tunic I was wearing, too, and forget you saw me tonight."

The sodden heart of Rome overflowed with oxcarts and horse-drawn wagons bringing in building materials and goods for the morning markets. Hundreds of drivers helped nighttime Rome live up to its reputation as the noisiest place in the empire. There was much comment tonight on the unusual presence of soldiers. They were everywhere... poking their smelly, pitch-soaked torches into every alley, bar, corner, and doorway, shouting inquiries about a lame woman in a bright red tunic.

Meanwhile, the object of their search rode straight through the city astride a dray horse, enshrouded in the hooded cape of a laborer. No one paid her any attention.

It had been years since Theodosia's catastrophic last ride, and this horse was a far cry from her beloved Lamia. His back was wider than any she had ever ridden before. Tomorrow, the muscles in her legs and hips would stab like knives, but for now she was thankful to take the pressure off her throbbing joints.

She made her way without incident out of the Subura, along the Via Sacra, past the forums of Julius and Augustus to the Pons Aemilius... the ancient bridge where the Via Aurelia crossed the gusty, swollen Tiber.

Only then did things begin to go wrong.

The bridge was guarded. Theodosia backed the horse into a cluster of shrubs and counted the men by their smoking torches. There were seven —two of them mounted—just this side of the bridge.

Suspecting that Nero would order the road leading to her home guarded more carefully than the others, she turned the horse toward the city, intent on finding another route. But then, the two mounted guards left the group at the bridge. Once again, Theodosia guided her horse off the pavement, stroking his stout neck in a plea for silence.

After the soldiers splashed past, she surveyed the situation. There were no more horses near the bridge.

Time for courage.

She kicked her mount into a trot and approached with as much nonchalance as she could muster.

"Halt!" shouted a voice as she drew near.

Grateful that her old ally, Juno the moon, had seen fit to be elsewhere tonight, Theodosia pulled her horse up some distance from the guards.

"Where you headed, fellow?" the voice said as the torches began moving forward.

Gambling on their curiosity, Theodosia sat still, measuring her opportunity as the bobbing line of lights drew closer. Her nose wrinkled at the acrid odor of blazing pitch, but with each moment that she waited, the gap between the five men and the bridge grew wider.

Finally—when she dared wait no longer—she kicked the horse as hard as she could with her right leg. The animal whinnied and lurched ahead.

Theodosia leaned low over his neck, smacked the reins, and rammed through the fire and smoke and soldiers. There was a pungent smell of burning wool... a bright flame at her shoulder that sputtered and died in the downpour. She kicked again and sent the horse racing across the bridge, out into the blackness of the Via Aurelia.

She could hear the guards cursing as they ran after her, their breastplates clinking fainter and fainter. Flashes of lightning illuminated the road ahead. Theodosia's main fear was that the dray horse would lose his footing on the slick stones, but there was no way she could let him slow down. Fleet cavalry riders might be after her even now.

The horse was breathing heavily. Obviously, he was used to steady pulling, not the quick burst of speed she had demanded, so after a while she eased up on him. With luck and a gentler pace, maybe he could hold out till they reached the villa. Or Caere, at least.

Caere!

Theodosia lifted her head in sudden comprehension.

"You're to ride with me to Caere... escape with the others... tomorrow will be too late!"

Oh, gods, that's why Titus was wearing his uniform at the banquet, instead of a toga... to make sure nobody would stop us on the road. It would've been so easy!

And he was trying to tell me... Alexander and Antibe aren't at the villa after all, but somewhere in Caere. Vespasian's house, most likely.

Clever Flavia! Antibe's illness was just a ploy to get Alexander out of the palace. Flavia must have dropped him off at Vespasian's house in Caere, where Antibe was waiting. Titus was supposed to take me there... then Alexander, Antibe, and I would have been gone by morning.

Juno, it would've been so damn easy!

She rode a bit further, then gasped at a new thought.

Do I even want to go with them? What kind of odd threesome would we make? Alexander and his wife and his former mistress... who now owes her life to him.

But there were few options. She had to go somewhere.

A lightning bolt crashed into the forest on her right, and the horse lurched in terror onto the left shoulder. Theodosia held on and guided him back to the road. He had kept up a steady pace for an hour now and might not have much strength left, but she had to push on. Caere lay only a few miles beyond.

Theodosia knew this stretch of road well. Not far off lay the rugged land—and the villa—that had once been hers. She could smell the sea in the rain on her face. Tears of longing and nostalgia overflowed her eyes, but she shook the mood off.

Concentrate! Don't get sentimental now!

To give her mind something else to do, she began singing one of the poems that Alexander had brought to the banquet, the first one she had selected... that haunting, perfectly rhymed lyric about lovers reunited under perilous circumstances. She sang it over and over, very softly, with an inexplicable, growing sense of elation.

She was about to cross a small stone bridge at a stream when her ears picked up the muffled beat of hooves on the pavement ahead. A squad of mounted soldiers emerged from the dark before she reached the bridge.

Theodosia held her breath and offered another prayer to Juno. She couldn't hope to outrun them; she'd have to bluff her way through.

Slouched under his hood, the laborer on the exhausted hack halted on command.

"No," he said with a yawn, he'd seen no one on the road.

"Yes," the soldiers posted at the Tiber had questioned him already.

"Yes," he was headed home to Caere.

"Of course," he'd notify the local authorities if he saw anything unusual.

Apparently satisfied, the officer in charge ordered his men to let the sleepy fellow through.

Pulling his hood down further against the rain, the laborer nudged his horse past the long line of soldiers who sat atop their mounts, eyeing him closely as he moved between their columns.

If I make it through this, I'm safe.

A short distance along the road, however—just when she had begun to breathe normally again—Theodosia heard new sounds in the darkness behind her.

A sudden disturbance among the soldiers...

A clatter of hooves heading in her direction...

A single voice shouting obscenities...

Without pausing to consider what she was doing, she tugged her horse off the road and plunged into the woods. The profane shouts and hoof beats followed and grew louder.

Theodosia recognized the voice and knew she was headed for the ride of her life. Otho was pursuing her into the thicket.

CHAPTER THIRTY

It was with bittersweet ambivalence that Alexander came back to the house where he had served as a slave. Here he had found renewed self-respect in his expert management of the Varro estate. Here he had been slapped for teaching a child to read. Here he had met Theodosia Varra, alternately argued and jested with her, and grown to love her.

The servants were asleep when Flavia's carriage pulled up; they had not been advised that she would be home tonight. Even the new steward, sleeping now in the cubicle that Alexander remembered so well, missed his predecessor's return.

Only Nicanor was in on the plan. For weeks, he had been riding to Caere to buy food and wine for two friends living in the necropolis. Now he rushed through the atrium, bowed low to Flavia, and threw his arms around Alexander.

This had been an awkward, stressful night for Alexander—more than just the ordeal in Nero's palace—as the runaway slave and the Roman who was helping him escape again tried to make conversation in her carriage.

There had been much to talk about on the journey into Rome from Caere, where Alexander had joined Flavia. His first getaway with Stefan and Lycos... The months in Antioch... Theodosia's physical and mental condition... Final details of tonight's plan...

But the return trip to Flavia's villa was something else. The easy banter of those long-ago days in Theodosia's pergola could not be recaptured. Flavia Domitilla was a slave owner herself now, a wealthy woman married to the emperor's counselor, and the sister of a rising star in the eagles. Although she had guarded Alexander's secrets and done her best to secure Theodosia's freedom, Flavia was still very much a Roman.

Alexander knew he would always be a slave in her eyes.

And if I hadn't gotten away when I did, I'd be her property now, too, just as Nicanor is.

Flavia handed her cape to Nicanor in the atrium, then turned to Alexander with a smile as she gestured around.

"It's all the same, see? No changes that you'd notice."

Alexander's eyes climbed the marble pillars, taking in the frescoed walls before shifting to the stairway, lit by a single lamp. His mind's eye saw Theodosia there on her way to Vespasian's party... radiant and flirtatious in her deep green silk... sparkling with the emeralds that Alexander had selected for her.

"No," he said, unable to control the irony that crept into his voice. "No change at all, my lady."

Flavia frowned, and for a moment he feared he had offended her. Then the smile returned and broadened to a grin... giving him a glimpse of the impish girl he remembered.

"Well, we shouldn't have long to wait. Titus," she said, letting him in on the last part of her plan, "has promised to see Theodosia safely to the necropolis. She and Stefan should get here in plenty of time."

Flavia turned to Nicanor.

"Go watch for them. Let me know the instant they arrive."

Nicanor bowed again and disappeared into the peristyle.

"Well, Alexander, where shall we put you while we wait?"

Do I dare ask for some time in the library?

His glance must have betrayed his thoughts.

"The library?" Flavia guessed.

"Would you mind? I used to spend a lot of time there."

"I know. Sure, why not? I'm going up to change."

When she was gone, Alexander stepped through the library door and closed the sapphire-colored curtain. There was a lamp burning on a table by the couch. He felt his way to the desk and sat down... enjoying the renewed contact of his fingers with the fine, polished wood. Reminders of the past—sight, sound, smell, and touch—were everywhere.

The old house quivered under Neptune's fury as rain pounded the panes and lightning pulsed through the black sky.

Just like that other stormy night.

Alexander turned his eyes to the couch where Theodosia Varra had sat... playing her cithara and singing to her two spellbound slaves.

Thank the gods she's safe with Titus!

Needles of rain stung Theodosia's face as she maneuvered the tired horse through the undergrowth. Rubol's long cloak billowed in the wind and repeatedly snagged on the branches, forcing her to stop each time and jerk it loose. Finally, she untied the cords and let it drop.

She could hear Otho cursing in the dark behind her. His horse was surely faster and more agile than hers, but Otho would be just as blinded by the downpour as she, so she felt no panic.

Besides... she had two major advantages. She knew exactly where she was, and she knew exactly where she was going.

It had come to her in that brief, peaceful interlude before she encountered the soldiers at the second bridge, when Alexander's evocative refrain—"And she met her lover where the dead heroes lay"—began echoing in her mind.

The Etruscan necropolis lay buried in the woods on the northeast side of Caere. Under normal circumstances, Theodosia could have found it easily. But in this storm, the trip was anything but easy, and—even if it were—she couldn't go there straightaway. She had to lose Otho first.

Free of the encumbering cloak, she leaned forward and started talking to her horse, patting his neck, asking for one more burst of speed. Little by little, the animal responded, pushing steadily through the brush until at last Theodosia heard what she was listening for... the splatter of rain on water, mud, and stones.

Memories of another horse and another riverbed swept over her.

I've made it this far. Mustn't panic now.

She wrapped her arms around her mount's sturdy neck and by the pressure of her elbows guided him down the embankment. In the distance behind her, along with the splash of a different horse's hooves, she could still hear Otho's threats and curses.

Once in the riverbed, she again asked the dray horse to give her a bit more, and they sped off in the rocky corridor as the wind whipped her sopping-wet hair and tunic.

A couple of miles downstream, the river bent abruptly to the right, and in another flash of memory—a summer ride to the necropolis... a picnic at the bend of the river... her own remark about that bend: *"almost like a sign from the gods"*—she saw her best hope to shake her pursuer.

She let the horse slow a bit for better footing, then tugged the reins firmly to the left. With remarkable strength, he surged up the embankment and burst over the top, snorting as if his lungs were about to explode. Theodosia pulled the exhausted animal into a patch of bushes and waited for the sounds that would tell if her ploy had succeeded.

Moments later, she heard the other horse splash by at full speed through the water. As Otho's shouts faded around the bend, Theodosia patted her horse's heaving neck once more and let him rest while she made sure her knife was still securely strapped to her right thigh.

She had no idea how far Otho might follow the river before realizing he had lost her, but with luck he wouldn't know exactly where it had happened. If her sense of things was right, the necropolis lay just a short distance away through the woods.

The rain was beginning to subside. With no sign of Otho, Theodosia eased the pressure on her mount. But if the ride was slower, the brambles were thicker than before, and by the time she spotted the first beehive-shaped mound, her face, arms, and legs were scratched and bleeding.

Antibe will wonder why such a scrawny, scraped-up woman was worth risking their lives.

That thought made her chuckle a bit. Well past vanity—and resigned to Antibe's presence in her life from now on—all Theodosia wanted at this point was rest and warmth and something dry to wrap herself in.

The ancient tombs stood black and silent against the retreating thunder and lightning.

Alexander and Antibe... where can they be?

Theodosia slid off the horse's back, looped the reins over his head, and began leading him along the muddy, murky street of the dead. His hoof beats echoed against the tombs as the fragrance of crushed mint rose from underneath.

Halfway down the street, Theodosia heard a crunch behind her. She had been through too much to panic now, even though she knew that both she and her horse were too tired to struggle further. The footsteps might be Alexander's... or Otho's.

Either way, my journey's over.

She turned and held her breath for an endless, mind-numbing moment. Then she sobbed in relief and disbelief as Stefan reached out of the darkness and took her in his arms.

Stefan sat down beside Theodosia on a stone bench in the same underground tomb that they had explored with Alexander years before. She snuggled gratefully into the blanket he had wrapped around her.

He hasn't changed a bit. I can only imagine how dreadful I must look to him right now.

"I wasn't expecting you to come alone," Stefan said.

"And I wasn't expecting to find *you* here."

"Expecting the emperor, maybe?"

"Maybe. After tonight, I wouldn't be surprised at anything. When will the others get here?"

"They're waiting for us at the villa. If you hadn't arrived soon, I'd have had to go on without you. That would've been tough!" He took her hands. "I didn't return from Greece just to leave you behind again."

"Gods, Stefan, you know what they'd do to you if they caught you. Whatever made you come back?"

He pressed her bony hands between his own enormous ones, then bent and kissed them.

"Love for you."

"And she met her lover where the dead heroes lay."

A cold chill ran down Theodosia's spine.

So, Alexander's long-lost lover wasn't metaphorical, after all, but literal... meant to be Stefan.

She shuddered with sudden guilt. Stefan had risked his life to come back for a woman who for the last two years had dreamed only of Alexander. And Alexander had risked his life—*Antibe's, too!*—so Stefan and Theodosia could be together. Stefan couldn't have come alone, couldn't have pulled this off alone; he was even more recognizable than Alexander. So... Alexander had stepped into the mouth of the Roman lion for the sake of two friends who, he assumed, loved one another.

Oh, Juno, help me!

"Stefan, you shouldn't have... I'm grateful—I really am!—but to think of you and Alexander and Antibe... all of you running such horrible risks for me. I couldn't bear it if—"

"Antibe?"

"Isn't that her name? Alexander's wife."

"Antibe ain't here. Where'd you get that idea?"

"The messenger at the banquet said Alexander's wife was ill."

"So, you believed—"

"Well, I saw it was a ploy to get him out of there, but when I realized he'd sent me clues, I just assumed they'd be hiding here. It never occurred to me that *you* would also—"

"Alexander's at the villa with the lady Flavia, or at least he should be by now. But, miss, Antibe is dead."

"Dead." Theodosia's mouth formed the sound, but the word made no impression on her mind.

Dead?

"She died in Syria years ago."

Antibe? Dead?

"And his son?"

"That's the happy part. Niko's alive. Alexander bought his freedom with two of your rubies. Niko and Lycos are both safe with friends in Greece." Stefan released her hands and stood up. "We should leave now. It's not long till dawn, and we'll ruin the escape plan if we're late."

Theodosia rose, reluctantly leaving the warm blanket on the bench.

Antibe is dead.

As in a dream, she followed Stefan up the narrow stairway leading to the old, rutted street; then she hopped out of the way as he unexpectedly jumped backwards.

Otho was advancing through the door, jabbing the tip of his sword into Stefan's chest.

"Thought you'd lost me, didn't you, bitch?" Otho growled in Theodosia's direction as he forced Stefan at sword point against the wall opposite the door. "Give me that document you had at the banquet, or come morning they'll find this fucking runaway with his throat cut and his balls stuffed in his mouth."

I can't tell him I left it with Rubol.

"I don't have it. I threw it away in the forest."

"Liar."

With his left hand, Otho pulled a large knife out of his belt and pressed its edge against Stefan's gullet. It was the same two-weapon assault he had once made on Alexander. Stefan was wearing a knife in his belt, too, but he couldn't get to it.

"One more lie and this slave takes a bath in his own blood."

"Just let us go. We're trying to leave. We're no threat to you."

"That document you were planning to show Nero has my name on it, doesn't it? My seal?"

"It does." Despite the danger, it gave Theodosia a thrill to twit him with her discovery.

"Then that document is a threat to me. Hand it over if you want this miserable lover of yours to survive the night."

Remembering the feel of her own knife at Nizzo's gullet, Theodosia knew how easy it would be for Otho to slit Stefan's throat.

He's not my lover any more, but I'll be damned if I'll let you kill him.

"If I do give you the document," she took a step closer, praying that Stefan wouldn't move, "will you let us go?"

"Of course! That's all I want."

"He's lying," Stefan said, barely moving his lips.

"Shut up, slave."

"Very well, here it is," Theodosia said with resignation, reaching under the hem of her tunic.

As her fingertips touched the handle of Phoebe's knife, she glanced up. Otho shifted his eyes from Stefan to watch her.

Stefan reacted instantly to the opportunity. He knocked the dagger away from his throat as the sword flew out of Otho's hand, crashing against the opposite wall.

Otho jumped as Stefan whipped his own weapon out of his belt. The men circled around the chamber, daggers in hand. Theodosia was moving backwards in the direction of the sword when Otho retreated a few steps and seized her arm. He pulled her in front of him and aimed the point of his blade straight into her heart.

"Drop that knife and kick it over here," he said to Stefan as he crushed Theodosia against him with his left arm.

She closed her eyes and waited. A moment later, she heard the clatter of Stefan's dagger hitting the floor, then the *swoosh* before it also crashed against the wall.

"Get in there. Pull the door shut behind you."

Theodosia opened her eyes and saw Otho gesturing to the burial chamber. He would throw the bolt, entombing Stefan.

"No," said Stefan.

Otho twisted his fingers into Theodosia's hair—just as he had on that horrible day in the garden years before—pulled her head back, and slid the long blade of the dagger along her throat.

"I'll kill her if you don't obey me."

"You'll kill her anyway."

"No. I have plans for this gimpy little whore." Otho laughed. "Don't worry, slave, you won't die in there. I have plans for you, too."

Paralyzed by the pressure of his blade, Theodosia could barely breathe, much less talk.

Stefan stepped to the threshold leading to the inner chamber.

"If you harm her, then you better leave me locked in here. If I get out and learn you've hurt her worse than you already have, I'll hunt you down and kill you." He walked into the chamber and pulled the door shut.

Otho dragged Theodosia to the door and shoved the bolt.

"Now, give me that document."

"I don't have it!"

He twisted her arm behind her and groped around her breasts, producing a crackling sound.

"What's that?"

"My certificate of manumission."

"Toss it over there."

Theodosia did as she was told.

"Now," he said after the parchment landed on the floor, "what really happened to that drawing you wanted to show Nero?"

"I told you. I threw it away in the woods."

"Don't lie."

"I'm not lying! It's true. Nobody will ever find it. And with all the rain, the ink has probably washed away already."

"You'll find it or you'll die."

Otho dragged her to his sword and shoved it into his scabbard; then he pushed her in front of him up the stairwell. The stone that Stefan had once brought to prop the door open was still there, still propping the door open. Otho pushed it with his foot, letting the door shut. To make sure, he leaned on the edge and listened for the click.

Despite her distress, Theodosia smiled to herself.

Bless Father for showing me the mechanism.

Without a word, Otho untied the reins of Theodosia's mount and the one that Flavia had provided for Stefan, slapped both animals on the rump, and sent them galloping away. Then he boosted Theodosia onto his own horse, leaped behind her, and headed out of the necropolis.

Theodosia rode silently until they were deep in the forest. The rain had dwindled to a drizzle, but lightning still flashed in the distance.

At last, she turned and looked at Otho over her left shoulder.

"Did you really murder Gaius as part of a scheme to marry me? I might almost feel complimented!"

"You vain bitch. I never gave a damn about you."

"Just my money."

"Just your money."

"You murdered Gaius to get your hands on our family fortune."

"Good enough reason, wouldn't you say?"

"And to stop 'the viper' and others from blackmailing you."

"An equally good reason." He laughed in her ear. "Zeus, haven't you been busy digging up the dirty past."

"And Nero went along for sport, didn't he? For that variety of entertainment he craves so much... just like the night before last, in the street of the potters."

"Clever little Theo. You've got it all figured out."

"You made sure Gaius' slaves in Rome weren't put to death, because you hoped to get them—along with his mansion on the Caelian Hill—by marrying me. You lured Alexander to Rome on the day you intended to murder Gaius. You were confident the Praetorians would blame him for it and leave me without anyone to rely on when I inherited the estate."

"Why didn't you ever show such analytical talent before?"

"And then," Theodosia said, still speaking over her left shoulder as her right hand began sliding down her right thigh, "when that didn't work, you tried to make me so afraid of Alexander that I wouldn't want to live in my home alone. You even got Lucilla to plant that idiotic couplet to make it look like Alexander was threatening me."

She felt a hard object under her tunic, just above her right knee.

"How did you find out he wrote poetry? Stefan and I were the only ones who knew that. Did Lucilla worm it out of Stefan and tell you?"

"Among other things."

"I thought so."

Her fingers had reached the hem of her tunic.

"You tried everything you could think of to get your hands on my money, didn't you?"

Her fingers crept up under her tunic, to that snug band of cotton.

"You promised Nizzo the funds he needed to buy my farm... on the condition that he lie about my mother. And then—assuming you intended to honor that promise at all, which I doubt—you would have used my own money to pay him off when your efforts to marry me succeeded."

Her fingers touched the smooth bone handle under the cotton.

"But in the end, when you saw that your schemes weren't working, you couldn't stand to watch the Flavians get their hands on everything you'd hoped would be yours. So... once you realized that nothing you'd done—not bribery, not blackmail, not murder—none of it was going to get you what you wanted, you set out to destroy me any way you could."

"And that was the simplest part of all. Gods, Theodosia, you made it easy! Riding horses. Playing music. Wearing courtesan colors. Throwing yourself at a stable hand. Fraternizing day and night with your slaves, even in Rome." Otho laughed again. "Poor little Theo! After so much low-class behavior—such a shameless display—it was simple to make the case that you were slave-born, a murderer, and a usurper."

317

"There's one thing you forgot."

"I forgot nothing."

"You forgot that my father raised me with enough spirit to—"

In that instant, she turned her head to the right to see her target.

Her hand flashed up and down, plunging the knife to its hilt into Otho's thigh. He screamed in pain as she yanked the long, bloody blade out and sank it again, with equal force, through his exposed calf.

"You bitch!"

Otho released her and reached for the weapon.

Seeing him distracted and leaning far out over his right leg, Theodosia seized the reins and swung the horse sharply to the left.

Senator Marcus Salvius Otho—descendant of Etruscan kings and best friend of the emperor of Rome—tumbled sidelong to the ground, cursing in pain and frustration and fury.

Theodosia spun the horse around, kicked his flank with her good leg, and took off for the necropolis.

Theodosia and Stefan rode Otho's horse through the woods until they came to the clearing by the sea, where on one beautiful September evening—a hundred years ago, it seemed—they had made love.

It was now barely an hour before dawn. The drizzle had stopped, and there was a hint of moonlight through the film of clouds. Across the curve of the shore, Theodosia's beloved villa lay dark and lovely in its sleep.

Antibe is dead.

The thought kept running through her head.

And maybe Alexander did come back for me.

"Pull up a moment, Stefan. There's something I have to tell you before we go on. All those years in the Carcer Tullianum, I had time to think and— Oh, this is the hardest thing I've ever had to do! I care so much for you. I always have, you know, since we were children. And then that spring, when I first came home... you were so magnificent. I think I was in love with the idea of loving you."

Stefan's arms encircled her as he kissed her hair.

"I've loved you every moment of my life," he whispered. "There's been other women—you know that—but none I ever truly cared for. Not like I cared for you. Gods, when I saw you out there tonight, skinny and wet and all tore up—" His voice broke. "Theodosia, I want to make up for everything that went wrong between us."

There was silence as Theodosia struggled to find the words she needed. But Stefan went on before she found them.

"I hear there's land up north, where the Romans don't go. Land for crops and animals, with good water and trees for building a home of our own. We can find a safe place there, raise a family…"

Desperate to make him stop, she shook her head. But he didn't stop.

"Well… Greece then. Won't be quite as safe, but we'll do all right."

"Stefan, please! I've got to tell you something… no way around it." She took a deep breath. "I'm sorry but… I love someone else. Gods, this is awful! You risked everything coming back for me, but so did he, and honestly, I think I loved him years ago. Just couldn't bring myself to admit it in those days."

"Alexander," he said, after the briefest of pauses.

Theodosia's eyes filled with tears, and she nodded.

"I never thought I'd ever have to face this decision. Never thought I'd see either one of you again. Never dreamed he'd—"

She bit off the words *come back for me*.

"It made me happy to think of him with Antibe. He loved her so."

"Yes, he loved her," Stefan's tone was odd, "for what they shared and the baby they had. All those years when he was a slave here, he honored his commitment to her. He grieved hard for her when he found she was gone."

Stefan's voice fell to a whisper. Theodosia pressed her shoulder against his chest to catch what he was saying.

"But he loved you, too, just as surely… all the way back to that night when—"

"But he—"

"No, wait!" Stefan pressed a finger to her lips. "All the while you was letting us pretend to be the friends we knew we couldn't never be with you… All the while you was playing Titus and Otho off against each other… All that time—and ever since—Alexander has thought of almost nothing but you."

Too tearful to speak, Theodosia waved her hands to stop him, but Stefan took them again and wrapped her in another gentle hug.

"He fell in love with you that night of the storm, but he resisted every temptation to tell you how he felt… out of respect for you and loyalty to a wife who was already dead before you and he ever met."

"But it was Alexander who urged me to go out to you in the garden, after I'd been shunning you. And it was Alexander who convinced me to marry Titus."

319

"And it was *Alexander*," Stefan added his own emphasis, "who risked everything by writing to Flavia Domitilla, when a word from her would have brought Roman soldiers to his hiding place in Antioch. And it was *Alexander* who made the decision to return to Rome. And it was *Alexander* who went into the emperor's palace tonight. Don't you see, Theodosia? He did all that for love of you."

Theodosia freed her hands from his and dabbed at her wet cheeks.

"Why are you telling me this?"

"I guess it's because... if there's another person in the world I love as much as you, it's Alexander. He's always looked out for me, too, you know. Just as he has for you."

"I know."

"And here's the best proof. Was there a line in one of his poems that guided you to the tombs tonight?"

"Sure. 'And she met her lover where the dead heroes lay.' Didn't he mean *you*?"

"He *did* mean me. That's just my point. He assumed all this time that I was the one you loved."

"You mean... he loves me so much that he would risk his life and his freedom so you and I could be together?" Theodosia shook her head. "Nobody's that unselfish."

"Alexander loves you too much to be selfish. And never, ever, has it occurred to him that *he* might be the one you actually love."

The last of the clouds had blown out to sea when they reached the villa. Juno the moon was riding high above the water. Stefan dismounted and lifted Theodosia off the horse at the foot of the stairs, as he had done so many times before.

She pulled him down to her height and gave him a kiss on the cheek.

"Thank you, my dear old friend. You're very special to me, you know."

"I know."

As she released Stefan, she spotted a short, stocky figure with a torch running around the corner of the house. Nicanor came to Theodosia, stuck his hand into the breast of his tunic, and drew out a leather pouch. Then—bowing with embarrassing reverence—he handed the bag to her. Its weight surprised her.

"What's this, Nicanor?"

"You saved me and my family, lady. Maybe I can help save you."

Theodosia opened the pouch and scooped up some of its contents with her fingers. It was a collection of gold coins… far more than a slave like Nicanor could hope to accumulate in a lifetime.

"Did you steal this?"

"No, miss." It was Stefan who answered. "That's the reward he got from Vespasian for finding you in the riverbed."

"I never knew about that." Theodosia poured the coins back into the bag and raised her eyes. "This money would buy your freedom, Nicanor. I can't take it."

Nicanor nodded firmly.

"Take it, lady. I got no need for money or freedom."

Theodosia would have argued with him, but at that moment Flavia appeared at the top of the stairs.

"You were supposed to call me, Nicanor, as soon as they arrived."

"Don't scold him, Flavia. Please."

With the bag in her hand, Theodosia looked again at Nicanor. His eyes were fixed on her face.

It's a matter of pride for him. Maybe the best chance he'll ever have to show he's a man.

She nodded and whispered, "Thank you!" Then she forced her legs up the stairs and—after a hesitation—threw her arms around Flavia.

"My truest, most loyal friend… can you ever forgive me? I had no idea what you were doing. I was so rude!"

"I didn't blame you. Who would, under the circumstances?" Flavia pulled back and stared at Theodosia's scratched face and arms and the coarse, soaked, torn tunic she was wearing. "What in blazes happened to you tonight?"

"A hard ride. It doesn't matter now."

"But Titus was supposed to—"

"He tried. Just please thank him for me, will you?"

Flavia nodded.

"You're welcome to stay here, you know. Forever, if you wish. You're free now, and this will always be your home."

"Thank you, Flavia, but… much as I love this place, I've found something more important." She hesitated again and smiled shyly. "Where's Alexander?"

Flavia's lips also curled into a soft smile.

"In the library."

Theodosia breathed deeply as she pushed aside the sapphire-blue curtain and stepped into the blackness of the room that had meant *home* all her life. A single lamp burned on the table by the couch, perfuming the air with its well-remembered sweetness. Instinctively, she looked toward the dark corner where the desk had always stood.

"Theodosia." His voice was tender. "Thank the gods you're safe!"

"And you, Alexander."

Aware that he could see her in the dim light, though she could not yet see him, Theodosia moved toward the desk.

"I almost didn't recognize you at the banquet," she said.

"That was the whole idea. You found Stefan?"

"He's outside." She set Nicanor's pouch on the desk. "I'm so sorry about Antibe. I was certain you'd find her."

Alexander made no response.

"You've been on my mind a lot these last years," Theodosia went on, not sure how to say what she wanted to say. "Thinking of you helped me survive." Her hand rose timidly to his face. "I guess what I'm trying to say is... I don't know why I never realized back then—back here—how very much I cared for you. How very much you meant to me."

She could make out his eyes now, looking into hers.

"I've wanted to tell you for so long, but I thought I'd never see you again." She took another deep breath. "I love you, Alexander!"

"But Stefan—"

"He knows. He understands."

"Do you mean what you're saying? You really mean it?"

Her answer was to slide her fingers around his neck and press her lips to his.

Alexander's hands encircled her waist as he responded with a passion that thrilled her. It was better than any other kiss she had ever known... real or imagined in the Carcer Tullianum.

When he released her, she pushed away, suddenly anxious.

"You haven't seen me yet. I'm a sight!"

"I have seen you. At the banquet, remember?"

"And you don't care?"

"Not a bit."

"But I'm even worse looking than that now."

"Impossible!" The corners of his eyes crinkled.

"And I'm not the same woman I was before."

"What? Not that haughty, stubborn, imperious Roman I remember?"

Theodosia began to laugh.

"You haven't changed a bit. Still mocking me."

Alexander drew her close once more.

"We don't have much to start a life on, you know. Just a couple of second-hand rubies."

"And this, from Nicanor." Theodosia picked up the pouch on the desk and handed it to him. "I didn't want to accept it, but it seemed so important to him." She touched his beard again. "I've learned so much since you and I first met, right here in this room."

"Such as...?"

"Well, for a start... I've learned that things almost never are as they appear. I know to look at what people are inside, not at what the world says they are. And I realize that I don't need things like this villa to be happy. All I really need is *you*."

She rested her head on his shoulder.

"Oh, Alexander, that haughty, stubborn, imperious Roman you were talking about... You'll never see her again. She died a long time ago in the Carcer Tullianum."

After a moment, Alexander eased her away from his shoulder and kissed her forehead.

"The boat's waiting. We'd better get going."

As they neared the door, Theodosia slipped away, ran her fingers along the carved wood of Aulus Terentius Varro's couch, and let her eyes wander around his library one last time.

"Good-bye, Father."

She turned back to Alexander.

"Be gone, fellow!" she said with mock sternness and an impatient flick of her fingers.

Then, with a smile, she took his hand and followed him into the atrium.

HISTORICAL NOTE

Marcus Salvius Otho did achieve his most ambitious goals... to marry Poppaea Sabina and become emperor of Rome. Unfortunately for him, neither situation lasted long.

In A.D. 62—six years after the end of *Rubies of the Viper*—Emperor Nero divorced Empress Octavia to marry Poppaea, although by then she was already married to Otho. To get rid of his friend and rival, Nero had banished him to faraway Lusitania (now Portugal) to serve as governor. According to ancient author Suetonius, who wrote *The Twelve Caesars*, the following ditty was soon on everyone's lips in Rome.

"OTHO IN EXILE?" "YES AND NO;

THAT IS, WE DO NOT CALL IT SO."

"AND MAY WE ASK THE REASON WHY?"

"THEY CHARGED HIM WITH ADULTERY."

"BUT COULD THEY PROVE IT?" "NO AND YES;

IT WAS HIS WIFE HE DARED CARESS."

Otho governed Lusitania for years, earning a surprising reputation for moderation and common sense.

Meanwhile, Poppaea bore Nero a daughter. She was pregnant again in 65 when—infuriated by her complaints about his returning home late from the races—the emperor kicked her to death in the stomach.

The unsavory recreational activities attributed to Otho and Nero in *Rubies of the Viper* are based on fact, as is the relationship between Otho and his conservative father.

In 68, Nero was forced by rebellious troops to commit suicide. His last words were, "What an artist the world loses in me." His death led to a period of civil war called the Year of Four Emperors, which began with the accession of Servius Sulpicius Galba, the first emperor not of the house of Julius and Augustus Caesar.

In January 69, Galba was overthrown by Otho, who was angered by Galba's refusal to declare him his heir. It was the first time in Roman history that an emperor was murdered by his successor.

Otho, then 37, wore imperial purple for only three months, during which time troops loyal to him battled troops loyal to Aulus Vitellius, who had been proclaimed emperor by the army in Germany. When defeat became imminent, Otho announced that he would "add one extra night to life." He went to bed, slept soundly, and stabbed himself promptly upon awaking at dawn. Suetonius reports: "The sensation caused by Otho's end was, I think, largely due to its contrast with the life he had led... Thus many who had hated Otho while alive, loved him for the way he died."

Otho was followed by Vitellius, who ruled the empire from April to December, when his forces were defeated by others loyal to Titus Flavius Vespasianus the Elder, then age 60.

Vespasian ruled shrewdly and frugally, with great popular support, from 69 to 79, when he died of a chill.

It was Vespasian—acting through his son Titus—who in 70 sacked Jerusalem and destroyed the Temple. The Arch of Titus, which still stands in Rome, was built to celebrate his victory over the rebellious Jews.

In 79, Titus Flavius Vespasianus the Younger—by then almost 40 and known as the conqueror of Jerusalem—followed his father on the throne. In the first year of his reign, Vesuvius erupted, burying Pompeii and Herculaneum, a disaster that tested his abilities. He conducted an active building program, which included finishing the Flavian Amphitheater, known today as the Colosseum. A popular and able ruler, Titus died under suspicious circumstances only two years after assuming the throne. Persistent rumors focused on his brother, Domitian, known to be resentful of the close relationship between Vespasian and Titus, but nothing was ever proved.

Titus Flavius Domitianus, not quite 30 when he became emperor in 81, earned the name "second Nero." Murdered in 96 by court officials after fifteen years of tyrannical rule, Domitian was replaced by the gentler, more-capable Nerva (96-98) and Trajan (98-117).

Vespasian's daughter, Flavia Domitilla, died young, before her father became emperor. Years later, as emperor, her brother Domitian had her deified and placed her image on imperial coins. Her daughter—also named Flavia Domitilla—became a Christian saint (in the Greek Orthodox Church). The husband attributed to her in this novel is fictional.

The reign of the Flavians is significant for Vespasian's and Titus' capable leadership and for being the first dynasty after the Caesars. It is interesting to speculate on how different the final decades of the first century might have been had Titus—"mankind's darling," according to Suetonius—survived to rule the years that were given over to his brother, Domitian, known as the "second persecutor" of early Christians.

Theodosia Varra is, of course, a fictional creation, but the great-grandfather attributed to her here, Marcus Terentius Varro—the prolific author of hundreds of books on sound agricultural, health, and library practices, among other things—did live in the century before Christ (116-27 BC). Born at Reate, close to where Vespasian was born a century later, Varro was considered the greatest Roman scholar of his time.

A PERSONAL MESSAGE FROM MARTHA MARKS

Reader reviews and word of mouth are great ways to help a novel you like find a wide audience.

After you've finished *Rubies of the Viper*, please take a few minutes to post online an honest review that will help others decide if they want to read it, too. Booksellers that carry reader reviews are linked from my website: **marthamarks.com**.

If you know people who might be interested in this novel, please tell them about it. You can email friends a free PDF sample, available on my website.

Rubies of the Viper is published in both trade paperback and e-book formats. Search for it by name or find direct links on my website.

Thank you for helping me build a buzz around my book!

And... I would love to hear personally from you. Feel free to send me an email with feedback of any kind: **martha@marthamarks.com**.

ABOUT THE AUTHOR

Martha Marks earned her Ph.D. in Spanish literature and linguistics at Northwestern University and subsequently served on the faculties of Northwestern University and Kalamazoo College. She enjoyed studying and teaching the novels, plays, and poetry of great Spanish and Latin American authors, and she believes that *Rubies of the Viper* is a better novel because of her in-depth exposure to their work.

During her academic career, she also co-authored three popular college-level Spanish textbooks: *Destinos*, *Al corriente*, and *¿Qué tal?*

Since retiring from academia, Martha has become an accomplished wildlife photographer and an enthusiastic member of the growing "indie" author movement (similar in concept to the indie bands and indie filmmakers). Martha and other independent authors use today's liberating new technologies—e-books and Print on Demand—to maintain full creative and quality control over their work. Like all authors, they rely on reviews, word of mouth, and the Internet to promote their work.

Please visit *marthamarks.com* to view Martha's high-quality wildlife imagery. Anyone who has enjoyed reading *Rubies of the Viper* and would like to send a free PDF sample to friends will find it there, too.

Martha lives with her artist husband, Bernard, in Santa Fe, New Mexico. *Rubies of the Viper* is her first novel.